THE DARK PLACE

STEPHANIE ROGERS

Also by Stephanie Rogers

1

Issy

SHE PULLS UP IN the car, turns off the engine, and sits outside the house for a minute, her heart skittering a brief, crazy rhythm at the sight of it. The house is a neat, small semi, with a well-manicured front garden; nothing special or remarkable about it. Bright sunlight reflects off the gleaming windows, causing Issy to shade her eyes. Home. The place that's supposed to be a sanctuary. She tries to quell the tremors in her hands by jamming them under her thighs, while thoughts of what's to come crowd her mind.

When the front door opens and three-year-old Noah appears, she opens the door and gets out. He belts down the drive past her mother's car in a war charge, in T-shirt, shorts and bare feet. His over-long blonde curls flap behind him. The muscles around her heart clench tight at the sight of her son.

'Waah!' he roars, putting on a spurt and heading straight towards her.

Issy's mother chases after him as best she can, but he's too quick. He careens straight into Issy and she picks him up before he can run into the road.

'He's heavy,' she says to her mum.

Issy has no hips to speak of, certainly not child-bearing ones, and he continually slides down. His chubby little arms

1

grasp tight around her neck and she turns away from the little boy smell that's making her stomach flip over.

'Darling, welcome home. We're going to have a great summer. Dad's been so excited.' Her mother beams at her and pulls her into a hug.

Issy puts a struggling Noah down, and he's instantly drawn to a beetle crawling along the base of the front garden wall. He pokes it with a tentative finger and squeals when it flips over onto his toe. Issy smiles brightly at her mum. Her mother won't notice she's not right. She's missed so many clues along the way. People only see what they want to see.

'Is Dad at work?'

'Yes, but he's arranged to come home early. We're all going out for tea. His treat. Aunty Pam and Uncle Justin are coming too. And Sammy and Joey. Carl's got football practice, as usual.'

Playing happy families then. Her heart thuds once, hard. She nods. 'Mmm, lovely.'

Noah tires of the beetle and scurries back inside the house, holding an imaginary sword aloft and yelling, 'Charge!'

Her mum tuts. 'He's got that from your dad. They've been playing 'battles' again. Oh, it's so great to have you home, love.' Her mother pulls her close and hugs her tight again, her hair tickling Issy's face. The smell of *Charlie* gets up her nose and Issy tries not to breathe it in. She's never liked it. For God's sake, who uses *Charlie* these days, anyway?

Together they unload the boot, dropping a jumble of plastic bags, holdalls and suitcases onto the pavement. The accumulation of a year's worth of life.

'Crikey, Issy, I'd forgotten how much stuff you'd taken to uni,' her mother says at the sight of it all.

They gather up the luggage and struggle up the drive with it, dumping it in the hallway. Issy looks at the massive pile— why did she need all this stuff, anyway? She won't need any of it soon. She wonders if her mother can sense she's different. Doesn't seem like it. Noah runs out of the kitchen, straight past them and up the stairs, clutching a toy car in his fist. At the top, he stops, turns and tosses the car down the stairs. It hits the bottom stair, bounces off and smacks Issy on the shin, then drops onto the floor where it lays upside down like an overturned insect, abandoned and forlorn, its wheels still spinning.

Issy looks up at him, ignoring the sting in her leg where it hit her. He watches, biting his lip, waiting to see what she's going to do. Issy picks it up, walks into the kitchen and throws it into the bin, right into a blob of what looks like discarded custard. Through the spindles of the staircase, Noah sees her and shrieks. *Serves him right*, she thinks, as she rejoins her mother at the bottom of the stairs.

Her mum is looking at her in dismay. 'Issy! You didn't have to throw it away. He'll carry on forever now. It's one of his favourites.'

'Well, he should have thought of that before throwing it. He's nearly four!'

'I know, and I've been telling him,' her mum says. 'It's just a phase.'

Issy rubs her leg while Noah's cries continue. 'Want car! Want car!'

She blanks the noise out and goes back to the kitchen to get a drink of water. Her mum is making her way up the stairs to him. She's way too soft with him, and it's about time he learned. Issy leans against the worktop, gulping down a full glass of water. Her mum gave up her job when she had Noah, so she could carry on at school and then go to uni, and Issy still feels bad about it. Her mum loved that job. She'd thought, when she'd got pregnant, that she would be able to cope, that she would get used to Noah, but it hadn't happened. She fills the glass again, and it clinks against her teeth when her hand shakes with the thought of what she's about to do. She'd planned to do it tomorrow, but she knows without a doubt that she can't stay a night in this house, delaying things. It has to be today. Soon. Before she can change her mind. She won't change her mind.

An hour later and it's time. She's done her duty and spent time with Noah, reading him three stories. When she closes the book, he protests loudly and tries to prise it open again. 'More!'

She holds the book firmly closed and his fingers wrench at it. 'No. That's enough for now, Noah.'

He lets go and looks up at her. She puts the book down on the bed and he picks it up and drops it on the floor. She leaves the book face down on the carpet, wondering how long these fits of anger will last. She's no idea; she's missed every phase he's been through. He climbs onto her knee and puts his head on her chest. A lock of his silky hair slips through her fingers and she grips it tight, then lets go. Suddenly, she buries her nose in his curls and breathes in deeply. Something twists inside. A small cry escapes her and he looks up at her curiously. She slides him onto the floor.

'Go and play,' she says.

He sighs. 'Okay.' He runs out of the room and into his bedroom, slamming the door. The crash it makes seems to bounce right off her as she sits on the bed, staring out of the window.

There's one thing she has left to do. She stands and turns to face the bed, gazing at the framed beach scene hanging above it. Her favourite picture. She first saw it when she was walking along the beachfront with her parents on holiday in Fuerteventura a few years ago and had to have it, refusing to move until they bought it for her. In the picture, the sea is wild, crashing onto the shore, the beach deserted except for a tiny figure in a bright red dress standing knee-deep in the waves. The woman's long black hair is being swept around her head and her flimsy dress is flying up around her thighs. But it was the sun glittering on the sea that drew her to it the most. Despite the blustery scene, the picture had always made her feel calm, with nothing but sand and sea visible for miles. Now, she's drawn to the faceless, lonesome figure of the woman. Faceless and desolate, like her. Lost.

She's already composed the note, having gone over and over it in her mind for the last few weeks. She pulls it out of her pocket and removes the back panel of the picture, tucking the note behind it, but leaving a good amount sticking out. If anyone turns the picture around, they'll see it. She's decided to leave whether or not it gets found up to fate; a fifty percent chance either way. It seems for the best. Once her parents have read the note, they can never go back to not knowing, and that's not a decision she feels she can make. She knows it's a cop-out, but it's all she can manage right now. She puts the picture on the wall again, tilting the bottom right-hand corner down a fraction, as it's always been.

Five minutes later, after one last look around her room, she takes a deep breath. She's sweating, but certain. She doesn't dwell on what it will do to her parents. They'll cope. They have Noah to focus on. Issy goes back downstairs and puts her shoes on at the front door.

'Mum, I'm just popping out for half an hour.' She keeps her voice steady.

'Where are you going? You only just got here.' Her mother comes out of the kitchen, frowning and clutching a tea towel.

'I need to pick up something special for you and Dad. Something I organised earlier. A surprise.' She meets her mother's eyes and does the acting job of her life. Something she's become good at.

Her mother looks pleased and carries on wiping her hands on the towel. 'Oh, okay, love. Don't be long.'

'I won't.' *She will. Go now*, she urges herself.

She walks out of the house carrying only her car keys. Her phone is in her bedroom, along with her bag and purse. A tremor runs up her arm as she turns the ignition key, her mind already following the route she's mapped out. At the end of the road, she turns left and drives towards town, where the roads get steadily busier and ten minutes later, she pulls up at the crossroads. The main road is the one lorries use to get to the by-pass. Her dad always complains that this crossroads needs traffic lights. He says it's dangerous, as the lorries are leaving the town, descending a slope and gathering speed. She hopes he's right.

There's one car in front of her and gaps are hard to come by as the traffic picks up speed. It takes a full two minutes before the driver ahead can turn right, and her heart collides painfully with her ribs as pure adrenalin floods her veins. The steering wheel glistens when she takes her hands off it. She can't risk screwing this up. She puts the car into first and waits. Three lorries pass, nose to tail, and she revs the engine. Behind her, in the mirror, she sees a car pull up and a man with glasses and sticky-up hair glances both ways. He yawns and taps his fingers on the steering wheel. She meets his eyes in the rearview mirror and looks away. A large gap opens up, more than enough to cross both carriageways. She waits. The man behind mouths something and waves his hand in a *go* gesture. To her right, a lorry is accelerating, having come round the bend and started to descend the hill. It's big, but not too cumbersome. Is it too slow? Not big enough?

In the car behind her, the man pips his horn. He can't understand why she's still sitting here. This lorry's perfect, but it's still too far away. It's leaving the thirty-miles-per-hour speed limit behind and is heading for sixty, the limit on this stretch of road. Getting closer. The man behind thumps his steering wheel in frustration.

She can see the lorry driver quite clearly, high up in his cab. He looks about thirty, quite fit actually, and he's watching the road intently. She's about to wreck his life. Fifteen metres left for him to gain enough speed. Will it be enough?

Ten metres. She pumps the accelerator, checks she's in first gear and releases the handbrake. The car moves forward a few inches, closer to the white Give Way line. Her leg quivers and a horrible thought crosses her mind. What if she stalls the car? What if she's badly injured, but doesn't die and is doomed to life as a paraplegic or something? She can't risk still being alive after this. She puts more revs on and moves forward again. She looks at the lorry driver and his eyes slide to meet hers. She mouths, 'I'm sorry,' and his eyes open wider. Five metres. Three metres. Two.

The car doesn't stall, and the clutch doesn't slip. The little Fiat responds beautifully, and she shoots out in front of the lorry. One metre. Then none.

2

Jon

'MEL? WHERE'S ISSY? HER car's not here. What time did she get back from Newcastle?' I call out.

I dump my laptop bag on the floor and kick the front door shut. Noah is playing with his cars in the living room off to the right, shouting, 'Broom, broom,' and pushing them over the rug. 'Grandad!' he shouts when he sees me go past.

My wife is in the kitchen, sitting at the table, reading. She looks up from her magazine as I enter the room. She frowns and picks up a cup of tea, curling her fingers round it. 'She got back about two, was in an hour then went out again. I thought she would have been back by now.' She glances at the clock.

'Where'd she go?' I sit at the table opposite her.

'To be honest, she never said. She just said she had to go out and get something. For us. Before I could ask her, she'd gone.'

'Have you phoned her?'

She pulls a face. 'No. You know how she gets if she thinks we're checking up. I'll give it a little more time.'

'Oh. Well… okay.'

I've driven home as fast as I dared, hitting the brakes hard when I saw one of those mobile speed cameras. I've been so looking forward to her coming home for the summer for weeks now, and I can't wait to see her. Mel always says I spoil

Issy too much, but she's nearly as bad. 'Did you tell her we're going out? We need to start getting ready soon. It's four o'clock now and the restaurant's an hour away. Table's booked for six.'

'I told her we're going out, but that's it. You never told me anything else.' She flips a page and sips her tea.

'I booked that new place in town, that world buffet.'

Town is Harrogate, fifteen miles away from where we live, Luxton, a much smaller town with no notable features. From right behind me, Noah lets out a shriek that makes both of us jump a mile. He keeps on doing that just lately and it sets my nerves jangling every time, but the more he thinks it gets to you, the more he does it.

'Noah,' I scold him. 'That's naughty. Stop it.'

I'm rewarded by a beguiling grin as he holds out his hand, offering me the little red car nestled there. This child can melt my heart at the same time I'm losing my temper with him, creating an odd juxtaposition. He's exactly like his mother used to be and still is. He's the spitting image of her: his blonde hair (although Issy has taken to dying hers black recently); his features; his quick-to-flare personality. To compare photos of them both when Issy was three, they could be the same child. Issy's always been able to manipulate me, and Noah's just the same. I sit him on my knee and he wraps his chubby little arms around my neck.

'Sorry, Grandad. Sorry,' he says and kisses me sloppily on the cheek. Then he presses his car into my hand. Now I have proof he truly loves me. No one can wrestle his cars out of his grip, ever.

'I need a shower,' I tell Mel, putting Noah back down. It's been baking hot today. 'If she isn't here when I get down, I'll ring her, whether she likes it or not.'

'Well, okay, but Pam and Justin should be here soon, so be quick.'

I stand to go and lean over to kiss her cheek. She stiffens slightly, a tiny movement, and edges away a fraction. I pretend not to notice. She fixes me with cool green eyes that don't betray what she's thinking.

At the bottom of the stairs, I glance at a photo of Issy. She's about fourteen in it and has a guarded look in her eyes. To look at, she's definitely an amalgamation of both Mel and myself. She's petite and delicate like Mel, but with my fair colouring. Even though I'm excited to see her, angst clutches at me. Issy's not the easiest person to be around. Introverted as a child, she got worse as she got older, becoming more sullen, argumentative and difficult when the mood took her. But she can also be a joy when you handle her right.

After I've showered, I hear voices in the living room. Good. Issy must be back. I take the stairs two at a time and rush into the living room, but it's only Pam and Justin sitting there on the sofa, drinking tea. I force the smile to remain on my face, pleased to see them but annoyed it's not her. *Where is she?* Justin, a giant of a man a good eight inches taller than me, stands up when he sees me. Patches of sweat are blooming under his armpits, staining his pale blue T-shirt darker. His face crinkles into a smile, and he slaps me on the back with a massive hand.

'Alright,' he says.

'Oh, hi. I thought you were Issy,' I say.

'Sorry to disappoint,' says Pam, archly. 'Where are we going for this meal, anyway?'

I tap the side of my nose and watch my sister-in-law bite.

'Where?' she asks again.

'You'll find out when we get there.'

Her mouth purses slightly. When I first met her, I couldn't believe she was Mel's twin. There are virtually no similarities between them, either in looks or character.

Justin gets up and stands in front of the bay window with his hands in his pockets, checking out the street in both directions, then looks at his watch. 'Sammy and Joey are meeting us there,' he says. 'I think they reckon it's okay to eat with us if we're buying but not to be seen in public with us any longer than is absolutely necessary.'

I laugh. He's not wrong. Pam's wearing a new summer dress and matching high-heeled shoes. 'What happened? I thought you were getting dressed up,' I quip.

Her mouth gapes open. 'You what? This is new!'

'Yes, the label's still on it, at the back. Size sixteen?'

She screws round and tries to look down her back. 'You cheeky sod! I'm a twelve! Where...?' She twigs and fixes me with a hard stare when I laugh, trying not to laugh herself.

'Shouldn't she have been here by now?' Justin asks, checking the street again.

'I'm going to phone her,' Mel says. She finds Issy's number on her mobile and rings it. 'No answer. Straight to voicemail. It didn't even ring. Like it's switched off.' Her eyes lock onto mine and my heart does a tap dance in my chest. 'Where can she be?'

'I don't know,' I say. 'Are there any friends she might have gone to?' My voice sounds strained.

'Blam, blam,' shouts Noah, dashing into the room and shooting each of us with a plastic golf club. No one pretends to die. 'Uncle Jussin,' he yells and grasps Justin around the knees.

'Hey, little fella.' He lifts him high up into the air and shakes him about, making Noah screech with laughter, then turns him upside down and holds him by the feet.

'Careful,' warns Pam, but Noah's loving it.

'I'm starting to get really worried,' says Mel.

I turn back to the window. I am, too.

'What time did she go out exactly?' asks Pam.

'Over two-and-a-half hours ago now. She said she wouldn't be long. She knows we're going out.' Lines crease Mel's forehead.

'She'll be okay. She'd have phoned us if there was anything wrong,' I say. I want to believe it. I've always thought if she was in trouble, I'd just know. I'd be able to feel it. So why can I feel sweat pooling under my armpits? It's not that hot now. Mel rings her again while we all watch.

'Voicemail again,' she says, biting on her bottom lip. Her eyes search mine.

Justin carries Noah away from the window, righting him and swinging him by the arms like a monkey.

'More,' shouts Noah. 'Again.'

'My back is killing me,' moans Justin. 'I'm an old man now, Noah. You need to go easy on me.'

A police car slides into view and stops at the kerb. Right outside our house. My blood seems to freeze in my veins and pound in my ears at the same time. I hear Mel take a breath in.

'Jon…' she says. I nod, my eyes not leaving the police car.

'What?' Pam stands up and Justin turns around. He slowly puts Noah down on the floor. The four of us stand frozen and watch as two coppers get out of the panda car, a man and a woman. Now they're coming through the gate with grave faces. A second later, the bell rings.

3

Mel

AT THE SOUND OF the doorbell, I rush to the door on wobbly legs. This can't be good. I wrench the door open and just stand there, unable to speak.

'Mrs Warner?'

'Yes?' I try to swallow, but my throat is closing up.

The policeman clears his throat, his colleague's gaze flitting between us. I feel Jon right behind me, breathing down my neck. He steps forward.

'Does an Isabella Warner live here?' the policeman asks.

I think I nod. I can't move my frozen face and my limbs feel like lead.

'A Fiat Panda, registration ISS 4Y is registered to this address in her name?'

The private plate Jon bought her.

'Yes.' Prickles of fear stab my scalp and I clutch the door frame. 'What is it?'

'May we come in?' asks the man. 'I'm Sergeant Dawson and this is PC Carter. I'm afraid there's been an accident.'

'Is she dead?' I blurt out.

Jon shakes his head. 'Don't be stupid…' he says, his voice tight.

'Please, may we…?' The policeman gestures to come in and I stand back. His face drawn, pinched. *He hasn't said no yet. Hasn't answered my question.* My heart is fluttering in my chest like a butterfly bashing itself against a window.

'Of course. Through here.' Jon directs them through to the living room, past Justin and Pam, who are hovering in the doorway.

They sit down when Jon points to the small sofa. The four of us sit on the larger one opposite.

'Are these family members?' asks PC Woman.

'Yes,' I say. 'My sister and her husband. You can say whatever in front of them. We've been sitting here waiting for her to come home. Please… where's my daughter?'

The woman leans forward and clasps her hands in her lap. A blush tints her cheeks. She blinks twice. Swallows. 'I'm so sorry. Her car was hit by a lorry. I'm afraid she died at the scene.'

A loud, piercing wail fills the room, and it takes me a second to realise it's coming from me.

'No, there… there must be some mistake,' Jon is saying, shaking his head. 'She only came back from uni a couple of hours ago. We're going out for tea. It's all arranged. We're going out.'

He's gripping my hand and I can feel his thigh trembling against mine. This must be a mistake. But the police don't make mistakes like this, do they? They don't tell you your daughter is dead if she isn't.

'Sir, we'll need someone to identify the body,' the man says quietly. 'I'm so sorry.'

The body. My daughter is a body now? A corpse. A mangled mess.

'Where did it happen?' whispers Justin. His eyes are stretched wide, and he's shaking his head.

I look at Jon, who's closed his eyes. He seems to be having trouble breathing and is gulping air. His face is grey, and he's no longer holding my hand. I don't recall him letting go.

'Hill Lane crossroads. She wasn't indicating, so it was assumed she was going straight across. A lorry was coming from her right and she drove right out in front of it.'

'You make it sound like she did it on purpose,' says Pam, frowning.

'We're not saying it was anything other than an accident at this stage,' says PC woman.

At this stage? They think she——?

'Issy would never kill herself. She had little Noah here. He meant the world to her.' Jon sounds incredulous.

'I'm sorry but we, ah, need someone to identify the body?' The woman is looking at me now and I want to hit her. How can she sit there, tell me my daughter's dead, suggest that she may have killed herself, and then ask me to go and look at her body?

'I can do it if... I mean, am I allowed?' asks Justin.

Jon gets to his feet. He looks shaky. 'I'll go. I want to see her. I won't believe it unless I see it for myself.' He stumbles to one side and I think he may be about to faint.

I shrink back when he looks at me. I should go with him, but I can't. I can't do it. I'm going to take the coward's way out and let him go, even if it means he'll hate me for it. If he says it's true, that she's dead, *then* I'll believe it. I'll have no choice. Until then, it's all a terrible mistake.

'Thank you, sir,' says PC Man.

'Do... do I have to go now?' Jon is shaking violently, tremors rippling through him.

'We can take a minute here, if you need. She's been taken to the hospital.'

I have a vision of her, cold and dead and lying on a slab. 'She's in the morgue? But what if she's not properly dead? Have you checked?' My voice has risen to a screech.

The policewoman sits down beside me. 'Can I make you a cup of tea?' She touches my elbow gently.

I shake my head. 'No. No, thank you.'

'I'll do it now. It won't be her. This is all a mistake. Any minute now she'll come through that door, kick her shoes off and dump her bag on the floor. You'll see.' Jon wipes a hand over his face. He looks to have aged twenty years in ten seconds.

Then he's gone with the policeman, with Justin trailing in his wake. At the doorway, Justin stops, looks back at me.

'I'll look after him,' he says and disappears.

Noah climbs onto my lap, subdued and sucking his thumb, and I realise, horrified, that he's heard all this. Pam comes to sit next to me and the woman PC keeps shooting me sympathetic glances. I wonder how many times she's had to do this.

'I'll put the kettle on,' she says and leaves.

I look at Pam. 'What's going on? She can't be dead. She's only nineteen. It won't be her.' My voice has a hysterical note to it. When I touch my face, it's all wet. 'I should have gone with Jon,' I say.

My arms are tight around Noah, who's looking up at me in concern. It's like looking at Issy again, all those years ago. I close my eyes and a tear slips down my cheek. It has to be a mistake. Things like this don't happen to people like us. Jon will sort it out. He'll go to the morgue, see a different girl lying there, some other poor woman's daughter, and Issy will be home soon. We'll all go out to tea as planned, and this nightmare will be over. I sit rocking back and forth and patting Noah on the bottom until his eyes close and he nods off, still sucking his thumb.

'Jon will sort it. He'll be home soon,' I say.

Pam grabs my hand. She doesn't believe me; I can tell without her saying a word.

'You think Issy is dead?' I say.

Her mouth opens, but she doesn't speak.

'Do you believe she's dead?' I ask again.

'If it was her car, and it had her number plate on it, who else would have been driving it? I hope to God it's not her, of course I do, but...' She shakes her head and her face crumples. She's always the one who knows best, the bossy one who's always right, and at this moment, I hate her for it. Just then, the policewoman comes in carrying tea. She looks terrified and I realise she's younger than I first thought. Her blonde hair is scraped back into a ponytail and her face is devoid of wrinkles. She brought this bad news into my house and I can't stand the sight of her any longer.

'I don't want tea. Please leave.'

She's startled, and the tea slops out of the cups as she puts the tray onto my coffee table. 'Mrs Warner...' she stutters, but I cut her off.

'Please, just go. I don't want you here.'

She nods but doesn't look happy. She leaves, closing the door behind her. I can see her out of the front window, leaning against the front wall, talking into her radio. Pam is shooting wild glances at me, her sister, the quiet, mild-mannered one who never says boo to a goose. Me, the younger sister, younger by a whole seventeen minutes, as I've been informed my whole life. Her mouth is hanging open, and she looks as if she's considering her words very carefully. She says nothing and we sit in silence.

Inside, I'm terrified and my stomach is churning. Issy hasn't come home yet, and I'm beginning to wonder if the police are right. Eventually, after what seems like an age, the police car pulls up outside again, and Jon and Justin get out. Before Jon turns around, the policewoman intercepts her colleague, her shoulders hunched and stooped. Probably telling him I kicked her out. When Jon turns to the house, I quail—his face tells me everything. He has to be supported all the way back into the house by Justin, who's propping him up under his arm. My insides are like ice; *it's true then.* My eyes meet his as he comes into the room and shakes his head. I've never seen such pain and anguish in someone's eyes.

'No! No! No!' I scream and collapse into his arms, but he's in no fit state to hold me up and he sinks into the sofa.

'We'll take Noah home with us,' I hear Pam say, her voice thick with tears.

For the next twenty-four hours, I can't remember anything else, other than wishing it was me who was dead instead.

4

Jon

IT'S BEEN TWENTY-FOUR HOURS since the horror that was waiting for me at the morgue. I will never, ever get over seeing that. I could only just identify her. Her face was swollen and bruised black, but I could just about see it was my daughter. She was wearing the same two rings she always does—a silver one with a large blue stone and another in the shape of a tiny black and silver skull. I don't know where either of them came from, or who bought them. Apart from her arms, everything else was under a white sheet, lumpy and misshapen somehow. They said most of the damage was to her chest and lower body. I couldn't think about what lay underneath that sheet. There were scars all over her arms that looked like cut marks. The pathologist confirmed that's what they were. It seems Issy must have been self-harming for a long time, cutting herself to shreds by the look of it, and I never knew a damn thing. They asked me if she always wore long sleeves, and I had to think about it. Yes, she did. I'd never made the connection. I'd never noticed. What kind of father did that make me?

Justin never saw her. I don't think, deep down, he really wanted to. I made him wait outside and he didn't argue. He didn't ask me about it on the way back. Just having him there was a sort of comfort. When I got back, Mel, unable to believe it, wanted me to describe it in great detail, every last sickening bit, then begged me to say it wasn't her. I hated her for it. I shouted at her that if she'd wanted to see it for herself, she should have gone instead of me. That sent her upstairs in floods of tears. All night and day I've sat in this chair, barely speaking, moving only to go to the bathroom to be sick and purge myself of what I've seen, but it hasn't worked.

I've barely spoken since. I think I've shut down, unable to move on from what I saw on that slab. The police are certain it wasn't an accident. The lorry driver and a man in the car behind hers both say it was deliberate. The man behind her said she sat through several opportunities to pull out when it was safe, then, when the lorry was almost upon her, she shot out with no chance of getting across safely. The lorry driver is in such a state he can barely speak. He wasn't injured but spent the night in hospital, under observation. Apparently, he's in shock. Well, why wouldn't he be?

Every time I close my eyes, I see my little girl's mangled body. Did she really do this to herself? If so, why? She had everything going for her. And I can't blot out the sound of Mel's weeping. I should go to her and console her, but I just can't. I can't see past my own grief, can't feel anything other than my own pain. Several people come to the house: the police again, counsellors, various friends and neighbours, Pam and Justin. Everything's a blur. I speak to none of them. If I concentrate hard enough, none of them are there. I blot them all out and retreat into blissful nothingness. In my chest, where a warm human heart used to be, now sits a stone-cold lump of concrete. I hate the fact that it still beats. If I could will it to stop, I would. Eventually everyone leaves, and Mel and I are alone again.

She comes to sit on the arm of the chair beside me and grasps my hand in hers. She feels ice cold. It's the most she's touched me in ages.

'Jon, you have to talk to me. Or, if not me, someone else.' Her voice is choked with tears.

I don't look at her. Inside, I can feel something churning, growing and trying to get out. It's bubbling within me,

19

funneling and spiralling upwards. Something big. I don't know what it is, but it propels me to my feet, almost knocking her off the arm. I open my mouth and roar. It's a guttural, raw sound, and comes from some primal part of me I've never connected with before. It's pain, agony and rage at what's happened, all rolled into one big ugly ball. I don't know how long it lasts, but I turn and see Mel looking shocked. I kick the coffee table as hard as I can, using every last reserve of strength. It hits the wall and chunks of plaster shower the room. The glass top shatters, making an almighty crash. Mel gasps, then flinches and covers her head with her arms. She doesn't know this side of me. Nor do I. I've never met this man, but at this moment, he is me. There, amongst the fragments of glass, I stand, breathing hard for a minute or two, then I'm spent. I lie down and curl up into a ball.

Something else is filling me now, something just as gigantic. Pure grief, and I'm suddenly crying so hard I can't breathe. I'm choking and gasping for breath and shuddering violently. I feel arms wrap around me as Mel cradles me from behind, lying in the glass with me, speaking soothing words. My grief is all-encompassing and the only thing I can feel, but eventually, after what seems like hours, the tears run dry. The shadows have lengthened through the living room window, until one small shaft of sunlight is all that remains, becoming ever narrower until that too closes up and the room gets darker and colder.

The glass has shattered into tiny, round pieces. Safety glass. Should have realised it would. I wanted it to cut me into millions of tiny pieces. Mel sits up, brushes herself down, and holds out a hand to me. My face is stiff with salt from dried tears as I allow her to pull me into a sitting position.

'I can't be strong for you, Mel. I'm sorry. I just can't. Please don't ask me to.'

'I know. I don't expect you to be. I shouldn't have let you go alone. It was wrong of me. I'm sorry.'

She smooths my hair back and holds my face. The glass may not have cut me, and my bones may be intact, but I'm broken all the same.

'Never ask me about it again. Please.' I whisper.

She chews her lip and shakes her head. 'I won't.'

I can see she wants to know, needs to know, but it's for the best. Her sleep will be less haunted than mine if she never has to visualise it. She hauls me to my feet and together we survey the mess.

'Let's go to bed. We'll clear it up tomorrow,' she says. 'Are you hungry? You haven't eaten a thing all day.'

'No. I couldn't swallow.'

'Me neither.'

I follow her up the stairs and climb into bed beside her. She's crying again.

'I've been so frightened today, Jon. You really scared me, sitting there like that, not speaking, just shutting down.'

'We do what we have to. We're going to have to get through this any way we can. There's no rule book.'

We lie together, the only thing touching is our little fingers. I sleep fitfully and wake up before dawn with a heavy weight pressing on my chest; the heavy mass of grief. And terror about how I'm going to get through the rest of my life without Issy.

At ten o'clock, a knocking on the door drags me out of bed. Mel looks tired, strained, and older. I guess I must look pretty much the same. I hear the front door opening and when I get to the top of the stairs, Justin and Pam are in the living room, surveying the mess from the smashed coffee table. I go back to sit on the bed. Mel is weeping silently. I feel useless, unable to cope with my own grief, let alone someone else's.

'Justin and Pam are here,' I say.

'I don't want to see them. I don't want to see anybody.'

'I know. I don't either, but they're here. I'll go down. You stay in bed.'

She doesn't argue and I go back to the top of the stairs on leaden legs. I can hear them talking quietly in the living room.

'What do you think happened?' Pam is saying.

'Looks like one of them lost it.'

'Jon?'

'Probably. Let's just clean it up.'

As Pam leaves to go into the kitchen, she spots me at the top of the stairs and stops dead in her tracks.

'Jon... um, how are you?'

I stare at her. My daughter's dead. How does she think I am?

At this moment, I don't think I've ever hated anyone more. Her crime? Her children are alive, breathing, laughing, eating, joking, sleeping. If one of hers died, she'd still have two more. My hands clench into fists. I just want them to leave but I know, ultimately, Mel will want her sister here. She needs Pam just as much as she needs me. More, probably. I don't speak, just shrug.

'We were just about to clear this up.' She doesn't ask what happened.

I somehow make it downstairs. Justin is sitting on one of the sofas with his head in his hands. His whole body is shaking. Through his splayed fingers, I can see tears dripping onto the floor. I forget what Issy meant to him and Pam sometimes. She was like a daughter to them, just as their sons are like my own flesh and blood. Even so, I still feel it's not right they're alive and Issy is dead.

I sit on the other sofa and wait for Justin to compose himself. For a few minutes, he doesn't know I'm there, and his grief reignites my own. When he looks up, tears are sliding down my face.

'I... I'm sorry, Jon. You don't need me losing it. It won't help, but...' He wipes his eyes with the back of his hand and sniffs.

I nod. 'She wasn't your daughter, but she was the next best thing.'

'Yeah. I loved her like my own.'

'I know.'

Pam comes in with a dustpan and brush and stops when she sees us. She makes to back up and I stop her.

'It's okay, you can come in. Where's Noah, anyway?'

'He's at home with the boys. He wanted pancakes for breakfast, so they're making them. God knows what sort of a...' Her voice tails off, and her eyes are moist. 'How's Mel?'

'Not good.'

'What happened here?' She nods at the remains of the table I smashed.

'Me. And my foot.'

'Ah, right. You know, Jon, if you need anything, anything at all, you only have to say. You know that, don't you?' She removes a tissue from her pocket and dabs her eyes with it before blowing her nose.

'Yeah. I do know.' *Can you bring my daughter back? No? Didn't think so.* I stand up. 'I'll make Mel some tea.'

'I can do that,' says Pam, automatically.

'I'll do it,' I say, and walk out of the room.

In the kitchen, a thought occurs to me—last year, Justin and I were waiting at that very junction and we were stuck for ages trying to get out. I remember the women had sent us to Ikea, one of my top five hated places of all time, to get a new wardrobe for Issy's bedroom. We'd gone in Justin's car as it's longer than mine, and I remember looking out of the window and seeing some cameras there. I'd never noticed them before, and we'd had a discussion about Big Brother watching. We were on opposing sides of the argument. I said I can't see a problem with them if you're a law-abiding citizen, but Justin thought they were an infringement on human rights. He hated not knowing who may be watching. Not traffic cameras, obviously, but other cameras. The thought hits me that the accident must have been recorded. I need to see it for myself and make my own mind up whether she did it deliberately or not. I don't want to tell Mel anything—I need to find out first, one way or the other, then I'll decide what to do. In a normal situation, I'd tell Justin, and we'd go together, but it's not a normal situation. It's something I have to do on my own. I have to find out.

I rattle some cups about and put the kettle on to boil. As it starts to make a noise, I grab my keys, slip quietly out of the back door, along the side of the house and into my car, parked on the drive next to Mel's

5

Mel

I'M IN BED, STARING at the ceiling, when there's a soft knock on the bedroom door.

'Can I come in?' Pam says.

'Yeah,' I mumble, my throat closing up tighter.

The door opens, and my sister pokes her head around it. I can tell she doesn't know what to say to me for the first time in our lives. Now there's a major difference between us; only one of us has a dead child. I pull the sheet up to my chin. Her eyes are puffy and red, and she takes her shoes off, lifts the sheet and clambers in beside me, like we always did as kids. We haven't done this in years. That's what husbands are supposed to be for, isn't it, to offer comfort and support in this intimate way? Not that mine does.

'I'm so sorry,' she says, as tears slide down her face.

Does she think this will help me, showing me her tears and her hurt? But I know she can't help it. My heart is so broken that I don't see how it can ever mend. The pieces don't fit together anymore.

'I can't believe she's gone. I keep expecting her to walk through the door any minute,' I sob.

'I know, so do I.'

We're quiet a while, then she says, 'I've cleared up the glass downstairs. What happened?'

'Jon lost it completely last night. I've never seen him like that. He just went berserk. But, there again, he's never had a reason to go crazy like that, has he? Do you know, Pam, I have absolutely no idea how we're supposed to get through this. I just want to die. If it wasn't for Noah, then...'

She puts her arms around me, and I can feel anguish radiating from her. 'Please don't say that. Please don't. I can't bear the thought of you not being here.'

I begin to cry again. Thoughts of Issy consume my mind. All I can hear is her voice, I can see her face, and smell her smell, the Soap and Glory and Lush products she used to like. She always insisted on us stocking up on them for her at Christmas, so she'd have plenty to last throughout the year. I need to smell her. I disentangle myself from Pam, throw back the sheet, and thrust my arms into my dressing gown while I run into her bedroom. In the doorway, I just stand looking. Her bags are still dumped on the floor from when she came back. She was barely in the house for an hour and hadn't unpacked anything. There may be a clue as to why she's done it in there somewhere.

I open her suitcase and the other bags and tip the contents onto the bed. A jumble of everyday, normal things tumble out. Make-up, clothes, tampons, books, pens. I stop when I see her phone. It's switched off. There'll be missed calls from me when it's turned on. Why wouldn't she have taken her phone? My heart speeds up when a diary falls out. I never knew she kept a diary. I leaf through it, but all that's in there are lecture timetables and notes about work due in on her English course. The last time I saw her, at Easter, she said she was enjoying life at uni and her course. Now I wonder if she was lying, or telling me what she thought I wanted to hear to make me happy and not worry about her. It seems there's so much I didn't know about her, my own daughter. She could be so secretive when she wanted to be, the biggest secret she's kept until now being the identity of Noah's father. She said it was some boy at school (but not her school) who'd moved away by the time she discovered she was pregnant. She wouldn't say who or which school he was from. She didn't know where he'd gone. She was adamant about it. In the end, we'd had a big row, and I asked her what she was protecting him from. She'd just said, 'Nothing.' I always thought I had all the time in the world to get her to tell us. Only now, time's run out.

She didn't tell us she was pregnant until well after the time she could have had a termination. The curve of her belly did that one morning, when I walked into her bedroom as she was dressing. I think she was hoping the problem would just go away, like fifteen-year-olds do sometimes.

I throw the diary to one side and root through the other things, but everything's so normal. There's no clue as to why she's done it. Eventually, I stop my mad scrabbling, sit back on my heels and glance over my shoulder. Pam is standing in the doorway, hugging herself, looking helpless.

'What are you looking for?'

'Anything. Anything to explain why she's done it, if it wasn't an accident like the police suggested. I need to know what was so bad she couldn't confide in me or her dad about it.'

Just then, the front door slams and I hear voices in the hallway, followed by Noah's high-pitched giggle.

Pam glances in the direction of the noise. 'The lads have fed him and played with him, but he kept asking to come home all last night.'

Noah rushes into the bedroom and clamps himself onto me like a limpet. I haven't stopped to think about him in all of this, not once. But now it hits me; how do you tell a three-year-old his Mummy is dead? I can tell from how he's acting that he's scared. I think back to what we said when the policewoman was here, what he might have heard, but I can't recall. He's sucking his thumb again. He saw Issy so infrequently he might not even miss her. It never occurred to me when I gave up my job, my life, to look after him that Issy would take such a small role in his life. She didn't come home from uni for months at a time, and I can't help feeling Noah has been dumped on us and we've been dumped on him. I love him, of course, but Issy often didn't seem to want to be around him. She wouldn't admit it, but I could tell. I hoped that would change over the years. Now we'll never know.

'I'll tell him if you like.'

It seems Pam has read my mind. I don't question it; for us, it's normal.

'Would you? I can't...'

'Yes, I will. When you want me to.'

'I don't know when. Not yet. Not today.'

She looks at me for a long time, then nods. 'No, not today. When you think it's right.'

I can hear the boys whispering downstairs: Sammy, at twenty-three, four years older than Issy, tall, blonde and strong, and still doing law at uni after starting two years late; Joey, fifteen, studious and, some would say, a geek; and Carl, twelve, with his dad's intelligent green eyes and easy-going nature, sporty and full of mischief.

Pam puts a hand on my shoulder. 'I'll go check everything's okay.' She leaves, closing the door quietly behind her. Downstairs, I hear her speaking in hushed tones to her sons.

Noah, still cuddling up to me, loosens his grip, struggles to sit back up, then scoots to the end of the bed and slithers off, out of the room. I listen to him rooting around in his bedroom and he's soon back, clutching his favourite picture book.

'Read please, Grandma,' he demands, climbing back onto the bed and thrusting it towards me.

My throat closes up as an image of Issy demanding a story fills my mind. She was always a bookworm and loved one story after another until I practically ran out of voice. Noah's just the same, but it won't be his mum reading to him every day. Not that it ever was. Truth is, if we hadn't shown him pictures of her on a regular basis and said 'Mummy', I don't know if he would have recognised her when she came home.

I'm lost in my thoughts when he jabs me in the ribs with the hardback cover.

'Read,' he says again, reaching up to pat my cheek with his fat little hand.

I can't read it to him because I can't find a voice to speak with. After a few deep breaths, I say, 'Sammy will read it if you ask him. Grandma's tired now.'

Noah looks as if he's considering what I've said. He can't resist Pam's sons. He idolises them, especially Sammy.

'Okay,' he says, and leans over to peck me on the cheek. His lips are soft and very wet. 'See later.'

For a while, I'm alone in the silent bedroom. Issy is everywhere and nowhere. Eventually, I go back to my own bedroom and get back into bed. Pam comes in with two slices of toast and a cup of tea. I know I won't be able to swallow any of it. Why do people think they have to force feed you at times like this?

'Just try one bite,' she says, holding a slice up to my mouth as if I can't feed myself.

I know she'll insist if I refuse. I try to chew, but it's as if there's no saliva in my mouth. A sip of tea helps it go down, but I can't face any more. I'm not convinced even that tiny piece will stay down and I push the plate away.

'I'll just have the tea,' I say as my sister's face tightens. I know she's worried about me, of course. Hell, *I'm* worried about me. And Jon. I truly don't know if we'll survive this.

'Where's Jon?' I ask her.

'He said he was making you a cup of tea, but he went out. He didn't say where. Justin saw him pulling out of the drive in his car.'

That's odd. It's not like him to not tell me where he's going or why these days. My next thought is *what if he's gone to her?*

'There is something I need help with,' I say to Pam.

She takes my hand. 'Anything.'

I try to say the one word I know won't come out. The word I've been dreading.

29

'I don't know how to plan a... a... her... funeral.'

As soon as the word is out of my mouth, my shoulders heave and I'm crying again. You shouldn't have to plan your child's funeral. It's not right. In the midst of this, Justin calls up the stairs.

'There's a man here to see you, Mel. I don't know who he is, but Jon's not here.'

'Just give us a minute, love,' Pam calls down to him. 'Take your time. They can wait,' she says to me.

I get out of bed, shove some clothes on and go downstairs. A man I've never seen before is standing on the doorstep, wearing jeans and a T-shirt. He looks young and his eyes are red and puffy, like he's been crying. Like my own.

'Mrs Warner,' he says, struggling to speak. 'I'm so sorry, but I had to come. I'm the lorry driver from the accident with your daughter.'

6

Jon

I'M STANDING AT THE junction where it happened. My feet feel hot and sweaty. I look down and see I'm still wearing slippers and pyjama bottoms with a baggy T-shirt. People are turning to look, but I don't care. I could be stark bollock naked and I wouldn't care. I was right. There is a camera there, pointing right at the crossroads. It will have recorded everything.

The road is open, and the traffic is running smoothly. It's busy, as usual. There's absolutely no trace that my daughter died here twenty-four hours ago. I scour the tarmac for any signs of blood or tyre tracks, but there's nothing. She's been wiped away, as if she didn't exist. My eyes sweep over the verge opposite and I see something nestling in the over-long grass. I have to dash across the road to get it, and a car horn pips at me as I see a gap and race across. My eyes are glued to the small piece of turquoise metal, and I scramble onto the grass verge next to it. Exhaust fumes from the lorries thundering by are directed straight into my face. I cough and splutter, even as my fingers are closing around the metal. It's part of Issy's bumper. I'd know it anywhere.

I can remember the day we went to buy a car for her when she'd just passed her test two years ago. It was the colour that took her fancy more than the car itself.

31

'It's bright, Dad, and fun. The colour of the sea in the Caribbean on those holiday adverts. I love it.'

And that was it. She had to have it. And the personalised plate I paid an arm and a leg for. Mel still doesn't know how much it really cost. I couldn't say no to Issy, even though I wouldn't have been seen dead driving it. The memory dies as the words sink in; *she did die driving it*. I turn the metal over in my hands. It's twisted and buckled and has obviously borne the brunt of a terrific force. There's nothing else here to see, and the fumes are clogging up my nose. I stand up and walk to the pedestrian crossing, still clutching the bumper part to me. It leaves black streaks all over my white T-shirt. People are still looking at me from their cars as I get back to where mine is parked: the nutter in the PJ's, slippers and filthy T-shirt. Let them look. I stow the piece of bumper in my boot.

In my wallet is a card. Inspector Steve Jackson's number is on it. He was one of the people who came round yesterday, the day after Issy had died, the highest-ranking officer to come so far. He gave it to me himself and said to call anytime, so I will. In person. It's only a short drive to the cop shop and when I get there, I'm in luck. He's in.

'Hello, Jon,' he says when he comes to fetch me. He shakes my hand. He reminds me of a fox, with his thin, angular face, not helped by the sandy colour of his thinning hair and over-bright, inquisitive eyes. The light brown suit is rumpled, his tie slightly askew. He has a keen, serious air about him, like not much gets past him. 'Come through and we can talk.'

He leads me down a maze of corridors and dreary little rooms into his office. It's as dull and nondescript as the ones we've just passed and there are several desks in there, but no other people.

He points me to a chair. 'What can I do for you?' He takes a seat opposite me and clasps his hands on the desk, wearing his most sympathetic face. If he's noticed my strange attire, he hasn't alluded to it.

'I want to see the footage from the camera at the junction.'

His mouth tightens. 'I see. Any particular reason?'

'To see for myself.'

He's silent for a few seconds. 'Are you sure that's for the best?'

'Yes. I'm sure.'

I cross my arms over my chest and lean back, locking eyes with his. He stares back at me, then his shoulders slump slightly. His eyes flick towards the door, as if measuring his escape. Then back at me.

'If you're absolutely sure, I can certainly arrange that.'

I breathe out and my muscles unclench a bit. 'When?'

'Maybe tomorrow...'

'No, today. Now.'

He looks startled but doesn't argue. Gives a tiny nod.

'I'll see what I can do.'

His chair legs scrape on the hard floor and he stands up slowly with his hands spread on the desk. His fingernails are not bitten or ragged, but nicely rounded. Nice, clean, pink, healthy nails. Not misshapen or rough at all, nor are his hands calloused. A man who doesn't get his hands dirty during his police work. No grubbing around in the dirt for him. Or pulling dead bodies from car wrecks.

He's gone half an hour. During that time, my phone rings three times; all Mel. I ignore it. If I decide not to tell her where I've been, I'll make something up later. I return it to the pocket of my pyjama bottoms and stand up when Jackson comes back into the room. He has a beaten look about him. He doesn't want me to do this. Probably not for any other reason than he's a decent man who doesn't want me to make things worse for myself.

'It's all set up for you, Jon. If you'd like to follow me.'

As we reach the door, he puts his hand on my arm. His fingers are cool on my skin.

'Are you absolutely sure about this? Once we start down these roads, it can make things worse. We can't change what's done, and—'

33

'I'm sure. Thank you.' I stare at his hand until he removes it.

I gesture for him to lead the way and follow him down more corridors to a room where a single desk and chair is set up. A monitor is waiting, the screen dark, with a keyboard in front of it. Jackson points to the chair, then leans over from behind me and presses the space bar. He steps back, out of my eye line, but I can feel him there. I lean forward as the screen comes to life.

There's an image of the crossroads. It takes me a few seconds to orient myself with the road layout. The camera is on the main road and I can see Issy's car from the front, passenger-side on. I can make her out in the driving seat. I have a clear view of the road and she clearly misses several opportunities to cross. The man behind her is waving his arms about, getting agitated at her not moving, and time goes by agonisingly slowly. These are the last precious minutes of my girl's life. My heart is thudding a painful, crazy rhythm in my chest that I'm sure must be audible in the room. Sweat blooms under my armpits and on my temples, but my eyes are fixed on the screen. Issy's lips move. I can't make out what she says, but it looks like *sorry* more than anything else. Her eyes are fixed on whatever is travelling from the right. I can't see it yet. There's no audio with the picture and, without warning, Issy's car lurches forward, straight into a lorry that has no chance of stopping. Even though I knew it was coming, it takes me by surprise and I shoot up from my chair, which clatters to the floor behind me. The crash it makes coincides with the impact on the screen, and Jackson leaps forward a foot into the air. I look back at the monitor. Issy's car is a total mess as the lorry ploughs into the driver's side, swerving and taking the car with it onto the wrong side of the road. It's a miracle it doesn't hit anything else. The lorry stops when it spins round a full one-eighty, ending up facing the other way, with Issy's mangled car still stuck somehow to its front end. I can see the stricken face of the driver in the cab. As I watch, the cab door opens, and the driver jumps out, running around and clutching his head. Other cars have stopped and people are beginning to leave their vehicles, several with phones in their hands. The driver is on his knees now, his eyes fixed on Issy's car. There's no movement inside the car and, after going to the morgue, I know why.

'Jon?' A quiet voice comes from behind me. 'Let's turn it off, eh?' A hand reaches for the space bar and I let him hit it. The action on the screen freezes, and the horror in front of me stops.

'Come on,' says Jackson and opens the door. I'm trembling violently as I follow him back to his office and sit down, trying to quell the rising nausea spiralling up inside me. I remember passing a toilet down the corridor and I propel myself out of the chair, down the hall and into a cubicle just in time to drop to my knees and throw up burning acid. There's no food inside me to come up. The toilet bowl smells bad and makes the retching worse. I push myself up and wash my face at the basin, swilling the taste out of my mouth. When I open the door, Jackson's waiting for me in the corridor.

'Alright?'

I nod but can't speak. I'm too busy reliving the horror on the screen. It was conclusive, if nothing else. She did it on purpose, without a doubt. I try to take a step, but my legs are so wobbly I lurch to one side.

'Maybe you should go home, Jon. Want me to drive you?'

I'm still shaking. 'No, my car's outside.'

'Are you in a fit state to drive it, though?'

'Probably not.'

He touches my arm. 'I think you're in shock. Understandably. Let's go get a drink somewhere away from here, and talk about it.'

I don't want to talk about it, but I could use some time to recover before I go home. A Starbucks is opposite the police station and I follow him there. We get two cappuccinos and sit at a table near the door.

'Do you have any kids?' I ask, feeling calmer away from the oppressive air of the cop shop.

He looks almost guilty for a second, then nods. 'Two daughters.'

'Keep them safe.'

'You poor bastard,' he says, shaking his head. 'No one deserves what's happened to you. Anything I can do to help, anything, you call me. Okay?'

'Yeah. Thanks.'

We sit in silence for the next ten minutes, sipping coffee. I appreciate him not pushing me, and the silence isn't awkward.

'Anything to eat?' he asks more than once.

'No. Thank you.' I stand up to go.

'The offer to drive you is still there.'

'I'll be alright, now. Thank you for your kindness. It's noted.'

He accompanies me to my car outside and lifts a hand as I drive away. I know what he's thinking: how sorry for me he is and how he's glad it isn't him. It's what I'd be thinking. I drive like a robot, on autopilot, not really seeing, just reacting to things, and when I pull onto my drive, I feel numb. There's a car parked outside my house, one I've never seen before. I hope it's not going to be an endless stream of visitors again, like yesterday. I trudge through the door, wondering whether I can sneak upstairs instead, but Mel comes out of the living room with a face that looks as though the blood has been drained out of it.

'Jon,' she says. 'You need to come in here now.'

I follow her into the living room. Framed by the sun coming in through the bay window is a man who looks familiar, but I can't quite place. Pam and Justin are standing at the far end where the dining table is.

'Jon, this is the driver of the lorry. He just got here a minute ago. He says he has something important to tell us.' She looks down at my slippers and pyjamas, frowns at the black smear on my front. I take a step past her.

The man is young, maybe thirtyish, and his dark brown, curly hair is fashionably too long. He has tattoos running down both arms, and his hands are thrust into the front pockets of his jeans. He's trembling and in his eyes I see a haunted look, probably like the one in my own. After all, I've now seen what he saw. His voice is husky and tremulous.

'I'm sorry, but I need to tell you what happened before she drove her car in front of me. She looked at me and mouthed 'I'm sorry'. I read her lips, plain as day. It's all I've seen since then. It was no accident. Your daughter killed herself and used my lorry to do it.'

Mel is shaking her head. 'No, it was an accident,' she says, at the same time as I say, 'Yeah, mate. I know she did.'

7

Mel

'I'M SORRY, WHAT DID you say?' I ask Jon. 'You know she did? How could you know?'

Jon's face is strained and pinched tight. He says, 'I know it was suicide. It wasn't an accident.'

'What do you mean? And where've you been, dressed like that?'

Jon rubs a hand over his face and sighs heavily. 'Mel, love, the police said as much. It wasn't your fault... er, sorry, I don't know your name...' He tails off, gesturing at the man who looks like he'd rather be anywhere but here.

'Greg,' he says. He looks relieved at what my husband has just said.

Whereas I want to batter him into a million pieces. He killed Issy and now he's turned up here, large as life, saying it was her fault.

'But why would Issy kill herself?' I sink into a chair as my legs give way. 'She was happy.' *Wasn't she?*

'I don't know,' says Jon, sounding weary.

I don't know what's come over him. How could he possibly think Issy would do this? He's taking Greg's side when, really, Greg's probably trying to avoid going to prison for dangerous driving or something. I see Pam at the other end of the room, wringing her hands over and over, as if washing them endlessly. Justin is standing next to her, his hands thrust into his pockets and head down, listening to every word we're saying.

'What proof have you got?' I say to Greg, 'That it wasn't you going too fast? That you didn't just drive into her?'

Greg swallows, and his Adam's apple bobs up and down. He looks nervous, darting glances between me and Jon. 'There are cameras at the crossroads. Traffic cameras. I've seen the video, watched it with the police. They agree there was nothing I could have done.'

At this, Jon's head snaps up and his eyes slide towards me. His expression is unreadable.

'I want to see it,' I say. 'Then I'll believe it.'

'No,' says Jon, sharply. 'You don't.'

Greg sinks onto the sofa behind him, and I realise he's crying when his shoulders shake.

'Please, Mrs Warner. You have to believe me. I'm a good, careful driver, with a clean record. Driving is my job. I know how dangerous that junction can be. Plus, why would she apologise if she wasn't planning it? Why?'

I can't stand to look at him right this minute. I have no words to say to him. He's lying. He must be.

'Get out of my house,' I finally blurt out. Then I scream, 'Get out!'

I take a step towards him. In my mind, I'm scratching at his face, kicking and punching him, punishing him for his lies. I take another step, my hands bunched into fists. Jon grabs my wrist and pulls me roughly around to face him, startling me.

'He's telling the truth, for God's sake.'

'How do you know? Get off; you're hurting me.'

Instead of releasing me, Jon grips me tighter. His face is so screwed up I barely recognise him. He leans in towards me and the pain in his eyes terrifies me. His breath is sour and I turn my head away from him.

'Because I've seen it too. That's where I've been. I know there are cameras there and I demanded to see the footage. It's true. Everything Greg says is true.'

Greg looks up at this, his eyes fixed on Jon. 'Really?' he whispers. 'You've seen it?'

'Yes.' Jon drops my wrist and looks at the driver. 'How old are you?'

'Thirty,' Greg answers.

I rub my wrist where Jon's fingers have left red marks.

'Please, sit down. We need to talk about this. Would you like some coffee or tea?' asks Jon.

I don't believe this. He'll be inviting him for dinner next. *Stay over in Issy's room. She won't be needing it now.*

'Er, coffee please, yeah.' He sits down on the sofa, looking at me, uncertain.

'I'll make it,' says Pam. She hurries out of the room, leaving Justin standing there, shuffling his feet. He'd probably rather be somewhere else. I know I would.

My legs no longer feel like they'll hold me up and I sit heavily on the nearest chair, twisting round to look at Jon. 'You've seen it? Today? Why didn't you tell me where you were going?'

'It was a spur-of-the-moment thing,' Jon says distractedly, and goes to sit beside Greg. 'Please. Tell me everything. And thank you for coming. It can't have been easy.'

I feel numb. But if Jon's seen it, it must be true. He wouldn't lie about a thing like this, would he? He's lied to me before, loads of times, but that was different. I take in the man sitting in my living room, his face buried in his hands.

'I haven't slept since it happened,' he says, in a choked voice. 'Every time I close my eyes, that's all I see. Her car.' He lifts his head and looks at me. 'I'm sorry. You have to believe me. I didn't mean to come here and break down like this, but I wanted you to know who I am. It's important. I don't want people thinking I killed somebody recklessly. I couldn't live with that.'

Jon is sitting quietly, twisting his fingers together in his lap. I wish I knew what he was thinking. He looks haggard, with his unshaven face, unkempt hair, and haunted eyes.

'If you came for forgiveness, you have it from me. It wasn't your fault,' Jon says.

I can hardly believe what I'm hearing. I can't say the same about forgiving him. It feels like Jon's betraying me. I can't listen to them anymore.

'I'm sorry,' I mumble and flee from the room, passing Pam in the hallway, carrying a tray with cups on.

'Mel?' she says, as I rush past her and up the stairs.

I reach the sanctuary of my bedroom and slam the door whilst grief overtakes me. There's no point in fighting it. I can hear Jon downstairs, plus Justin's deep rumble and Greg's huskier voice. I wonder what they're talking about. Me, probably. The nutty woman. Someone raps on the door, breaking into my thoughts. I know it's Pam before she speaks.

'Can I come in?'

'Not right now. I need a moment.'

Still weeping, I stand near the window and look out on the back garden while she goes back downstairs. I can hear her soft tread and the creak on the third and eighth stairs. Outside, it's a gloriously sunny June afternoon. Pam's boys are playing football with Noah in the back garden, on the weed-free, neatly trimmed grass, in the child-friendly zone of the garden, well away from the sandstone patio and the lush borders. It's a normal, tranquil scene with no clues as to the horrors of what happened yesterday. I watch them for a while, my stomach churning constantly.

I can see into next door from here, where our neighbours, two young women tenants in their twenties, are lying on sun loungers in bikinis. There's no fat on either of them and I envy them their youth, their freedom, their slim bodies, their happiness and their unwritten futures. I think of my own body after just one child. Stretch marks, saggy skin, breasts like empty sacs at the top. I used to look like them once. Not that I care now. Meanwhile, they laugh and chat, with their whole lives ahead of them. Issy was like that a couple of days

41

ago. I wasn't. I've had the responsibility of Noah weighing on me for the last three years.

Obviously, it wasn't what I wanted for Issy, getting pregnant at fifteen. What mother would want that? She could only go to uni and carry on with her life if I gave up mine to look after him. There was never any question of Jon giving up his job as a freelance garden landscape designer. After all, real men have to go out and earn money, don't they? My job in the office at the high school was no big deal, was it? Even though I loved it and didn't want to give it up. So it was down to me to make the biggest sacrifice of all.

When you find out your fifteen-year-old daughter is pregnant, it feels like the end of the world. She'd always been a quiet girl, sometimes secretive. Not the kind of girl to ask for help with anything, and she never seemed to want or need to confide in me. She'd become snappy and tearful but I didn't suspect she was pregnant, didn't even know she was seeing anyone, let alone having sex with them until that day I walked into her bedroom and saw her belly. By then, she was too far gone to have a termination. She was six months and busy hiding her head in the sand. Much as I love Noah, if he'd never been conceived or born, our lives would have been very different, mine especially. I'd looked forward to being a grandma many years down the line, not while my teenage daughter was still a child herself and living at home. I'd envisaged enjoying some freedom when she left home, enjoying my job and going to her wedding at some point, then children after that. None of that had happened, nor would it ever, now.

All she would say was that Noah's father was a boy she'd met at a party. She got drunk and slept with him, and he was never her boyfriend. She said he wasn't from her school and she'd never told him she was pregnant. Didn't know where he lived or how to find him. Then she told us he'd moved away. Now we'll probably never find out who he is. He has the right to know he's got a son, surely? And his parents are grandparents, too.

42

Over the back fence is a playing field, just visible over the line of small trees and bushes Jon planted when we moved in. This house had the biggest garden of all the ones we'd looked at, despite having the smallest square footage inside. For Jon, it's never about the house. It's about the outside space, where he can indulge his wildest dreams with landscaping and planting. It's certainly beautiful—he's good at what he does. But I'd have liked a bigger house. You don't live in the garden, do you? But he wouldn't budge. There's a game of football going on in the playing field and some kids on a slide and some swings. It's a nice area, this, with modest houses. We're not wealthy people by any means. We were so proud of Issy when she got a place at uni, although my heart sank when I realised she would barely be around to parent Noah. They'd both miss out, and I'd be the one at home all day. The truth is, he wears me out. He's easy to love but can be strong-willed and stubborn when he wants to be. Issy could be like that sometimes as well.

Outside, Noah shrieks as Joey squirts him with water from a water bottle and wriggles away from him, still squealing. If Joey knew there were near-naked girls over the fence less than five feet away, he wouldn't be so calm and collected, despite his geek persona. His male hormones would be racing round his body, controlling his brain. I remember when Jon was consumed by his urges and we gave into our passions at every opportunity. Then he gave into them with someone else. Now, after what's happened, we'll probably never be happy or carefree enough to make love again.

I go to the door and pull it open. I can hear the three men downstairs, the rumble of three distinctly separate low voices, but I can't make out what they're saying. I stop dead when I see Pam sitting on the bottom step, but it's too late. She's seen me.

'Okay?' she asks.

No, of course I'm bloody not. My child is dead. I somehow manage to nod, my head feeling stiff and almost fused to my neck. I go back to the unanswered question from earlier. 'So, will you help me plan the funeral?'

8

Jon

TODAY IS THE WORST day of my life. I can't believe it's really happening. Outside the church, I hoist Issy's coffin onto my shoulder to carry it inside. Justin is at the other back corner, looking as uncomfortable in his new funeral suit as I feel in mine, and we glance at each other. His mouth is set in a tight, grim line and he nods at me, willing into me the strength to move my feet, one in front of the other. *One step at a time* is all I can think. The doors open and we begin to go forward. I try to suppress the tremors and the nausea that start up, but they don't go away. Two of the funeral directors have the front end and I focus on the straight, black-suited back of the one in front of me.

The church is packed, and every inch of space seems to have someone sitting or standing in it. The church wasn't my idea. Issy never set foot in a church. Instead, Mel insisted. She said that it was important for Issy's soul that the service was presided over by a vicar. Personally, I can't stand the places or the people in them; I've always found them to be a bunch of hypocrites. Churches give me the creeps. Mel's not religious either, but goes to church on certain occasions; Christmas, weddings, christenings. And, of course, funerals.

We continue our slow walk down the aisle to the mournful music of the organ. The collar on my new shirt is stiff and cuts uncomfortably into my neck. Everyone's looking at me, their collective sympathy like a tidal wave. I can feel them thinking *poor bastard–I'm glad it's not me*. I'd be thinking the same. The thought of dropping the coffin fills me with fresh horror. Visions of Issy's mangled body tipping out flood my mind, and panic starts to spiral out of control as beads of sweat form on my brow. Apart from the undertakers and the pathologist, I'm the only one who knows what Issy actually looks like inside the coffin. I haven't told a soul about the cuts on her arms. Maybe her legs were the same. I should have checked, pulled the sheet down and looked when I had the chance.

Calm down, breathe, I repeat inside my head, all the way up the aisle. Mel's not far behind me, following the coffin, and I can hear her wailing and sobbing. Pam's supporting her on one side, and their mother, Kitty, is on the other. Three generations of females in their family, and it's the youngest one being buried here today. No; cremated, I mean. When we get through the horror of this, we have the further nightmare of the crematorium to face. I gulp deep lungfuls of air.

We're halfway down the aisle now, and I try to focus on the people who are there. I can't believe Issy knew all these. I don't know half of them, apart from a few of her friends and teachers from school. Because Mel used to work at the high school, there are staff from there who've come to the funeral for her and because they knew Issy. Some of them deserted us like rats on a sinking ship when Issy got pregnant, and it riles me that they've come today. Talk about judgemental. Issy went from quiet schoolgirl to slag overnight. The whole thing was horrible, but she stuck it out as long as she could. After Noah was born, she didn't go back. She went to college instead, where no one knew her.

Some of her friends are with their parents and, everywhere, people are crying. Out of the corner of my eye, I see Justin glance over his shoulder at his wife. He looks as stricken as I feel. Issy's death has hit him and Pam as hard as me and Mel. They were so close to her. They'd babysat for her many times over the years, as we had for their sons. Their place was home from home for Issy and, with them only living round the corner, their boys were forever running in and out of our house. It was normal for me to come home and not know how many were going to be staying for tea.

We'd been on holidays, spent Christmases together, birthdays, everything. When I'd met Mel, Pam was already going out with Justin and I kind of left my other friends behind. It wasn't intentional, but the four of us just had no need of anyone else. We were a tight unit and stayed that way. It's just the same now. Pam and Justin have been a great support, rallying round and arranging the funeral. Plus, Noah's stayed with them a lot over the last two weeks, since Issy died, whilst we've struggled to cope.

Two whole weeks since she came home and went out to die. I missed her by an hour. Before that, I hadn't seen her since the Easter break, which means it's been three months since I held her, saw her, kissed her. By now, we've reached the front, and I face the task of placing the coffin on the wooden stand in the middle of the aisle. It's like some sort of public test—can the man who couldn't keep his daughter alive put her coffin down without dropping it? Before we came in, the funeral director ran us through what happens, for mine and Justin's benefit. I can barely hear the organ playing for the rushing sound of blood inside my head.

On a visual signal, we lower the coffin down carefully into place. That's when I hear it; a slight thud. For one split second I think it's Issy, then I stumble forward when something hits the backs of my legs and I jump to the side, away from the wooden stand. It's Mel, behind me. She's fainted and is lying, crumpled, half in the nearest pew. Her eyes are closed and her face is bone-white.

'Mel,' I say, kneeling to cradle her.

She hasn't overheated. This place is cold, even in June, with its expanses of cold stone and concrete floors. The organist falters, as flustered as the rest of us, and plays some wrong notes. It sounds comical and I can imagine Issy rolling her eyes and saying *For God's sake, you lot!*

Mel groans and turns her head to one side. Her eyes flutter, skittering over her surroundings, flitting over my black suit, then spring open. She struggles to get up and I help her to stand, leading her into the pew at the front that's been reserved for us.

'Are you okay?' I ask her.

Tears are sliding down her face and she just shakes her head.

I put my arm around her. 'Let's just get this over with, eh?'

Her eyes slide to the coffin, resplendent with its purple and red sprays of flowers, Issy's favourite colours, on the top. I'd imagined the next time Issy would have been surrounded by flowers in a church would have been at her wedding, but there again, she probably wouldn't have got married in a church at all. She told me once she couldn't see the point of marriage.

'It's not natural to be monogamous. People cheat all the time,' she'd said. It had taken me by surprise, how fiercely she said it, especially as she was only about thirteen at the time. I didn't even think she knew what monogamous meant. A lot of her friends' parents were divorced, and she'd seen her friends go through hell because of it. The fact that her mother and I were still together didn't seem to occur to her.

Mel tugs at my sleeve and I realise I'm the only one left standing. The rest of the congregation has sat down and the vicar is waiting patiently to start, his eyes moving over the crowd, wearing a pious expression. His face irritates me. If his God is so wonderful, why do things like this happen? I sit down heavily, the pew hard against my back. I try to listen to the vicar as he talks about Issy as if he knew her, but it's all crap. He's never met her. She would have hated this place with all its formality and pomp. I can hear her whispering *It gives me the creeps, Dad*. I hear a giggle, her giggle, bright and sparkly and not heard often enough. I look around, half-expecting to see her, and realise it's in my head. She isn't here. She isn't in the coffin either. What's left of her, the best parts, are in our memories. Mel is sobbing loudly into a bundle of soggy tissues. After this is over, I don't know how she'll cope.

Last night, I found her sitting on the bed with various pills in packets spread out in front of her. She must have gone through every drawer in the house, stockpiling tablets. There were ibuprofen, paracetamol, aspirin, co-codamol, stuff collected over the years from doctors and hospital visits. I never knew we had all this stuff. Some of them must have been well past their use-by dates. My heart had lurched when I'd walked into the bedroom and seen it.

She'd jumped a mile and said, 'Oh, I thought you were in the garden.'

Evidently. 'What are you doing?' I'd asked, kneeling on the floor beside her.

She'd shrugged, glanced at me, then dropped her eyes. 'Trying to make the pain go.'

She knew there was no point in denying it. These last two weeks have sent us to hell and we're still there. Every day has started with us in a black hole and ended the same. I may never climb out. As well as the pain of losing my daughter, I'm now in fear every day of what Mel may do. She can't cope with looking after Noah on top of everything else, and he's been at Pam's most nights. He's been crying to come home, but I don't feel he's safe with us. We can barely look after ourselves, let alone him.

There's a nudge in my ribs from Justin. Everyone's stood up to sing a hymn. For one rebellious moment, I want to stay sitting and not sing about how great God is, but it's Issy's funeral. It's about her, not me. I can't sing a note, can't even mumble the words, so I stop trying, and slump back onto the pew when it's over. Pam is next to Mel, and Kitty is on the far side of Pam. She's a small, frail woman who had her twin daughters late in life. When her husband died, not long after Issy was born, it seemed to knock the stuffing out of her. Now, she's lost her only granddaughter, and she idolised Issy. As Issy's only living grandparent, they were remarkably close, and she was always there for Issy. She was the only one who could get away with calling her Isabella, her full name. 'It means beautiful and you are,' she'd say.

She bows her head now, in prayer. I stare at the black trousers of my new suit.

'You should have worn red trousers, Dad. Added a bit of colour to this place,' I hear Issy saying. I know it's in my head, but I can't help glancing round. Everyone else is still, heads bowed, and the vicar drones on about how good God is.

Good? If he's that damn good, he wouldn't have taken my daughter, would he? I imagine how it would feel to stand up and scream this at the top of my voice. I'd do it, but Mel would never forgive me. But it's true. Issy would find it funny. *Go Dad!* I can hear her say.

The service manages to both drag and fly at the same time, and then we're following the coffin out of the church, trooping into bright daylight, to clamber into waiting cars to begin the drive to the crematorium. Mel seems to have recovered from fainting earlier, but she's pale and quiet, and has a small red mark on her forehead. We sit in our own worlds. It took a lot for me to convince her that Issy had driven in front of the lorry deliberately. She tried to deny it so many times, but in the end, she had to believe me. Since I told her I'd been to see the traffic camera footage, she's treated me like the enemy, on and off. She thinks I sided with Greg, but he was telling the truth. It's like another wedge has been driven between us, this one a wedge that used to be our daughter. Some days we've barely spoken to each other.

All the way to the crematorium, Mel looks out of the window, averting her face from the rest of us in the car. Justin, Pam and Kitty share the car with us and Sammy. Joey and Carl are in another car behind. My own parents are dead and my sister, Jenny, lives in Australia. We're not close and she hasn't come over for the funeral. She sent a card and some flowers. She's twelve years older than me and we have nothing in common, never have done. The last time I saw her was at my father's funeral seventeen years ago, after he died from a heart condition no one knew about. Mum had died of cancer two years before that. It was a bleak two years of my life, but nothing compared to this. Jenny hadn't come over when Issy was born—why would she come now?

We turn into the crematorium. This is the last interaction of anything to do with Issy. After this, there will be only memories. We shuffle obediently into the little chapel where there's nothing to focus on except the coffin. There are fewer people here, but it's still full. All I can think about is the burning and roaring of the furnace they're going to shove my little girl into until there's nothing left. I swallow hard and look around.

There's no one from my work here because I'm a one-man-band. Self-employed. I'm a freelance landscape garden designer and I love it. These days, I mainly draw up plans, rather than do the actual heavy work. When I set up on my own, it was a struggle at first, but word-of-mouth meant my business grew steadily, and I'm constantly busy. People from all over the country send me photos of their gardens and tell me what kind of thing they're after. I interpret it into a working design they then give to their chosen contractors. Mel says I get so much work in because I don't charge enough. Maybe that's true. Occasionally, I get my hands dirty on a local job and that's where I'm happiest, making my design really come to life.

Working on my own means there are no colleagues offering their support here, no sympathetic handshakes or pats on the shoulder from bosses claiming *take as much time as you need.*

The service is mercifully quick, without all the stuffiness of the church. When we were asked if Issy had a favourite song to play at the crem, I was stumped. Since when had I not known what music she liked anymore? I could name her favourite bands and songs right up to her being about fourteen (she'd been heavily influenced by the bands I favoured) but after that, no. It wasn't cool to like the same music as your dad. Of all the things to feel a failure for, not knowing her current favourite song is miniscule, so why did it feel huge? Thankfully, Mel had some suggestions and I listen to the winner being played now, some pile of shit I've never even heard before where some bloke says *YO* a lot and eff-words are blanked out. Did she really like this stuff? It's not even proper singing.

Five minutes later, the curtain closes on the coffin and it's all over. Back to some pub for a good old knees-up. It feels wrong, and I make a snap decision not to go.

Outside in the sunshine, I tell Mel, who's standing with her mother.

She looks aghast. 'Not coming? What do you mean? You have to come. How will it look?'

'I don't care how it looks. I'm not going. She's not there, Mel, and I'm not spending time with these people. I don't know most of them.'

She's angry now. 'So it's okay for me to go alone and have to explain where you are?'

'No. You don't have to do any of those things. You can come back with me now.' I glance over the sweeping green lawns of the crematorium towards the street. Towards freedom. I'll be home in half an hour if I walk. 'So, what's it to be?'

She sets her jaw and judging by the mutinous look on her face, I'm in the doghouse.

'Of course I have to go. One of us has to.'

'Okay.' I start to walk away from the funeral party and a voice calls me back. It's Kitty. She walks towards me. Mel has moved away, disappeared somewhere.

'Jon, be sure of this. If you regret it, you can't turn back the clock.'

'I am sure.'

Her eyes fix on mine, clear and unwavering, and then she nods. 'Go on then. I'll look after Mel.' Then she takes hold of my hands. 'I do understand. Completely.'

It shocks me that I've found an ally in such an unlikely place.

'Thank you, Kitty.'

I spot Mel, standing with her back to me, her shoulders stiff and unyielding. I leave the throng of mourners and walk out of the car park, past flowers and benches and plaques and the big chimney stack with smoke belching out of it. Are they burning her already? Instead of turning left towards home, I turn right, in the direction of the police station. It's hot and I take off my jacket and tie, stuffing them into the first bin I see. As I get nearer to the town centre, shops begin to line the street, tatty junk and charity shops at first, then restaurants, pubs and clothes shops. One has men's clothes in the window and I go in. The interior is dark and cool after the burning sun outside. Some black jeans and a blue T-shirt will do, along with some black trainers. I leave my new trousers, shoes, and shirt in the dressing room. I never want to look at a suit again.

9

Mel

MY HEAD THROBS WHERE I hit it on the pew, and I rub the lump that's there. I never thought he'd have the nerve to come. When I saw him, I just keeled over. Not only did we bury my daughter today, but the man who was responsible for her death, whether intentionally or not, was there. I'd almost reached the front of the church, staring fixedly at Jon's back, which was better than looking at the coffin itself, when I glanced to one side and saw *him*. Greg Evans. I couldn't believe it. What did he think he was doing? He surely couldn't have thought he'd be welcome. I felt the blood drain from my face, then before I knew it I'd fainted, hitting my head on the pew as I fell to one side. Right in front of everyone. Issy would have been mortified, and she would have scolded me for making such a spectacle of myself. I can hear her now saying, '*MUM!*'

And now he's here at the wake, walking straight towards me. He's here, but my husband is not. It's laughable, but not funny. My hand shakes, and tea slops out of the cup and into the saucer as he gets closer. The nerve of him! I want to get away from him, but I can't. Where would I run to? To be fair, he looks terrified and I get a small shot of satisfaction from that. He's scared. Of me. He looks like a small, frightened child. His suit is too big, as if he's lost inside it somewhere, and he looks desperately uncomfortable. At least his bloody awful tattoos are covered up and his hair's been tamed a bit. His eyes are a pale, diluted blue; they remind me of a wolf's I saw on some wildlife programme once. Chilling and cold. Like him.

'Mrs Warner, I hope you don't mind. I had to come.' My cup makes a *chink* sound as it rattles. Mind? Of course I bloody mind. No words come out when I open my mouth. I wish Jon was here. Or maybe I wish that, like Jon, I wasn't.

'Um... how are you?' he asks me, dipping his head slightly in my direction.

What a stupid question. Anger burns within me. 'I've just buried my daughter. How do you imagine I am?'

'Sorry. That was stupid.' He thrusts his hands in his pockets and studies the floor. 'Perhaps I shouldn't have come, but I had to. I haven't slept since. I... I can't get back behind the wheel.'

A muscle twitches at the corner of my eye, once, twice. Then again. 'Am I supposed to feel sorry for you?' I put the cup and saucer down on the nearest table and fold my arms. I feel uncomfortable in this itchy black dress. It's making me sweat.

'No, God, no. Of course not. I just don't want you to think that I'm not affected by what happened. This... ' he waves his hands around uselessly, 'What happened haunts me. I know I can't do anything to make it right for you.'

'No, well, someone can't un-die, can they?' I glare at him. 'Maybe you should leave. Just go.'

He recoils as if I've slapped him, and I'm relieved—he's going to leave. Then his eyes flash. He lifts his chin and pulls his shoulders back, towering over me. I never realised he was so tall. When he came to the house before, he seemed cowed and shrunken.

'Mrs Warner, I'm not responsible for this. Your daughter could have killed me as well with her little stunt. Do you understand that? There were several road users that day. Any one of us could have died because *she'd* decided not to go on living.'

I'm startled at the change in him and take a small step back. His tone has changed from wheedling to cold and forceful, and it hits me that he's right. She could have taken someone else's life with her reckless act. And it was *her* reckless act. Jon's seen the proof. I can't deny it any longer. As I watch him stride away through the room, wearing his hurt like a mantle, I realise how much it's taken for him to come here. I'm not sure I would have dared. Hot shame stabs at me at how I've treated him.

'Wait,' I say, hurrying after him. People turn to look as I rush by, red in the face with a still-twitching eye. He doesn't hear me. Or, if he does, he doesn't stop.

I finally catch up with him outside, at the bottom of the steps that lead up to the entrance. He turns when I call out to him again, his mouth a taut slash in his face.

'Please,' I say, in what I hope sounds like a conciliatory voice. I gesture to the low wall that borders the front of the pub where we can talk in private. 'Sit down with me?'

He pauses, then nods, looking wary. I wonder if he thinks I'm going to rip his head off. We walk over the grass and sit on the low stone wall, away from the other mourners and pub goers. My bubble of righteousness has finally burst. I lace my fingers together in my lap and stare at them, hard.

'I'm sorry. I know it wasn't your fault. What you just said now—I've not thought of it that way. Please forgive me for my appalling behaviour.' I glance up to find him looking intently at me.

He looks gob-smacked at first, then a small smile begins as he accepts the olive branch. 'Thank you. Of course I will.'

'Let's start from scratch. Would you like a drink?'

'Yeah, thanks. I'll have an orange juice. But I'll get them, Mrs Warner. What would you like?' He stands up.

'Orange juice would be nice. Thank you. There's some in the main reception room, over near the door. And it's Mel.'

'Understood. Coming up.'

He strides back over the grass and I sit, snarled up with confusion inside and twisting my wedding ring round and round until he comes back, carrying two glasses.

'Thanks.' I take mine and swallow some, along with my last vestiges of pride. 'It must have taken a lot for you to come today. Thank you for bothering.'

He gives a small shake of his head. 'I had to come.'

He leans forward with his elbows on his knees and stares out across the grass, still holding his glass. There's a small fishpond in the middle and a toddler runs round it, chased by his dad. Or Grandad. I think of Issy at that age and it hurts my heart.

'Truth is, I've no idea how to move on from this,' I tell him. 'Issy had a child, Noah. Did you know that?'

'Yeah. I overheard someone at the church mention him. How old is he?'

'He'll be four in a couple of months.'

'Right. Where's Jon, by the way?' He turns to me and nails me with his stare.

I've spent most of this afternoon telling people Jon's gone home because he wasn't feeling well, but suddenly I wonder what's the point in lying? Why should I?

'Honestly? I don't know. He walked out of the crematorium, and I haven't seen him since.'

His eyebrows shoot up. He hasn't heard. 'Oh. I see.'

'I'm a bit jealous now that I didn't do the same. He always does what he wants and leaves me to do the right thing.'

A note of bitterness creeps in. I sense I've made him awkward as he glances down and clears his throat. In unison, we take a sip of our drinks.

'Tell me about Noah,' he says.

'He's a typical boy. Looks like an angel but can be a devil, you know. But he's also very loving. He's got Jon wrapped around his little finger. The child-minder is dropping him off here in a bit. He's way too young for all this. He'd probably have charged around the church with a Lightsaber, shooting the vicar.'

Greg smiles at that. 'How come he lives with you? Oh, I'm sorry. That sounds really nosy. I don't mean to pry. I'm just interested.'

I wave away his apology. 'Issy got pregnant at fifteen, had him at sixteen and I gave up work to look after him so she could finish school and go to uni.'

He raises his eyebrows. 'That's a big thing you did. She was lucky you did that. How did you feel about it, giving up your job?'

Amazingly, he's the only person ever to ask me that. Should I tell him the truth or say what I'm expected to? In other words, lie. I'm grateful he's bothered enough. To my horror, hot tears prickle and I blink them away, determinedly. *Tell the truth. See how it feels.*

'Let's see, well, actually I felt quite resentful that I was just expected to give up my life and go back to looking after a baby, that all the responsibility would fall on me.' It feels quite liberating to say it, and I get the feeling that he won't judge me for it.

'I'll bet,' he says.

'And now, am I going to be his mum forever? To be honest, the thought terrifies me. Before, I always thought she'd take him and live somewhere else one day, in a little family of their own.'

Greg asks the million dollar question. 'What about the dad? Is he not in the picture?'

Well, while I'm airing my dirty linen, might as well go the whole hog.

'We don't know who he is. She would never tell us, and now we have no chance of ever finding out. It was just some boy at a party, like a one time thing.'

'Wow,' he says, and blows out a breath. He looks at me like he's really seeing me for the first time. 'This whole deal is really rough on you, Mel.'

My name sounds weird coming from his lips, but so much better than *Mrs Warner*. It makes him more my equal somehow. I'm only ten years older than him, but up to now it's seemed like a gulf. He's smack-bang in the middle of me and Issy in age, but I've been thinking of him more like her generation. Now I see he's not. He could be married with half-grown kids of his own, for all I know.

But now the words are out, feelings of betrayal start to rear up and swell like that foam stuff you spray into cracks in walls. I try to shake them off. I shouldn't have told anyone how I really feel. It's disloyal.

'Do you have kids?' I ask, sipping more orange.

He shakes his head, then smiles. 'Not that I know of. It's not my thing. Well, up to press, anyway. I might feel different one day, who knows.'

When I look at him again, I see the man, not the boy. His wavy hair is thick and curling way below his collar, and stubble is beginning to dot his chin. Dark hair on the backs of his hands disappears under his jacket sleeves. It's not unattractive. Does he see a middle-aged woman when he looks at me? Possibly. I'm suddenly angry with Issy for ruining his life as well as mine. He didn't deserve it.

'I'm sorry for what my daughter has done to you. She's wrecked your life, hasn't she?'

When he looks at me, his eyes are shiny. 'A bit, yeah, I suppose.' He tries a weak smile. 'Thank you for understanding.'

'What will you do if you can't go back to driving?'

'I don't know. It's all I've ever done. I'm not qualified for anything else. When I was little, I wanted to drive big trucks, and that's what I did. Always enjoyed it. 'Til now.' He pulls a rueful face.

If he can't work, what will he do? I know how horrible it is to have a job you love swiped from under you for reasons beyond your control. How could my daughter do this to someone? Did we not bring her up properly or something? It occurs to me we can't have. She did get pregnant at fifteen, after all.

'Where did you used to work?' he asks.

'At school. In the office. Issy's high school, actually, Ridge Academy. You know, admin-type stuff. Quite a few people I used to work with are here; teachers and dinner ladies and such like. I haven't seen any of them since I left four years ago. I don't know what to say to them. But it was nice of them to come.'

'Yeah. It always amazes me, though, how people you haven't seen for years make the effort to go to funerals. It's weird. People need to know how much they're thought of while they're alive. It's too late when you're dead.' He takes a sharp breath in and I know why. He's scared of saying the wrong thing. Everyone at the funeral is. It's almost laughable; we're at a funeral and frightened of upsetting people by saying the 'D' word.

Just then, Elaine, our occasional child minder, appears, walking up the front path and holding Noah by the hand. She hasn't seen me. I'm just about to stand up and call to her when Sammy approaches her and picks him up. They both look towards me and she nods, leans in to say something to Noah, then walks over the grass to me.

'Hi. I'm not going to stick around. I've got to get back,' she says. 'Jodie's parents' evening.' She flushes slightly as she says it. After all, her kid is still alive.

'Okay. Thank you, Elaine.'

She walks off quickly, looking eager to get away. I don't blame her. Sammy puts Noah down and Noah reaches up to hold his hand, beaming at him. Beside me, Greg is speaking again.

'That must be Noah.'

'It is. That's my sister's boy, Sammy, with him. She's got three lads and they're all brilliant with him. He's like their baby brother.'

'Mel? I've been looking for you everywhere.'

My head jerks up at the sound of my sister's voice and I turn to see her striding towards me. Her eyes slide to Greg and back to me. She nods a greeting at him.

'Sorry to interrupt, but people are beginning to leave. They want to say goodbye. Shall I send them out here?'

'No, I'll come in.' I stand and hold out my hand to Greg to shake. 'Thank you again.'

He grasps my hand and shakes it as he stands up. 'No, thank you,' he says.

On impulse, I say, 'Come by the house if you need to talk. Maybe we can help each other get through this.'

He looks pleased and smiles. 'If you're sure. I'd like that. Thank you.'

Pam loops her arm through mine and leads me back over the grass. 'What was that all about?'

'Forgiveness, Pam. Pure and simple forgiveness. On both our parts, I think.'

10

Jon

BY THE TIME I reach the police station, I'm sweating in the blazing sun. My new T-shirt has wet patches under the armpits, and the trainers are rubbing my feet. Several times on the way here, I've thought about ringing Mel, but I haven't done it. I'll suffer for it later, not going to the wake, but I couldn't do it, sit there making small talk with everyone. I'm a practical man, and I need to do something practical now. Grieving can wait. I need to find out what made Issy decide that taking her own life was better than living. She had everything to live for. Or so we'd thought.

On the walk here, I've had lots of time to think. When we'd found out she was pregnant, my first assumption was that her life was over, she wouldn't be able to finish her education and get a good job, but we pulled together as a family and Mel had given up her job to look after Noah. I was surprised when she offered. She loved her job, but she's always had a strong sense of family, of duty, of doing the right thing. For me to give up work to look after Noah was out of the question. It takes all my time to keep the business going. Besides, it's not what men do. We need to provide, not be at home all day looking after kids. If I'm honest, it was enough of a shock coming home from work every day to find a baby in the house again. It took some getting used to. Even though I adore Noah, part of me is furious with Issy for abandoning us and expecting us to bring up her child. Haven't we done enough already? It burns me up, also, that the kid's father has got away scot-free while we deal with the consequences of his dick. If I ever find out who he is, I might rip his spotty head off his shoulders. So there's two things I need to find out: why she did it and who the father is. I can't sit around being idle while there are things to be done.

The man behind the desk is the same one from when I viewed the traffic camera footage. He looks up as I step out of the sunshine and into the foyer. It takes my eyes a second to readjust.

'Help you, sir?'

'Is Steve Jackson available, please?'

'I'll check. Remind me of your name again, sir.'

'Jonathon Warner. I saw him before...'

He nods and picks up the telephone. 'Take a seat, please.'

I go to sit on one of the hard plastic chairs arranged along the dirty grey wall. The only other occupant is an old man in the corner, in filthy, torn clothes and stinking of stale booze. I wonder which park bench he'll call home tonight. A bottle peeps out of one of the carrier bags at his feet. Vodka, I think. He stares resolutely out of the window, avoiding my eyes. I pick the furthest chair away from him and spend the next few minutes trying not to breathe in his smell. Maybe next time I'll ring Steve rather than just turn up. Just then, the desk sergeant beckons me over.

'He's out at the moment. He'll be about an hour. I don't know if you want to wait or come back...'

I think of the smell in the corner. 'I'll wait outside. Thanks.' A corner of the sergeant's mouth turns up slightly and his eyes slide towards the tramp, then away again.

Over the road is a newsagent, between the Starbucks we went to before and a pub. After getting a newspaper and an ice-cold coke from the fridge, I settle down on the grass, in the shade of a large tree at the front of the station. I lay down and prop myself up on one elbow while flipping through the paper, mainly looking at the headlines and pictures. It's all bad news and celebrities, so it takes all of five minutes to reach the end. I spend longer on the sports pages, even though I'm not a sports fan. Fifty-one minutes left to wait. I stretch out on my back on the grass and close my eyes, reliving the funeral and the service at the crem. In some ways, life without Issy begins now. The time that's passed since her death has been taken up with organising and funeral arrangements; even with Pam helping, there's been a lot to do. When I get back later today, there'll be just me, Mel, and a whole lot of nothing. Sure, we'll be busy with Noah, but the reality will hit then that Issy's never coming back. Tears sting my eyes and a swell of panic rises up. This is real; my daughter's really dead. For the rest of my life, I'll be Noah's surrogate dad instead of grandad, with all that entails.

Over and over in my mind tumble questions with no answer. Issy had given no indication that she was unhappy. Maybe something at Uni wasn't right. Perhaps she was being bullied. But I've never thought of her as the type bullies go for. She may have been quiet, but anyone who's ever been on the receiving end of her temper knows she has no trouble sticking up for herself when she needs to. Or needed to, I should say. She seemed happy enough with her course at Easter and said she was keeping on top of her work. In the year she'd been there, she'd made some new friends. So she said. Images of her sitting alone in the Halls of Residence night after night now fill my mind. Had she lied so we wouldn't worry? We never met any new friends. At school, she'd made friends easily enough, hadn't she? I saw no reason to think that would be different at Uni. And she was always close to Mel. I'm sure if she couldn't confide in me, she would have confided in her mother. I'm positive. So what made her take her own life?

'Jon?'

My eyes fly open to find Steve Jackson standing over me. I get to my feet, brush myself down, and shake his hand. He's a good few inches shorter than me; he must be five seven at the most.

'Inspector, thank you for seeing me.' I glance at my watch. He's thirty minutes early.

'Call me Steve,' he says. 'So, what can I do for you?'

'Well, you said I could call on you anytime. About this business with my daughter.'

He nods as I pause, trying to gather my thoughts together about what I need from him. 'I remember.'

'Okay... well, I need to find out what made my daughter kill herself. No one does that for no reason. I need to find out why.'

He chews on the inside of his cheek, his eyes narrowing. 'And how do you intend to do that, exactly?'

'I don't know. Ask around her friends, possibly.' I can't tell from his expression whether he thinks it's a good or a bad idea.

'Where do I come in?' He regards me keenly.

'The first place to look is her computer and her phone. Do the police have a department that does this?'

'We do, but only as part of an ongoing investigation. Your daughter's death has been ruled as suicide, so there is no investigation.'

'I know that, but she did it for a reason. I'm going to find out why, however I can, if it's the last thing I do.'

Jackson looks at his watch. 'My shift ends in half an hour. How about we meet over there then?' He nods his head at the Black Bull, the pub over the road.

'Are you sure?'

'Yes. Get me a pint in. Fosters,' he calls from over his shoulder, as he makes his way back to the police station.

I watch the door close behind him. He's either going to tell me he'll help or that there's nothing he can do and maybe he's thinking a friendly chat over a pint, man to man, will soften the blow. I've got to wait half an hour to find out which.

By the time he joins me in the pub, I've downed two pints already through nerves. If he won't help, I'll be back to square one. Or rather, I'll stay at square one, seeing as I'm already there. Mel hasn't rung me all afternoon. Maybe it'd be better to stay out all night getting pissed and really have something for her to get upset about. At the moment, it's not an unattractive option.

'Cheers,' he says, pulling out his chair and sitting heavily on it. He's changed out of his suit and is looking a lot cooler in T-shirt and long combat-type shorts. A blissful look comes over his face as he takes a large swig of his pint. It's half gone when he puts the glass back down. Condensation from the glass glistens on his fingers and he wipes it over his face.

'God, that's good. It's still hot out there.' He leans back and folds his arms, settling into the chair.

I wait for him to speak, turning a beer mat over and over in my hands. I wonder how old he is. Looks about forty-five. I get the sense that he's a better friend than enemy, a good man to have on your side.

'So,' he says. 'I've been thinking about what you said. I can't help you in an official capacity, but there's nothing to say I can't help you in my free time.' He leans forward with his elbows on the table and rests his chin on one hand.

I'm stunned. 'Er, I don't understand.'

He fixes me with a clear, steady gaze. I get the sense he's deciding whether to tell me something or not. He looks down and away, towards the door.

'My mother took her own life when I was a lad, so I have personal experience of what you're going through. I suppose that's why I've taken a special interest in this since I met you. Also, I have two daughters of my own, fourteen and seventeen, and I can't imagine being where you are now. I wanted answers about my mother and never got any until I was a grown man. My father would never talk about it.'

'I'm sorry,' I say.

He takes a drink, and I mull over what he's said. He's willing to help me. I don't care what his reasons are. I've no wish to pry into his family business. If he wants to tell me more, he will. 'So the computer thing, is that the way to go? Kids these days, their whole lives are on their gadgets, right?

There might be a clue on there, maybe on her Facebook or email or something. Maybe something deleted, but still on her hard drive. Or a text on her phone. I just need a lead, a clue. Something. Anything.'

He clears his throat. 'I can't do it at work, but I know people who do this sort of thing. You'll have to pay them, of course, it's their job, but they're good. If there's anything there, they'll find it.'

A faint glimmer of hope ignites in me. 'So, what's the plan?' I ask. 'I don't want to take up your spare time, but I really appreciate you doing this. I wouldn't want you to get in trouble with your missus over this.'

He waves my comment away. 'Divorced. My girls live with their mum. Most nights, I go home to an empty house. I'm not complaining, I'm happier than I've ever been. We just weren't meant to live together. We get on great now we live in separate houses. In separate towns. So things like this, extra-curricular activities, if you like, are right up my street. I'm a nosy bastard, comes with the territory, and I'd like to help you. Truth is, I'd like to know why she did it, as well.'

I like the fact that he's not tiptoeing around the fact that Issy killed herself, like everyone else seems to be. People can't look me in the eye since it happened. Neighbours have even crossed the road to avoid talking to me and I feel like an outcast; the man who couldn't keep his daughter alive. What sort of freak must I be?

Jackson puts the beer mat down and drains his glass.

'Another?' I ask.

'I'll get these in.' He makes to stand up.

'No, it's the least I can do. Same again?'

He nods. 'If you insist.'

At the bar, I mull over what he's said. I can't believe a detective inspector is willing to help me. He's easy to get on with and I like him. Suddenly, I don't feel so alone. I know I've got Mel, but I don't know whether to tell her what I'm doing or just keep her out of it. I work better alone and the bouts of depression she's suffered from in the last few years make her difficult to predict.

There's no one waiting to be served, and the barman is quick. I pick up the drinks and head back to our table. The silence from my phone screams at me. I should go home.

'So, how soon do you think we could kick this off?'

'Fetch the stuff here, same time tomorrow, if you like. Are you including the missus at this stage?'

'I don't know. Maybe.'

'Well, that's up to you. You know her better than anyone. How would she take it?'

'Not sure. She's obviously not good at the moment. I don't know how she'd cope. But it's different for me. I can't sit back and do nothing. I need to know.'

'I would, too. You and me, we're a lot alike.'

I'm beginning to see that. In different circumstances, we could be friends.

'Are you absolutely sure you're prepared, though? You know, what if you find something you don't like?'

I breathe in hard. 'I thought there couldn't be much worse than finding out she was pregnant at fifteen, but this has trumped it.'

Steve nods. 'What about the kid's dad?'

'She wouldn't tell us who the boy was. He left the area soon after, or so she said. I've never been sure of the story myself; seemed a bit too convenient. I realised then, we never really know our kids, do we? She was the last person I would have expected to be a teenage mum. She had so much going for her.'

I stare into my pint, watching the bubbles rise to the surface. A small layer of froth sits on top, fast disappearing as the gas fizzes out of it. Steve doesn't speak.

'I really appreciate this. You're the first person to understand what it's like, having gone through it yourself. People don't understand. They don't know what to say, so they say nothing.'

He nods. 'True. How did the funeral go? It was today, wasn't it? I was going to come, but I got called away.'

'It went off alright, but it was awful. Mel fainted, knocked into me, and all I could think about was what would happen if I dropped the coffin. At the crem, it wasn't any better. I kept having to tell myself it wasn't all a bad dream, you know? The wake is still going on. I'll be in the bad books, actually. I ducked out of it and came to see you, so Mel's facing it alone. But I just couldn't cope with it. I keep thinking *how did it get to this?* I don't think it's sunk in yet. Maybe it never will, and I'll be stuck in this kind of limbo forever.'

'It is a bit like that. When my mother did it, I was ten and didn't have a clue what was going on. All I can really remember is Dad crying all the way through the funeral. Anyway, life went on, as they say. It just carries on in a different way. Nothing is the same after, it's true.' He picks up his phone and checks the time on the screen. 'I'd better get off. Things to do, you know. I'll see you tomorrow with her phone and laptop, yeah?'

'You will. And thanks again. I suppose I'd better go and face the music.'

We shake hands, and he leaves. Instead of going home, I order another pint and sit drinking alone, like some sad loser.

11

Mel

IT'S AFTER SEVEN WHEN the front door slams. So he's finally decided to come home. I don't know where he's been, and I'm damned if I'm going to ask him. I'm trying to concentrate on playing with Noah and his cars on the rug, but all I can think about is Issy and how we're supposed to live without her. The knot of grief and tension in my chest constricts further. A strong whiff of beer accompanies him when he walks into the living room. Has he been in the bloody pub all afternoon while I've been coping alone at our daughter's wake? Then I notice what he's wearing.

'Where's your suit?' The jeans he's wearing still have a label on them. Twenty quid.

'I got rid of it.'

'Well, where is it? It was new.'

'In the bin.'

I'm not going to ask. I can't be bothered. I don't care about his clothes.

'Hey, Noah.' Jon comes to sit on the floor next to us. Noah fashions a gun with his fingers and shoots him. Jon groans, flails about, and falls back onto the floor, lying still, with his eyes closed.

For God's sake. 'Don't encourage him,' I say. 'You know I don't like guns.'

'It's just make-believe. It's what boys do,' he says, his voice weary. His eyes remain closed and only his mouth moves.

He doesn't get up from the floor, and Noah jumps on him then lays on top of him, grabs his face, and kisses it. Jon curls his arms around Noah's little body and hugs him. I watch them, remembering when affection with my husband was so easy to give and receive. As I watch, my throat gets tight. Where do we go from here? What he did today has left me feeling hurt and betrayed, that he could leave me to go through it alone, but at the same time I understand exactly why he acted that way. I wish I'd dared run away like that— in fact, he told me to. I can choose to forgive him and move on, or I can make a big deal of it and we can fight and hurt each other more. I think we've been hurt enough without ripping each other to pieces. Pam would say that I shouldn't let Jon walk all over me, but if I forgive him, is that really what I'm doing? Don't we all have to cope in the way best for ourselves? I managed without him there and even cleared the air with Greg. A mean and spiteful part of me decides not to tell Jon what happened. He's not the only one who can harbour secrets.

Jon lets go of Noah, who runs upstairs, and sits up, hutching up next to me. I can't help what I do next; I breathe in the air, sniffing him surreptitiously for someone else's perfume. I can't smell any.

'I'm sorry,' he says. 'I shouldn't have left you there to face the wake alone, but I couldn't do it.'

'It's okay. I understand.'

'Do you really?' His eyes search mine.

'I think so. We have to get through this as best we can. If I support how you cope and you do the same for me, then we may be alright. Otherwise... what good is it if we just fight each other? Aren't we going through enough without that?'

He nods, looking relieved. We sit side by side in silence for a few minutes, listening to Noah playing noisily upstairs, while I gather my courage. I take a deep breath and tell him what I've been thinking about since I got back from the wake.

'There's one thing I have to talk to you about. I don't think I can spend the next twenty years being Noah's mother and nothing else. I know that sounds awful and I'm not saying I don't love him. Of course I do, very much, but I didn't choose this and I can't do it alone. I need some help and a life outside it.'

I feel like I'm failing Noah just feeling this way, but I can't help it. My fingers dig into the deep pile of the rug and twist it round and round. I'm not sure what Jon will think of what I've just said. He nods and eventually he speaks.

'Alright. What do you think is the best way to sort it out?'

'I don't know. Paid help, I suppose. A regular nanny, child-minder, something like that. But what about the money? These things don't come cheap.'

'We'll cope money-wise. Do you think Pam would help out?'

'I don't know. I'm not sure being more reliant on her is going to be for the best. For me, I mean.'

'How come?'

'Well, she works full time, for a start, so she's not there in the day, which is when I would need her. Also, it might sound daft, but part of me doesn't want to be beholden to her. I think I'd rather pay a professional.'

Jon is quiet. I know he worries about money, especially being self-employed and me not working. It's not fair that he should shoulder all the financial burden. He needs to know I want to go back to work.

'Um, there is maybe something that would help. I could go back to work part-time. It would help pay for the child-care but, more importantly, it might just save my sanity.'

I'm surprised when Jon traces his fingers over the back of my hand, softly and lightly, so relaxing. *Did he do this to her?* I slide my hand away under the guise of getting more comfortable and pretend not to notice when his mouth tightens slightly.

He clears his throat. 'Is that what you want? To go back to work?'

It all comes out in a big rush. 'Yes. More than anything. Does that make me a bad person? I feel like I'm letting Noah down, but the thought of staying at home, being a mother again for the next fifteen years makes me panicky. I can't do it, Jon, I just can't. By the time I got my life back, I'd be pushing sixty. I'd been banking on Issy taking him at least some of the time when she left uni and got a job. Noah would have been at school by then, and we would maybe have had him here some evenings or weekends. I wanted to be his grandma, not his mother.'

I swallow hard and blink away the tears. I have to start getting a grip, or I'm going to spend the rest of my life crying.

'If that's what you want, that's what we'll do. Feel better now?'

I blink several more times. 'Yes. It's going to be really hard, isn't it? Now and forever.'

'Yeah. It is. We'll have to pull together and be there for each other. And Pam and Justin will help us, I'm sure. They're the best.' He groans. 'God, I'll have to get off this floor. It's killing my back.'

Jon staggers to his feet and my first thought is that we're not getting any younger. He sits on the sofa and I stay on the rug, packing away Noah's cars into his toy chest.

'So, where did you go this afternoon?'

Jon pauses, and I feel a flicker of anxiety. I know from experience that this is the crucial time when he decides whether to tell the truth or not.

He sighs and meets my eyes—a good sign, surely. 'If I tell you, promise you won't go mad?'

'Alright. I'm listening.'

'I've been to the police station. To see that copper, Steve, the one who said we could ring him anytime.'

'What for?'

'Mel, I need to find out why she did it. I can't just sit back and not find out why. He's going to help me.'

Is that it? He hasn't been with *her*. The relief is enormous.

'I feel the same. I need to know, too.'

Jon is looking at me with relief on his face. 'So you're okay with it?'

'Jon, do you think I'm not eaten up with questions, either? I've wondered why every second since she did it.'

'I know that, of course. It's just, it might not be easy delving into parts of Issy's life we're not familiar with. We might find out things we don't like. I wasn't sure how you'd cope with that.'

'I don't know how I'll cope either, but, like you, I have to know. So, what's the plan?'

'I'm taking her mobile and laptop to Steve tomorrow to see if there are any clues on it. I won't rest until I find out why she's done it, Mel, I just won't.'

I know that resolute set of his jaw. Nothing could stop him, especially not anything I could say.

'Did you really think I'd just lie back and give up?' I ask.

'Well, you *were* piling up pills the other day. It scared me.' His voice is small, barely there.

'It was a moment of weakness. A lapse on my part after everything. I wouldn't go through with it. I wouldn't do that to you.' Now I'm the one lying. The truth is, the way I feel now, I could easily swallow a bottle of pills and leave everything behind.

He searches my face for a long moment; he's making up his mind whether to believe me. I know he wants to.

'Okay,' he says, finally. 'Come with me tomorrow. We'll do it together.'

'Alright.' I think about the pills upstairs, stockpiled in places he won't look. Just a precaution. A safety blanket. I'll never need them. Hopefully.

12

Jon

I'M NOT PROUD OF the fact I had an affair, but stuff like this happens and you have to deal with it and move on. What Mel doesn't know is that it was more than just an affair; I was ready to leave her for Adele. That only changed when we found out Issy was pregnant.

I'd hooked up with Adele again through a school reunion I didn't even want to go to. I'd been dragged along by Eddie, an old school pal who I'd kept in touch with sporadically.

'It'll be a laugh,' he'd said, trying to persuade me to go.

I didn't really fancy it and told him as much, but he wouldn't have it. Eventually, I agreed to go just to shut him up.

It was over twenty years since we'd left school. I hadn't kept in contact with many friends since meeting Mel and had no particular desire to find out how any of the people from school were doing. My reasoning was that if I was bothered about any of them, I'd have kept in touch, anyway. I hadn't thought about Adele in years, and it'd taken everything I had to forget to think about her. We'd dated for two years in high school, and she was my first serious girlfriend. There were a few others in between splitting up with Adele and meeting Mel, but no one special. Adele had dumped me for someone else, and it took me ages to get over it. At first, I thought I never would. When I walked into the reunion and saw her, it was like being hit by a thunderbolt and catapulted back through time. She looked incredible in a tight-fitting, low-necked dress, easily the sexiest woman in the room. My first thought was that she'd hardly changed and God, she was still sexy. She was laughing with friends when she turned and looked straight at me, as if she could feel me watching her. As if pulled by magnets, she came towards me.

'Well, well, well... Jonathon Warner,' she said simply, her eyes seeming to capture mine. She didn't let go. 'Fancy seeing you here!' She tossed her hair, still long and blonde, over one shoulder, like she did when she was seventeen.

'Adele Hunter,' I replied, my tongue sticking to the roof of my dry mouth. All I could think about was the incredibly hot sex we used to have when we were teenagers. Every detail seemed imprinted in my mind in glorious technicolour, every fold, crease, and line of her amazing body. It looked just as amazing now, better, if anything. Curvier and fuller. We smiled, sat in a corner and talked the whole night, about ourselves and our lives and about other people in the room, who was wearing well and who wasn't.

She was Adele Thomas now, divorced and childless. She told me she'd married a wealthy workaholic and had spent most of her married life feeling side-lined and invisible. I couldn't believe any man could ignore her. She also told me she regretted dumping me and considered it one of the biggest mistakes of her life. Said she'd realised too late I was her soul-mate, an expression I've always thought stupid, yet when she said it, it somehow wasn't.

'I've thought about you so often over the years,' she said.

I was flattered, and it set me reminiscing. If I'm being absolutely honest, even though sex with Mel had always been good (up to my affair), with Adele it was something else. I spent most of the evening trying to hide my raging, treacherous dick, but I needn't have bothered. She was up for it, I could tell, the way her fingers kept twisting into her hair and touching my arm before moving to rest gently and briefly on my thigh at regular intervals. The bolts of electricity shooting straight to my groin had been hard to ignore, and the inevitable had happened, a six-month passionate affair, and I was getting deeper and deeper in, until Mel uttered those fateful words: Issy's pregnant. Selfishly, my first thought had been for myself.

Adele was convinced it was fate, us meeting up again at the reunion, and that we were destined to be together. We fell desperately back in love with each other, and so I made up my mind to leave Mel. I'd figured that, at fifteen, Issy would get over it. Then came the pregnancy bombshell. I had no choice but to break it off with Adele, telling her about the family crisis I was going through. Instead of understanding, she was devastated, then went crazy and texted Mel, telling her all about us.

At the very worst time in my life, my teenage daughter was pregnant, and my marriage was on a knife-edge. Then followed Mel's depression, which I'm not sure she's ever really come round from, with Issy thinking it was because she was pregnant and blaming herself, which only added another layer of misunderstanding and misery to the mix.

But we are where we are and life, as they say, goes on. Mel and I reached an uneasy truce, pulling together for Issy's sake, and have limped along since then. Our sex life has been practically non-existent too, after that text from Adele. There've been a few aborted attempts and a couple of passionless successes. Mel bounces between blaming herself for not being a good enough wife and blaming me for being a cheating bastard, and every so often she drags it all up and uses it as a weapon to beat me with. It'll never be gone from our lives. I haven't heard from Adele since she sent the text to Mel and blew everything wide apart. I texted her back saying it was over and that was it, but I've thought about her often since, and wondered if I did the right thing. Deep down, I still miss her like crazy because I'm still in love with her.

The odd thing is, I still love Mel, but she doubts it now more than ever, and it's not the passionate love that I need and I crave that. I know it crossed her mind when I pulled my disappearing act after the funeral that I might have gone to see Adele. Or maybe a different woman. What sort of a shit would do that? But I live in a world of suspicion now, and it's my own fault.

I'm glad she's with me now, as I take the laptop and phone to Steve Jackson. I feel I did the right thing by telling her. She climbs out of the car, pretending not to notice the hand I hold out to her. It's not lost on me, the subtle snubs she regularly metes out since the affair. She says she's forgiven me, but she hasn't, not really. If we only stayed together for Issy's sake, what happens now? The same, but for Noah's? I'm not sure I can live like this forever.

'Where do we go?' She's stopped outside the police station and is looking at the windows.

'Over there.' I point at the pub over the road. 'A kind of after-hours thing.'

She looks puzzled, then shrugs. 'Okay.'

We make our way over the road and into the cooler interior of the pub. Steve is already there and stands up when he sees Mel.

'Hello,' he says, smiling at her. He raises his eyebrows at me as she goes to sit down. I don't know whether he approves of the fact I've brought her or not.

'Do you want a drink?' I ask her.

'Just water,' she says.

I hear her talking to Steve as I go off to the bar. When I get back with two pints and some water, she's listening intently to him as he explains what they're going to look for, then asks, 'What if they've got passwords? You know how teenagers are about privacy with their phones. I can't see that it wouldn't have.'

'They'll get in, don't worry about that. They're usually something obvious. If it's a better one, which I doubt, you answering some simple questions will probably sort it out.'

I'm not so sure. It seems there were large parts of her life we weren't party to. I slide onto the bench next to her and put the drinks down.

'Thanks,' says Steve.

'How long will it take?' Mel asks.

'I'll try and have them back in a week, but if something comes in needing their time, it may take a bit longer.'

'Okay. Well, thank you for agreeing to do this for us. We're stuck in a dead end at the moment.' Her bottom lip quivers and she catches it between her teeth.

Steve nods. 'I am so sorry, Mel, that this has happened to you. It's not fair, I know.'

Mel's eyes fill up and she swallows several times. 'It wasn't an accident. Our daughter did this to us. No need for you to feel sorry.' She dabs her eyes with a tissue from her bag.

Steve's eyes dart to mine, clouded with uncertainty. He picks up his pint, and says, 'I'll have to make it quick. I want to get these delivered tonight so they can make a start first thing. If there's anything on them, we'll find it.'

'What exactly are they looking for?' asks Mel, still sniffing.

'Emails, messages, pictures, anything that doesn't seem right. Something we might be able to trace back to someone who might be able to tell us what was going on in her life. Because, believe me, something must have been going on. This can't have been completely out of the blue. Something triggered it. We need to find out what. How much about her life at uni do you know?'

Mel looks at me, then down at the table. When she speaks, her voice is quiet. 'Obviously not as much as we thought. You see, Issy was always a very private girl, secretive, you could say. Happy and outgoing as a child, then becoming moody when she hit the teenage years. But that's normal, isn't it? Then she got pregnant and everything got much worse, like not telling us who the father was. So that's one big mystery we never got to the bottom of right there.'

'Mmm.' Steve's lips are pursed, and he's in full-on copper mode. I can see the cogs turning. 'Did you ever have any feelings or suspicions about anyone it could be?'

'Well, I never did, no. Did you?' She turns to me.

I shake my head. 'No. But I never believed the one-night-stand thing.' I slide a beer mat over to the corner of the table and begin squaring it up, so there's no overhang on either edge, a millimetre one way, then the other. It's pointless but soothing.

'And so, if it was someone else, where and when would she have got the opportunity to meet up with him? Evenings, weekends? Did she go out much around that time?'

'A bit more than normal, but she was at her friend, Ellie's, a lot of the time or with other groups of friends. Or, at least, that's what she said. She was always in at a decent hour, though, so it didn't seem like a problem,' Mel says.

'Did you ever speak to Ellie? Could she verify it?'

Mel grimaces. 'God, I wouldn't have dared. She'd have sulked for weeks if she thought we'd checked up on her.'

'What about you, Jon? Anything jump out to you from around that time?'

'Not that I can think of.'

'Jon was really busy with work around that time, weren't you? Sometimes he was too busy to come home at all.' Mel smiles at me sweetly, but there's no mistaking the edge to her voice, the sarcasm only I would pick up on.

She's saying I was too busy shagging my mistress to notice what was going on with our daughter. Maybe she's right. I'd used work as an excuse to see Adele, but suddenly I'm sick of the snide remarks and holier-than-thou attitude. I watch her as she turns her attention back to Steve. Has he noticed the tension between us? He can't have failed to, really. I stay silent and begin shredding the beer mat into tiny pieces, dropping them onto the table where they sit in a puddle of beer and condensation. The conversation swings between the two of them. I hear nothing I don't already know, and I can feel Steve's eyes flicking towards me from time to time. Maybe I shouldn't have brought Mel in on this. I could have just kept it to myself, and it might have been better. I wouldn't have been sitting here feeling like a fool now. Steve drains his pint

80

and draws me back to reality when he bangs his empty glass down.

'I'll have to go. I'll be in touch when I know anything. Jon, I'll ring you, okay?'

'Yeah. And thanks again, Steve. For what you're doing for us.'

'No problem. Glad to help.'

He picks up the phone and laptop and walks out of the pub. I turn to Mel. She shifts in her seat and suddenly looks nervous. I glare at her, stand up and weave my way through the chairs, leaving her there. By the time I get outside, she's almost caught me up.

'Jon, wait.'

I spin around.

'What the hell was that about? *Really*, Mel? Is this really the time? Are you going to use our daughter's death as another way to get at me some more?'

She's crying now. 'I'm sorry. It just came out. I didn't mean it.' She clasps a hand to my arm, but I shrug it off.

'No, that's just it. You did mean it.'

I'm almost at the car now. I don't want to argue in the street, so I stay silent until the car doors are closed. 'How much longer are you going to throw this back at me? Okay, so maybe I deserve it, but *today*? God, Mel!'

I start the engine and shove the gearstick around so violently I'm afraid of wrenching it off in my hand. But I'm not finished.

'Were you trying to humiliate me back there? Trying to make me feel small? Because it worked. And you know what else, I don't know if I can live with someone as perfect as you any longer. I don't measure up, I know. It's like living with a bastard saint.'

'Jon, please. It's not like that. I never said I was perfect...' A sob stops her voice.

Usually I can't stand to hear her cry, but just now, it makes no difference. After everything that's happened these last couple of weeks, I'm incapable of feeling anything at all. I'm driving too fast and I ease off the accelerator, as what happened to Issy floods my mind.

'Jon, I'm sorry. Please. I don't want to fight.'

'Maybe you should have thought of that earlier, then. You can be such a bitch sometimes, you know? Do you think it's any of Steve's business, our life, our marriage? Shit that it is.' The last four words are muttered, but not quite so much that she can't work out what I've said.

After a couple more aborted attempts on Mel's part to speak, we sit in silence. I need to calm down so we can walk back into the house where Pam is looking after Noah, and appear 'normal'. She thinks we've been out for tea, and neither she nor Justin know about the affair. I think it's the first time Mel's kept something from her sister. Or, at least, she told me Pam doesn't know. On reflection, though, I think she's telling the truth. If Pam knew, I don't think she'd be able to treat me the same.

With acting abilities that deserve an Oscar, we both plaster smiles on our faces and relieve her of her babysitting duties.

'Did you have a nice meal?' she asks, muting the TV when she sees us.

'Lovely,' says Mel brightly, even though the three of us know Mel's hardly eaten since Issy died and is struggling to find her lost appetite. Her clothes now look at least two sizes too big.

Pam looks at me. I shrug and she leaves shortly after, leaving Mel and I to spend the evening in different rooms, her in the bedroom and me in the living room. Afterwards, I go to sleep on the sofa bed in the attic where I've spent many nights alone since the affair came to light. Our house is bursting at the seams and, when Noah came along, we had to convert the attic leaving us with no savings. We could afford to have the basics done, but it's a long way from finished. It's still a small space, mainly used for storage, with boxes piled at one end. Issy's bedroom is empty, but I can't sleep in there, not yet. It's still full of her stuff.

I throw my clothes on the floor and cover myself with a thin blanket, stretching out on the sofa bed with its thin base and protruding springs. The pillow is too soft and flat and always makes me wake with neck ache in the morning. If I sleep at all, that is. Too many things are whizzing about in my mind for me to sleep tonight. I need to go back to work, or we'll have severe cash flow problems on top of everything else. Everything looks bleak and I can't see a way out of it.

13

Mel

IT'S BEEN A STRAINED week since Jon and I took Issy's things to Steve Jackson. We've both been on tenterhooks, waiting to hear from him, but Jon's hardly spoken to me. He's still angry with me for the dig I had at him in the pub. I shouldn't have said it, but the hurt never truly goes away. Sometimes, I think he only stayed with me because Issy got pregnant. I daren't ask him if that's true, in case he says it is. I've seen pictures of Adele Hunter on Facebook, on his laptop, when he's been at work. He has a Facebook account he never uses. There's stuff on there from years back, but nothing since Issy got pregnant. She's still listed as a friend on it, though. How telling! Adele Hunter updates her page sporadically, and I still check it every month, or so. She puts pictures of herself on from exotic destinations around the world. I don't know how she affords it, working in a bank, but she seems to go on lots of holidays: Adele in a bikini and sarong on a beach in Thailand, big-boobed and still toned; Adele in shorts and a khaki shirt on safari somewhere in Africa; Adele in a full-length gown on a cruise in the Caribbean. By the look of it, she did well in her divorce settlement. She's one of those knockout kind of women most of us can't look like.

I don't know why Issy killing herself has raked up Jon's affair for me again, but it has, possibly because of the disappearing acts he kept pulling straight afterwards. It's how he was when he was seeing *her*. Jon told me everything (or so he said) but only because he was forced to. How long he would have kept it up for if things hadn't changed, I can't say. Some days I can't look at him and I don't want to be near him. Up until now, were things getting better? Possibly. But maybe I was learning to live with it which, apparently, is what you do. That's not necessarily the same as things getting better.

I was glad when he returned to work earlier this week. I think he thought I'd be upset, but I prefer the house without him in it. It's easier, especially if we're barely speaking. Justin and Pam took a couple of weeks off after Issy's death and have both gone back to work now, Justin as a sales manager for a company selling something industrial for factories— machinery parts or something—and Pam as an English teacher in the local college. Their kids have been in childcare practically since they were born. As much as Pam loves them, she adores her job and spends a lot of the holidays working, planning stuff for the next term.

They always seem so happy together; maybe that's why I never told Pam about Jon's affair. She has the perfect marriage, and I don't want her to know how far short my own has fallen. So now, I'm here on my own all day with Noah while everyone else is working, carving and crafting a living. I make finger paintings and Play-Doh animals, and sit watching toddlers' TV until I think I'm going to go mad. Noah is more clingy lately, unsettled and wanting me all the time.

While he has a sleep on the settee, I search for jobs online. I meant what I said. Only the thought of going back to work is keeping me sane. I rang Julie in the school office where I used to work and asked if there was any chance I could come back.

'I'd have you back like a shot, Mel, but the budget's been squeezed so much we haven't replaced you. We were told we'd have to spread the load ourselves, so there is no job anymore. I'm so sorry. I wish it were better news.'

'Okay. If you hear of anything similar in another school, will you let me know? I'm desperate. I can't sit at home much longer.'

'I will.'

At the time, it sounded hopeful, but it was over a week ago, and I've heard nothing, so I'll have to find something else. The trouble is, the story's the same everywhere. *Not hiring at the moment, thank you. Too much economic uncertainty*. So what am I supposed to do? I've never been good at anything. With no outstanding skills or attributes to shout about, I'm Mrs Decidedly Average, whose husband looks elsewhere for love.

While I sit going through the same adverts a second time, the phone rings. I don't recognise the number.

'Hello?'

'Hello, is that Mel?'

'Yes.'

'It's Steve Jackson.'

My heart speeds up. I thought he was going to ring Jon, not me.

'Hello, Steve. Any news?'

'Um, is Jon there?'

'No. He went back to work. He's at the office space he rents, on the outskirts of town. Do you have his number?'

'Yes, but it's actually you I wanted to see. Are you home now?'

'Well, yes. What's up?'

'I can be there soon. Thirty minutes. Is that alright?'

'Yes. Sure. See you shortly.'

He hangs up and I sit with the phone in my hand, wondering what that was all about. It sounds a bit cloak and dagger. And why would he want to talk to me and not Jon? Does it have something to do with Jon?

I decide to have a quick sandwich before he gets here. Half a slice of bread and one cheese triangle forms my lunch.

It's more than enough. After I've eaten it, I make a jam sandwich for Noah for when he wakes, and I'm just wrapping it in clingfilm when the doorbell goes.

'Hello, Steve. Come in.' I step back so he can enter. I can't read his expression. 'Can I get you some tea or coffee?'

'Tea, thanks. White, no sugar.'

He follows me towards the kitchen, and Noah stirs as we walk past the living room door. I really need him to stay asleep so I can talk to Steve with no interruptions, but I'm not that lucky and, right on cue, his eyes spring open. Within seconds he's rolled off the sofa, and he's up in my arms, eyeing Steve.

'Hello, little fella,' says Steve, leaning in to talk to him. Noah turns his head to the other side so he can't see him. 'Shall I put the kettle on? Seeing as you've got your hands full.'

'Please. Noah, do you want to watch TV? Grandma's got to talk to Mr Jackson.'

'Okay. Scooby Doo.'

He settles down happily to watch it with his sandwich in one hand and a drink in the other. I find Steve in the kitchen, hunting around for the drawer with spoons in.

'So,' I say to Steve, 'You've got me worried. What did you find?' I hand him a teaspoon, and take teabags and sugar out of the cupboards.

He takes two mugs off the mug tree and finishes making the tea. I can tell he's working out how to deliver the bad news. 'I wanted *you* to see this, not Jon. You might decide it's something he shouldn't see. Well, anyway, you be the judge.'

He presses some keys on Issy's phone and hands it to me, whilst clearing his throat and looking at the floor. I can tell from his body language he's uncomfortable. I bring the phone closer to my face and gasp at what's there. It's a photo of Issy on her bed in her uni room. She's naked and spread-eagled, and the photo looks like she's taken it herself. You can see everything. It's pornographic by any stretch of the imagination. There's more of her on display than when she gave birth to Noah with me holding her hand. It's disgusting.

'There's more, if you swipe right,' says Steve, quietly, still with his head down. Whether it's to spare his blushes or mine, I don't know. I feel sick that he's seen these. The pictures of her displaying herself get worse, if that's possible. I know why Steve showed them to me and not Jon. With her dyed jet-black straight hair, pale skin and heavy eye make-up, she's a porno Goth queen. I can feel my cheeks flaming and my stomach roils with nausea. I sit down heavily at the table as my legs threaten to give way.

'Oh God, I don't know what to say. Have you seen all these? Of course you have. Stupid question. How many people?'

'The three people in the team. One of them is a woman, if that helps.'

It doesn't. Not one bit. I can't believe my daughter would do this. Why? What for? Who for? My stomach lurches at the realisation. 'Did she send these to someone?'

He nods. 'Yes. That's what I wanted to see you about.'

'Who? Did she text them?'

'Yes. We traced the person she sent them to, although, we hasten to add, no laws have been broken in doing so. She's over the age of consent and did it of her own free will, by the look of it.'

'Who?'

'One of the lecturers at the university.'

'Oh, my God. Are you sure?'

'Yes. A Peter C. Have you heard of him?'

'No. Have you spoken to him?'

'Not yet.'

'Well, why not? Isn't it a breach of trust or something? On his part, I mean, she's still a child.'

'Well, in the eyes of the law, she's not. She's just turned nineteen, hasn't she? Although I suspect they'd take a dim view of it at the university.'

I can't speak, as my mind floods with images and questions. If a lecturer has been taking advantage of her, they should be struck off, like a teacher at school would, surely. I sit down at the table with my head in my hands. How much worse can things get? I can't get the pictures out of my head, although the worst thing of all is the look on her face in them. I barely recognise her. It's a knowing look, full of sex. She knew exactly what effect the pictures were meant to have. Also, I feel angry. I'm at home looking after her baby while she was off displaying her lurid self for all to see when she was supposed to have been studying. What kind of creature had we raised?

Another thought hits me. What if she was making extra money by selling pictures or, even worse, her body, for sex? I've heard of students doing it to make money on the side. A groan escapes me and Steve sits opposite me, lowering himself into the chair.

'I know it's been a shock, Mel, but you need to decide if you want Jon to see them. You'll have to tell him, of course, but he doesn't have to see his daughter like this, does he?'

'No. You're right. He had to see her in the morgue, so maybe this is levelling up the score.'

Steve looks puzzled but leaves it alone.

'I'll let him decide. If he wants to see them, then that's his choice. There's no point in protecting her, is there? Not anymore.'

Jon looks thoughtful. 'Suppose not. What do you think he's likely to do? About the lecturer, I mean? The police won't be getting involved, but he might want to follow it up himself.'

'I think he will. If he wants to go up there, which is likely, I'll try and make sure he's in a calm frame of mind when he goes, but I never know what he's going to do. He can be a bit fiery, you see.'

Steve nods but doesn't say anything. Probably being tactful.

'What about the laptop? Have they looked at it yet?'

'Not yet. They're looking at it tomorrow. I didn't want to sit on this.' He points to the phone. 'I thought you'd rather know straight away.'

'Yes, but why would she do it? It just poses more questions.' I sink my head into my hands and cover my face.

'Small steps, Mel. That's how these things are solved. Small steps, one at a time,' he says.

The music from Scooby Doo pipes up, and Noah pelts into the room.

'Want socklit,' he demands.

'You can have chocolate when you've had a banana,' I tell him.

Noah is silent and I can see him making the trade-off in his head to see if it's worth it.

'Okay,' he says and goes back to the living room as the next episode starts up, clutching a banana and a Freddo.

I look at Steve. 'Thanks, I think,' I say, tapping the phone. 'You know, I'm feeling more and more like I never knew my daughter at all.'

He nods. 'I understand.'

But does he, really? When Jon learns about the pictures, I don't know what will happen.

14

Jon

'LET ME SEE,' I demand, holding my hand out for the phone. 'Are they really that bad?'

'I've told you what they're like. Of course they're that bad.' Mel's holding the phone down by her side.

I retract my hand and mull it over. What will looking at pornographic photos of my daughter achieve? There again, it can't be worse than the body in the morgue, can it?

'I need to know the full extent of everything to do with this. I can't be in the dark about anything. Show me.'

Mel hands me Issy's phone and I put it face down on the table, bracing myself and plucking up courage at the same time. For a brief second, I feel like I'm at the top of an obscenely high roller coaster and there's that pause before you know it's going to hurtle down, taking you with it. Then I turn the phone over and look at the screen and my stomach plummets. The feelings are worse than I thought they'd be; revulsion, disgust and horror. If I'd eaten anything beforehand, I'd be losing it about now. A moan escapes me and I slam my fist into my mouth to force the nausea back down while tears sting the backs of my eyes. The stupid little bitch! What the hell was she thinking, taking images of herself like these? Even though I must have looked at plenty of other people's daughters in similar poses over the years, it's not the same. Double standards, some would say, and I'd agree with them. I scroll to the end of them and almost break down at the sight of the last picture on her phone. It's a teddy bear, propped up on her pillow on the same bed. I hand the phone back to Mel, who's anxiously scanning my face.

'Who's seen these?' I ask her.

'Just the team checking out the phone and computer, and Steve Jackson. Plus Peter C, who she sent them to may have shown them to thousands of people or put them on the internet for all we know.' Mel's voice is rising and ends up bordering on hysterical.

If this Peter C has been encouraging my daughter to send pictures like this to him, I know what the C stands for. I resist the urge to hurl the phone at the wall and watch it smash to pieces, but only just. It's tempting. No one should see their daughter broken up in the morgue or selling herself like a piece of meat. I sit at the table with my head in my hands. Anger tussles with grief, sadness toys with fury and disgust, and I don't know how much more of this either of us can take. But we can't quit now; this is only the first hurdle. Once we've accepted, and tried to forget what we've seen, we can concentrate on getting some answers.

'What the hell was going on with her?' I say. 'I thought we might find an incriminating message from someone maybe threatening her or something like that, but I never expected this. If she's done this willingly, and it looks like she has, then she's the one responsible, just like the crash.'

'I know. Jon, what sort of monster did we raise? There must have been something seriously psychologically wrong with her.'

I throw up my hands in a helpless gesture, and she continues.

'Should we talk to this man, this lecturer, do you think, or wait and see what the computer might turn up?' She slumps forward onto the table and rests her head on her arms. 'I don't think I'll ever forget those pictures as long as I live.'

I know what she means. They're imprinted on my eyelids when I close my eyes.

92

Mel sits up again, and her eyes are blazing. 'What annoys me is that she was off doing that when I was at home, coping with her last mistake.'

I stare at her. 'You don't mean that. We love Noah.'

'Oh, I know we do. I didn't mean it like that, but he *was* her biggest mistake. She wasn't planning on getting pregnant, surely?'

We look at each other in silence. Where our daughter is concerned, we don't know what to believe anymore. Was everything she said lies?

I sigh. 'I'll go and bath Noah. You get some wine and put your feet up. I'll read to him after that and put him to bed. Then we'll talk some more.'

All the time I'm bathing Noah and reading to him, my mind is churning over what to do next about that lecturer. We should go and see him, but uni's broken up for the summer, and I also don't know if Steve would get his address for us. He's a straight-up copper and I wouldn't want him to do anything that would compromise his job, not that he would anyway. Noah settles down easily, and I'm only halfway into the second story when he nods off. It's a good night; I've known it take four or five books before he's asleep. When I go back downstairs, Mel's halfway down a massive glass. I'm not sure whether it's her first or not, and she's placed a can of beer for me on the table. I sit next to her, open it and slug half of it down, trying to wash away the nasty taste the photos have left.

'What's on telly?' I gesture at the screen with my can at the couple who are screaming at each other. Probably EastEnders then.

Mel mutes it. 'Nothing. I'd rather we talked.'

'I've been thinking about what to do next. What do you think?'

'Wait and see what the computer says. The more we know, the better for us to decide. He said they're looking at it tomorrow, all being well, so a couple more days won't change anything in the long run, will it?'

'No, you're right. Let's leave it until then. I've been meaning to ask, have you thought any more about the job thing?'

She pulls a face. 'Yeah, actually. I've been looking on the internet but apart from cleaners and sales, there's nothing much around. Cleaning? No. I want to do something stimulating. But we both know I'm no natural born saleswoman.'

We both laugh as we remember her working in Curry's, selling electrical items over Christmas years ago. She hated it. *I can't talk to people I don't know,* she used to say. She always sold the least, and I think they were glad when she quit. She'd shake like a leaf every morning when I dropped her off at the shop. Then she got the office job at school, where contact with the public was limited.

'I've had an idea,' I say, raising my eyebrows.

'Well? What? Don't keep me in suspense.'

'Remember those dance qualifications you got and never used because Issy came along?'

A spark of interest ignites in her eyes. 'Yeah. What about them?'

'The dance studio in town need a part-time teacher three evenings a week, teaching little ones tap and ballet.'

She sits up straighter. Dance was the love of her life when she was younger. I know she yearned to be a professional dancer but didn't make the grade. She was good enough to teach kids, though.

'Why would they give me a job? And it probably wouldn't fetch much money in, just three evenings a week.' She sounds doubtful, just like I knew she would.

'If you don't apply for it, you'll never know, will you? And we don't need you to make lots of money right now. I'm doing alright. I've got designs backed up, waiting to be done. We can afford for you to concentrate on doing something you just might love, like I do. Plus, I'm home in the evenings, so it wouldn't cost us extra for child care. And if we get really strapped for cash, I can always give up renting the office space and work from home.'

'But you said you didn't want to work from here, that Noah would be too much of a distraction.'

'I know I did, but maybe it was a stupid decision, paying out money for premises to look more professional when I don't think anyone really cares. Most of it comes from the internet anyway, these days.'

She sips her wine, mulling it over. I know she wants to do it. I knew she would. Time for the killer shot.

'Mel, it's time to put yourself first for once, not Noah, not me. You. Here's the phone number.'

I pull a scrap of paper out of my pocket and pass it to her. She looks excited, exhilarated, like the teenager she was when I met her. I can't remember the last time I saw her like this.

'Do it tomorrow.'

She nods. 'I might.'

I suppress a smile. Dancing's her Achilles heel. I know she'll do it. She has that faraway look in her eyes she used to have when she was younger, whenever dancing was mentioned.

'Do you really think they'd hire me?'

'They'd be daft not to.'

She smiles and turns away, staring at the TV. I can see she's working to put the pictures of Issy to the back of her mind, as am I. Before long, the wine she's had is making her nod off. I go upstairs to the attic where I'm still sleeping and take my phone with me. Sitting on the bed among the clutter and bags of stuff we don't need, I ring Steve Jackson. He answers after three rings.

'I wondered when you'd ring. I've been waiting for your call,' he says.

'I need that bloke's address,' I say, not pussy-footing around.

'I know you do.'

'Can you give it to me?'

'No. It's not in the phone book, so it's not in the public domain.'

'How can I get it?'

'You can't. I doubt the uni will give it to you. Staff files are confidential.'

'So what do I do now?'

'What are you going to do if you meet him?'

'Just talk to him. Get to the bottom of it.'

'Is that all?'

'Yes. Why?'

'You're not going to do anything stupid, like clobber him? Cos that's assault.'

'I know! I'm not going to touch him.'

'Do I have your word on that?'

'Yes.'

'Should I believe you?'

'*Yes*. I may want to smash his face in, but I'm not going to.'

'He may be innocent in all this.'

Yeah right, course he might. 'I know.'

'Then I may be able to help.'

'Okay. How?'

'Apparently, Peter C is a workaholic. I have it on good authority. So, even though uni's broken up for summer, he spends a lot of his time there, still working in his department, prepping for next term, plus he's studying himself, doing some doctorate. If you were to go to the uni, there's a good chance you might meet him.'

'Really?' This sounds too good to be true.

'Yes, really. But only if you weren't going to do something stupid. Because, if you did, I wouldn't be able to get you out of it.'

'I'm not. I'm not stupid.'

'Jon?'

'Yeah?'

He pauses and I can hear him breathe in sharply. 'I'm sorry about the pictures, man. I can't imagine how you're

96

feeling, but I knew you'd insist on seeing them, like you did the footage from the traffic camera. Hopefully I didn't do the wrong thing, taking them to Mel first?'

The lump in my throat makes my voice sound small and strained. 'No, it's okay. Steve, I felt so sick when I saw them. Like I didn't know her at all, you know? I know we're both men of the world, but I can't describe what it's like when it's your own. I'm disgusted. Devastated.'

'I know. I'm sorry I had to see them too. I'm going to forget them completely. Erase them from my mind.'

'Good. I hope I can.'

'Well, listen, I'll be in touch about the computer, maybe tomorrow or the weekend. As soon as I know anything.'

'I know. And thanks, Steve. I mean it.'

'Alright, mate. Goodnight.'

'Night.'

I hang up. So that's the next move right there. For Mr C, it's work as usual. Five minutes on the uni's website gives me his surname. There's only one Peter in the English department. Peter Cunningham. Time to pay the dirty bastard a visit.

15

Mel

'PLEASE PAM, COULD YOU have Noah overnight on Sunday for us? It's important or I wouldn't ask.' I grip the phone tighter, desperate for her to say yes. The college has broken up for the summer, so she's off work.

'Course. Actually, Justin's home, too, on Monday. You know how he loves spending time with him. We'll take him out somewhere, make a day of it—maybe Gulliver's Kingdom. What's so important?'

I'm glad I can't see my sister's face, and feel bad that I'm about to lie, but Jon and I have agreed not to involve anyone else in what we're doing. It seems easier and I don't want to have to explain the pictures; they're just too embarrassing. I've decided a half-lie is best.

'We're going to Newcastle to collect Issy's bits and pieces that she left there. We're going to drive up on Sunday and pick them up on Monday. Jon thinks a night away will do us good.'

Thankfully, she doesn't find any of it fishy even though Issy packed up all her stuff and brought it home for the summer.

'Okay, it's no problem. We'll pick him up on Sunday morning if you like.'

'Thanks, Pam. I don't know what we'd do without the two of you.'

'Well, thankfully, you don't have to. We're here, you know that. What are you doing today?'

'I'm going to see about a dance teaching job at the studio on Cleveland Road. Jon spotted a notice in the window about it.'

Pam's silent for a second. 'Well, good for you. I think you'd really enjoy that. God, do you remember that dance troupe we formed when we were nine, *the Dancing Kweens?*'

'Yes. We must really have got on Mum and Dad's nerves, twirling and pirouetting everywhere, even down the shops.'

She laughs down the phone. 'I know. Look, I'll have to go. See you Sunday, if not before.'

'Okay. Have a nice lunch with Sharon.'

She hangs up, and I look at the clock. I rang the studio earlier and a harassed-sounding woman asked me if I could pop in this afternoon, so, at short notice, the child-minder agreed to take Noah. Pam had told me yesterday she was meeting an old friend she used to work with for lunch and a shopping afternoon, so there was no point asking her to have him.

I have two hours to get ready and get there, looking more presentable than I have in weeks, having dug out a floral dress from the back of the wardrobe that I haven't been able to get into in years. Now, it fits perfectly, the tie-belt at the back meaning I can pull it in even more. It takes me ages to find my dance exam certificates, which makes me rush to get ready, then at the child-minders Noah plays up, not wanting me to leave him, and I end up with three seconds to spare standing outside the studio, looking up at the large window on the first floor, with sweat drenching my underarms, both from rushing and nerves. It's above a dry-cleaners, accessed through a staircase between that and the newsagents next door. The name *REEL THING DANCE STUDIO* stretches the full width of the window in sparkly silver letters. I take a deep breath, push the door open, and climb the stairs.

This place has been here about five years now, on the edge of Luxton, not too far from the junction where Issy died. I've never taken much notice of it, my dancing days being behind me, or so I'd thought. The stairwell is shabby and scuffed, probably from school bags being scraped against it. I can imagine the chatter and squeals of the little girls as they dash up the stairs, eager for their lessons to start. I was one of them once. It has a happy feel to it and I open the door at the top, out into a spacious studio, well-lit with a beautiful polished, sprung floor. The smell of the polish and the warm honey tones of the oak take me back years. I stand and breathe it in. It smells wonderful.

'Hi, you must be Mel.'

I turn to see a small woman in exercise gear sitting in the corner, rolling up mats.

'Yes, I am.'

'I'm Olivia Moore. We spoke earlier. Pregnant mums' aerobics has just finished.' She points to the pile of mats. I'd forgotten it was an exercise studio as well.

She scrambles to her feet and comes to meet me, shaking my hand. 'Shall we go through to the office?'

She leads the way to a door I never noticed at the back. The office is little more than a cupboard with a computer, desk and chair, and two shelves with folders on. Paper and clutter are everywhere. At least it has a window.

'Please, sit down.'

She removes yet more paper from the chair, most of it flyers for local takeaways, so I can sit down while she sits on the edge of the desk. I hand her my certificates.

'This place is mainly a dance studio, but I also rent it out in the day and some evenings and at weekends for exercise classes. It brings more money in, so it helps me keep it going.' She studies my certificates.

I watch her, and the familiar doubts pour in. She's one of those immaculate people: her frame is tiny and delicate, her hair long and dark brown, is pinned up low at the back of her neck. She looks really self-assured and confident, a proper dancer—not like me. I wipe my palms on my dress. She finishes reading and looks up.

100

'So, tell me about you.'

That's it, the dreaded interview question. There's nothing interesting about me. I think back to what Jon told me to say. *Don't say 'I'm just a wife and mother'. Talk about your dancing.*

'Well, I danced from the age of three right up to having my daughter.' I pause, swallow twice and dig my fingernails into my palm, hard, before images of Issy can flood my mind. I carry on. 'I danced with my twin sister. It was my life. I loved it. It was everything to me. I tried out for several top dance schools but didn't make it, sadly.' Oh great. That sounds stupid, like I'm a failure, a loser, which is about right.

'Only the lucky few ever do. I didn't either,' she says with a smile. 'But I just went in a different direction and opened my own school. I love teaching. It's different to competition and exhibition dancing, but just as rewarding in its own way.' A kind of energy fizzes off her when she speaks about dancing. It's contagious, and I can feel it rubbing off on me.

'I've never thought of it like that. I'd love to give it a go. I thought I would be too old now I'm forty, but that's silly. Age is just a number, right?' *Turn negatives into positives, Jon said.*

'It is silly. I'm thirty eight and there's no way I'd pack in. I've seen teachers going strong in their seventies.'

'Yes, actually, that's so true. Some of my ballet mistresses were sixty- and seventy-plus, and they were hard taskmasters. You can't put a price on all that experience, can you?'

'Exactly. Plus, I've employed a string of younger girls here and they're just not reliable. They don't seem to understand the concept of letting people down. I've just had to let the last one go. She only turned up when she felt like it or would swan in halfway through the class she was supposed to be taking. It's as if they thought my little dance studio was beneath them. I blame 'Strictly' and all those kinds of programmes. They feel that's what they should be doing, like it's their right, but they don't want to do all the hard graft it's taken those professional dancers to get there. I've decided not to go down that path again. Anyway, rant over. I didn't mention it in the ad, but I'm looking for someone nearer my own age, who's settled and not flighty, and wants the studio to succeed.'

I'm loving what I'm hearing and find myself nodding enthusiastically. 'Well, I've lived in Luxton most of my life and I know what teamwork is like. I used to work at the high school, doing admin in the office.'

Her eyes light up. 'Ooh! That would really help. I'm rubbish at paperwork, obviously.' She casts a hand around the place. 'I leave it until the last minute and then get in a mess worrying about it. Can you do accounts and stuff for the taxman?'

'Yes, no problem. It's just about being organised and prioritising. There's no magic formula. I find it quite therapeutic actually, watching something organised come out of chaos. I like neat and tidy.'

'I'm more like nature abhors a vacuum. Any available space I have gets something plonked in it. Mel, I think we could work well together. How do you feel? I can see you can do the job and more. Are you sure three evenings would be enough for you, though? I can only pay you eight fifty an hour.'

Don't mention too much about our home life, Jon had said. *Don't make them think you have problems that would interfere.*

'That would be perfect for me. And the money's not my main reason for doing it.'

'Okay, what about coming in on Tuesday evening and we can see how it goes?'

'Great. What time?'

'Seven o'clock. I take junior ballet then. You can watch and join in if you like. Pitch in as you see fit. Oh, there's no parking, I'm afraid, but you can park around the corner on Turner Avenue, the pay and display. It's free after six. Which way do you come?'

'Past the high school.'

'That's good. It's really busy the other way. That junction just up the road's awful. I've been stuck there for over five minutes sometimes. It needs traffic lights. They might put some there now after that bad crash a few weeks ago. Did you hear about it? Some poor girl died there; it's terrible.'

I sit there with my mouth open while the blood turns to ice in my veins.

'Mel? Are you alright? You look a bit pale.'

Might as well tell her and get it over with. Then she can rescind the job offer when she finds out my daughter killed herself. She might think being unstable runs in the family.

'Er, yeah, I mean... about the crash... it was my daughter. The girl who died.'

A tear escapes and I swipe it away. I refuse to cry now. I want this job, and crying won't bring Issy back.

'Oh my God! I had no idea! I'm *so* sorry.' Olivia's hand flies to her mouth, as if trying to cram the words she's just spoken back in but it's too late. Her face blanches, then flushes bright red as the full horror hits her.

More tears are escaping now, and there's not a damn thing I can do to stop them. My voice hitches. 'It's... okay. Why would you know? Don't w… worry about it.'

'Are you sure you're up to this now? I mean, hardly any time at all has passed. It's probably way too soon for you.'

I don't want to see the pity in her eyes, so I look at the floor.

'No,' I say. 'I *want* this job. I *need* this job. I need something else, to forget. Do you understand?' I look up fiercely and meet her eyes.

She looks hard at me, as if trying to see right inside me, then the moment passes and she nods. 'Well then, I'll see you at seven on Tuesday, but first, do you have time for a coffee and to look at my non-existent filing system?'

I smile gratefully. 'I'd be glad to.'

Everything else can wait. The child-minder, Elaine, told me not to rush back. Everyone knows about Issy, even though most think it was a tragic accident, and they're all making allowances. For the next hour, I forget about everything other than chatting to Olivia and sorting out her paperwork. I love it. It reminds me of the job I had to give up. And I'm coming back on Tuesday to start teaching. A small, very small, glimmer of hope has appeared on my horizon after all the bad, but I remember, driving home, that the bad's not over. The next hurdle is meeting the lecturer and seeing what the hell was going on with him and Issy.

16

Jon

THE DRIVE TO NEWCASTLE takes a little over an hour. Mel aborts several attempts to engage me in conversation and reads her Kindle for most of the journey, muttering something about monosyllabic men under her breath. My brain won't engage in small talk when all I can think about is what to say to this guy when I meet him, this Cunningham. This pervert.

We've booked into a Travelodge on the outskirts. Waste of good money, if you ask me, all this staying over, but it was Mel's idea. She wants me to be calm when we confront this guy, not all worked up from driving. She knows how I use driving time to think, or brood, as she sometimes puts it. Or maybe she just needed a break from Noah and used me as an excuse. It's money we can ill afford to spend, anyhow.

The room's basic but pleasant enough, and we sling our bags on the bed. At one time, if we had a hotel room to ourselves, we'd put the bed to good use more or less immediately, but I can see Mel eyeing it uneasily, probably hoping I'm not going to pounce on her. She hasn't asked me why I'm still sleeping in the attic room. I've been there since the row we had after the meeting in the pub with Steve. It just seems easier to go to bed there every night. Maybe it's just habit, or maybe it's something more. I slump into the tub chair by the window and two days' worth of stubble scrapes my hand as I rest my chin on it. I'm worried Steve's information's not good, and Cunningham's not going to be there. We'll have driven all this way and forked out for a hotel for nothing.

'He'll be there. Steve was certain.' Mel is leafing through the literature from the hotel. 'Stop worrying.'

'How did you know?'

'I can just tell. Maybe I should do the talking.'

'What? Why?'

'So you don't launch yourself at him and hit the guy. I know what you're like.'

'Don't be bloody stupid! What good would it do us if I ended up getting done for assault? I'm not going to hit him.'

'Maybe I should do the talking, anyway.'

'You hate talking to strangers.'

'Yes, well, maybe it's time I got used to it. I'll have to talk to parents with my new job, won't I? It'll be good practice. See how diplomatic I can be when necessary.'

I don't like it. She thinks I can't control myself? What if she screws it up? But she seems adamant.

'Whatever,' I say. I can always butt in if necessary. 'What do you want to do for the rest of today?'

'I dunno. The shops are just about to close, but we could have a mooch round, if you like, down by the river. Get an early dinner.'

'Alright.' We're both anxious about what we may find out tomorrow, so it would do us good to get out and take our minds off it. Plus, we need to get out of this place, where the bed is like the elephant in the room.

'I might have a quick shower first. I feel all sticky,' she says.

'Okay.'

I kick off my shoes and stretch out on the bed while she showers. It's still hot outside and I'm sweaty, but I can't be bothered to change or shower. I can hear the water running and then it switches off. Mel comes back wearing make-up and dressed in a floaty summer dress. She looks extremely thin, scrawny even. It makes her look older and drawn in her face.

'You look nice,' I tell her.

'Thanks,' is all she says, slipping on her sandals. She's the first to the door.

***

On Monday morning, we stand outside the building where Issy studied English.

'Do you think he's in there?' Mel asks, chewing her bottom lip.

'I don't know, but you need to swipe a security pass to open the door. I vote that we phone someone and ask them to let us in.'

'Phone who?'

I pull out my phone and google Newcastle uni. The first phone number that comes up is the one I dial. Not expecting anyone to answer, I'm amazed when someone does.

I tell her who I'm trying to get in touch with and who I am. Who I was the parent of.

'Can I get back to you on this number?' she asks.

'Yes. I'm outside the Percy Building now. I've been informed that Mr Cunningham is on the premises this week.' His name is bitter on my tongue, like poison.

'Leave it with me.'

For ten minutes, we sit outside the Percy Building in the Quadrangle, where Issy used to take some of her English classes. It's beautiful here; I've always liked it. Even when the students are milling around, and there are still plenty, mainly from overseas by the look of it, it has a tranquil, academic feel to it. I check my phone constantly, even though I know it hasn't rung. Mel is beginning to get fidgety. Me? I could wait all day as long as I get what I came for in the end. A door to the Percy Building opens, and a man steps out, blinking in the sunshine. I know it's him—*Peter fucking C*. He's mid-thirties and not what I expected at all. He's boyish and quite good-looking, I suppose, in that trendy, actor-type way, in black combats and a white T-shirt. His dishevelled, light-brown hair is slightly too long. He glances around and locks eyes with me. I stand up and the hair on the back of my neck bristles. This is the man my daughter prostituted herself for? I know I said I wouldn't hit him, but I really want to smash his chiselled face in.

He has an owlish look about him, accentuated by his thin, wire-rimmed glasses, like he always has his head in a book while the real world passes him by; one of those otherworldly beings unaffected by the real life the rest of us struggles with. Mel hears me hiss under my breath and turns to me.

'Jon?' she says, following my gaze as *Peter C* draws near. 'Oh!' she exclaims in surprise, probably taken aback by how handsome he is.

'Mr Warner? Mrs Warner?' Cunningham says, walking over to us with his hand extended. Mel shakes it, looking bemused. I stare at his hand pointedly and shove mine in my pockets. He looks flustered and drops his.

'Would you like to come in?'

'Er, yes, thanks,' says Mel, her eyes wide. She's practically salivating. *Why, of course, Professor.*

She wanted to do the talking, so I'm going to let her. We follow him into the building and down a corridor to a room at the bottom with his name on the door. It's small inside, with a desk and two chairs, one in front, one behind. He grabs another chair from behind the door and puts it with the one in front of the desk.

'Please, sit down.' He looks more flustered than before as he goes to the chair behind the desk. 'Er, may I offer you some tea or coffee…?'

'No, we're fine,' I say. I'm not accepting hospitality from him.

Mel shifts beside me in her chair but doesn't contradict me. Cunningham meets our eyes and doesn't drop his gaze in a stare that's almost challenging. Not flustered anymore, then.

'Before I speak, may I ask the purpose of your visit?'

I clear my throat and Mel jumps in.

'It's about some photos on our daughter's phone that she sent to you.'

He starts in his chair, a small movement, before he checks himself. 'Ah, right. Um, yes.' He removes his glasses and rubs his hand over his eyes, then settles back in his chair. His face is flaming as he puts his glasses back on.

My hands, resting on my thighs, ball up into fists. The bastard's not even denying it. *Ah, right? Is that all he can say?* He'd better not ask to see them again. He surprises me when he gets up and goes over to a filing cabinet next to the desk and pulls open a drawer. After replacing his glasses, he riffles through files and plucks one out. When he turns around, his face is still beet red. Is he embarrassed because of the content of the photos or because he got caught out?

'Issy did send me some, er, rather compromising pictures. They compromised her and me, I'm afraid. A most unpleasant business. In here are the records from a meeting I had with the head of department about the incident.' He taps the file with a forefinger, then opens it and swivels it around for us to read. Mel and I lean forward as one as I pull it closer.

The form on top details the date and time of the text messages, the content and the fact that Cunningham is logging it officially as a complaint. It also states that his preference is to involve Issy's parents from the outset. The form below is Issy's version of events, which corroborates Cunningham's and states that she is willing to change tutors and remain on the course if there is no repeat of the incident. She has signed the form, along with Cunningham and an intelligible squiggle which I gather is the Head's.

When I look back at Cunningham, he's leaning back in his chair with his fingers steepled under his chin. 'As you can see, I wanted to involve you from the outset, and Issy begged us not to. I haven't taught her since, and when she returns in September, she will be placed with a female lecturer. She's lucky to be returning at all, after what she did. I was all for kicking her off the course altogether. As you can imagine, I can't teach under those circumstances.' His voice comes out in a rush and he stops to take a steadying breath. 'It's a delicate issue, working with young, sometimes impressionable girls, but I would go so far as to call it stalking, what she did to me over several months. She could have ruined my career and my life. I have a wife and a young son. This has caused me no end of trouble.'

He shakes his head and holds out his hands, palms up. His hands are shaking slightly. 'It's been unbearable. My work is my life, and she put everything in jeopardy, everything that matters to me. I'm still angry with her, if I'm honest. Please believe me when I say if there's a repeat performance with me or any lecturer, Issy will be made to leave, no question. No more second chances. Frankly, I'm amazed she got away with it this time.'

I blink, and Mel does the same. I leave her to it when she leans forward.

'Mr Cunningham, Issy won't be returning in September.'

Cunningham looks relieved. 'Oh. I see. May I ask why?'

I can't hold back any longer. As Mel inhales, about to speak, I dive in.

'She's dead.'

The blood drains from Cunningham's face as his jaw drops, and he stays like that for several seconds. Then his eyes flick from side to side, panic building on his face. He looks like he's regretting everything he's just said.

'Oh God... when... I mean, how? I'm so sorry.' He shakes his head and takes his glasses off again to pinch the top of his nose with his thumb and forefinger. I watch him, feeling strangely detached. It hasn't escaped my notice that I can say my daughter's dead without grief taking over. Beside me, Mel makes a small, strangled noise, and I know she's struggling not to cry. I reach for her hand and squeeze it whilst addressing Cunningham in a low voice.

'So you never encouraged Issy at all in this matter? You weren't sleeping with her, were you, because if I find out you're lying, that you were shagging her, I'll kill you.'

'No, God, no. That's why I went straight to Pattinson and reported it. I would never, never do something like this. Ever.'

He is so vehement I have no choice but to believe him, even though I'd prefer to blame him still. It seems Issy wasn't so innocent. The more I learn about her, the less I know. Mel is weeping into a tissue beside me, and Cunningham is still looking shocked. A tiny amount of colour has returned to his cheeks.

'I'm so sorry for your loss. I can't believe it. What happened, if I may ask?'

I swallow hard. Twice. 'Suicide.'

Once again, his mouth drops open. 'What?' he whispers, sitting up straighter, then keeping going until he's hunched over with his head in his hands.

'She drove her car under a lorry,' I say. I've repeated it so often, it's like it's not real anymore. Just words. I have a feeling we're not going to learn much more here. Issy fancied her lecturer and sent naked pictures of herself to try and snare him. Apparently, it's not uncommon these days for girls to take intimate photos and send them to boyfriends. At least, given the circumstances, they won't have ended up on the internet somewhere.

'What did you do with the photos she sent?' I ask.

'After Pattinson witnessed them, we deleted them. No need to keep them as documentary evidence after we'd filled out the report. We didn't want to risk them falling into the wrong hands. You never know, these days.' He flaps a hand in the air. I know just what he means.

'Thank you,' I say, relieved. 'Er, when you confronted her about them, how was she? Embarrassed? Especially with Mr Pattinson seeing them as well?'

'Well, actually, no. It was as if what she'd done was no big deal. Like it was normal.'

'I'm sorry for what she did to you and what it could have cost you.' Mel's voice is small, and she's staring at her interlocked fingers in her lap. She sniffs and swallows hard.

I have no idea where we go from here. I take a deep breath and throw myself on his mercy.

'Mr Cunningham, we are finding out things about our daughter we had no idea about. How did she seem to you, over the months you taught her? How did she come across?'

He clears his throat and shifts awkwardly in his seat. 'You want the truth?'

Mel looks startled and blinks furiously.

'Yes. In your opinion,' I say.

He sighs. 'I feel awkward saying this, but I found her very forward, in a sexual way. She seemed very aware of her body and wasn't afraid to use it to get what she wanted. It was uncomfortable and embarrassing, the way she threw herself at me. I'm not that kind of man.'

'Mmm. Was she like this with other lecturers?'

'Not as far as I'm aware.'

'Did you know she has a child?'

He looks surprised and blinks several times. 'No.' He shook his head. 'No. That's news to me. I never heard her speak of a child at all. How old?'

'Three. Noah.'

'So she must have...' His eyes shoot up and look from left to right as if working something out.

'Been pregnant at fifteen, yes.' I sigh. 'Did she make many friends on her course, do you know?'

'I wouldn't know, to be honest. Who people make friends with is their own business.'

We all lapse into silence, each of us lost in our own thoughts. Then Cunningham speaks.

'Why, though? Why would she do that? A lorry? Christ.'

Mel leans forward, wiping her eyes and sniffing. 'That's what we're trying to find out. None of it makes sense. We thought she was doing well at uni. There was no sign of anything wrong, or, if there was, we missed it. Anything you can tell us might hold some clue. Anything at all.'

Cunningham leans back in his chair and looks first at Mel, then me. 'I have a lot of students, as you can imagine, and I don't see them really, outside of lectures, unless they're having any particular problems. Issy came to me a couple of times with things she said she was struggling with, but it didn't feel genuine to me; more like she was using it as an excuse to get me on my own. Her grades weren't good, and I don't think she'll have done particularly well in her exams. Such a shame, really. She certainly had the brain, it was more the application that let her down. She seemed to me to be a girl with issues, but it's not my job to deal with that. We have a counsellor at uni that the students can see anytime. That may be worth looking into, whether or not she ever went to see her. She was supposed to, after the, er, photos incident. Kim Brent, she's called. I can give you her number. Have you spoken to the students she was planning on sharing with next year? They might know something.'

Mel and I look at each other and shake our heads.

'We hadn't thought of that. We need to get in touch with the letting agent and tell them she won't be moving into the house. I don't know who she was sharing with. She was, as usual, not forthcoming about it,' says Mel.

'The letting agent will know. Were you guarantors?'

'Yes.' Mel looks at me. 'I can remember writing a cheque for the deposit months ago. We'll have to sort it out. I'll look it up.' I can see she's hoping it may lead somewhere.

'I'm sorry I can't be of any further help. If you leave me your numbers, if I think of anything that might be useful, I'll ring you. And I'm sorry, again, about everything. I can't imagine what you must have thought of me when you found those photos.' He blushes again and looks down.

'I'm sure you can,' I say.

He nods. 'Well, yes, probably. God, what a mess,' he mutters, shaking his head.

This time I'm the one to extend my hand. 'I'm sorry. For what she did.'

His eyes search mine. 'Thank you.' He shakes my hand, then Mel's.

'We'll see ourselves out, let you get back to work,' Mel says. 'And thank you.'

'I'll be in touch if I think of anything that might help,' he says as we leave.

Outside, still in bright early July sunshine, we look at each other.

'Nothing more to learn here. Let's go home,' I say.

She nods. 'Yes, let's go home. And find that bloody deposit form.'

17

Mel

'NOAH! PLEASE! DON'T DO that! It's naughty!'

Noah stands, glaring at me with his arms folded across his chest, then turns his back on me. We've reached a stalemate; I want him to stop throwing his toys around and clear them away before watching TV and he is refusing, making more mess by tipping out every toy he has on the floor. Frustration almost boils over as I look at the mess he's made. The house looks like an explosion in a toy shop. I've tried to be patient with him after all the upset we've been through. He's super-clingy, not wanting me out of his sight, yet won't do a damn thing I ask. He hasn't once asked where his mummy is, which breaks my heart. Sometimes he calls me Mummy, sometimes Grandma, but the former is increasing in frequency. I've even started answering to it. In true Noah fashion, his mood changes swiftly and he comes to sit on my knee, plastering kisses all over my face. 'Sorry, Mummy.' My eyes are wet and he pokes gently at them with his fingers. 'Don't cry, Grandma.'

He played up for Jon last night when I went to the dance studio. He knew I was going out and started to have a tantrum. Even when I cuddled him and told him I wouldn't be long, he wouldn't be placated. In the end, I was glad to escape, which only made me feel worse. When I got back, Jon's words were, 'He's been a right little shit!'

115

I taught my first class last night and, even though it was to tiny beginners, I was nervous about it. But in the end, I thoroughly enjoyed it. I was mainly helping Olivia so she could show me the ropes, and for long periods of time I didn't think about Issy and that's not happened since she died.

Noah gets up, picks up a car and puts it in the box, then glances over at me.

'That's right. Now let's clear the rest of them away and put Scooby Doo on.'

He starts to throw everything back into his toy box, happy to do it himself.

'Careful or you'll break them all and then you won't have anything left to play with.'

His bad mood appears to have passed, and he continues clearing away on his own. I sit back on the rug and watch, my mind wandering back to Jon. I'd checked *her* Facebook page on his laptop the other evening, when he went to the pub with Justin. There was no change or contact between them, but why am I still doing it after all this time? Maybe because he's still sleeping in the attic room. Every night, I listen for late-night phone calls coming from upstairs; I haven't heard any, but maybe he's texting or emailing her. I lean back against the sofa and stretch out my legs in front of me, relieving the stiffness in them. Funny, but back then, I'd never considered he would ever have an affair; didn't think he was the type. That's when I found out there isn't a type. Anyone's capable of it, even me. Ever since then, I've always thought if I find the right person, I might do it, just so Jon can experience that level of betrayal and what it can do to you.

'All finished.' Noah holds his hands out to me, and I look up to see all the toys cleared away.

'Good boy. Scooby Doo now?'

'Yes, please.'

I put the DVD on for him, and go to make a cup of tea. As I sit at the table with it, I think for the thousandth time about the meeting with Peter Cunningham and how we learned that we knew our daughter even less than we'd realised. I've never been so embarrassed—to have to sit in front of a man my daughter's sent explicit pictures of herself to in an attempt to seduce him. I thought I'd die of shame and he was so good about it, but, ultimately, it's only thrown up more questions. So where do we go from here?

As I sit feeling helpless and useless, with my brain churning endlessly round in the same fruitless circle, I suddenly think of something I can do. Ellie, Issy's old school friend, should be back from uni now. I could call round there. If I remember right, she went to Bristol to study something sciencey. She'd been Issy's friend all through school, and Issy still saw her whenever they were both back from uni. Come to think of it, though, she hadn't been to ours to visit for a long time. Issy always went to her place.

Yesterday afternoon, Steve Jackson fetched Issy's computer back, with the disappointing news that there was nothing of any significance on it. Just the usual Facebook stuff and uni work. At least she *did* some work while she was there. Her laptop is still on the kitchen table where we left it. Thanks to Steve telling us the password (first pet's name (Joey) and her date of birth), in no time I'm on her Facebook page. When I try to find Ellie, I find out Issy and she aren't Facebook friends anymore. Since when? Come to think of it, I don't recall seeing Ellie or her parents at the funeral but, there again, I sort of drifted through much of it in a blur. Maybe it's time to go and see her. She might know something.

I go and watch Noah as he sits far too close to the TV, entranced by a cartoon dog. His eyelashes are long, thick and dark, and they spill onto his cheeks in a fan shape every time he blinks, just like hers did at that age. She was chubby, blonde and smooth-skinned and I couldn't get enough of her, even though she was well into temper tantrums at that age, unbearably long ones made to test your patience. Until she was two, she slept between Jon and me. It was the only way any of us would get any sleep. If I left her in her own bed, she would cry all night if she had to. *Ignore the crying,* was the advice from the health visitor and doctor. And Pam. Easier said than done. She would never go back to sleep on her own. After weeks of Jon and I walking round like zombies, we just gave in and let her sleep with us until she decided she'd rather be in her own bed.

Thankfully, Noah was a different story, content to sleep on his own. He looks at me, screeching with laughter at the TV and pointing at the screen. As soon as it finishes, I tell him we're going out. I strap him into his car seat and drive over to Ellie's house. A small pink car is outside. Ellie's?

After my third insistent knock, I hear someone inside the house shout, 'God! I'm coming! Keep your hair on!'

When she opens the door and sees me, the scowl on her face dies away and is replaced by a heated blush that travels up from her neck and chest. Her hair is pinned up loosely in a teetering pile and she's wearing tiny denim shorts and a yellow vest, the ghost of acne still visible under her carefully applied makeup. I remember the hell she'd gone through because of it. Must be four or five years ago now. Maybe more. Her skin has a deep golden tan.

'Oh, Mrs Warner! Hello!' She looks uncomfortable. Her eyes skit about over my shoulder. What's she checking for? Is it uncool for your dead friend's mother to be knocking on your door?

'Hello, Ellie. Can I have a quick word?'

Ellie's eyes drop to Noah, standing by my side and gripping my hand tightly.

'Hello, will you play with me? Have you got any biscuits?' he asks.

Ellie looks taken aback and doesn't answer, but her shoulders relax a bit.

'May I come in?' I ask.

She steps to one side and opens the door wider so I can enter. The house is clean, uncluttered and quiet—everything I'd like mine to be.

Her eyes meet mine briefly and flit away, and I remember the first time I met her, when she came with two other friends to our house with Issy. The other two, whose names I've long since forgotten, bounded through the doorway, bubbly and chatty, and Ellie sort of slipped in behind them, looking at her shoes, crippling shyness radiating from every pore. It was painful to see how, in trying so hard to be invisible, she inevitably stuck out like a sore thumb. Every bit of her begged *please don't notice me, please don't look at me, please don't talk to me,* and the result was such that she might as well have had a neon sign illuminating her. I hope age and uni have given her a bit more confidence. A tiny, hesitant smile greets me and I can see she's wondering why I'm here.

'Are your parents away?' I ask.

'Yes, they've been in Spain since May. They have a house there and go every year for two months in the summer. They can both work from there. I've been over as well.'

So that's why none of them were at the funeral.

'Would you like something to drink?' she asks as we follow her into the kitchen.

'I'll have some pop,' shouts Noah.

'Noah! That's not polite,' I scold.

'She asked!' he says, confused.

'I've got orange juice,' Ellie says. 'Will that do?'

'Yeah,' he pipes up again.

'Sorry, no. Water will do fine for him. Nothing for me, thanks.'

'Don't want stupid water,' Noah complains, scrunching his face up.

I bend down so we're eye to eye. 'Water or nothing,' I say. 'You've already had orange juice today. What did the dentist say? Once a day only or he'll have to get the drill out.'

A black thundercloud descends, darkening his features, and he wrestles with what I've just said. He hates to lose, just as Issy did, but I'm not budging.

'It's your choice,' I say, folding my arms and straightening up.

119

He sighs, apparently suddenly being blessed with the wisdom of one much older. 'Water please, thank you.' His shoulders sag slightly. Round one to me.

'Water it is, then,' Ellie says, glancing at me for confirmation. I nod, and she fills a glass from the tap and hands it to him then looks at me. 'Er, is a glass okay? I don't think we have anything plastic.'

'That's fine. Be careful with it Noah, like a big boy, okay?'

Noah looks at me solemnly and grasps it with both hands and a great deal of reverence and concentration. I should use this big boy thing more often. It works a treat. We all sit at the scrubbed pine kitchen table with what looks like years' worth of scratches and scars etched into it; I can visualise the happy family mealtimes that must have taken place here, similar to the ones in my own house. The ones that will never happen again. Noah raises the glass and sips while his legs, dangling above the ground, swing back and forth, his left foot bumping against my shin on every swing forward, then scraping on the way back. The canvas pump is rough on my bare skin, but I ignore it.

'Ellie, I need to ask you something about Issy?' Bump. Scrape.

Ellie's eyes drop down to the table. 'I'm sorry about, you know, the accident. It must have been awful for you. Like, I don't know what to say... '

'It's okay. There's nothing anyone can say.'

'I was in Spain for the funeral, with Mum and Dad. I only came back two weeks ago.'

'Right. It's just, I was wondering when you last saw her and how she seemed to you? Was it Easter?' Scrape.

Ellie looks at me, startled. The strap of her little vest top slips down, and she yanks it back up, covering her pink bra strap. 'Did she tell you that?'

I move my leg away from Noah's foot. 'Yes. She said she was coming here when she came home for Easter break. How did she seem to you then? Was there anything out of the ordinary about her?' Bump, scrape. 'Noah, stop kicking me.'

Noah stops and glances around, his eyes widening when he sees an old, rusty swing in the back garden through the open French doors. 'Can I go on the swing?'

Ellie looks at me. 'Is that okay?'

'Yes. He'd love that. Come on, Noah.'

We all go outside and I lift him on the swing. He grasps the chains and I push him only just enough to get him moving.

'Noah, hold on tight so you don't fall off.'

Ellie clears her throat and goes back to my earlier question, her eyes fixing on mine for the longest time. 'Mrs Warner, I don't know why Issy told you that, about coming here. I haven't seen her at all since before she had Noah.'

I stiffen. 'You mean you haven't seen her in over four years?'

'No. I haven't.'

So where had Issy been going all these years when she told me she was 'just nipping round to Ellie's?'

'Right. When did you stop being friends on Facebook?'

'God, like, ages ago. I can't even remember.'

I swallow. Time to tell Ellie the truth.

'Issy always said she was coming here all through college and the holidays in uni. I thought it was funny that you never came round to ours. Do you have any idea where she would go or who she might see when she said she was seeing you?'

Ellie shakes her head. 'No. No idea at all. Why would she say that?'

I push Noah again and he chuckles, throwing his head back and sticking his legs out in front.

'I don't know. So, did you two have a falling out or something? At school, I mean?'

A mottled flush creeps up her chest and neck. 'Not an actual falling out as such, no.'

'But what? Something else?'

'Er...' I can see how hard this is for her, but I have to know.

121

'Please. Whatever it is, you can tell me. It might help me understand.'

She gazes at the floor. 'Well, it was years ago now. When we got to high school, Issy seemed to change, that's all. She didn't want to come out with us, me and Gemma, anymore. We tried everything, but she always said no.'

'Change how?'

She looks at me; her eyes, a soft, hazel brown, implore me to understand. 'Well, at first, she was quiet and really moody, snapping at us and biting our heads off if we said the wrong thing. Not like her usual self. She could be so funny and make us laugh when she wanted, before.'

'And it didn't just seem like teenage hormones to you?'

'No. It didn't seem like it. I mean, we were all going through the same, but she was far worse. And hers went on all the time. I even asked her once if you and her dad were getting divorced or something. She said no and gave me a funny look. Once she'd changed, I kind of kept expecting her to change back, like whatever was wrong would eventually sort itself out and she'd be 'Issy' again. But she never did. If it was her hormones, they were way off the scale compared to anyone else's. And no matter how many times we asked her what was wrong or tried to help her, she just said nothing was wrong and she was okay.'

I'm having a hard time believing that Issy and Ellie hadn't been friends for years and I hadn't suspected a thing. How could I not have noticed?

'Anything else?' I ask.

'Well, she was kind of like, argumentative and defensive all the time, as if she was getting in first before anyone said anything. She said she preferred being on her own to being with us and didn't want to hang around with us anymore. But whenever I saw her, she wasn't on her own. She was with lads, some of them a few years above us, laughing and joking around with them.' Her face flames again but she presses on. 'She was always flirting around them, you know, inviting them to touch her or kiss her. Before long, she had a, kind of like, bad reputation. A few of them said she'd let them put their hands up her skirt or down her top. It was common knowledge. So no one was all that surprised when she got pregnant. Not really.' She blushed furiously at the subject of Issy getting pregnant and being easy.

'Was Issy not popular then? With other girls? Is that what you're saying, that she didn't have many friends?'

'I guess, yeah. But it was her choice.'

It's so much to take in. My heart sits like a stone in my chest. 'I thought you two were so close, all this time. I had no idea.'

She shakes her head. 'Not for a long time, no. I'm sorry. I wanted to be friends with her, but she pushed me away.' She looks down at her nails and picks at them. 'I always assumed we'd be friends all our lives, you know? Until suddenly we weren't anymore.'

Noah pipes up. 'Push me.'

I push him again. Ellie and I glance at each other.

'Is there anything else?' I ask.

'I don't think so. I'm sorry.'

'No, you've been most helpful. I wish I'd known all this earlier. Thank you, Ellie.'

She nods.

'So, how are you finding uni?' I ask, feeling like I should show some interest.

'I love it. It's great.'

When I look at her, her eyes are moist and shiny. 'Do you think there's something I could have done, or helped her in some way, Mrs Warner? I feel so bad about what's happened, you know. We used to be so close. I think about her and I still miss her. In some ways, she was the best friend I ever had, for a long time, anyway.'

'I don't think you could have done anything. I feel the same, like there was something I could or should have done too. But if *I* didn't know, how could you? Don't feel bad, Ellie. None of us knew this would happen.'

I put my arm around her slim shoulders, like I have done many times when she was little. How come we don't notice people slipping away? She wipes her eyes on the backs of her hands.

'Ellie, if you ever want to come round, you're more than welcome.' I let her go.

She nods, but I know she won't. Too much time has passed and too much has happened.

On the way home, in the back seat, Noah sings loudly to his favourite CD, some Disney thing he can't get enough of. I tune him out and mull over what Ellie has said. But, really, what I've learned has left me no further on.

'Grandma?' he shouts.

I turn the music down.

'What?' I look at him in the rearview mirror to see he's stretching the neck of his T-shirt out of shape. 'What are you doing?'

'What... why... would my mummy want hands in her top? Like this?' He shoves his hand inside as far as it will go.

Christ! No, no, no.

'And in her skirt?' He's messing about with his shorts now, trying to get his fingers up the leg.

I have no idea what to say. I should have been more careful; he doesn't miss a thing. Ever.

'Oh, nothing, darling. Ellie didn't mean anything by it. Just forget it; it was grown-up talk. Ooh, shall we have ice cream when we get back? With sprinkles on?'

'Yay!' he shouts. 'Grandma?'

'What?'

'Put my song back on!'

I turn the music up and he continues singing happily to himself, clapping his hands to the beat. But his question reverberates in my head. Why would she indeed?

When I turn the corner onto our street and go to pull into the driveway, my heart does a double slam. Greg Evans is sitting on the front doorstep.

18

Jon

'DON'T YOU THINK THAT'S a bit weird? I wouldn't like that. The man who was driving the lorry that killed your daughter sitting in your house with your missus, large as life. No way.'

Justin shakes his head, lifts his beer, and drains the glass. We're in my living room while Mel's teaching her second class at the studio. We've had to move our regular Thursday night pub session to our house so I can watch Noah. It's either that or ditch it altogether, and neither of us wants to do that. It's been a long-standing tradition of ours and jealously guarded at all costs. Justin is away most of the week travelling, making wads of money, and Thursday nights are our time to kick back and relax.

'Well, what could I do? I come home from work yesterday and he's here, drinking coffee in this very spot. Apparently, at the wake, him and Mel cleared the air, became BFFs, or whatever they say, and agreed they would keep in touch. I didn't know because I wasn't there, was I? I also didn't know she'd told him he was welcome anytime. She must have 'forgotten' to tell me.'

I drain the last of my beer and get up to get us a couple more from the fridge. Justin turns on the TV as I'm pulling out the cans, and I can hear him switching channels at the speed of light; flick, flick, flick. I kick the fridge door closed and take the cans back in, hand one to him, then sit on the sofa with my feet on the coffee table. I don't mind drinking at home. Can't sit like this in the pub. Plus Justin's stumped up for the John Smith's. In my pocket is the list of names that Mel got from the letting agents yesterday. Surprisingly, or on reflection maybe not, all the names are male. Issy was planning to share a house with four men when she went back to uni. *Four* men. I find that unsettling, that there's not a single female on there.

Justin's settled on a Top Gear repeat whilst flipping through the telly mag at the same time. The folded list in my pocket digs into my thigh as I sit down and I shift it to one side. I don't want him to see it and start asking questions. He'll want to help, but I want to do this myself, sort of my last act for Issy. I'd rather Mel wasn't involved either, but she is. Can't help that now.

'So how many nights is Mel going to be working, did you say?' Justin asks, glancing at the supercar Clarkson is driving, before looking back at the magazine and turning to the letters page.

'Three. Tuesdays, Thursdays and Fridays. At the moment, anyway. I reckon she's going to do more, though. The woman there needs her to sort out her admin, and you know how Mel likes to do stuff like that. Pretty soon, she won't know how she managed without her. I can see it coming.'

He closes the TV mag. 'How is Mel? I haven't seen much of her lately. Pam says she's been acting a bit weird.' He picks up his beer.

I turn to him. 'Weird? Is that what she said? We've just lost our daughter. Don't we have the right to 'act weird', for God's sake? How are you supposed to act when your daughter takes her own life?'

He looks like he's realised he's said the wrong thing. 'I didn't mean it like that, mate. Sorry. Perhaps weird was the wrong word.'

'What did you mean, then?' I don't bother with my glass, just lift the can to my mouth. The trouble with drinking at home is I drink much more than I would in the pub by at least a factor of two.

Justin sighs. He doesn't want to get into this now, I can tell. He's my best mate; a good-looking, affable giant of a bloke, but with the knack of saying the wrong thing. *Blunderman,* I used to call him. He's put his foot in it more times than I've had hot dinners. If he would only think before he speaks, a lot of upset could be avoided. I've seen him get people's backs up by choosing the most inappropriate words many times.

'Nothing. It's just that Pam misses her, you know. They're normally so close. I think Pam wants to spend time with her sister, you know. Like before.'

'Like before Issy threw herself under a lorry, you mean?' I don't know why I'm being like this, really. It's not Justin's fault, but it's not fair he has three healthy, living kids and I now don't have any, is it? I glare at him. 'There is no *before* anymore, Justin. You can't go back from this.'

He looks at me with something like pity. It's horrible. I don't want pity. I want my little girl, the one I thought I had before all this. My throat feels like it's closing up and choking off, and tears prick the backs of my eyes. I blink as I sit up straighter, looking the other way from Justin.

'Grandad!' yells Noah from upstairs, saving me from continuing this conversation. He's been quiet up until now, playing in his bedroom.

I swallow hard. 'What? It's nearly bedtime. Are you ready for a story?' A wave of tiredness crashes over me after another rough night on the sofa bed, and I stifle a yawn.

'Yes,' he shouts. 'Ready, Grandad. Now.'

'You look done in. Want me to go, instead?' Justin offers.

'Yeah. If you like. Thanks.'

'No problem.'

He leaves the room and, when I hear his footsteps in Noah's bedroom above, I get the list out of my pocket and scan it: David Noone, Ryan Anderson, Nathan Brown and Michael Kelly. All English lads, by the sound of it. I thought unis were full of kids from all over, multi-cultural and all that. After a bit of wrangling with the agent about confidentiality and data protection, I managed to get addresses and phone numbers for them, telling them I needed to get the lads to find someone for Issy's room, as I couldn't afford to pay it. Given the tragic circumstances, they couldn't really uphold the contract and come out of it looking good if I complained online about it, so they agreed.

The names swim before my eyes: David Noone, Ryan Anderson, Nathan Brown, and Michael Kelly. I can't imagine what Issy would have in common with four seemingly random boys. I hope to God she hasn't slept with them all. The thought isn't a good one but, earlier, Mel told me she'd visited Ellie and, apparently, Issy had something of a bad reputation at school. Before I know it, I'm crushing the piece of paper in my hand, just thinking about it, all those boys touching her and sniffing round her. I smooth it out on the table and fold it into quarters. Perhaps they're on her course and that's how she knows them. They could all be English students; that would explain it. I've never heard her mention any of their names, but she never spoke much about her new friends at uni. It could be like getting blood out of a stone, getting stuff out of Issy.

I can hear Noah laughing upstairs.

'Grandad,' he yells. 'Come and see.'

I put the list back into my pocket and follow the chortles of laughter up the stairs. At the doorway to his bedroom, I stop to watch Justin acting out the characters from one of Noah's stories.

'Uncle Jussin's funny. He's doing silly voices and making funny faces.' Noah's eyes are twinkling and shiny in the dim lamplight.

Justin's face is just as animated. Noah turns his head to one side, and the light plays off his blonde curls. The trademark dimple appears in his right cheek, identical to the one Issy had. I have that dimple too, less pronounced now than when I was a boy. When I catch sight of it, my breath hitches in my throat. My little girl is gone, and the pain hits me afresh, as if it's the first time I've realised it. It feels physical, like a blow to my chest. With wet eyes, I escape to the bathroom and lock the door. On the edge of the bath, I sit and sob quietly into the bath towel until I'm an empty shell, purged of emotion. Justin and Noah's voices are muffled through the door, but Noah's squealing with laughter.

It's going to be hard, I know that, but I'm so glad that Issy had Noah. He's all we've got left of her. I know Noah's safe with Justin, so I take my time in the bathroom until I feel strong enough to go out. When I do, Noah's nodding off to sleep and Justin's just leaving his room.

He squeezes my shoulder, a brief touch of reassurance that I appreciate. If he knows what I've been doing in the bathroom, he doesn't say anything. We're just at the bottom of the stairs when the front door opens and Mel comes in. For a brief moment, she looks happy, but as she closes the door, her shoulders slump and her features draw down. I know it's this place doing it to her, sapping her energy and bringing her down with its gloom. I feel it too. It's as if the sunshine our family had is gone, leaving behind only storm clouds and rain.

'How did it go tonight?' I ask, the same time as Justin says, 'Hi, Twinkletoes.'

'Hey, you two. Yeah, it was good.' She smiles, but it looks like hard work.

'What did you do tonight?' Justin asks as we go into the living room, his arm slung around her shoulders.

'Tap class. But it descended into chaos. Some of the older ones ended up trying to teach me street dance. I reckon I'm going to ache like mad tomorrow. I've used muscles I'd forgotten I even had.' She tucks her feet under her on the sofa and closes her eyes, a massive yawn escaping her. 'God, I'm so tired. Has Noah been good?'

'Brilliant. Much better than the other night,' I say.

'How's Pam?' she asks Justin. A web of fine lines gather at the corners of her eyes and around her mouth. Have they got worse since Issy?

He glances at me, unsure what to say. 'Um, she's okay, but she's missing you. Says she hasn't seen much of you lately. She wants to know when she can come round and have a girly night, just the two of you.'

'I'll give her a ring tomorrow.'

Justin finishes his can. 'I'd better get going. Good job I'm working from home tomorrow. Had a couple too many of these.' The empty can makes a hollow thunk as he puts it on the coffee table next to mine.

He stands up and raises his eyebrows at me, indicating with a minute inclination of his head towards the door that he wants to talk in private. I follow him out of the front door and to the garden gate. You can almost see his house from here, around the next corner. It's bigger and fancier than ours, more bedrooms and a bigger garden, all landscaped by me. Bigger pay packet to cover it all.

'What's up?' I say.

'Is everything okay? Really?'

Looks like he's trying to finish what he started earlier.

'Yeah. Well, as right as they can be. I don't know what's right or wrong when your child dies. I can't even begin to explain how I'm feeling. As for Pam, just tell her to give Mel some time. She needs to grieve; well, we all do, you know what I mean? We're feeling our way through this bit by bit, just doing what feels right.'

He looks anxious. 'It's just, you don't have to shut us out. We're here for you, you know that. I suppose what I'm trying to say is that we feel useless and helpless. and it's horrible. It's always been the four of us coping with stuff together.'

'Yeah, I know. But we're not meaning to shut you out. I can't explain it; it's just hard.'

He nods, slowly. 'You know we're going through this with you, right? She was our little girl, too.'

'Yeah. I know. Do you know what kills me, though? The thought of telling Noah when he's old enough about what she did. When he asks why, what do I say? I don't know why.'

He shoves his hands in his pockets and shakes his head. 'I don't know. I've been wondering that, as well. There are no answers, are there?'

'No. Unfortunately not.'

'Have you rung those bereavement counsellors the police told you about?'

'No. What good will they do? Won't bring her back, will it?'

'No, but talking's supposed to help, isn't it?'

'I can talk to you, though.'

He looks pleased. 'Course you can. Anytime. I want you to. You know that.'

I nod and we say goodnight. I watch him leave with his head down and his shoulders hunched forward, silhouetted against the moonlight. He walks as though the weight of the world is on his shoulders, like Atlas. How long will this affect us all for? I lean against the wall with my back to the road and watch the moon, right above the house, disappear behind wisps of thin cloud. It's a balmy evening, still nearly twenty degrees. It hurts to think Issy will never look up at the same moon again. I used to get reassurance when she'd gone to uni that she could see the same sun and moon as me, no matter how far apart we were. She'd given me her usual derisory look, then laughed when I'd told her one day.

'You're so daft, Dad,' she'd said, rolling her eyes. I imagine I can feel her soft breath on my cheek and it almost forces me to my knees. The pain of her loss is staggering, and I can't see it ever getting easier.

I push myself off the wall and make to go back inside when a text alert vibrates my phone. I slide it out of my pocket to see it's from Steve Jackson.

Hi Jon, can you call at the station tomorrow in the afternoon sometime? I think I may have found Noah's dad.

19

Mel

'MRS WARNER, MRS WARNER, watch me twirl!'

Five-year-old Maisie hoists her arms aloft and staggers around in a clumsy pirouette. With damp tendrils of hair escaping her bun, and her face beet red, she looks like she has been dragged through the proverbial hedge backwards.

'Oh, Maisie, that's great. You're getting really good at it.'

Maisie pushes her hair out of her eyes and beams at the praise, which is quickly followed by more shouts, all demanding I watch. The class is just winding up and shrieks of laughter fill the air. I think of Issy at that age. I dragged her to more dance classes, trying to ignite a spark of interest in her, but other than messing about, she wasn't bothered.

'Okay, it's time to pack up now. If you want to, you can practice those new moves at home and have them perfect for next week.' Olivia claps her hands and the girls flit around quicker, grabbing up clothing and shoes and stuffing it all into backpacks. The mums are clearing up too, after spending the last hour leaning up against the wall, some chatting with each other and others glued to their phones. I notice there isn't a single boy in the class.

Olivia ushers the last of the girls out of the studio and down the stairs, huffs out a breath and flings herself down on the floor. 'I'm exhausted. What is it about five-year-olds that wears you out this much? They never give in. I wish I had half their energy.'

She closes her eyes and I look enviously at her figure once again. She's not much younger than me, but her body is slender and wisp-like, as if a stiff breeze could blow her away. Even taking into account the weight I've lost since Issy died, her body looks twenty years younger than mine, toned and tight, where I've got saggy skin. She looks fabulous in her Lycra leggings and vest top that hug every inch of her. I've seen the much-younger mums eyeing her figure with envy. In baggy trackpants and a T-shirt, I don't look half as good. I'm going to go and get some better exercise gear at the weekend, something that doesn't make me look like a bag lady. She opens her eyes and sits up, her back drenched in sweat. She never gives less than one hundred percent, and works all hours to keep her studio, her dream, alive and I admire her for that. Even though I've only known her a short time, already she's an inspiration to me, with her drive and focus and determination to succeed.

She turns to me and smiles whilst blowing her fringe out of her eyes. 'So, that's your first week over. How've you found it?'

'Tiring, but exhilarating. I've really enjoyed it.'

The prospect of four days of looking after Noah with no respite descends on me like a fog, heavy and all-enveloping. It must be echoed in my face as she's now eyeing me with concern.

'How's things with you, anyway? Any developments?' she asks.

For some reason, I've found myself telling her everything that's happened since Issy died. After every class, we've talked for ages and she's really listened. She's interested and non-judgemental, not like other people who've avoided me after Issy's accident. I know they're embarrassed, but it really hurts. Olivia's different; I feel like I can tell her anything and nothing would shock her. She feels sorry for everything I've been through, yet I don't feel her pity.

133

'Greg Evans turned up out of the blue the other day, when I was out with Noah. He was just sitting on the doorstep waiting for me, and it actually lifted me to see him, but I don't know why. Possibly because he's hurting as much as I am. Does that sound weird to you?' I start to put away the equipment we've been using in the class, piling it up in one corner.

'No. It sounds normal. He knows what you're going through and that must give you a common bond, if nothing else. I reckon people who are going through the same thing naturally seek one another out. What does Jon say about it? Does he mind?'

'I don't know. He turned up while Greg was there but didn't say much about it. I think he was a bit surprised, that's all.'

I look out of the window at the building on the opposite side of the road, where a pigeon is nestling next to the chimney, and fold my arms across my body, hugging where it hurts inside.

'I still can't believe she's gone, you know. Every morning when I wake up, for a split second there's a moment when I don't remember, then it comes back to me and it's like hearing it for the first time all over again. The weight of discovering it afresh crushes me every day.'

She nods. 'I can understand that. I can't imagine how awful it's been for you.' She comes up behind me and puts her hand on my shoulder. 'So, what did Greg want?'

'Nothing specific. Just to talk, you know. Just some company. He told me he hasn't gone back to driving his truck yet. We chatted over coffee, then he went.'

Olivia purses her lips. 'Well, there's no harm, is there? Did you tell Jon that you went to see Ellie?'

'Yeah. He's as baffled as I am. It's just more lies. She's been lying to us for years about Ellie still being her friend. Where's she been going all the time she said she was at Ellie's?'

134

'It is strange, I'll give you that. Why would she lie, though?'

'Maybe she's been skipping off to see Noah's father. Maybe he didn't move away at all.'

'Do you think that's likely?'

'Honestly, I have no idea. Nothing surprises me much these days, though, so why not?'

Olivia picks up her bag. 'Well, try and have a nice weekend, if you can, and I'll see you back here on Tuesday. I've really enjoyed this week, having you here, Mel.'

We leave the studio. Outside, it's nine o'clock and still light, and a warm breeze caresses my face as we step outside. Young people congregate outside takeaways, munching burgers and drinking from cans. Chatter floats towards us from a pub down the road, where people are milling around outside. Just around the bend is the junction where my daughter threw her life away. It's mid-July now and over a month since she died.

'Bye, Mel. See you Tuesday.'

Her light hand touches my elbow and I say, 'Night.' I'm still staring in the direction of the junction. Instead of walking to my car, my feet pull me to that fateful spot. The walk takes barely five minutes. At this time in the evening, much of the traffic has gone but lorries still use the route, supplying the shops, supermarkets and factories Luxton relies on twenty-four-seven. There's also a large warehousing and distribution centre across the other side of town, and lorries use this road on their way back to the motorway. They continue to thunder past as I walk briskly on the small footpath, which is bordered by a narrow strip of grass, all that separates me from the road. I'm slightly out of breath by the time I round the bend and can see the crossroads.

My feet slow as I approach it but my heart speeds up. A massive lorry with two trailers roars by, lifting my hair in its slipstream. The draught almost pulls me off my feet. If I reached out, my fingers would be mere inches away from it. If I slipped down the incline towards the road, I'd be under it in a second. I probably wouldn't know anything about it, wouldn't feel much, and there'd be no more Jon, Noah, or anyone else to worry about. A second lorry goes by, smaller than the first, but only just. I stand there, long seconds, imagining doing it but ultimately I know I daren't. I'm too much of a coward. That's the difference between me and Issy: she wasn't. But if I did dare, Jon would be alright without me. A nasty voice in my head whispers that he could go and find *her*. They could live blissfully together with no *me* around to spoil it.

I jump when someone bumps into me from behind and I turn to see a man with a large dog dragging him along.

'Sorry, love,' he says, his feet barely touching the ground as he hangs onto the lead for dear life.

My face is wet with tears when I bring my hand up to sweep my hair out of my eyes. I don't know how long I've been standing here, but it's beginning to get dark. My eyes fix on the very spot where Issy drove under Greg's truck and I try to imagine and understand what she went through. I have a sudden need to talk to the one person who was there and pull out my phone. He said I could ring him anytime.

'Hello?'

'Greg, it's Mel. Are you busy? I know it's short notice, but... do you want to meet up?'

'I'm not busy, just watching rubbish on TV. I'd like that. Where were you thinking of meeting?'

'I'm at the crossroads. There's a pub not far, the Wheatsheaf. I could meet you there.'

He doesn't ask which crossroads or what I'm doing here. 'I know it. I'll be there in twenty.'

The phone goes dead and I realise I'm smiling. I want to see him. When I get to the pub, it's quite busy as it's a Friday and I get myself a drink and one for Greg, find an empty table and sit down to wait.

20

Jon

I JERK AWAKE WHEN the phone rings and snatch it up.
'Hello?'

A male voice startles me. I was expecting it to be Mel. It's
after eleven. She should have been back from the dance
studio ages ago. Where is she?

'Ah, at last. The elusive Mr Warner, the Scarlet Pimpernel.
I've been ringing you all day.' I know who it is straight away,
and his snarky tone gets my back up.

Ken Wallace has been hounding me since nine o'clock this
morning about his garden design plans. What with Issy and
everything, I've got behind with my work, but this dickhead's
more persistent than most. I suppose getting his landscaping
done is more important than my daughter's suicide. Truth is,
though, my clients don't know what's happened to me.

'Hello, Ken. Sorry I missed your calls. I've been up to my
neck in it all day. It was too late to ring you when I got home.'
Lies and more lies.

'I'm not bothered how late you ring.'

'Yes, you might not be, but I am. It's after eleven. I'm not
at work now. Anyway, your design will be in the post
tomorrow afternoon. Ring me with any issues.'

I hang up. There's not much he can say to that, the
moaning bastard. I'll have to spend tomorrow morning doing
them now. Truth is, instead of doing them this afternoon, I

went to see Steve Jackson, following up on the text he sent me about Noah's dad. Potential dad, anyway. I'm not sure where it will lead yet. When I got to the police station, Steve was waiting for me.

'Well?' I said, as soon as I got into his office.

He closed the door and pointed to a chair. I sat.

'I've been doing a bit of digging. You said Issy told you that Noah's dad moved away before she had him and you couldn't find any information from any of the schools. Well, with this, you can.' He held up his Inspector ID and wiggled it at me.

My mouth dropped open, and I just stared at him. 'Really?'

'Yep. I checked all the schools in this area for lads who left within a certain time frame. There weren't actually that many. It seems people don't like to move their kids when they're in their last couple of years at school, you know, what with exams and that. Not good parents, anyhow.'

'And you got some names?'

He'd nodded. 'Well, to be fair, one name. Narrowed it down a bit. There were a couple of others, but...' He tailed off.

'What?'

'Well, I worked out when Noah must have been, er, conceived, from his date of birth. He wasn't early, was he? Mel said he came one day after his due date, so a doctor friend of mine helped me work out when he was conceived, give or take a few days either side.'

His face had got pinker, and he'd run a finger around the inside of his collar. He was embarrassed, talking about my under-age daughter. I knew how he felt. There's something seedy and shameful about it that's never gone away.

'So, the other names?'

'One had moved a month before and the other two weeks before, so I think we can more or less rule them out. If the other lad ends up a dead end, we can look at them again.'

'So, this lad—who is he?'

Steve had pulled a notepad towards him and read out what was scrawled there. 'Oliver Roberts. He was at Ridgeforth High School at the time.'

'Ridgeforth? That's only nine miles away. The kids from there come to Luxton all the time. They play Luxton Comp at sports and things. There's a good chance Issy could have met him through school activities or after school, hanging out with her friends.'

Even though I'd only half-believed Issy's story, I was positive it was him. Steve wouldn't get something like this wrong.

'What do we do now?' I'd asked, imagining this boy's puny Adam's apple under my thumbs as I squeezed.

'One thing at a time. I'm going to do a bit more digging into his background and timescales and stuff, make sure I haven't overlooked anything obvious that rules him out.'

'But you must have been pretty sure to have sent me that text last night, though?'

He'd nodded, trying to keep the smile from spreading over his face. 'I am, but ninety percent's not good enough. We need at least ninety-nine before we act.'

'Where did he live?'

Steve glanced down at his pad. 'Hayton Croft.'

'Six miles from here. And where did he go?'

'His parents split up. His mum went to Sheffield, and he went with her. His dad's still in their old house in Hayton Croft.'

My hands had curled into fists, and I'd shoved them under the chair. I needed Steve to think I was calm enough to handle this, but that little shit might still come round here to visit his dad. All this time, he could have been six miles away or less at any time. More than likely a right cocky little bastard. I could picture him, with his sullen teen eyes and floppy hair, out-of-control hormones rampaging all over his skinny white body and into my daughter's.

'Jon, are you okay?'

139

'Yeah.' I tried to relax my mouth. 'It's just a bit of a shock, that's all.'

'I bet. Did you tell Mel?'

'Not yet. She's been very up and down lately. I'd thought it might be better to see if anything came of it first, in case it's a wild goose chase.'

'Okay. You know best.'

'Can I come with you to see him? We need to get him to do a DNA test, don't we? Is it better to go to his home address or his new school? No, he won't be at school now, will he, if he's the same age as Issy? Has he gone to uni?'

Steve had looked at me with narrowed eyes, and I'd pushed my thigh down hard to stop my leg from jiggling. *Act calm, cool. You can do this.*

'It might be better if I go alone, in an official capacity, you know.'

And miss my chance? I needed to see the little shit. Steve was talking again.

'Let me make the initial contact and get his DNA. There'll be plenty of time after, if he is Noah's dad, for you to see him and meet him. Can you swab inside Noah's cheek for me if I get you a kit?'

'Yes, but I still want to come.'

'Jon, it could get me in bother if I take you. I'm not supposed to be doing this, remember?'

He had me, and he knew it. I felt my adrenalin dissipate, and I wilted into my seat.

'Alright,' I'd mumbled. 'But keep me informed, won't you?'

'Course.' He looked at his watch. 'I'd better crack on and get some work done.' He'd indicated the pile of paper on his desk. 'I should have something in a week or two. Try and forget about it and don't worry. If it's him, we'll know soon enough.'

I'd taken the hint, stood up and had shaken his hand, appreciating the firm grip. I knew this man was capable, and he'd already proved himself to be a good friend and invaluable ally.

'I can't thank you enough, Steve. I owe you so much.'

'No worries. Now get out of here.'

He'd touched me briefly on the shoulder as I left and closed the door behind me. For the rest of the afternoon and evening, I thought about what he'd said. *Oliver Roberts*. I'm going to rip his scrawny little dick off. Then his head. I can picture his spotty face now, and his hands roaming all over my daughter. *Oliver Roberts*. I even hate his name.

I brooded about him until I fell asleep after putting Noah to bed. The phone call from Ken Wallace woke me up, and now I realise Mel should have been home hours ago. My heart lurches at the thought that something may be wrong. Anything could have happened to her. I hit speed dial and her phone rings. I'm weak with relief when she answers, and it makes me snappy. She's sounds unconcerned and slightly drunk. *What the hell's going on?*

'Mel, where are you? Do you know what time it is?'

'No, why? What time 'sit?'

'Are you drunk? Where are you?'

'Where am I?' I hear her ask someone.

A male voice says, 'Wheatsheaf.'

'What? Who's there? Who are you with?'

'I'm having a little drink. Can you pick me up? 'Vad too much to drive.'

'Well, Noah's in bed.'

'Bring him.'

God. 'I'll be fifteen minutes. Stay there,' I order her. I stomp up the stairs, cursing under my breath, and pluck Noah out of his bed. Luckily, it's still warm out and he's fine in his pyjamas. What's Mel playing at? This isn't like her. And I still don't know who she's with.

Five minutes later, I finish strapping Noah in and pull away. It's a good job I didn't have a drink at home tonight myself. I'd looked at the beer in the fridge and thought better of it.

Outside the pub, I ring Mel's phone. I can't take Noah in there. He'll wake up for sure, plus what the hell would that look like? A man with a sleeping child dragging his wife out of the pub like some alkie? No chance.

'I'm outside,' I hiss when she answers.

'Right,' she says.

Two minutes later, she appears, weaving all over the place, with Greg Evans behind her, holding her elbow. He spots the car and comes over with her.

I wind the window down. 'What the hell's going on?'

He opens the door and Mel flops into the passenger seat.

He grimaces. 'Sorry, Jon. I didn't realise she was so drunk. She seemed okay, then all of a sudden, she couldn't speak. I'd been trying to persuade her to go home when you rang. I was just about to call her a taxi. I can't give her a lift because I've had three pints. Er, does she not normally drink? She's been on the shots.'

'Not like this, no. How did you come into it?'

'She phoned me earlier, after she finished her dance class, and asked if I was free. She wanted to talk about Issy and stuff, you know? I met her here just after nine. I assumed she must have told you about it.' He shuts her door, and I lower my window as he comes around the car to me. His face looks so earnest, I know he's telling the truth.

'Okay. I'll get her home. Bye, Greg. And thanks for looking after her.'

Mel's given up trying to put her seatbelt on and is just sitting there with her eyes closed and her head lolling onto her chest. In sloppy trackpants and a T-shirt, she's not exactly dressed for a night out. It's not a pretty sight, your own wife, hammered. I could kill her.

I click her seatbelt, slam the car into gear, and take her home, then get Noah out of his car seat. He slumps over my shoulder, stirs, and settles back down. Mel is harder to manoeuvre. She's snoring and unresponsive, so I leave her. I get Noah into bed, then have to go back outside to get her. In the end, I carry her up to bed, pull the covers back and practically sling her in. She lays exactly where I dropped her and snores softly. After I've taken her shoes off, I sit next to her, watching her. I can't help feeling I don't know this woman. The fact that she's going to suffer in the morning gives me a shot of satisfaction. She'll be glad it's Saturday, but I'm going to have to work on Ken Wallace's garden design, so I won't be looking after Noah for her. If she thinks she's going to have the luxury of lying in bed all morning, she's going to get a shock. Noah's rarely in bed after seven any morning.

Back downstairs, I open a can of beer and sit with the list of the four tenants' names in front of me. I have their home addresses and intend to visit them before uni starts, if I can. It will mean even more time off work, getting further behind and pissing more people off, but some things are more important. Mel doesn't need to know about any of it: the DNA test on Oliver Roberts or my plans to visit the four tenants. Especially after tonight, the less she knows, the better. If she's going to go round getting pissed or going to pieces, what good is she going to be to me? No, from now on, I'll go it alone.

21

Mel

WHEN I WAKE UP, my head is shot through with the most shocking pain and my eyes are glued together when I try to open them. For a few seconds, I can't think why, then it comes back to me: last night, I called Greg, and got absolutely hammered in the pub. I didn't mean to; it just sort of happened.

I hear a horribly loud shuffling noise beside me and force my eyes open. Jon has just come in and is standing beside the bed with his arms folded over his chest and his lips pressed together hard in a tight line. He's pissed off. I close my eyes quickly and groan. What the hell was I drinking last night?

'I've got to go into work this morning, to get some stuff finished off and in the post. You'll have to look after Noah. He's already awake.'

'What? You never said you were working today.' I think I might cry.

'Grandad!' Noah yells, the piercing noise barely muffled by the two closed bedroom doors between us. Something malicious sparkles behind Jon's eyes. He's enjoying this.

'God!' I pull the quilt over my head.

Jon pulls it back down again. A thousand needles stab my brain.

He leans in and narrows his eyes. 'I had to get Noah out of bed last night, just to come and get you. Your car's still

144

near the dance studio. We'll have to go and pick it up later. You'll probably get a ticket now.'

He stands up and runs his fingers through his hair as he goes to the door. Irritation seeps out of him.

'I've had to come get you before,' I complain. 'I suppose that's different, though, isn't it?'

Jon stops with his hand on the door handle and looks back at me. Anguish twists his features.

'I was worried sick about you last night. You didn't ring or let me know where you were or anything. I didn't know what to think.'

I didn't. He's right. 'Sorry.'

'Grandad! Mummy!' shouts Noah, again.

Jon leaves the room and opens Noah's door. 'Go to Grandma,' I hear him say. He's probably whispering to him to jump up and down on me in bed. Then he shouts, 'I'm off,' and the front door slams a moment later. It's not even eight o'clock yet.

Great! A second later, Noah bounds through the doorway and onto the bed, the motion making me feel sick. My stomach clenches with sudden nausea.

'Noah, lay down with me a minute. Grandma's not feeling well this morning. Poorly tummy.'

He slaps me right on the stomach with the flat of his hand. Even through the thick padding of the quilt, it makes me retch. I leap out of bed and dash to the bathroom, slamming the door shut behind me, only just making it over the toilet in time. They don't call it purging for nothing. Perspiration coats my forehead, underarms and back, and my legs feel like jelly. There's no way they'll hold me up if I try to stand. A spasm clenches my guts and I'm over the toilet once more, heaving. There's no way I can cope looking after Noah on my own today. There's only one thing for it.

'Mum,' I cry into the phone ten minutes later when I've managed to get downstairs. 'Sorry to ring so early, but is there any way you can help me today? I'm ill and Jon's working. I can't look after Noah like this.'

A glance out of the window onto the drive confirms Jon's car has gone. I swear he's doing this on purpose to punish me for last night. in the bathroom upstairs, I hear the taps running.

Mum comes through for me, as always. 'Course I will. And Pam's just arrived with my shopping. We'll come straight round.'

'Thanks, Mum. I really appreciate it. Got to go.'

I put the phone down and race upstairs on another tide of sickness. When I get to the bathroom, Noah has put the plug in and has filled the bath almost to the top. The taps are still running, and as I lean over to pull the plug out I start to heave. Noah jumps back in surprise when I push him out of the bathroom and slam the door. This time I'm in there for ages. I've only just made it downstairs when Mum and Pam come through the front door.

'Darling, you look positively green. Come and put your feet up,' says Mum, fussing round me as if I'm a child. It's just what I need, and I collapse onto the sofa.

'Where's Noah?' asks Pam. She frowns as she looks me up and down in my tatty old dressing gown. I haven't brushed my hair and may still have last night's makeup on, what's not smeared over the pillow. 'God, you look rough!'

'Thanks. He's probably flooding the bathroom again,' I groan.

Pam dashes up the stairs to find him, and I'm so grateful to both of them I could cry.

'You're probably dehydrated. I'll fetch some water,' Mum says.

I lay back and close my eyes. I've never felt this bad through drink, ever. What possessed me to drink shots last night? Greg must think I'm an alcoholic or something.

'How come Jon's working on a Saturday?' Mum asks when she comes back with a glass of water.

'Says he's fallen behind and needs to catch up. I think he's doing it to punish me, though.'

'For what?'

'For getting rat-arsed in the pub with Greg Evans last night.'

My mother's face runs the gamut of emotions from shock, surprise and disbelief to something else. She starts to giggle.

'I'm not even going to ask,' she says.

'What's this fixation with the bath?' asks Pam, as she comes through the door dragging a grumpy, wet-looking Noah by the hand. 'He'd put the plug in and filled it up again. It was going down the overflow. He says it's the sea, and he wants to play boats.'

I give him a stern look. 'Noah, if you can't behave, you can go to bed and stay there. Grandma's poorly and she needs you to be a good boy today. Can you do that?'

He looks surprised at the tone of my voice and nods solemnly. 'I'll be good. Don't want to go to bed. Can I watch TV?'

'Yes. Aunty Pam will put a DVD on for you.'

Noah toddles off and sits on the floor cross-legged, a foot away from the TV screen, the way kids do. Pam drags him back a few feet, and he's already oblivious, tantalised by the credits on Winnie the Pooh.

'What's up with you, anyway?' Pam asks.

Mum fills her in, trying not to laugh. Pam looks surprised, then pulls an *I'm impressed* face.

For the next few hours, they're both great, looking after me and Noah. Mum keeps making me drink water. Jon doesn't ring to see how I'm coping, which I don't know if I'm relieved or irked by. Justin drops by after lunch, 'to check on the invalid', carrying a large holdall.

'How are you doing?' he asks. I can see he's trying not to laugh.

I just shake my head, then stop when it hurts again.

Noah, who's now thoroughly sick of watching TV, colouring and playing garages with his cars, launches himself at him and wraps his arms around Justin's legs.

'Hey. What's up?' Justin says.

'Bored,' he says, sighing.

'Bored? Well, we can't have that, can we? Go and look what's in my bag over there.'

Noah's head shoots up as he looks for the bag. He runs to it, struggles to pull back the zip, and huffs exasperatedly when it won't open. He sits back on his heels and cups his chin in both hands, resting his elbows on his knees.

'Can't do it,' he sighs, sticking out his bottom lip and shaking his head.

Justin opens the bag and stands back.

'What is it?' asks Noah, yanking a plastic cricket bat out of the bag, followed by another one. He brandishes one as if it's a gun.

'Noah, have you ever played cricket?'

He frowns. 'Crickid? No.'

'No?' gasps Justin. 'Then you don't know what you've been missing. Cricket is a noble game, played by gentlemen. Are you a gentleman?'

Noah shrugs. 'Dunno.' He looks at me. 'Am I?'

As if!

'Well, you can be,' Justin says. He looks over at me. 'Any better?'

'A bit,' I say with a weak smile.

'Good. Come on, Noah. Let's give the ladies some peace.'

He hoists the bag up onto his shoulder, and Noah follows him into the garden. The next half hour is punctuated by shrieks, screams, shouts, and laughter as Justin tries to get Noah to listen to instruction. We watch from the window as Noah holds the cricket bat like a rounder's bat and takes wild swings. He connects with the ball only rarely, and I marvel at Justin's patience.

'I don't know how you lot do it,' I say. 'I feel so bad-tempered all the time. It's not fair on him.'

'It's easier when you're not with them all day, though,' says Mum. 'You do a brilliant job, Mel, and don't let anyone tell you different.' She looks at me and stops when she sees my eyes brimming with tears. 'What's wrong, love?'

I breathe in deeply, steeling myself to speak.

148

'While you're here, will you both help me with something? I need to go through Issy's stuff and start sorting it out, but I can't do it on my own. I feel like it's hanging over me, waiting to be done. Jon won't talk about it, just tells me he can't do it. You know, maybe start with clothes and stuff.' A massive sob catches in my throat.

'Are you sure it's not too soon?' Mum places a hand on my arm.

'No, it needs doing. I can't go in there as it is. I'm not saying I'll get rid of anything. If we can just make a start sorting it out and get some things in bags, that'll do.'

'If it's what you want, of course we'll help,' says Pam.

We hear the bat thwack the ball as the three of us troop slowly up the stairs. Noah cheers loudly. I focus on putting one foot in front of the other. *I can do this. I have to do this.* Issy's not coming back, and I can't keep her bedroom as a shrine. It's not healthy. Outside her bedroom door, we stop dead. I place my hand on the doorknob, and my sister and mother look at each other, then at me. The doorknob is slick with sweat from my palm and my mouth is suddenly dry. I slowly push open the door. I've been in here many times since Issy died, but not so much in the past two weeks. As time's passed, it's got harder to come in, probably because I know I can't leave it like this forever. For a start, it's a mess. Issy dumped her bags on the floor when she came home and I tipped them up, searching for clues as to where she'd gone that day. It's not been cleared up since. The pink and purple checked duvet cover is rumpled and hanging unevenly off the bed. Her suitcase is open, the contents spilled out.

The north-facing room, at the front, is dim and cool. Its pale pink walls add no cheer, and it has an air of abandonment about it. I venture in, bolstered by my mum and sister, hoping they'll give me courage to do this final thing. They each take one of my hands and we stand like that for some time, crying silent tears. Eventually, Pam speaks.

'Where do you want us to start?'

I point at the heap of clothes on the floor. 'Here's as good a place as any. I think Issy brought back a lot of dirty washing.'

We all grab a handful of garments and begin sorting them.

'How about a pile for washing and another for...' Pam's voice tails off. *Getting rid of,* I think she means. *Dumping.*

'Alright. Anything that needs washing, throw it over here. Everything else we can bag up.'

'Have you got any bags?' Mum asks.

Damn! 'I've left them in the kitchen, sorry.'

'I'll get them,' says Pam, disappearing back off downstairs.

I steal a quick glance at Mum. She looks frail and fierce at the same time. I realise the fierceness is because she's determined to do the right thing for me. Maybe I shouldn't have asked her to do this with me. It's as hard for her. She squeezes my hand and I squeeze back.

'You don't have to do this,' she says in a steely voice. 'Pam and I can do it for you.'

At this moment, I love her more than I ever have. I shake my head.

'I need to do it.'

The hardest bit is to get started. When Pam comes back, we bag up clothes, shoes, bags, books, and what I call *miscellaneous stuff.* The washing pile grows huge, and Pam goes to put the machine on. Everything else has fit into four black bags. I can't cope with anything else today, so we shove the bags against the wall at the far side of the bed. From there, they can't be seen when you come into the room. Seems like the best solution for now. A couple of times I have to fly off to the bathroom when the nausea resurfaces. Both my body and Issy's bedroom have been expunged by the time we've finished. It's a small step, but it's a start, one step on the road to accepting my daughter won't ever walk through the door again. I can't say it's been therapeutic—it's been hell—but I feel it's a step on the road to healing and moving on.

I don't know how Jon will feel about it, but I asked him to help, and he refused to even talk about it. As if that's going to get us anywhere. He copes in his way, and this is mine—to do something practical and not ignore things. He thinks I don't know he's off meeting that policeman behind my back, delving and digging, trying to find things out. Probably doesn't want to tell me, reckons I can't handle it, but he's wrong. I'm stronger than he thinks.

When we're done, we sit on the edge of the bed like three garden birds in a row. The bedroom looks like a sterile guest room with no particular occupant. Justin opens the door.

'I wondered where you lot had got to. Everything alright?'

Noah races past him and leaps onto my knee, patting my face and squeezing my cheeks before kissing me. I put my arms around him and hug him tight, inhaling his earthy, sweaty, little-boy smell. He's tired from the garden and rolls off my knee onto Issy's bed, where he's sucking his thumb and nodding off within minutes. We all sit watching him, each of us lost in our own thoughts.

Justin hasn't moved. Eventually he says, 'Shall I make us all a cup of tea? I could certainly do with one.'

'Yes, please,' says Mum, and Justin goes back down the stairs.

I've decided I'm going to sit here until Jon gets home, no matter how long I have to wait. He needs to know what we've done and, that with him or without him, things still have to get sorted.

22

Jon

DESPITE SPENDING MOST OF Saturday in the office, I get no work done whatsoever. Instead, I clear my desk and lay out Issy's laptop, phone, and the names of the students she was due to share with in September. I keep meaning to complete the drawings for Ken Wallace, but somehow, I never get around to it.

First, I ring each of the students on their mobiles, even though I'd originally decided not to when I'd got them from the lettings agent. The possibility that one of them may know something is just too great. Not a single one bloody picks up. I don't leave any messages. I open up Issy's laptop. Their profiles come up as friends of Issy on Facebook, and they seem like normal students to me. David Noone, Ryan Anderson, Nathan Brown and Michael Kelly. I have all their home addresses, but there's no point in rushing off to visit them. She spent her first year in the halls of residence so, as she hasn't been sharing with them in her first year, I can't see that they'll know much, anyway. Again, the thought occurs to me that she might have slept with them all. It's not good to contemplate. So back to the Facebook pages.

David Noone is blonde and has his arms around a girl on his Facebook page. She looks about the same age and her name is Julia. It says he met her at the Students' Union, and they've been a couple for six months. So Issy probably never slept with him, then.

Nathan Brown has long, scruffy hair, a beard, and small glasses, sort of like a hippy version of Harry Potter. He looks like a good scrub wouldn't do him any harm, either. He and his mates are all holding up full pint glasses and there's no mention of a girlfriend. He could have slept with her, but I don't think he's her type. Not clean enough. But what do I know of my daughter's life and sexual preferences? Absolutely nothing, that's what.

Ryan Anderson and Michael Kelly are a couple by the look of things. This is looking better. Perhaps my daughter wasn't the proverbial *village bike* after all, which is what I've been scared of all along.

I decide to leave them all for now. I'll go and see them after uni starts if I still need answers. Mel hasn't mentioned going to see them at all. Probably forgotten all about them with the excitement of starting her new job and all. Suits me. It means I can do things in my own way, in my own time, without any interference from anyone.

Still on Issy's laptop, I download and print out her phone bills. Now we know her password, it's turned out she used the same one for everything. She's had the same phone contract for over two years now and it takes some time, but I print out twenty-seven phone bills, going back to when she was still in college. Most months run to two pages and I staple them together and put them in date order on my desk. Starting with the most recent, I study them in detail. I get to know the most frequently called numbers quickly and write the names of the people from her contacts list against the numbers on the bills. There are lots of people on her contacts list that I've never heard of, as I would have expected, and many of them don't appear on her bills either. Her mother and me feature, of course, as does her Grandma Kitty. Justin is on her contacts list, along with Pam, but it seems she rarely phones them, which isn't surprising. She didn't phone us that much either. By far, the most dialled number is someone

listed in her contacts as *Lamech*. This person also calls her a
lot too, but I've no idea who it is. Even more mystifying is
the fact this Lamech appears right on Issy's first phone bill,
so it's not someone from uni. A Facebook search shows no
results for that name on Issy's page. Some of the calls
between them are half an hour or more in duration, so it
seems whoever it is, Issy talks to them far more than anyone
else. I have a hunch that if I could find this person, they might
be able to fill in some of the blanks.

Out of curiosity, I ring it from her phone, but it goes
straight to voicemail. I don't leave a message or expect a
return call. Maybe Steve Jackson can trace the number, but
it's probably an unregistered pay-as-you-go, knowing my
luck. I wonder if whoever Lamech is even knows she's dead.

It takes over two hours and several cups of coffee to go
through the bills and contacts list to get to feel I know them
inside out. All the while, I keep meaning to finish Wallace's
plans, but this is hugely addictive, like linking a series of
puzzles together. I should ring Mel and see how she is but,
again, I keep putting it off. If she's suffering, it's her own
fault, anyway. Over a cup of coffee and a break halfway
through, I wonder if I should be jealous that Mel spent the
evening with hunky young Greg, but I'm not. Everyone needs
someone other than their partner to turn to, like I've been
using Steve Jackson, so maybe Greg fills that need in her. By
the way Mel still stiffens every time I come near her, and the
fact that we haven't had sex in ages, I can't see her doing it
with him, but you never know. She once said to me in yet
another blazing row, 'what's good for the goose...' Maybe she
should jump in the sack with him. Might loosen her up a bit
and do her some good.

I lean back in my chair and stretch my arms above my
head, feeling my neck crack. Thinking about Mel freezing
every time I go near her makes Adele spring to mind. Despite
how it ended, I can't think about her without getting turned
on. She was a woman with no inhibitions. *If it feels good, do it,*
she used to say, and boy, did she know how to do it. I close

my eyes and conjure up an image of her fabulous body. I can remember every glorious inch of it; what it looks like, smells like, the feel and taste of it. How many times since have I wondered if I did the right thing leaving her? She made me happy, and I loved her. Letting her go was agony for me, a huge sacrifice. Would we have been happy together and made a go of it? Possibly. Probably. I could check her Facebook page, but looking at her actually hurts. Best not to do it then.

I shake the image of her out of my head and get my mind back on the job. The bills take another two hours to go through, and after that I go for a long walk, trying to clarify things in my mind before heading home. Ken Wallace rings again and I shove the phone into my pocket. As soon as it stops ringing, I turn it off. Sod him!

Both Pam's and Justin's cars are parked outside when I get home and alarm bells start to ring at the sight. Two separate cars? Visions of pills and Mel lying on the bed fill my mind. Or has something happened to Noah? I pull onto the drive and bolt into the house. There's no one downstairs, and I run upstairs to find them all in Issy's room, silent and still. Four black bin bags are lined up along one wall. They all turn to look at me as I burst in, panting. Noah is sleeping on Issy's bed. They're all okay. I'm so relieved I sag against the wall and tears prick my eyes at the thought of what they've been doing and how they must have felt. Mel's been asking me to help her do this for a while now, but I just couldn't. It felt like we would be clearing Issy away, getting rid of her, and throwing her out. Eradicating her from our lives.

I sit on the bed next to Mel and hold her hand in mine. She doesn't pull away. She looks so small, broken and deflated.

'I'm sorry I couldn't do this with you,' I whisper.

She looks nervous and I realise she's been scared of how I might react at what she's been doing while I've been hiding away, avoiding things here and also avoiding doing any actual work. I'm suddenly ashamed.

'How've you been?' I ask her.

'Hungover. Really bad.' She gives me a small, rueful smile. 'I had to get Mum over to help. I'm sorry about last night. Really.'

Kitty stands up and places her hand on Mel's shoulder.

'I might get off now Jon's home, darling.'

She looks tired. 'Shall I take you home, Kitty?' I ask. It's the least I can do.

'It's okay, Jon, we'll take her.' Pam stands up and takes her mother's arm.

'Do you want us to take Noah tonight?' asks Justin.

'No. He's been too unsettled lately. He'll be better off here, in his own room,' I say.

Mel nods.

'Okay,' says Pam. 'We'll get going then.'

'See you later,' I say, as they see themselves out.

The front door bangs when they leave. I gesture at the room. 'You've been busy.'

'I started to sort some of her things out. Mum and Pam helped. We don't have to get rid of the bags yet, if you don't want to. I just thought it would be better to make a start.'

'You're probably right,' I say. But it still hurts to see Issy's life bagged up like this.

Mel looks directly at me. 'I need to ask you something and I need you to be honest with me,' she says.

I pause. 'Alright. What?'

'What have you been doing with Steve Jackson? I know you're up to something and I also know that you think you're protecting me, but I want to know. Tell me.'

I tell her about Steve finding the boy who left school and getting a DNA test done. She sits up quickly and looks at me intensely. If she's going to have a go at me for not telling her in the first place, this'll be it. But she doesn't.

'Imagine if we found out it's him.' She looks thoughtful. 'Have you ever thought, though, if or when we do find his dad, he might want to see Noah? Are you prepared for that? Maybe his biological father could legally take him away from us.'

'I hadn't thought of that, actually, no. Would you want that?'

She chews her lip. 'I don't know. It would be odd, but he would be in his rights. I don't know where we'd stand.

Do you think her phone could tell us anything more?'

'I don't know.' I don't mention Lamech, whoever it is.

She nods. 'I know what we could do next.'

'What?'

'Phone Peter Cunningham and ask him if we can arrange to see that student counsellor he told us about.'

I sit up straighter and Noah stirs in his sleep as the bed moves, then settles down again.

'I'd forgotten about her! How could I have forgotten? And see if Issy went to see her, you mean?'

Mel nods.

'That's a good idea, yeah. I'll ring him tomorrow.'

23

Mel

'COME AND GET A drink, Noah!'

He ignores me and carries on racing around Pam's beautiful garden in his sweat-stained T-shirt. His hair is plastered to his head in the heat of the afternoon sun. He stumbles and falls into one of the borders, snapping the stem of a plant in full flower. Pam will go mad if she sees it. My glass hits the table a little too hard as I put it down.

Jon turns to me. 'Leave him. He's fine.'

'He's going to wreck everything. And I'm bloody sick of him ignoring me. Some days he doesn't do a damn thing I say.'

'I know, but let's just relax today. Chill out, will you?'

I move my arm away from the condescending pat I know will be coming. It's as irritating as the too-soft tone of voice he's started using with me. I'm glad it's Sunday afternoon and I'm not coping on my own with Noah.

Near the house, Justin is manning the gas barbecue in his much-prized outdoor kitchen, the one Jon designed and they built together. We all know it's the only time he ever does any cooking. Pam is running in and out of the house, carrying plates and glasses and cups and bottles. Mum's helping her, but at half the speed, and carrying half the amount. Up to now, the pair of them have refused all my offers of help and

158

I'm sitting around like a spare part, drinking wine I don't want.

I rest my head on my arms, slumping over the table, trying to fight off another wave of despair. Everyone's anxiety and their concern is enveloping me like a suffocating blanket. I didn't want to come today, but all I got was how much better I'd feel if I made the effort. But I don't feel better. I want to be left alone. In many ways, I feel worse now than when Issy first died. It's as if the disbelief and shock cushions you in the early days, with the lead up to the funeral, then the anger and the overwhelming grief keep you busy. Now, there's nothing but acceptance and that's the worst thing. Finally, you know it's true and not a bad dream.

'Another drink?' Jon asks.

I lift my head. 'Sure. Why not?' Maybe drinking to oblivion will help.

I hand my glass over and he gets up with a sigh. I know this is just as hard for him as it is for me, but somehow I can't care about what he's feeling at the moment. Pam's three boys are milling around, playing with Noah, helping Justin and generally trying to avoid being too close to me. They don't know what to say to me or how to act. Nobody comes near me until Jon sits down again and passes me another glass of wine.

'Did you ring Steve about the DNA test?' I ask.

'Yeah, he said he rang the lab yesterday. They're backed up and because he's not acting in an official capacity, he can't press them on it. They said they should get to it before the end of next week.'

All we seem to do is wait. When Jon rang Peter Cunningham about fixing up an appointment to see Kim Brent, the student counsellor, she'd just gone on holiday. She's due back tomorrow, and Peter has said he'll ring us when he's spoken to her.

I sigh deeply. Not that anything will change. Whatever we do or don't learn, Issy will still be dead. Some days, I don't know why we're even still trying to find out why she killed herself. If she wanted us to know, she'd have left a note or something, wouldn't she?

'Are you sure you won't go to the doctor to get some anti-depressants? They're bound to make you feel better,' says Jon, quietly. 'I hate seeing you like this.'

'I'll go next week,' I say, to get him off my back.

I've got no energy, yet I can't sleep. I can't eat, and I cry at the drop of a hat. Mum says I look gaunt. What do they expect? There's no rule book telling you how to act when your child dies. Kills herself, I mean.

'Mum says do you want to eat yet?' Sammy's voice makes me look up with a start. He's standing opposite me, the table acting as a buffer between us.

'I'll eat when everyone else wants to. I'm not very hungry, though. Tell her I don't want much, will you?' My stomach roils at the thought of burgers and sausages.

'Alright.' Sammy shoves his hands in his pockets and looks me directly in the eye. The eldest of my sister's sons has had his problems over the years, going through a wayward phase, but he seems to have sorted himself out now. Although he's four years older than Issy, he's only in his second year at uni, thanks to two lost years around his A' levels when drink and drugs were preferable to study. But he and Issy always got on and were very close and, at one time, she idolised him. I was a bit worried she was going to follow him down the wild road. Now I wish she had, and that was all I had to be worried about.

Justin waves Jon over to where he's standing behind the barbecue. I can't hear what they're saying. Sammy sprawls in the chair Jon just vacated and lights a cigarette.

'Are you looking forward to going back to uni?' I ask Sammy, making an effort to look interested.

'Yeah, I suppose. I should get my exam results next week.' He takes a deep drag.

'I'm sure you'll have done well.'

He blows smoke out of the corner of his mouth. 'I'm not. They were really hard.'

'I'll keep my fingers crossed. You've probably done better than you think.'

'Aunty Mel,' he says, his eyes sliding to where Carl is playing cricket with Noah. Or rather, Noah is charging after him, wielding the cricket bat. 'It doesn't seem fair, does it, that I'm going back and Issy's not?'

At last. Someone's mentioned her. Just lately, I've felt like she's been swept under the carpet by everyone in a desperate bid not to make me feel worse. I'm surprised that tears *don't* spring to my eyes for once. I fiddle about with the stem of my glass.

'No, it doesn't.'

He dips his head and nods. 'I still can't believe she's gone, though. It doesn't feel real.' He flicks ash onto the grass. As Pam doesn't approve of smoking, she doesn't have ashtrays anywhere.

'Sammy,' calls his mother from a few feet away. 'Can you give me a hand?'

She's probably heard him talking about Issy, and she's trying to get him away before he upsets me. His eyes flit to her, then back to me, and he takes another pull on his cigarette.

'We're alright,' I call back. Pam doesn't answer, but I know she's still trying to listen.

I lower my voice and lean towards him. 'Sammy, did she ever say anything to you? I know you were close at one time. Was she upset about anything?'

'She didn't say anything to me, no. I was completely shocked by what she did. We only kept in touch on Facebook, and not that often.'

'Did she ever give you any clues about who Noah's father is? I mean, suppose Noah had some inherited medical condition on his father's side that we didn't know about; it could be really bad. We need to find him.'

He looks uncomfortable, and a red flush creeps up his chest and neck.

'No. She never told anyone, did she?'

161

'No. You know how secretive she could be when she wanted.'

He nods. 'You're right. I know.'

I smile sadly. Noah squeals, and we both look over.

'Noah hasn't had that cricket bat out of his hand since he got it,' I say.

He's still chasing Carl around the garden with it, now waving it like a wand and shouting something.

'It's *expelliarmus,*' shouts Carl, sprinting away from him easily. 'Not *experamus*. You can't cast a spell if you say it wrong.'

Carl stops and turns to face him, smoothing down his thatch of unruly blonde hair and quoting lines from Harry Potter. Noah tries, but fails, to get his tongue around the magic words, whilst twirling the bat round dangerously. With his broad shoulders, Carl looks much older than twelve; he lives for sport and has declared it his mission to turn Noah into a decent cricketer before he starts school.

Joey, as usual, has his head in a book. His chosen place is under the branches of a large cherry tree in the corner, swinging in a hammock, taking advantage of the quiet and the shade.

'What's Joey reading?' I ask Sammy.

'At the moment, anything and everything about Rome and Roman Emperors. Until his next obsession.'

'What that lad doesn't know about history isn't worth knowing.'

'I know. It's as if he never forgets anything he's ever read. I wish I was like that, especially now. I just went blank in one of the exams.'

'I'm sure you've done just fine.' I take a glug of wine. 'Issy soaked things up like a sponge as well. I remember her wanting to know about every American President. I didn't know anything about them. We learned it together.'

Sammy nods. 'I remember. She asked me, too. I didn't know many of 'em.'

'Grub's up,' shouts Justin, waving a fish slice in the air. Grease drips off it, sizzling as it falls back onto the barbecue. The smell and sight of it makes me feel sick. A mountain of burgers and hotdogs are piled on a plate.

'Yay,' Noah yells, turning instantly and rushing towards the barbecue.

Justin hands him a burger, as he wheels by without stopping. He grabs it and takes a bite, still brandishing the cricket bat. As he runs towards Joey, who's still under the tree, oblivious to what's going on around him, I notice Jon stood with his back to everyone, huddled over his phone. *Who's he talking to? Her?*

Sammy finishes his cigarette and grinds it out under his trainer, then stands up, leaving it on the polished sandstone. Pam won't like that. He sees me looking.

'Should put some ashtrays out then, shouldn't she? Shall I fetch you something to eat?' he asks.

'Er, yes, okay. But not much.'

Sammy walks over to the barbecue and picks up two burgers then heads back to me.

'Any sauce?' he asks.

'No, thanks.'

'I'll just get some coke,' he says, striding away again and munching on his burger.

Jon slips his phone into his pocket and shoots me a look across the garden. He comes over to me, stopping to grab two hot dogs from Justin along the way, then sits beside me, dragging his chair up close.

'That was Peter,' he says, conspiratorially, leaning in towards me.

My heart, which had been slamming hard, slows down, but not by much.

'He's had an email from Kim Brent. She's agreed to see us on Friday morning in her office at Newcastle.'

'Oh. What about work?'

'Sod that. I'll work over the weekend to catch up. I'm not too far behind anyway, now. We're going.'

163

'Of course we are. What about Noah, though?'

Pam is glancing our way, obviously wondering what we're whispering about. I feel mean not telling her what we're doing, but it's something Jon and I have to do together. If she and Justin knew about it, they'd probably want to help and end up taking over like they usually do.

'Erm, I don't know. We'll have to take him with us.'

'Would he sit long enough for us to talk with her, do you——?'

'Here's the chef! Great food.' Jon holds up his hot dog and takes another bite as Justin appears behind me. I hadn't noticed him coming over.

'Glad you're enjoying it.' He pulls out a chair and sits down, putting his beer on the table. 'Jon, your glass is empty. Want another?'

'In a sec, mate. I'll get it. You sit down. You've been slaving away over there. Sweat's pouring off you. You must be exhausted.'

'Get lost,' says Justin, laughing at Jon's sarcasm. 'It's hard producing food of this calibre, you know. I have to keep up my three Michelin stars. Not that you'd know what a Michelin star is.' He stuffs the last of the hot dog in his mouth. 'You probably think it's something to do with tyres.'

'Yeah, right,' says Jon. 'I'm no match for a connoisseur like you. Gourmet hotdog sausages, out of a tin, and shop-bought rolls. Brilliant.'

'It's all in the cooking, though. Getting it right. There's definitely an art to it. I wouldn't expect you to understand.'

'Is Dad boring you again about how great he is at barbequing?' asks Joey, appearing behind me and sitting down next to Justin. He throws several packets of crisps down onto the table and Sammy and Carl make a grab for them.

'You always take the last salt and vinegar,' complains Carl, pulling a glum face at the cheese and onion in his hand. 'Mum, is there any more salt and vinegar? Greedy arse has nabbed the last one, as usual.'

'Arse!' yells Noah.

'Carl! Mouth!' scolds Pam, coming to stand next to him. 'Sammy!' she snaps, bending down to pick up his discarded cigarette butt.

'You're just not quick enough,' quips Sammy, cramming a large handful of crisps into his mouth and rolling his eyes. 'This is good. Really vinegary *and* salty. Mmm.'

I take a bite of my burger. It's fatty and greasy and feels horrible in my mouth. My throat closes up when I try to swallow it, and I wash it down with a large glug of wine.

'I'll just get some water,' I say to Pam, standing up.

'I'll get it. Sit down.'

'No, don't be daft. You sit down and finish your meal.'

I hurry inside, hoping no one will notice me dropping the remains of the burger in the bin as I pass it. In the house, I can hear the TV on in the living room, where Mum is watching Antiques Roadshow. Whatever she's doing on a Sunday, she never misses it. Pam comes in as I'm running the cold tap and reaching for a glass. Her hands are full of piled-up plates and cutlery.

'Are you okay?' She puts the plates down on the side.

I nod and shrug. 'Yeah. Considering.'

'I hope Sammy wasn't upsetting you earlier.'

I spin around quickly. 'What, by mentioning my dead daughter? Pam, I want to be able to talk about her without people feeling embarrassed. I appreciate him bringing her into the conversation, if you must know. She did exist, after all.'

Pam gawps at me, then quickly pulls herself together. 'Sorry. It's just, you've been so down lately. I'm worried about you.'

I press my fingers into my temples, hard, massaging the flesh. 'I know. And thanks for caring, but it's going to take a long time. I'm fine. Well, I'm not, but I might be, one day.'

'God, I'm being overbearing and suffocating, aren't I?'

'No, not really. Well, maybe a bit. But there's no rule book on grief, is there? No right or wrong way. If it takes me ten years, then it takes me ten years, but I need to talk about her, Pam, whether it makes you uncomfortable or not.'

'Of course. It doesn't make me uncomfortable at all. I love talking about her. I don't know why you think that.'

'You know, it's at times like this, more than ever, that I miss her the most. Even though she said she hated these family things, the older she got. But I can picture her out there, her and Sammy with their heads together, her rolling her eyes at us for not being cool or whatever it is these days. You know how she used to follow him around all the time. Funny how we stopped doing these barbeques after Noah was born, though, wasn't it?'

'Yeah, I know. I've been thinking that, too. Why did we stop?'

I get my water and drink the full glass down. 'I dunno, really. Listen, I might go soon. It's been lovely, but I'm exhausted.'

'Still not sleeping?'

'No. Jon wants me to go back to the doctors.'

'Probably a good idea. Why don't you?'

'They've already given me anti-depressants. I've had a few, but I don't like being dependent on tablets. It kind of feels like an admission of failure, like you can't cope.'

'There's nothing wrong with that, Mel. I think you've coped brilliantly so far, with what you've been through.'

'Do you? I'll see. I know I'm depressed, but I want to get better on my own. The dance studio's helping a lot. I love it there.'

Justin wanders into the kitchen. 'What are you two gossiping about?'

'Not much,' I say.

I pick up my glass to go. Noah is on Sammy's knee, still eating and dripping ketchup all down his front. As I walk off, I hear Pam say, 'Aw, look—our Sammy will make a lovely dad one day.'

Outside, I make my way over to the hammock Joey has vacated, away from everyone else. For some reason, Pam's words stay with me as I sit watching Sammy. I remember how uncomfortable he looked when I asked him if he knew who Noah's dad was. He drops a kiss on the top of Noah's head, almost absent-mindedly, and wraps his arm around the little lad in a natural, almost proprietorial gesture. I don't like the thought that's gathering, but I can't stop it. Could it be so obvious, right under our noses, and we haven't seen it? But I must be wrong, surely. To be right is unthinkable.

24

Pam

'WHAT'S UP WITH MEL?' Justin asks quietly, so Kitty won't hear if she's on the prowl. He wipes his hands down his burger-grease-spattered chef's apron. She wrinkles her nose at the strong smell of barbeque smoke coming off him.

Through the kitchen window, Pam's gaze leaves her sister, and she turns to her husband behind her, her hands still seeking out the cutlery in the bottom of the washing-up bowl.

She whispers back, 'I don't know. Do you think she's acting stranger than normal?'

Justin leans closer, his eyes sliding back to Mel, sitting alone on the hammock, hunched over and hugging herself as if in pain, her fingers curled around a glass of water. Everyone else is at the table, and the area surrounding her is like an evacuation zone. Ground zero.

'I don't know. Maybe. It's hard to tell these days, isn't it? Did you hear her earlier, shouting at Noah? The kid was only doing what kids do, but she was straight down his throat, like he's the worst-behaved child there's ever been. It's not fair on him.' Justin shakes his head.

Pam sigh and lifts out a knife and fork, rubbing them clean. Justin picks up the tea towel. Funny how the lads are never anywhere to be seen at cleaning up time. In the corner, the over-full dishwasher hums quietly as it starts its long cycle.

The droop of Pam's shoulders mirrors that of her mouth. 'I really don't know what to do anymore. It's like whatever I say is wrong. She either rips my head off or doesn't want to talk. I know what's happened is terrible, but I just want to help her. Do you get that feeling from Jon that things are happening that we don't know about? That they don't want us to know about?'

Justin pulls her close, and she feels her back relaxing into him, as usual.

'Yeah, I do. But we can't make them tell us stuff, can we?'

She sighs again. 'No. I know. You're right. We'll just have to carry on being there for them if they need us.'

Justin removes his arm as Mel stands up and looks across the garden at Jon.

'Are they going?' asks Justin.

'Looks like it.'

They go outside as Mel shouts to Noah that it's time to go. Pam's chest constricts as Noah ignores her and Mel goes marching over the grass to drag him away from where he's chasing Carl with the cricket bat.

'Uh-oh,' Pam mutters.

Justin's hand tightens on her arm and she holds back.

Noah starts to shriek, and Jon picks him up.

'Do as you're told,' Mel shouts at him, her face red and angry.

'Mel, calm down,' Pam hears him say. She dries her hands on a tea towel and steps outside. 'Are you going?' she asks her sister brightly, going to meet her.

'Yes. Thanks. We've had a lovely time.' Her voice is flat and insincere. The smile doesn't reach her mouth, let alone her eyes. She's watching Sammy intently and frowning, and Pam wonders what's going on. Has he said something to upset her? They were fine earlier.

Pam puts her arms around her, shocked again at how her chest and shoulder bones are jutting out. Mel is wasting away right in front of her and there isn't a damned thing she can do about it. She's suggested shopping trips, long walks, weekends away, even offering to pay for them both for a week somewhere hot, and all for nothing. 'I can't,' is all her sister ever says. 'Sorry.'

She watches as the three of them leave, a grumbling Noah being carried by Jon, still clutching the plastic bat. The further away they get, the more she can feel the air lighten as the tension goes with them. Next to her, Justin exhales slowly, puffs his lips out and raises his eyebrows at her.

'Thank God that's over,' he says, as the gate closes behind them and they disappear.

'Don't,' she says, immediately feeling disloyal to Mel for wanting to agree with him.

Sammy is walking slowly around at the bottom of the long garden, smoking. She watches him blowing out a spiral of smoke that curls into the air and disappears. There's nothing more she can say to him about the evils of smoking. The more she nags him, the more intent he seems on doing it. He turns, sees her looking and walks over the grass towards her, throwing the cigarette butt into the border. She tuts and rolls her eyes, knowing she can't leave it. She'll have to fish it out later. Sammy seems to think they rot down, but she finds them months later, still whole.

'Wow,' he remarks as he draws level. 'What was that all about?'

'What?'

'Aunty Mel. She was okay at first, then she just changed and started staring at me. Weird.'

'I don't think she would have meant anything by it, love. She goes off into these trances more and more. I think she just stares at whatever's in front of her. This time, it happened to be you. Don't worry about it.'

'Alright. Anyway, I'm going out tonight.'

'Anywhere nice?'

'Date.'

'Oh? What's this one's name, then?'

'Ha! As if! I'm not telling you so you can nag me to death about it. Dream on.'

She laughs, and he gives her a peck on the cheek before going into the house. Pam watches him go, all six feet one of him. Her *blond sensation*, especially since he's sorted himself out after his 'going off the rails' episode. She wishes he wasn't going out, dreading asking him if he's driving. Ever since Issy, watching her kids leave the house causes a massive wrenching sensation in her chest that they won't come home again. The relief when they come back through the door every time almost brings her to her knees.

Joey and Carl are kicking a ball around, Carl treating it like the FA cup final and Joey looking like he'd rather be having teeth pulled at the dentist. His glasses keep slipping down his nose and his face is bright red. His eyes continually slide back to the hammock and the book that is face-down on the grass next to it.

'Come on, Joey, put your back into it, lazy-arse,' Carl complains, as Joey makes minimal effort to stop the ball floating past him into the goal.

Joey is hot and sweaty, and smiles gratefully when Justin offers to take his place.

'With pleasure,' he says, slinking back to his book.

With laughter and the echo of the football being kicked ringing in her ears, she goes back into the kitchen to finish clearing up, unable to sit down until every last thing is back in its place. It takes her a couple of hours until everything is just how she likes it. Eventually, after finishing, she hangs up the tea towel and pours herself the remains of an open bottle of wine to take into the garden. The house is quiet, Kitty having left earlier, not long after Mel. The barbeque still needs cleaning, but that's Justin's domain. The sun has slipped lower and Carl and Justin are lying on the grass, staring up at the sky, and she goes to join them. Carl rolls over onto his stomach.

'I'm hungry,' he says.

Even after all the burgers, crisps and cake he's consumed, neither Pam nor Justin are surprised when he gets up and goes into the house, no doubt to raid the fridge. Pam puts her glass down carefully on the grass and lies down next to Justin.

'Pam?' he says, frowning.

'Yeah?'

'You're not going to like this, but do you think Mel needs help?'

'I am trying to help her.'

'No, I mean... professional help.'

Pam takes a deep breath in. 'God, Jus, I don't know. I can't say that to her, can I?'

'But it's so obvious she's depressed. Is she likely to get better on her own?' He brushes a wisp of her hair off her face with a finger.

'I don't know.'

Justin takes her hand and kisses her knuckles. 'I'm glad I married the sane one.'

She punches him on the arm. 'Don't be horrible. She's not mad. She's depressed. Could you try talking to Jon and try to find out what they're doing?'

Justin rolls onto his back, squinting at the sun. '

I'll try. But I don't know when.'

'Just when it feels natural, you know. Don't tell him I put you up to it.'

'I'm not that stupid. And anyway, he'll probably guess.'

Pam sighs. 'It feels horrible, doesn't it? Like we've always been so close and now we're not.'

'Yeah, it does.' He sits up, a roll that wasn't always there jutting over the waistband of his jeans. 'Listen, I've got some emails to do for work. Sorry. And I've got an early start tomorrow, so I'll be leaving at five.'

She sighs, barely suppressing her irritation. Emails on a Sunday again? 'Okay. You work too hard.'

'Yep, so you're always telling me. But it's got to be done.'

'Er, and what about the barbeque? You can't leave it in that state.'

'I'll do it later.'

172

Course you will, she thinks. When that pig flies across the sky. Even though Pam knows he takes his role as North of England Sales Manager seriously, sometimes she hates his job. She definitely resents the time it takes him away from them, and it's got steadily worse over the years. Sometimes she feels like they have one or two days a week where they're both in the house together and the rest of the time, he's phoning her from one hotel room after another. What annoys her is that he seems happy whether he's at home or not. She wants him to miss her and complain that he's not home often enough. But he doesn't. Instead, he just accepts things, always ready to go with the flow. And he says the same things over and over—*People rely on me, I have responsibilities; I have no choice; so, what, you'd rather I was working in Asda on minimum wage? We wouldn't be living in this house, that's for sure*. So she's stopped nagging, but it still bugs her. He used to tell her he appreciated her more when he'd been away, but that had stopped long ago.

Justin groans and clutches his back as he staggers to his feet. 'I'm getting old,' he grumbles, walking off nevertheless, to shut himself away in his study for the rest of the evening, no doubt leaving her to watch Sunday night TV on her own. She finishes her wine, determined not to let it bug her. Thoughts of Mel come back into her mind. The only time Mel seems content is when she's talking about her new job at the dance studio. Apparently, Olivia is brilliant, a good friend, and so easy to talk to. Does that mean Mel's talking to Olivia instead of *her*? And where does Greg fit in? Mel's definitely been getting closer to him. They'd had their heads together at the funeral, for God's sake! It has crossed her mind more than once that she's jealous of these two new people in her sister's life, that they're taking her place, while Mel is closing down and shutting her out. She knows she ought to be glad that Mel has other people she can talk to but, deep down, she isn't. She likes that Mel has always come to her, needs her and looks to her, and she doesn't like it that it's changing. Her sister means the world to her.

173

She stands, goes into the house and shuts herself in the living room with just the TV for company, picking up her phone every half hour but putting it down again, determined not to crowd her sister and to give her some space. Later, after she gets into bed with no sign of Justin, she realises the barbeque is still dirty.

25

Jon

'NOAH, PLEASE BE QUIET!'

I glare at him in the rearview mirror. He stops banging the two metal cars together and rests his hands in his lap. He's been noisy most of the way up to Newcastle, alternating between squeezing a toy duck that quacks loudly and playing with a book that has a bell that rings on it. Mel's done nothing but snap at him. She's tetchy and looks tired and didn't eat a thing for breakfast this morning. She has her eyes closed now, resting her head on one hand and leaning against the door. Noah meets my eyes in the mirror. The kid looks anxious and I smile at him.

'Sorry, chief. I didn't mean to snap. I'm not angry with you. Just play quietly for a bit, eh? Grandad has a headache, that's all.'

When we get to Newcastle, the parking's a nightmare and we have a twenty-minute walk to the uni, me carrying Noah as he just dawdles otherwise. Kim buzzes us into the building and I take the stairs two at a time, with Noah laughing at being jiggled up and down.

At the top of the stairs, a young black woman, smartly dressed in a grey trouser suit and red blouse, stands waiting. Is this her? She looks in her thirties, I'd guess. Against her dark, unblemished skin, her teeth stand out pearly white and straight. She looks like an ad for cosmetic dentistry.

175

'Hello, I'm Kim Brent.' She extends her hand first to Mel, then me. Most of her fingers have rings on and a bracelet jangles around her left wrist. She has a beautiful smile, but I get the sense it's tempered with sympathy. Noah turns his head away from her and looks over my shoulder at the wall.

She ushers us into a spacious, uncluttered room with a desk at one end and a sitting area with two sofas at the other. The room smells of something sweet and flowery. It's not unpleasant. She gestures at the sofas, and Mel and I take one while she sits on the other. Noah shuffles round on my lap and beams a megawatt smile at Kim. I don't believe it.

'Hello,' she says, leaning forward. 'You must be Noah. Would you like to see what I have in my bag?'

He nods and sits up straighter. 'Yes, please.'

Kim picks up a large white handbag from the floor beside her and rummages around inside it, then plucks out a small electronic gadget. A Game Boy.

'Want to play Pokémon?' She flicks a switch, and it lights up.

Noah is mesmerised by it. It's now buzzing and making all sorts of odd noises. He nods and holds out his hand.

'Can you play with this while Grandma and Grandad talk to me?'

'Yep,' he says and scrambles off my knee, eyes fixed on the prize.

Kim shows him to a beanbag I hadn't noticed in the corner and settles him down. I'm gobsmacked. She's just won him over without even trying. She smiles at the astonished look on our faces.

'I have a four-year-old myself,' she explains, as she sits back down and crosses her legs.

'Ah. Okay,' I say. Maybe we should get one of those things instead of him watching DVDs all the time. It's not great, I know, replacing one screen with another, but at least games are interactive. Mel looks like she's thinking the same thing and raises her eyebrows at me.

'Maybe we should get with the times,' she whispers to me.

In the corner, Noah is rapt. It seems he already knows how to use it. How do kids automatically know this stuff?

'Can I get you some coffee, tea?' Kim asks.

'No thanks, not for me,' I say, wanting to get this over with. Mel shakes her head and says, 'No thanks.'

'So, what did Peter tell you exactly? Do you know why we're here?' I ask.

My fingernails are digging into my palms and there are droplets of sweat at my hairline. One trickles its way down my temple, and I swipe it away. Although it's hot in here, it's not that hot. Mel sits silently and a tiny muscle in her jaw tightens. I'm filled with a sudden dread at what I may find out.

'Peter told me everything about the conversation he had with you. I'm so sorry about Issy. It's just terrible.' Her hands clasp in her lap, bracelets jangling slightly, and she looks at me, concern clouding her eyes.

'So you know we want to find out if she came to see you, in your professional capacity?' asks Mel.

'Yes. And I'll help you all I can. I just can't believe what's happened.'

'Okay.' Good. At least she's not going to pull the 'patient confidentiality' bullshit. 'Can we go back to the beginning? When did she first come to see you?'

Dark brown curls tumble around her face, and she pushes them back. Her nails are short, functional and unpolished, not the hands of a woman for whom appearance is everything. Somehow, daft as it sounds, it instils confidence in me as to her abilities as a counsellor. Although she's immaculately turned out and made-up, looks aren't everything for this woman.

'I only saw her once, after the incident with Peter Cunningham. She had to agree to see me as a condition of remaining at the university. I'm not sure I found much out, I'm afraid. There was still a lot of work to do.'

My heart plummets like a stone. *She can't help us. We've come all this way for nothing.* The noises coming from Noah playing on the game are starting to get on my nerves. Kim speaks again.

'You need to come next door. Noah will be okay here. I'll watch him. Please.'

Mel gets up without a word and follows her. Part of me wants to stay right here on this sofa, but I have to do this. Next door is a much smaller room, containing only a small desk with a computer sitting on it. Two chairs are facing the screen. It reminds me of when I watched the footage from the traffic cameras at the police station.

'I record all my interviews. It's easier if you just see it for yourself and make of it what you will.'

We sit behind the desk and she leans over Mel's shoulder, positions the mouse and clicks it. She disappears out of the room and closes the door behind her. *Does that mean it's worse than we thought?*

It's a total shock to see our daughter on the screen, sitting there looking frightened and cowed. Her head is bowed and I can't see her face properly. Before I can take another breath in, tears are choking up the back of my throat, closing it off. I hear a sob from Mel. I reach for her hand and she grips my fingers tightly.

'Oh,' she says at the sight of Issy. 'Oh. Just look at her.'

The urge to touch the screen and run my fingers down her face is overwhelming. Instead, I shove my free hand under my thighs. She's not there.

On the monitor, Kim's voice is the first thing I hear. 'So, Issy, you understand the need for this meeting today?' Kim speaks in a soft, soothing but sincere tone. If she spoke to me like that, the urge to spill my darkest secrets would be too much to resist.

Issy nods and looks down at her hands, which are folded neatly in her lap. She's wearing a black, long-sleeved top and I'm shocked by how scrawny she looks. Why hadn't I noticed before? Was she anorexic? I know now the long sleeves were to cover up the cuts on her arms. I want to ask Kim if Issy

178

said anything about cutting herself, but Mel is here so I can't. Maybe I should email her later and ask.

'Yes,' Izzy mumbles.

'Can you tell me why?'

'It's because of what I did. Sending those pictures to Peter Cunningham.' She grabs one sleeve and pulls it over her hand then does the same with the other. Her eyes flit to the camera and then away again. The black top she's wearing makes her skin look so pale it's almost translucent.

'Why did you send them, Issy?'

She shrugs and picks at her nails, keeping her head down.

Kim asks again, 'Can you tell me why? What did you think might happen by doing it?'

'I like him.' She shrugs again. 'I thought it might make him like me back.'

'In what way?'

She looks towards the camera, just off to one side, obviously to where Kim is sitting. 'I 'like-liked' him, if that's what you mean.' She makes quote marks with her fingers in the air and smiles uncertainly.

'Fancied him?'

'Yeah. I mean, he's really sexy, isn't he? All the girls like him.'

'Do they?'

'Yes. But I'm the only one willing to do something about it.'

'By sending the pictures—is that how you express the fact that you like someone? Showing them your body?'

She looks up and seems a bit baffled, pulls the sleeves down over her hands again, puffs her fringe out of her eyes. She looks so young and vulnerable.

'Well, yeah. Everyone knows that.' She doesn't add the *duh!* that hangs in the air.

I'm shocked. We never brought her up to think that. I feel Mel clutch my hand tighter. She's staring at the screen with a deep frown, taking in every word. She shakes her head in denial and sits up straighter.

'Why would you think that, Issy? Who told you that's right?'

She shrugs again. 'How else is there?'

On the video, Kim coughs in the background. 'What about other ways? Getting to know someone, talk to them, going on dates. Plus, did you know Mr Cunningham is married?'

She pulls a disinterested face. 'Yeah. So what?'

'So that doesn't bother you?'

'No. It's his business. And it doesn't always stop them.'

What does that mean? She targets married men? I'm more bewildered than ever. This isn't the daughter I know. I don't know this girl at all.

'So you've been with married men before?'

'I never said that!' Issy sounds defensive. Her eyes dart around the room as if seeking to escape.

'Issy, I don't understand about the pictures. You haven't said why you think it's okay to do that.'

Issy sighs. 'It's how you get what you want. It's how they love you.'

'They?'

Issy looks over at Kim scathingly.

'Blokes. Whoever you want to like you.'

She flings an arm up to push some hair out of her face and the sleeve rides up, revealing livid red slashes all the way up her forearm to her elbow. She tugs it quickly back down.

Mel gasps at the sight. 'Look at that! What in God's name . . .?'

Do I tell her I already knew? Admit I've kept something else from her? Mel lets go of my hand and covers her mouth with it, doubling over and sobbing. 'Was she s-self-harming?'

Issy scowls at the camera, blushing at her arm, another secret, being exposed. 'Can I go now? Are we done yet?'

'Not quite. Why do you think exposing your body to men will make them like you?' Kim doesn't mention her arm, but she must have seen it.

Issy tuts. 'I've always known it. He said if I loved him, that's what you do. You show them *that* bit.'

He? My bowels seem to clench and my gut spasms.

'Who said that?'

She's suddenly more animated and irritable. The change is sudden and unexpected. 'Look, I've been here, talked like you wanted, and I'm not saying anything else.' She leans back in her chair, crosses her legs and folds her arms. A defiant look creeps over her face. When she tilts her chin up, dark crescents clearly stain the skin under her eyes. Kim tries again.

'Who's *him?* Professor Cunningham?'

Issy shouts, making Mel and me almost leap out of our seats. 'No, not him. Are you fucking stupid? I don't have a choice, can't you see? This is how I am now. Look, I came here like I had to; I want to leave.' She stands up sharply, and a little bag I hadn't noticed falls from her knee. She stoops to pick it up and I can see she's crying. 'Can I go now?'

'I'd prefer it if you stayed so we could talk more.' Kim's voice is soft and calming, in complete contrast to Issy's. 'Issy, the cuts on your arm? Did you make them? Is someone hurting you?'

Issy shakes her head but doesn't sit back down.

'Why have you cut yourself?'

'It stops the pain. Well, covers it up with another one.' She pulls her sleeves up and shows her arms to the camera. 'There! Happy now?' Fresh cuts oozing blood run in parallel lines up her left arm. She's right-handed. Probably manages a better job of it. I feel sick and dizzy at the thought of the blade slicing into her young, soft flesh.

'Is someone hurting you?' Kim asks again.

Issy laughs. 'No. I do a good job of that all on my own.'

'Issy, have you spoken to your parents about anything that might be worrying you?'

My heart gives an almighty lurch at what she might say next. Mel goes even more rigid and we both lean forward.

'No. There's nothing wrong.' Her face is blank, devoid of any expression or emotion. Like a robot. It's horrible.

'Are you close to them? Can you talk to them about stuff?' Kim asks.

She turns to leave. I desperately want her to answer the question. Can she talk to us? Are we close? Before all this, I would have said *yes* without a second thought. I'd have laughed at the suggestion otherwise. I knew she didn't always *choose* to confide in us, but that's not the same thing as *can't*, is it?

'Will you come and see me again?' Kim asks. 'I can help you. We can work together.'

Issy looks at the woman sitting to the side of the camera. Side-on, she's very thin and her legs are like twigs, the skinny black jeans hanging off her frame. She wasn't this thin at Easter. What happened between Easter and summer? She seems to have been set on a path of self-destruction. Why didn't she talk to us?

'Maybe,' says Issy. 'Will I get kicked out if I don't?'

'I don't know. It's not my call to make. But you have at least attended this time, so possibly not. I do want to help you, though, Issy.'

'You can't help me,' Issy says, in a voice thick with sadness. She looks down at her feet. 'No one can.'

She turns and walks out of the room, leaving the camera filming thin air. Then it's switched off. Mel and I turn slowly to look at each other, and I wonder if my face is as ashen as hers.

'What the hell was that about?' she whispers. 'Who was she talking about? Who's *he*?'

All I can do is shake my head, as what feels like a million thoughts tumble about on a fast spin through my mind.

I know who she's talking about. 'Noah's father. That's who. Without a shadow of a doubt, Mel, I know it.'

'Are you thinking what I'm thinking?' Mel says slowly, in a tortured voice.

'What are you thinking?' I can't be the one to say it first.

Her eyes are wild, confused, and full of hurt when she looks at me. 'Do you think Issy was raped? Or abused? That Noah wasn't born because she was careless at a party?'

It sounds even worse when Mel says it out loud than it did in my head.

'That's exactly what I'm thinking.'

'But why wouldn't she have told us, confided in us?' Mel tips her head back to look up at the ceiling, then closes her eyes. 'Oh God,' she whispers.

A polite cough announces Kim's presence, and I look over to see her standing in the doorway.

'That was a week before uni broke up for the summer. I was intending to follow it up and try again. Some of what she said was very disturbing, don't you think?'

'Yes. Kim, did anyone here know she had a son?' I ask.

Kim shakes her head. 'No. Well, I certainly didn't. The first I knew about Noah was when Peter told me you'd mentioned him. I don't think anyone here knew about him.'

I need some air. We're not going to get any answers here today. All it's done is throw up more questions.

'I think we need to go,' I say.

She nods. 'I'm sorry I didn't get the chance to help her more. I was going to try to continue with it all when she came back.'

'Right. Well, we have a lot to think about. Can we ring you if we need to?'

'Of course. Anything I can help you with, I'm only too happy. I hope you find the answers you're looking for. Here's my card.'

She hands me a small white card. Her phone number and email address are on it.

'Thank you.'

Noah isn't too pleased when we take the Game Boy from his grasp. He's totally absorbed by it.

'Want it,' he wails, his face contorting in misery.

'It doesn't belong to us, Noah. You can't take someone else's toy, can you?' Mel's voice is firm.

'Why not?' he asks.

'Noah, we have to go home now,' I say, grabbing him under his armpits and lifting him up.

He begins to cry. 'I want it!'

'We'll get you one for Christmas,' I say, knowing he has no concept that Christmas is months away. It appeases him a bit, at least, but he's still crying, muttering, 'Want it.'

'I'm sorry,' Kim says, nodding at Noah. 'I seem to have made it worse.'

'Don't worry about it,' I say.

'Bye,' I hear her say quietly as we leave her behind.

Mel and I walk back to the car in silence, stopping off at a Tesco Express to get sweets for Noah. Within five minutes of leaving he's asleep, and we can finally get some peace to talk. But, other than repeatedly asking the new questions that have been raised, we don't. Now, more than ever, we need to find out who Noah's father is. And when we do, I'm going to kill the bastard.

26

Mel

'PUT THE PHONE ON speaker,' I say when Jon rings Steve Jackson to update him about the meeting with Kim. I hear Steve's sharp intake of breath when Jon tells him what Issy said, the insinuation of abuse.

'We really need that DNA test,' Jon says.

'Mmm. This puts a different slant on things. I'll chase it up.'

'Thanks, Steve.' Jon hangs up and turns to me. 'I have to catch up on some work,' he says. 'I'll try not to be too long.'

'Okay. I'll just take Noah into town then.'

He doesn't look pleased. He knows I'm getting a Game Boy for Noah to stop the relentless nagging and pleading he's done since playing on Kim's. I know we can't really afford any unnecessary expense, but he's driven me round the bend with it. Thoughts of how much it will occupy him have also tormented me. I need the space.

Noah's the perfect angel in town, probably because he knows he's getting his own way, and the trip is peaceful, pleasant even, but the racks of clothes, shoes, bags and such like hold no appeal for me. We're back within an hour and Noah bounds into the house, eager to start playing on his new toy.

'How much has that set us back?' Jon asks with a sniff, checking out the two games I've had to get for it.

'Eighty pounds, on special offer at Argos,' I say, hoping he doesn't see the receipt for a hundred and fifty quid. The rest of it is my dance studio money that I've put aside.

I hope he won't check the catalogue. He's been nit-picking over every penny just lately, so he must be more worried than he's letting on. I could do with more hours at the dance studio, but there aren't any. I knew that when I accepted the job. Maybe I should look for something else in the day, something part time.

Steve's as good as his word, and first thing Monday morning he rings with the news we've been waiting for. I don't know if it's good or bad, but it's conclusive; the boy isn't Noah's father. He's never even heard of her. It's what I was expecting. I think Jon was, too, especially since speaking with Kim.

Jon comes home from work on Monday running a temperature. He looks dreadful and keeps running to the bathroom with stomach cramps. He's too ill to look after Noah, and I don't want to bother Pam at short notice. When I ring Olivia, she tells me to bring him with me.

'Anything to encourage boys to dance,' she laughs. 'I've thought of press-ganging them in the street before now. And I'd love to meet him.'

Noah has a great time, more due to being the centre of attention than the actual dancing itself. He throws himself into it with gusto, doing the ballet moves with the grace of a baby elephant. Dressed in T-shirt and shorts, and with bare feet, he takes his place at the barre, right in the centre, and copies everything everyone else does. Instead of running around tearing the place up, like I thought he would, he's concentrating hard on getting the moves right. Olivia is totally smitten.

'Aw, can I have him?' she pleads.

'Most days, with pleasure.'

'He's gorgeous. I could eat him.'

Noah's dimple appears as he smiles and clasps his hands behind his back. This kid can charm the birds out of the trees. Only I know he can be a little monster most days.

When we clear up, Noah's in helpful mode.

'Mummy, where do these go?' He's holding up some ribbon streamers that the girls have been twirling in an effort to improve their grace.

'In the blue box over there, please,' I say, ignoring the fact he's called me Mummy rather than Grandma once again. I continue cleaning the barre with disinfectant spray and a cloth; a few of the girls have colds or sniffles, and I'm not taking any chances. I've already done the door knobs. 'Thank you, Noah, you're being so helpful.'

Noah sits down to roll up the ribbons like Olivia's shown him. It should keep him busy for a while and he's right at the other end of the room so he can't hear us. I take advantage of the break to tell Olivia what's happened since I last saw her. Her face falls when I say the DNA test was negative.

'I'm sorry. So you're no further on?'

'No.' I quickly fill her in on the meeting with Kim from Friday.

She gasps at each revelation. 'Raped? Surely not. How would she have managed to keep a secret like that? And why? Surely she'd have wanted him punished.'

'That's the bit that doesn't add up to me. I've thought about it all weekend, and it doesn't make sense. If she'd been raped, I don't think she could have hidden that. And why would she?'

'Yes, I know what you mean. And the self-harming?'

'I had no idea about that, and nor did Jon. He was as shocked as me. He was speechless. All I can do is keep asking myself why—what would be so bad that she'd cut herself to blot it out?'

Olivia shrugs helplessly and blows her fringe out of her eyes. 'You poor thing! I don't know how you're coping.'

'We're not, really. Just getting through each day, I think.'

'So what's next?'

187

'I honestly don't know. But we're not giving up.'

'God, no. Let me know if I can help at all. Anything I can do . . .'

'Thanks.'

Just then, she gets a text, and she stifles a smile when she reads it, covering her mouth with her hand.

'What?' I ask, glad of the distraction.

'Oh, nothing.' She slides her phone back in her pocket and starts to sweep the floor vigorously. I watch her for a while, and she pretends not to notice.

'So come on; what's his name?'

She looks up, startled.

'Who?'

'The bloke who's put that smile on your face. You've had a crazy, dreamy grin on your face all night.'

'I have not!'

'Don't come that indignant stuff with me! It won't work. Anyway, it'd be nice to hear some good news for a change.'

'Is it that obvious?'

'It is to me.'

She smiles. 'Okay, you're right. I met someone.'

'I knew it. Who? Where?' I stop cleaning the barre.

'At my sister's birthday party on Saturday night.'

'What's he called?'

'Nick. He's divorced, like me. He's thirty-two and gorgeous.'

'Thirty-two? You cradle snatcher!'

She laughs. It's a brilliant sound, unfamiliar to my ears of late. 'I know. Are you jealous?'

'You bet I am! What does he do?'

'He's a police dog handler.'

'Well, he should be good at keeping you in line, then.'

She snorts out a laugh, and we both cast a glance at Noah, who's trying very hard to roll up ribbon as neatly as he can, using Olivia's example as a guide. His head flicks between it and his own in exaggerated movements, the tip of his tongue poking out between his lips.

'So, when are you seeing him again?' I rub hard at a sticky smear. God, it looks like snot. Children are so disgusting sometimes.

'Tomorrow night.' She looks so happy.

'What are you doing?'

'We're going out for dinner. Maybe see a film. I don't really care.'

'It's about time you had some fun.'

'I have fun all the time,' she protests.

'I mean grown-up fun.' I lower my voice. 'You know. With a man.'

She gives me a dirty grin. 'Don't worry about that. I intend to. I've been out of the saddle far too long after *that scumbag*.'

That scumbag is her cheating ex-husband, Dominic. I've heard plenty about him and none of it good. He left her for one of her so-called friends after cheating on her for over a year. I know what that feels like. It was a bit too close for comfort when she was telling me. My heart was going like the clappers, but she didn't notice anything.

We finally finish up and go out into the evening, Noah's hand clasped firmly in mine. It's dull and drizzly and we rush around the corner to our cars. She hugs me while Noah clambers into his car seat.

'If you need me, you know where I am.' She says this every time we say goodbye after work.

'Thanks. Have fun tomorrow.'

Noah's good in the car on the way home. Playing Pokémon. It's a bit old for him, but he's happy just pressing the buttons.

'Can you be good for Grandad when we get home? He's poorly.'

'Yes, I am good,' he says, not looking up. 'Where's my mummy?'

My heart nearly stops. *What?* It's the first time he's asked that, and I have no idea what to say. In the mirror, I can see him. He keeps on playing his game; beeps, buzzes and

189

terrible, tinny music punctuate the silence. I pull over at the side of the road and turn round in my seat.

'Katie Capstick says my mummy is dead,' he states matter-of-factly, his thumbs stopping working for a split second. Lights dance across his face from the console screen, turning his blonde hair green.

'Who's Katie Capstick?' My throat is dry and my tongue feels like it's stuck to the roof of my mouth.

'Katie Capstick is seven.'

'Okay. But who is she? How do you know her?'

'At 'Laine's house.'

His thumb sweeps over a button, and he presses it and squeals.

'You know Katie from Elaine's house?'

'*Yes*,' he says exasperatedly, shaking his head.

Elaine, the child-minder. He doesn't understand. Yesterday, though, he did fetch a picture of me and Jon with him and Issy on it. I never thought anything of it.

'What's *dead*?' he asks. He stops playing his game and looks at me, his face expectant and open.

A big sob hitches in my chest, and tears blur my vision. 'Can you remember Mummy from the picture?'

'Yes,' he hisses at me like I'm an idiot, shaking his head.

'Mummy was my baby, remember? My little girl. She's gone to heaven, Noah. Jesus wanted her to live with him and he took her to heaven. She lives up in the sky with the stars now.' This is awful. I've had all this time to prepare something to tell him, and I haven't managed it.

'Oh. Okay,' he says and shrugs. And that's it, it seems.

I drive home on autopilot to find Jon flat out on the sofa when I get there. He's trying to sleep but looks ill. His stomach is still cramping up, and he's sweating as if the room's on fire. Noah goes straight up to his bedroom, still pressing buttons on the Game Boy as he walks upstairs.

'Hi,' he croaks, looking at me in that pathetic way men do when they're ill.

'How are you feeling?' I sit far enough away from him that I might not catch it, but near enough to not make it obvious.

'Shit,' he says. 'I think it's a virus. How was work?' He tries to sit up a bit, and gives in, grimacing.

'Good. Until Noah asked on the way home if his mummy is dead.'

Jon's eyes widen. 'What did you say to him?'

'I said she's with Jesus in the stars. What would you have said?'

'Honestly? I haven't a clue.' He reaches out and grasps my hand in his. I let him. I can wash it as soon as I leave.

'Who told him that?'

'Some girl at Elaine's house. Do you think we should find a new child-minder?'

He thinks for a bit. 'No. He had to find out sometime. Perhaps she did us a favour.'

'Maybe. It was horrible, though.'

We're both silent for a bit. I know he's thinking about Issy and the paternity thing again. He's obsessed by it these days, and he never seems to switch off. He's always on the computer, looking things up, or on the phone to Steve Jackson. Being ill must be driving him crazy.

'Can you fetch me my laptop?' he asks, right on cue. 'It's doing my head in doing nothing in here.'

'Okay.'

I promptly forget about the laptop until after I've bathed Noah. When I remember to take it in, Jon's asleep, so I leave it on the floor and creep out again to the kitchen. My mind goes back to Olivia's news about Nick and how he's younger than her. I decide to text Greg.

Hi, how are you? Fancy meeting up when you've got time? I type an *x* then delete it, then replace it with two more, then delete those. Finally, I press send before I can change my mind. Since when did a simple letter cause so much anxiety?

Within a few seconds, my phone rings. I feel irrationally happy to see his name, and I snatch it up.

'Hi Greg. You didn't have to ring me now. It would have waited,' I say, keeping my voice soft and quiet so as not to wake Jon.

'It's alright. I wasn't doing anything special. What's up?'

I spend the next few minutes going over everything that I told Olivia earlier. I wonder why I can't seem to stop rehashing it with people I barely know, but Greg's such a good listener that I always seem to go into great detail about how I'm feeling. He talks about things as if he cares. He's silent for a minute when I finish speaking, and I can feel the shock waves coming down the phone. *Abuse? Self-harm?*

His voice is so quiet I can barely hear him. 'God, Mel, this is serious. Look, I'm not doing anything much tomorrow. Do you want me to come over and we can talk some more?'

'Erm, I'd love to meet and talk about it, but not here. Jon's ill, and by the look of him he won't be well enough to go to work tomorrow. Can we meet somewhere else?'

'You can come to mine if you like, but don't expect much. My flat's tiny, nothing special. You'll have to take it as you find it, but I'll run the hoover round.'

'Don't be daft. That would be great. Noah's at the child-minders in the afternoon. We could do it then.'

'Okay. I'll text you my address. Two o'clock?'

'Yes, that's good for me. I drop him off at half one.'

'Come straight round after that, if you like. I'll be in.'

From that, I infer he's still not gone back to driving. I feel happy when I put the phone down. I'm seeing Greg tomorrow at his place. He's a good friend. An extremely good-looking male friend who's an attentive listener. A sensitive man. Plus, he knows what I'm going through.

I turn on the small TV and flick round the channels faster and faster, but the picture that's permanently in front of my eyes is the sight of Issy's arms on that video, cut to shreds, bleeding and scabby. It won't go away.

27

Jon

I TURN THE ALARM off, feeling weak and drained, like someone's kicked the shit out of me after the virus yesterday. *Man flu*, Mel always calls it, in that snidey way women do when talking about how much men exaggerate when they're ill. I can't take the day off work, so I get up. I can't afford to get any further behind.

At the barbeque the other day, I told Mel that I've caught up but it wasn't true. I'm further behind than ever. Since Issy died, my focus has gone completely. Nothing feels important now, compared to what's happened. When your kid tops herself, it has a way of putting things in perspective. But the bills haven't stopped coming and now I desperately need to get some money in, so I have to go to work. A couple of ibuprofen should dull the headache a bit. My neck is killing from the damn sofa bed. Maybe I should broach the subject about sleeping in Issy's bed. Or maybe I won't. That would just swap one pain in the neck for another.

In the office, the phone's ringing constantly with people wanting to know when their drawings will be ready. I resist the urge to snap, *I'd get your job done quicker if you'd get off the pissing phone and stop harassing me,* at every one of them. On the plus side, I completed the job for Ken Wallace, so he's off my back. A tetchy cow called Karen Butler is now the worst. She's a female version of Ken Wallace. Many times just lately,

I've wished I hadn't taken her job on. It's been dragging on for months now, mainly due to her changing her mind all the time. The only good thing about her is that she lives in Scotland, so she can't drop by.

She's wanted everything from a Mediterranean garden, then a Japanese-inspired one, then one with Romanesque pillars and columns and now, the most recent one (since she joined the National Trust and started visiting gardens), an English country cottage garden with herringbone brick paths, arbours, and a stone folly nestling in trees. She lives in a three-bedroomed, ex-local authority semi. The plot is okay size-wise, bigger than the new-builds they do these days, but not worthy of the grand scheme she's after. I've told her it'll look daft, but she won't listen to any advice and keeps ploughing on with the changes then complaining when they aren't ready. Many times I've wanted to throw in the towel and tell her to get stuffed.

I'm making notes on a new project when the phone rings. I grab it without thinking and get a sinking feeling when I hear her nasal, whiny voice.

'Jon?' she snaps. No, *Hello, how are you? Sorry to hear your life's gone to shit at the moment.*

'Hello, Karen,' I say, closing my eyes and massaging my temples, my pencil still in my hand. *Shit!*

'I've been expecting the drawings back all last week. Have you sent them?' Snippy.

I speak very slowly, as if she's intellectually challenged, hoping this time she'll listen. 'I told you, that was for the Roman design, not the new one. Then you changed it again, remember?'

'No, Jon, it was for the new design. I know what you said. My contractor's due to start on Monday and I have nothing to show him.'

'Karen, we've been through this. Every time you want the design changed, it adds to the time. And you've only paid me for the first lot of plans, before you decided you didn't want them. What about the other two lots you haven't paid me for yet? It's not my fault you keep changing your mind, is it?'

She explodes. 'Oh, that's it, is it? I should have known! Well, I'm not paying a penny until I have the design in my hand.'

For a minute, I can't speak. Then I find my voice. 'As of now, you owe me fifteen hundred: five hundred each for the two scrapped designs, which I completed and sent you, and five hundred for your new ones. *Before* I do them.'

Her voice rises an octave. 'You must be bloody joking? How stupid do you think I am?'

I swallow, breathing hard, and snap the pencil I'm holding in two, wishing it was her neck. 'Karen?'

'Yes?'

'As of now, you need to find another garden designer. I'll see you in court for what you owe.'

'Well...' she says, spluttering. 'I don't think—'

'You just asked me how stupid I think you are. Well, I think you are the stupidest woman I've ever met. Oh, and go fuck yourself,' I add, just for the satisfaction of it.

Just before I put the phone down, I hear her sharp gasp. I cut the call and then turn my phone off. I'm rid of her and if I never get paid, I'm just glad that she's no longer my problem. The relief at not having to answer to her any more is immense. I turn back to my monitor, feeling lighter and freer at the lack of her.

Two hours later and I've done more work than I have all last week. Instead of avoiding the pile that's built up, I've sorted it into different piles. I'm prioritising and it feels good. Tetchy, impatient people are no longer skipping to the front of the queue. Instead, I'll do the jobs in the order they come in, which is what I used to do before everything got on top of me. If people don't like how long it's going to take, then it's just hard luck—they can find someone else. And the ones that have been stalling payment will have to settle up fast. I'm owed thousands. If that comes in, it'll tide us over.

I'm about to finish a complicated job, but then I realise the drawings are at home on a memory stick and there's no copy on my laptop. Shit! I can't print them out and send them from here. It's lunchtime, so I may as well eat at home. It's a fifteen-minute drive home and I manage it in ten. Mel's car isn't on the drive, which is odd. She should have been back from dropping Noah off at Elaine's by now. Maybe she's gone shopping. My gut clenches at the thought of her going on a spending spree we can't afford.

I make a sandwich and have just sat down when a car pulls up outside. Two young men get out, eyeing the house, dressed in jeans and T-shirts. They look vaguely familiar as they walk straight up the drive and ring the bell. I brush crumbs off my front and am still chewing the last mouthful when I open the door.

'Hello?'

The two men look at each other. One is slight and dark and the other, bigger-made and blonde. They look a bit effeminate and it niggles me that I can't place them. I've definitely seen them somewhere before.

'Mr Warner?' asks the smaller one, in a soft voice. Acne scars dot his cheeks and he has razor rash on his throat.

'Yes.'

'Erm, I'm Ryan Anderson and this is Michael Kelly.'

It falls into place, helped by the crescent-shaped scar above the blonde one's eyebrow that I've seen before on Issy's Facebook. The two who looked gay.

'We were due to share with Issy next year at uni,' the blonde one, Michael, explains.

'Yes…' is all I can manage.

'Could we come in?' asks Ryan.

'Of course. I'm sorry. Please.' I open the door to let them in and lead them into the living room.

'We just heard about Issy from the lettings agent in Newcastle. We're so sorry. We just had to come.'

'Thank you.' My chest feels its usual tightness at the sound of Issy's name coming from someone else's lips. 'I was actually going to come and see you when uni starts back. I got your names from the letting agent.'

Ryan and Michael look uncomfortable, hovering in the middle of the room.

'Can I get you anything to drink?'

They both shake their heads. 'I'm good, thanks,' says Ryan at the same time Michael says, 'I'm okay.'

'The agent wasn't sure of the details but said something about a car accident.' Ryan looks down at his hands.

It's better to just state it baldly, I've found. 'She killed herself. Drove her car under a lorry. That's why I wanted to speak to you, to see if you might have any clues as to why.'

They both stiffen, but I can see it's not come as a complete shock.

'Sit down, lads.' *Before you fall down.*

They sit.

'How well did you know Issy?' I ask.

Michael clears his throat. 'We were really good friends from about last Christmas. We're on the same course and started hanging out together. You have to pick your housemates for the second year pretty early on, so we teamed up with David and Nathan and all decided to share.'

'I rang them and they didn't answer.'

'No, David was going travelling with his girlfriend over the holidays and Nathan's got a summer job, so he'd most likely have been working. But they're good lads, nice people, you know. We've told Nathan, but David's still out of the country. We've left messages for him, but he hasn't contacted us yet.'

'Right. I appreciate your coming. Erm, one thing... did you know Issy had a child?'

They nod. 'Yes, but we didn't for a long time. She was always, like, a bit on the quiet side, you know?'

'So, how did you find out? Did she tell you? When?'

They look at each other. 'When would it have been?' Michael asks.

'When that bloke turned up? About March? April?'

A rush of adrenalin propels me forward and the hairs on my arms stand up, electrified. 'What bloke?'

'We were coming out of lectures one day, talking about going to the pub, then Issy just stopped. She said *I'll see you later* and just walked off. We carried on, but she walked over to some guy and they went the other way,' Ryan says.

'Yeah,' Michael adds. 'We didn't see her until the next day and we asked her who it was. She said it was her kid's dad. We were gobsmacked. We hadn't known she had a kid.'

My heart is scudding fast against my chest wall now. 'What did he look like, this man?'

'We only saw him for a split second, mostly from the back and the side.'

'Please, think. Anything you can remember. What colour was his hair, for instance?'

They look at each other. 'I think he had a woolly hat on and a big winter coat. That's all I remember. It was freezing,' Ryan says.

'Are you saying you don't know who the kid's father is, then?' asks Ryan, frowning.

'Yes, that's exactly what I'm saying. We don't know whether or not he could hold the clue as to why she killed herself. Plus, she was fifteen when she got pregnant, so that's an offence in itself. We think now he may have raped or abused her.'

'Why would she have gone off with him if he'd raped her?' asks Michael, looking aghast. 'That wouldn't make sense.'

'No,' I agree. 'It wouldn't. Lots about it doesn't make sense. At this stage, we're just guessing.'

'What makes you think she was abused?'

I pause. I'm not sure how much to tell them. I don't even know them. 'Just something someone said. I don't know for sure. Listen, was that the only time you ever saw this guy?'

'It was for me, yeah.' Ryan looks at Michael.

'I never saw him any other time, either.'

'How many boyfriends at uni did she have?' I ask, dreading the answer.

'I don't know. She used to disappear off campus a fair bit. She never told me where she went or who with. It was a bit of a standing joke,' Michael says.

Disappear? She didn't know anyone there, did she? Where had she been going?

'From when she first started?' I ask.

'Yeah. Pretty much. I'd go to her halls to see if she was coming out and she sometimes wasn't there.'

'I see. Did you know anything about her and Peter Cunningham?'

Their eyes widen. 'Cunningham? No. Did he do something wrong?'

'No, he didn't but she could have got him into trouble, that's all. If she didn't tell you about it, just forget it. He's a nice guy. Didn't do anything wrong.'

'Yeah, everybody likes him. He's, like, married with a kid, isn't he?' Ryan asks Michael.

'I think.'

I realise how little of what goes on around them teenagers actually notice if it doesn't affect them.

'Are you both the same age as Issy?' They nod. 'These other flatmates, Nathan and David—I hate to ask this, but have either of them slept with Issy? I mean, it's odd, don't you think, that she's sharing with all males?'

Ryan shrugs. 'She didn't have any female friends, I don't think. But David's been with Julia a while now, and he was after her for months before that.'

'Yeah,' Michael agrees. 'That's true. He's been obsessed with her since they met. I don't recall him ever being with anyone else at uni. And Nathan's more interested in sports. He says he's too busy for a relationship. And we certainly haven't.' They share an embarrassed glance.

We sit in silence for a bit and I think everyone's said what they need to.

'Well, thanks anyway, for what you could tell me. And thanks for coming to see me; it's very good of you. I really appreciate it.'

'I'm just sorry we missed the funeral. We would have come, you know.' Ryan stands up and holds his hand out to me. I shake it and then do the same with Michael.

'Thank you. I know you would have. I'm sorry you found out too late. If you think of anything, anything at all... no matter how insignificant you might think it is, please get in touch.' I pull two business cards from my wallet and hand them over. 'All my contact details are on there.'

I show them to the door and stand on the step until they've driven away. It's good of them to come and see me, and at least I've learned something. Then a tidal wave of despair crashes over me.

It's three o'clock now. Where the hell is Mel? I try her phone, but she doesn't answer. All those good intentions I had for ploughing through this afternoon have gone. I don't know where my wife is and the day's just gone to shit. Before I know it, I'm pulling the whisky out of the cupboard and savouring the burn as it disappears down my throat.

28

Mel

I CLUTCH THE PIECE of paper with Greg's address scribbled on it and look up at the window. Surely this can't be the place—a minging flat over a Chinese takeaway? The window above the shop looks like it hasn't been cleaned in decades and the frame has hardly any paint left on it. Grotty isn't the word. I know he said not to expect much, but I wasn't expecting this. My phone rings. It's him.

'Are you going to stand out there all day? Come up; the door to your left.'

He hangs up and, glancing up, I see a shadow move behind the dirty net curtain. The door to my left is in the same state as the window; badly in need of attention. Still, it's unlocked, so I go through it and up the concrete stairs, my feet echoing loudly. He's at the open door when I reach the top, wearing jeans, a tight white T-shirt and a big smile. I don't want to think it, but he looks very attractive, all rumpled, unshaven and dark. I'm glad I made the effort to do my hair and put on some make-up and a decent dress.

'Hi,' he says. 'Come in. You look nice. It's good to see you.'

We stand awkwardly, weighing up whether to hug or not, then he stands aside to let me in and the moment's gone. I wonder whether I might have just imagined it. I catch a whiff of musky aftershave as I step past him. Inside, I stop dead.

201

'Wow!'

The flat's gorgeous. The net curtain is off-white, not dirty, like it looked from outside, and the place, although small, smells fresh and clean. It's immaculate.

'Coffee?' he asks, closing the door behind me.

'Yes, please.'

'Coming right up. Have a seat.'

I sit on the pale green chenille sofa with the furry cream cushions. The green and cream tones of the room complemented by the stripped wood floor. Large, framed photographs of cute dogs hang everywhere. I love it; it's quirky and modern but with a homely feel. I flip through a lifestyle magazine that's lying on a coffee table while I wait for him to come back. In the kitchen, amid a clattering of cups, I hear a whoosh and hiss of what sounds like steam.

'Did you decorate this?' I ask, as he fetches two cups of coffee in on a tray, with sugar and a packet of Jammie Dodgers. 'It's really lovely.'

'Yeah, actually. It was a dump when I moved in. Still is, from the outside. I need to find time to paint it—it's next on the list. It had really bad damp issues and was disgusting, but the landlady said I could rent it dirt cheap if I did it up. Now it's finished, I still pay the same. Win, win, I'd say.'

'You have great taste and a good eye for colour. And a decent landlady, it seems.'

'Thanks.' He laughs. 'But it helps that the landlady is my mum. The last tenant left it in a right mess, and I needed somewhere after my divorce.' He shrugs. *I didn't know he was divorced.*

He sits on the arm of the sofa, at the other end. There are no other chairs. When he smiles, his face just comes alive. It's very attractive.

'I like the photos,' I say, pointing to a Cocker Spaniel with a ball in its mouth.

'Oh, it's a hobby of mine. Those are copies of some of the portraits I've done for people. Not that I've done many lately.'

'You took all these? Wow! They're brilliant.'

'Thank you.'

'You're a man of hidden talents.'

'Like you with your dancing.'

I smile. 'Yeah.'

He stands up. 'I can give you a guided tour, if you like. Shouldn't take more than about, er, twenty seconds, I'd say. Thirty, if we stretch it out.'

'Go on, then. I'd like that.'

I follow him into the kitchen, which has the most fantastic golden light coming through the window. Filtered through a slatted blind, the sun bounces off the cabinets (cherry?) and onto the slate floor. Despite being small, the kitchen has everything you'd expect, even a state-of-the-art coffee machine, which accounts for the noise earlier. The rich aroma of fresh coffee fills the room, and a round bistro table and two chairs fit snugly into the space beneath the window. I long to sit there, bathed in the light, and I resist the urge to pull out a chair.

'I thought you said I'd have to take you as I found you. Well, I find it immaculate.'

'Yeah, well, compared to your house, it's a poky dump.'

'Don't be daft. Mine's only a two-bed semi, plus a box room and too much clutter. And this is amazing inside.' Although it's true, the view from the window isn't that great. The kitchen window looks down on the backyard from the takeaway and is littered with cardboard boxes and rubbish.

'It's a bit of a losing battle,' he says, standing beside me and looking down at the scene. The scent and proximity of him unsettles me slightly. 'Anyway, come on.'

He leads me back through the living room and into the bathroom; dark grey and white with a gleaming shower cubicle and a strong smell of bleach coming from the toilet.

'Do you have OCD?' I'm picturing him on his hands and knees, scrubbing the loo, wearing rubber gloves and brandishing a toilet brush.

'No,' he says, a tad defensively. 'I just like things clean.'

I smile. 'You could always get a job as a cleaner.'

'Maybe I will.'

'You'd be good at it.'

There's only the bedroom left now. I feel hot and flustered at the thought of us in his bedroom. It's bound to be small and intimate, like everything else in the flat.

'And last but not least,' he says, opening the one remaining door. I just stop myself from saying 'where all the magic happens', thank God!

He steps back to let me in. It's at the back, next to the kitchen, and has the same stripped floor as the living room. Again, slatted blinds filter the sunlight, this time casting stripes of light and shade across the pristine white bedding. Once more, there's nothing out of place. Apart from the metal framed bed, oak chest of drawers and wardrobe, there's not much in here. A slim TV stands on the chest of drawers and a photography magazine lays open, face down, on a bedside table, next to a reading lamp. A picture jumps into my mind, of him lounging in his white bed, bare-chested and watching TV. I try not to look at the dark hairs peeking out above the neck of his T-shirt, yet I imagine the way his naked torso would look. A glance round tells me no women live here. It doesn't look like any females even stay here. It's not so much masculine as uncluttered, but there are no feminine knick-knacks anywhere. No hairbrushes or deodorants in the bathroom, or perfume or bits of women's clothing in the bedroom. He's definitely still single, then. Not that it matters to me, of course.

We go back into the living room to drink our coffee. Three hours until I need to pick Noah up. Three hours of pure, uninterrupted adult conversation without a demanding child at my elbow. Bliss.

'So, have you not gone back to work yet, then?' I ask, trying not to refer to the fact that he's here, available at a moment's notice, in the middle of the afternoon.

We're sitting at opposite ends of the small sofa. About a foot of space separates us, twelve inches that seem to me to be electrically charged. Not that any of it is coming from him. *What the hell is wrong with me?*

He sighs and shuffles forward, planting his feet squarely on the floor and resting his elbows on his thighs. He studies the floor and rubs one palm with the other thumb.

'I'm due to start back this weekend. They've let me have two months off due to stress, which is good of them. I'm taking a load to Harwich docks. Truth is, I'm dreading it.'

I don't know what to say, so I say nothing. When I don't answer, he speaks again.

'Mel, what if I get back behind the wheel and can't do it? What if I freak out or freeze or something? What then?' This time, his eyes fix on me. His face is contorted with anguish and I feel desperately sorry that my daughter has reduced him to this. He doesn't deserve it, and I can't help him.

'I'm sorry,' I say. 'It's Issy's fault, all Issy's fault.'

He looks away and shakes his head. 'I don't think I can do it,' he whispers.

'Greg?' He looks back at me, his eyes searching mine. They're a much deeper blue than I remember them being at the funeral. 'You *can* do it. You're going to be fine. There's no need to worry.'

I reach out, grip his fingers and squeeze them, then let go. I sounded much more confident than I felt just then. I hope he buys it. A spark of hope flickers in his face.

'Do you really think so?'

'Yes, I do. What happened can't possibly happen again. Let's face it, it's not likely, is it?' I take a sip of my coffee.

'I guess not.' His shoulders relax. 'Well, whatever happens happens, right?'

He takes the packet of Jammie Dodgers from the tray, rips it right down the side and places it on the table in front of us.

'Not very grown up, I know, but they're my favourite. Can't resist them. Or custard creams. Don't know why people make so much fuss over Hob-Nobs—they can't hold a candle. Help yourself.' He takes one and dunks it in his coffee, then crams it into his mouth in one.

I take one too. 'There's just something about biscuits, isn't there? One of the small pleasures in life.' I bite half of mine.

'Definitely.' His body language changes; his shoulders go up a notch and he sits up straighter. He takes a deep breath in and puts his coffee down. Here it comes: the real reason I'm here. 'Look, on a serious note, I was shocked yesterday to hear you say the counsellor suggested Issy may have been abused or raped. Do you think she may have been?'

The biscuit sticks to the roof of my mouth and I try to swallow it down. 'I don't know. I can't see she would have been able to keep that from us. Do you know what I really think? I haven't told a soul this, mind.'

'What?'

'It may sound daft but my nephew, Sammy, my sister's son... it's crossed my mind lately that what if it's him? He's four years older than Issy, and they were so close. But for a couple of years, he went off the rails, actually around the time Noah was conceived. I've been considering the fact that something may have happened between them. He was the one Noah was with after the funeral, at the wake, when we were outside, remember?'

His eyes go wider. 'Oh, yeah. The one who took him off the childminder? Really? You think it could be him?'

It's the first time I've voiced the thought that's been growing in my head since the barbeque, and it doesn't gain clarity from being spoken aloud. Is it feasible or am I a madwoman, clutching at straws?

'I never thought it until just lately, but I've been watching him with Noah. He's so natural with him; he really loves him. Like a father.'

'Would a DNA test be any good? After all, it proved the other boy's not his father.'

'Yes, but how do I go about it? Everyone would think I've lost the plot. I'd have to do it in secret.'

'Have you told Jon?'

206

I shake my head. 'What if I'm barking up the wrong tree? It could cause an awful lot of trouble in my family if I accuse him of it and he's innocent.'

'Well, you wouldn't be accusing him at this stage, would you? You could do it without him knowing and if it's negative, then there's no harm done.'

He makes it sound so simple, but I really don't think it is.

'You really think I could get a sample of his DNA and send it off? Like… hair or something?' Greg's making me think perhaps it's not so far-fetched and I'm not imagining it. Like it could be a real possibility.

'Don't see why not.' He turns to face me. 'What about the self-harming, though? What do you make of that?'

'I felt sick when I saw it. God, Greg, it was awful. Her poor arms, covered in those horrible cuts.' I fight hard not to let the tears out. I've cried so much I'm surprised there are any left. 'We really didn't know anything about her at all, did we? How can that happen?'

'Kids tell you what they want you to know, I suppose.'

'But what was so bad that she couldn't confide in us? Nothing's that bad, surely. To feel driven to do what she did. And now we might never know.'

'Don't give up looking for the truth, Mel. Perhaps you will find out.'

Deliberately, I steer the talk away from Issy and onto more general things; politics, the weather, TV, and before I know it, it's time to pick Noah up. Just as I'm getting up to go, his phone rings.

'Hi, can I call you back in five minutes? Okay. Seven o'clock, yeah. I'm looking forward to it, too. See you soon. Bye.'

My ears prick up at the warmth in his tone.

'A date?' I raise my eyebrows and he nods.

'Yeah, actually. We've been out a couple of times. We're going out tonight.'

An irrational stab of jealousy comes from nowhere when he mentions he's seeing someone. He looks happier than he's looked all afternoon and I realise I've been stupid, harbouring some silly crush for him. Thank God I haven't acted upon it or I'd be mortified now. What would he see in me, anyway? I'm ten years older than him and I look like a train wreck. My face feels hot and I turn away.

'Well, have a great night. I'll see you soon. You can let me know how it went.'

I leave quickly without looking back, glad my dignity's still intact, and arrive slightly early to pick Noah up from Elaine's. I could tackle her about what that girl said to Noah, but it's not her fault. The child only told the truth. Noah is pleased to see me and jumps up, clinging around my neck and hugging me tight. When I get home, Jon's car is on the drive. *Why isn't he at work?* The house is quiet, and I put my head around the living room door. He's flat out on the sofa, with an empty glass in his hand, a soft snore escaping him. An empty whisky bottle is lying on its side on the floor. This isn't looking good. I know what happens when he drinks whisky.

'What's matter with Grandad?' asks Noah, gripping my hand tighter and looking up at me anxiously.

'I think he's a bit poorly. Can you go and play in your bedroom? You can play Pokémon for a bit if you like, and I'll come up in a minute.'

He bolts out of the room and up the stairs. I wait until his bedroom door slams before going into the room and kneeling beside Jon. The whisky fumes nearly knock me out.

'Jon?' I shake him by the shoulder and he snorts, stirs.

'Where you been?' He's slurring and not focusing properly.

God! He's legless! Drunk on the sofa in the afternoon? It's bloody disgusting, and he has the nerve to question *me*? 'How much have you had to drink?'

'Dunno. Not enough. Why?'

'Because it's four in the bloody afternoon. You were still ill from yesterday when you went to work this morning. Why are you here now?'

He turns over, his face squashing into the back of the sofa, and goes back to sleep. Great! I don't know what can have made him drink in the middle of the day like this, but I know one thing: it's a complete waste of time asking him now. I'll get no sense out of him. As I stand up, I see his phone on the floor, half under the sofa. The bloody thing's switched off. Good job I didn't need to ring him for anything. I pick it up and wander into the kitchen with it. When I turn it on, several emails, texts and missed calls flood in.

His password is an old telephone number of ours; he hasn't changed it since the affair. Proof he has nothing to hide? It's a bit obvious. What's to stop him having another phone? I read his emails. Some are the usual marketing ones, but there are quite a few from irate-sounding people, demanding to know why their plans aren't ready. When I scroll through them, I see most of them have emailed him already, several times. It's the same with his texts, again more disgruntled customers complaining. With a sinking heart, I listen to his voicemails. One is from a woman called Karen, and she's shouting. Reading between the lines, he's been rude to her earlier today, and she's not happy, saying something about court in a thick, Welsh accent. She's not the only one. There are more like it, two threatening to take their business elsewhere.

I put the phone down and sink into a chair, resting my head in my hands on the table. At this rate, he'll have no customers left. What will we do for money then?

'Grandma, want some tea,' says Noah, from right behind me.

I didn't hear him come down the stairs. He climbs onto my lap and I wrap my arms around him.

'Okay, let's have a look what there is, shall we?'

As I carry him around the kitchen, opening cupboard doors, my feelings of alarm grow. What's Jon playing at? At this rate, he's going to lose the business he wanted and worked so hard for. As if losing our daughter isn't enough. And why hasn't he told me? Once again, he's shutting me out.

The thought that there's lots I haven't told him lately gets locked in a box right at the back of my brain. That's different.

29

Jon

'WILL SAMMY BE THERE?' asks Noah, right by my ear.

I'm carrying him and we're walking around the corner on our way to Pam's house for Carl's thirteenth birthday. The atmosphere between me and Mel is frostier than the inside of our freezer. We haven't spoken since Thursday, ever since Mel came home to find me pissed on whisky on the sofa. It's now Sunday.

We had a holy row the day after I got drunk. I was still not right from being ill the day before. That must have been why the whisky affected me so much. I crawled off the sofa, went to bed and didn't get up until the next day. Mel was livid. She'd found texts and emails on my phone from customers complaining about my bad service and flipped out about it. She asked what other secrets I've been keeping, and we then had another row about her snooping through my phone. As we weren't speaking after, I never told her the real reason I got drunk that day, after Michael and Ryan visited. Maybe I won't now. It might be better if I try to track down Noah's dad on my own properly, like I wanted to in the first place. If I'm going to be accused of being secretive, then I bloody well will be.

Mel has Carl's brightly wrapped present in her hand. I don't know what's in it. That's another thing she'll have a go at me about when we're speaking again: she always has to buy birthday and Christmas presents *and* wrap them as well because *I* never bother. And so on, blah blah blah. I think I prefer it when we don't speak; at least that way, she can't go on at me all the time.

'Grandad?'

'Yes, Sammy will be there,' I answer Noah.

'Yay. I love Sammy,' he shouts.

From my left, I hear my wife make a strange noise, a bit like a hiss, but I don't rise to it. Whatever's up with her now, I don't want to know. Out of the corner of my eye, I can see Mel's face, and it's not a happy one. We go into the house and Mel veers straight off towards Pam, no doubt to huddle in a corner and talk about me. If they had an effigy of me, no doubt there'd be pins sticking out of it everywhere, especially the nether regions.

'Alright?' says Justin, clapping me on the back and giving me a bro-hug. 'Hey, Noah. High five. Don't leave me hangin'.'

'Where's Sammy?' Noah demands, ignoring Justin's outstretched hand.

'Charming! In the garden, I think, buddy.'

He struggles to get down and I almost end up with a black eye as he head-butts me in the face in his attempt to get down quicker.

'Ow! For God's sake, Noah!'

He runs through the house and out of the back, yelling for Sammy as he goes.

'Drink?' asks Justin. 'It's not like you have to drive home.'

If I get pissed, it will make things far worse. Mel will probably never speak to me again. 'Yeah, I'll have a beer for starters, thanks.'

Justin frowns. 'How long has it been since the days when we used to get properly hammered?'

'God knows. Back in the good old days. When life was fun.'

Justin glances at me, but he doesn't comment. We get beers from the fridge and go to sit in the garden. It's cool and quite overcast, but at least it's not raining. Mel and Pam are standing just outside the kitchen door, and she glances at me, hostility all over her face.

'What's up with the missus?' asks Justin quietly, raising his eyebrows in her direction.

'Ah, you know—what's *not* up would be easier to answer. She's having a strop about something; I forget what exactly.'

He gives me a look. He knows damn well that I know what's up with her.

'Come on, what are you in the doghouse for this time?'

'Got pissed on Thursday afternoon. She found me.'

'On an afternoon? Why?'

'Just... stuff, you know. I'd been ill and felt like shit, and everything got on top of me. Anyway, cheers,' I say, opening my beer. I can tell Mel's glaring at me, and I drain half the can in one gulp. What's wrong with a man having a drink, for crying out loud?

Justin's lads are milling around, as well as some of Carl's friends. It's noisy, and Noah's made his usual beeline for Sammy, who's now holding him by the ankles and swinging him gently, like Justin sometimes does. Noah seems to have a thing about being upside down; he shrieks with laughter.

'Careful,' snaps Mel, and Sammy looks at her in surprise. 'Don't swing him about like that. He's not a toy.'

'Sorry,' Sammy mumbles, obviously embarrassed by her outburst. He lowers Noah down onto the grass and he rolls over.

'Again. Do it again, Sammy.'

Sammy eyes Mel. 'No, mate. Grandma doesn't like it.'

'She *is* in a mood, isn't she?' Justin whispers.

I shrug and drink some more. 'Don't worry about it.'

But he does look worried. 'So, how are things in general, you know?'

'Honest answer? I don't know how things are. I'm not sure I care, either, at the moment. It's hard living with Mrs Sanctimonious over there.'

'That bad, eh?'

213

'Yup.' I drain my can. 'Are we having another beer? Or something stronger?'

'Beer's fine for now,' Justin says.

I grab four beers from the fridge, two for now, and two so we don't have to get up again. Mel's face is a picture. I know exactly what'll be going through her mind right now. *He's going to drink himself stupid and leave me to see to Noah. What if I want to get drunk? Why do I always have to be the responsible one?* and so on and so on. She wasn't so responsible when she was hammered in the pub the other week, was she?

I'm sick of it and I'm sick of her. I'm sick of everything.

'Are you sure you're okay?' Justin asks when I slam myself back down into the chair and place the four cans on the table. 'Only you're acting a bit weird.'

Despite my resolve to keep things to myself, I lean into him and lower my voice. 'I've been trying to find out who Noah's father is.'

His eyebrows shoot up into his hair. Or nearly into it. For the first time, I realise his hair is thinning at the front. It used to come down much further than this.

'Why didn't you tell me? I would've helped.' He looks wounded.

'I know, mate, but we agreed it was something we wanted to do together, just me and Mel.'

'Yeah, yeah, I can understand that. Have you found anything out yet?'

'Not really. But we've ruled out the boy from school, the one she said she slept with just before he left.'

I can tell he feels left out. 'I knew there was something. How did you find that out then?'

'A copper's been helping me. Off the record, like. He shouldn't have really, so keep it to yourself, okay?'

'Course, yeah.' He picks a fresh can up and pops it open, takes a long swig, then puts it back down.

He starts to speak again when I hear Mel shouting. She's still with Pam, but she's irate about something. Again.

'That's not the point, though, is it?' she's saying.

What's not the point? Everyone turns to look at my wife, making a show of herself in the garden. Carl and Joey, who've been kicking a ball around until now with some of Carl's friends, stop and stare, then look at each other. Joey shrugs. At fifteen, women's moods are an alien concept. He'll learn that it doesn't change. Sammy glances at his dad, who gives a tiny shrug, then he looks at me and walks over, with Noah clinging like a limpet to his legs.

'What's up with Aunty Mel?' he asks, with an unlit fag clamped between his lips. He sits down and lights it up.

Noah climbs onto Sammy's knee. Sammy holds the cigarette out to one side, far away from Noah.

'I don't know. Just ignore it, she'll get over it.'

'She had a right go at me earlier.'

'I know, mate, I heard. Sorry about that. I don't know what's got into her.'

Sammy nods. 'Anyway, I'm heading out now. Got a date. Noah, sit on Uncle Justin's knee.'

'Really? With Rachel again?' asks Justin, holding out his hands as Noah shuffles onto his lap.

Sammy taps his nose and takes a drag, blowing smoke out of the corner of his mouth. 'No one you know.' He stands up, ruffles Noah's hair, and walks off into the house.

He's probably glad to get away. Mel is tainting the atmosphere with her bad mood. It's settling over the garden like a toxic fog.

'Remember what it was like at his age, playing the field?' Justin says, leaning back with a faraway look in his eyes.

'Not really, no,' I say. 'We were both married.'

'Right, yeah,' he says, wistfully.

'We can't carry on like this,' I hear Mel say. She glances over at me, then away.

So she's telling Pam all about it then, my drunken afternoon. About how I'm neglecting customers and how, if the business goes belly up, we could lose the house. Typical of her to turn a molehill into a mountain. The business will get back on track in no time, it's just I have other things taking priority right now. We can manage on less money if she stops buying ridiculously expensive kids' toys and lying about how much they cost. She's acting like we're going to be on the street living in a cardboard box. It's bloody ridiculous. Justin's silent, as are Joey and Carl. She's making everyone feel uncomfortable. I have to stop her.

I walk over to where she's sitting on the wall, holding a small glass of wine. She glares at me when she sees me.

'What are you doing?' I hiss, trying to be quiet. 'Stop making a show of yourself. You're spoiling Carl's birthday.'

'Or what?' she says, loudly. 'What will you do? Go and get drunk or have another affair?'

The words hang in the air, and I can feel a collective gasp. *Did she just tell everyone I had an affair?* I'm speechless, standing there in shock, with my hands curled into fists at my sides. Never before have I wanted to hit her. Never! But I do now. I bite my lip, spin on my heel, and leave her there, marching around the side of the house and up the garden path. I'm so livid I can't even think straight. What does she think she's doing, telling everyone our private business? My one mistake and she can't get past it. It's done, dead and buried, yet she can't let it go. *What the hell is wrong with her?*

Out in the street, I stop and look left, then right, unable to decide where to go or what to do. I hate her! At this moment, I actually hate her, and I wish I'd left her for Adele when I had the chance. She's ruined Carl's birthday, humiliated me, snapped at Sammy, and embarrassed everyone. She's acting like a crazy person and all because I got drunk and she read a few emails? There must be more to it than that. I don't buy it. On impulse, I turn right and stride off up the road. Fast walking always helps me think, but this time it's not working. Before long, I hear my name being called out, and I turn to see Justin running up the road with Noah in his arms, grinning at being jiggled up and down so hard.

'Wait, Jon. Hang on.'

I wait for him, trying to calm down for Noah's sake.

'Where are you going?' he asks.

'I don't know.' I start walking again, slower this time. My office is this way, so maybe, subconsciously, I was heading there, even though it's a good forty-minute walk or more.

Justin puts Noah down and he grabs both our hands. 'Swing me,' he begs. We swing him, and he giggles.

'Well, I might as well do some work. That's if Noah will let me.'

'Mind if I come along? We can talk if you like, or I can take Noah off somewhere and amuse him for the afternoon, so you can get some work done.'

'What about Carl's party?'

'It's okay. He's itching for a chance to disappear with his mates, and I think he's just found it.'

Suddenly, a wave of despair crashes over me. Talking would be good. I can't talk to Mel anymore. The only other person I could think of is Steve Jackson, but I don't know him anywhere near well enough to tell him about my infidelity. Or *shagging around*, as Mel refers to it.

'Okay. Sounds good to me. I'm sorry about her ruining the party.' We lift Noah into the air again, swinging him forward, then setting him back on the ground.

'I'm sure Carl will get over it. He didn't want a family party anyway, he said. He wanted to go out with his friends instead, but Pam insisted. I didn't want to make him. He's not a little kid, and he hates it when she treats him like one. To be honest, I think she thought it'd do you and Mel good.'

'You're fu— bloody joking, aren't you? I don't think either of us are up to family gatherings, pretending everything's like it was before Issy died. It's the last thing we need.'

Swing. Forward. Back. Down. Giggle. 'Fuh. Bloody,' Noah says. I ignore it.

It starts to spot with rain and before long, we're dashing to the office, down side streets and past shops, pubs, the library (now boarded up), and into the small business park

217

where I rent my office space. The rain's beating down on us when we get there and I'm carrying Noah.

We burst into the small space, dripping wet and cold. None of us has a coat.

'I'll put the heating on. It's chilly in here.'

Justin looks around the office, noting the mess strewn across my desk.

'Good filing system. Organised.' He raises an eyebrow. 'It didn't look like this last time I came here. What happened?'

Might as well tell him. 'Well, since Issy and everything, I've got a bit behind. It's one of the reasons Mel's mad at me. She saw some messages from customers complaining their jobs hadn't been done.'

'Ah. Um, is he alright doing that?'

I turn to see Noah has opened one of the drawers in my desk and is now pulling things out.

'No. Noah, stop it! That's Grandad's work stuff.'

With a sigh, he shuts the drawer and hoists himself up in to my chair, swinging his dangling legs. His shoulders slump and he sighs again. 'I'm bored.'

He pouts and pulls the corners of his mouth down. He looks so like Issy I have to look away as my chest tightens. There's nothing here for him to do. Justin shouldn't have brought him. I turn on my computer and search for toddler games on the internet. In just a few minutes, he's happily playing one.

When I turn around, Justin's making coffee. He passes me mine and we go to stand by the window, which gives us a whole three feet of space from Noah in which to talk.

'That other thing,' he whispers. 'What was that all about?'

He's talking about the affair. I could kill Mel for blurting that out. I'm thinking of what to say when he asks if it's true. *No point lying.* I nod.

'When?' He looks surprised.

'Just before Issy got pregnant.'

'Really? Who with? Anyone I know?'

'No. Someone from way back. You don't know her.'

He takes a breath in then blows it out, pulling a disbelieving face. 'How come you never told me? You're turning into a right dark horse.'

'It's not the sort of thing you go blabbing about, is it?' I hiss, checking to see if Noah can hear us. He's engrossed in his game, with that look of total brain-washing that kids get around computer games.

'No, s'pose not. How did Mel find out?'

'Adele got her number off my phone, texted her, and told her everything when I tried to end it—after Issy dropped her pregnancy bombshell.'

'Adele. Mmm.' Justin sips some coffee and gazes out of the window at the view of the dumpit site at the back. He shakes his head as if trying to process the information.

'Have you ever been tempted?' I ask, suddenly curious. He's not a bad-looking bloke, I suppose, if you like that friendly, clumsy giant sort of thing.

He shakes his head. 'Pam would chop my knackers off for sure. It's not worth the risk. I've had offers, yeah, but I never acted on it. So what was it like?'

'Sleeping with someone else? What can I say? Exciting, amazing, it made me feel alive? All of those things. I was really going to leave Mel for her, but then... back to reality. Mel's never going to forgive me, you know. She dredges it up all the time, picks at it like a scab, and uses it as a stick to beat me with.'

'From how you just described it, maybe this Adele was worth it, mate.'

'Maybe she was. Sometimes I think we should split up, anyway. I should just go.'

Justin looks gob-smacked. 'Really? Would you, though? Just go?'

'Maybe.' I shrug, looking out of the window. It's stopped raining now, leaving everything coated in a damp, grey film. 'I don't know. I can't stop thinking she might do something stupid. You remember when she got depression before, when Issy was pregnant?'

'Yeah. What about it?'

'The pregnancy wasn't the reason. It was then that she found out about Adele.'

It feels better than I thought it would, unburdening myself like this, and I find I like talking about Adele. I miss her more than I've admitted to myself. Plus, he's a good mate and a good listener, and never judgmental.

'Done it, Grandad, finished.' Noah scoots down from the chair and grabs my hand, pulling me over to the desk. He's right; he has done it. He's finished the game; all twelve levels. He's somehow worked them out by himself.

'The little feller's a genius,' says Justin, over my shoulder.

'A regular Einstein. Hey, Noah, well done, mate. High five.'

We slap hands, and Noah scoots back up into the chair.

'Another game, please.'

'How about we leave Grandad in peace to get some work done? Are you hungry? We could get pizza or ice cream or something,' Justin says.

'Burger. Can I have a burger? With ketsup?'

Justin looks at me. 'Can he?'

'Course. And thanks, Justin. For everything.'

'I'll bring him round to yours later.'

'Okay. I'll have to stay here and get some work done. Mend some bridges.'

'If you need to talk, you know where I am.'

'You've been watching too many slushy films. We're men, remember?' I say, trying to sound happier than I feel. 'We don't talk about our feelings.'

'Course, yeah. How stupid of me. Maybe see you later, then.'

'Okay.'

I watch him as he leaves. I wish I had his life. Good job (if not probably boring), sane wife (if not somewhat bossy), nice kids (still alive). I rest my head on the desk and close my eyes. I don't know if all this mess this can be sorted out. But Mel's right about one thing. If my business goes under, how will that help? I fought for this business and I'm damn well going to keep it. I sit down and start to do some work.

30

Mel

AFTER JON STORMS OUT of the party, everyone gawps at me. I vaguely register Justin grabbing Noah and shooting off after him. I can feel the heat in my cheeks warming my face. Pam's mouth is opening and closing rapidly like a fish. It would be funny, but there's no way to unsay what I've just said. Jon will kill me. He'll never forgive me. But so what? Why should I keep his dirty little secret? I wasn't the one who did wrong. But I shouldn't have blurted it out in front of everyone like that. A sob bursts from me and I run into the house, away from the puzzled stares on the boys' faces. Pam follows, and catches up with me as I'm trying to wrench open the front door. She puts her hand on my shoulder and spins me round.

'Mel? What you just said...'

Hot tears are spilling down my face and I can't speak.

'Is it true?'

I nod. She glances back towards the kitchen. Through the window, we can see the boys huddled together, obviously discussing what just happened. Poor Carl; what a birthday, and all thanks to me and my big mouth. Pam pulls me into the front room and closes the door behind us.

'When?'

I swipe my hand over my eyes and only succeed in smearing the wet all over. I can hardly get the words out.

'Before Noah was born. Jon was shagging some woman he went to school with.'

'Really? But why didn't you tell me?'

'I don't know. I was embarrassed... he was repentant. What was the point?'

She looks upset at the thought I kept something this big from her; more upset at that than what I've just told her Jon did to me. It's ridiculous how she carries on sometimes, her and her stupid, perfect life. A mean, spiteful spark has ignited in me and it's going to be hard to stop it. I'm consumed with the thought that Noah is Sammy's. I can't shake it off. If he is, would Pam know? Would she go to any lengths to protect him? After how I've behaved today, to even bring it up could do irreparable damage, but I need to know. But she's still harping on about Jon's floozy.

'Did you know her?'

'What? Oh, no. I've seen her on Facebook. Jon keeps tabs on her, or he did. I don't know if he still does. Anyway, it's not important. I just said it because I was mad at him. I'm supposed to be *over* it.'

'I noticed things weren't exactly peachy when you arrived. What else is wrong?'

'He was supposed to be working the other day, and I came home to find him drunk on whisky on the sofa. In the middle of the day. We had a big row about it, and he reminded me that he had to pick me up drunk from the pub not long ago when I'd been drinking with Greg. Anyway, we weren't speaking when we got here. We haven't spoken for about three days. He's been sleeping in the attic room for ages now and letting his work slide, and I'm constantly worrying about money. So is he, to be fair.'

'Why was he drunk in the middle of the day?'

I think for a bit. 'I don't know. He didn't say.'

She's quiet for a minute. I want to ask her about Sammy. I *need* to ask her about him. The words are practically burning my mouth to get out.

'Do you think Sammy could be Noah's father?'

She turns white right before my eyes. 'What?' she whispers. She's totally horrified. 'Sammy? Are you mad?' She recoils from me. 'You can't really think that, can you? Is that why you were horrible to him earlier?'

I stare her down. 'He could be. They were thick as thieves around that time. She adored him, you know she did.'

'He would never... ever... have touched her in *that* way. Have you gone completely mad?' Her voice is white hot with fury.

'What if he did?'

'I think you'd better leave.'

'Think about it. Who says I'm not right?'

'Mel, just go. I won't have you here in my house, spitting venom and bile about my son. I'm sorry for what you've been through, you know I am, but *this* is NOT on.' She narrows her eyes and folds her arms, her body rigid. I can see her trembling with anger as I stand up.

'I want him to take a DNA test,' I say as I brush past her.

I turn round before I open the front door and meet her eyes. She's looking at me like I'm the enemy. A niggling voice starts up at the back of my mind. What if I'm wrong? Before it can take hold, I slam out of there and hurry around the corner back home, dashing through the rain that's pelting down. Maybe Jon will be there. My heart skitters at the thought of facing him.

When I get home the front door is locked and the house is empty. Thank God! I flop down on the sofa and grief engulfs me like a tidal wave, knocking the breath out of me. All I want to do is see my daughter, touch her, smell her. But she's gone, and she's not coming back. Something inside me splinters open and haemorrhages. Something that can't be put back together. I need to be close to her, my Issy. Upstairs, her bedroom awaits, and I climb into her bed. I washed the bedding when she went back to uni at Easter, and she wasn't in the house for even one night in the summer. Nothing in the room smells of her. The grief now seems worse than when she first died.

The pills. I can make the hurt stop for good and be with Issy. I throw back the covers and collect the pills from the various places I've hidden them around the house. Places Jon wouldn't think to look. Like under the bag in the cereal he doesn't like and behind the icing sugar box that rarely comes out of the cupboard. I gather them all up and take them upstairs with a glass of water, back to her bedroom. I'm numb as I climb into her bed and tip the pills onto the duvet. There're loads. More than enough to do the job. If I do this, I need to be sure it's for good. I need to take enough. I sort them into piles of ten with trembling hands, dropping them as they slip through my fingers. Seven piles of ten and four strays.

The house is silent around me, apart from the ticking of the clock on the windowsill on the landing. Calm and rhythmic, slow and steady. I pick up the first pill, then put it down, then pick it up again. I listen for Issy, to see if I can hear her in the room. Is there any trace of her here? No. What did I expect? I put the pill on my tongue and wash it down with water, then pick up a second.

31

Pam

WHEN JUSTIN RETURNS, NOAH is with him. Pam hears him shouting as they come up the stairs and into the bedroom, looking for her. She sits up on the bed and rubs her eyes as Justin opens the door. Noah runs in. A wave of nausea engulfs her. She's not sure she can do this now, be with Noah.

Justin stands in the doorway. 'Has Mel gone home?'

Pam nods. 'What's Noah doing here?'

Justin looks surprised at her harsh tone. 'Jon had some work to do at the office. He's snowed under. I said I'd bring Noah back and take him home if Mel wasn't here.'

Pam bites her lip. She's dying to tell Justin what Mel said but can't in front of Noah. She blinks back the tears that are threatening to spill out.

'What's the matter?' He sits next to her on the bed.

'Can I play outside?' Noah asks.

Pam sits up, looking at the child. It's a ridiculous notion that Sammy could be his father. If it was true, then Noah would be her... grandson.

'Yes. Go find Joey and ask him to read you a story or something. Tell him I said.'

'Love? You look awful. What is it?'

Pam waits until Noah's gone, sighing at her husband's propensity to say the wrong thing. She knows she looks awful; he doesn't have to tell her. The fact that she's done nothing but cry since Mel left has made sure of it.

'I can't believe what happened when you left. It's just too awful,' she says, sniffing.

'Tell me.' He takes her hand and squeezes it.

'I can't believe what she said. She started talking about Noah's father. She thinks she knows who it is.'

He's speechless. Then, 'Who?'

'Sammy!' she blurts out with a sob. 'She thinks it's our Sammy.'

Justin goes pale, and his mouth opens and closes several times. Finally, he says, 'I don't understand. Why would she think that?'

'I don't know. We had a massive row. It was horrible. She said some awful things. I really think she's gone insane.'

Justin sits forward and put his head in his hands. 'This just gets worse. This whole thing is just one bloody great big mess. Damn Issy!'

Pam is shocked by his outburst. 'Justin! The girl's dead!'

'Yes,' he snaps. 'And look at the state everyone's in. The bloody stupid girl! I know, it sounds awful, but what she did is ripping our family to bits, Pam. And there's nothing we can do about it.'

Pam is silent. He's right. Just a few weeks ago, everything was great and now… But it sounds so bad to say it out loud. She's even been thinking lately that Issy was just a stupid little slut, an attention seeker that did the biggest thing anyone can possibly do for attention. The first time she thought it, she hated herself, but what if she's right?

'What did Jon say, anyway?' she asks.

'About what?'

'I don't know. The affair? Whatever it is they've been up to that they won't tell us? We have a right to know, if they're going to go round blaming our family.'

'He said he had an affair with some woman he knew from school. He used to go out with her.'

'What a bastard!'

'Don't judge people, Pam,' he says, sharply. 'You don't know what goes on in someone else's marriage, really, do you?'

She looks startled. 'No, I suppose not, but...' She tails off. 'Anyway, what happens now? Mel says she wants Sammy to do a DNA test.'

'Oh, Christ! This just gets worse. Sammy's not Noah's dad. She's bloody mad alright.'

'I know. He's not doing any test, anyway. We know our own son. He wouldn't sleep with his own cousin. It's disgusting.'

Justin gets up from the bed. 'So, what do we do with Noah? Do I take him back home or keep him here? I don't even know if Jon's going home today. It didn't look like it.'

'He should go home. He's not our responsibility is he, really? Maybe we've done enough to help. If she's going to throw it back in our faces, then why should we?'

'It's not the kid's fault, love. He's been through enough.' He puffs out his cheeks. 'I'll take Noah back in the morning. He'll be okay here tonight. Give Mel a chance to calm down. She'll see reason when she's had time to think about it. You see, she'll be round here apologising before you know it.'

32

Jon

A BLOOM OF SWEAT trickles down the centre of my back as I stand across the street from the bank in the middle of Harrogate where she works, leaning against a wall, waiting for her to come out. Christ knows what sort of reception I'll get when she sees me. Fireworks? Cold shoulder? Knowing her, it could be either. Maybe she'll fly at me, try to gouge out my eyes. It's not like I don't deserve it. My heart is trying to thud out of my chest with nerves. I'm about to find out.

At five-thirty prompt I see her, and the slam in my guts almost has me doubled over. She leaves by the main door of the old brick building, descends the five stone steps and places an unlit cigarette in her mouth. She cups her hands around it as she lights the end. When did she start smoking again? Her blonde hair holds no traces of grey and swirls back from her face somehow. She still looks younger than her forty years. She hasn't spotted me yet and I shift my weight from one foot to the other. It's now or never. I push myself away from the wall. All I have to do is put one foot in front of the other, yet it's like learning to walk all over again. It takes a while to get the hang of it.

As I cross the street towards her, she glances up, sees me. Looks away then straight back, like it hadn't quite sunk in the first time. Her expression is neither welcoming nor hostile.

229

Almost as if, even after all this time, she's been expecting me to just turn up one day.

'Adele...' I begin. I don't know what else to say.

She doesn't speak but leaves me to fill in the blanks. Her eyes travel the length of me, appraisingly, and she takes a long pull on her cigarette, blowing the smoke out of one side of her mouth, away from me. It should be unattractive, but it's not.

'Well, well, well,' she says. 'Isn't this a turn up for the books?' Her voice is devoid of emotion.

'It's good to see you,' I say, haltingly. She's not giving anything away.

'Is it?' She turns and begins to walk away from me. The cold shoulder, then. I can't help but watch her hips sway in her tight black skirt as she clips down the street in high heels with her head high. She must know I'm watching. She tosses her head back and quickens her pace, and I have to hurry to catch up with her.

'Can we talk, just for a minute?'

'What for?' In her voice I hear the hurt, and I'm sorry for what I put her through. She loved me and wanted a future with me, and I dropped her and cut all contact. Why shouldn't she hate me? She has every right.

'Please. Just for a minute.'

'No.'

She turns the corner and heads for the small car park at the rear, fishing her car keys out of her pocket, walking faster still. Stopping next to a white BMW, she points the remote at it and the lights flash. The doors unlock with a thunk. I can feel my chance slipping away. I can't let it, and I rush to get between her and the car as she reaches out for the handle.

'I'm sorry. For what I did to you. It was a mistake, I know that. I'm sorry I hurt you.'

She stops and some of the tension in her shoulders goes. Finally, she looks at me. Her eyes are hard.

'Okay. You're sorry. Bye then.' But her voice is softer.

I point at a coffee shop across the road. 'Have you time for a coffee? Please. It's important.'

She hesitates. The air between us is thick, with anticipation or hostility I can't tell. Her eyes flit around, settling everywhere but on me. I'm still not sure I haven't screwed up here big time.

'What's made you turn up out of the blue after all this time? Quite the bad penny, aren't you? Or has wifey kicked you out?'

I remember she used to call Mel *wifey* when we were together. It somehow made Mel sound small and insignificant. It was her way of coping, I think, with the fact that she had to share me. For a moment, I scrutinise her face. She is still beautiful. The tiny lines around her eyes and mouth don't detract from her looks. Not one bit. I want to touch her, hold her hand, but I don't dare. It occurs to me that she might not know about Issy. She lives and works here in Harrogate, and was never one for reading the papers or watching the local news. Also, she hadn't kept in touch with many people from school and had gone to the reunion on her own, as I recall, just out of curiosity, she said. She takes another pull on the cigarette, drops it on the floor and grinds it out, then reaches past me for the door handle, just inches away from me.

'Bye, Jon.'

'Issy's dead,' I blurt out.

She stops, then blinks twice. A third time. It's a reaction I've become familiar with. I give her a little time to process what I've said. Slowly, her eyes sweep up to search mine and her hand covers her mouth.

'God. Really?' she whispers. 'I... I'm sorry, Jon. Really sorry. How? Was she ill?'

I shake my head. 'Suicide.' The word is cold, hard and short and never any less shocking, no matter how many times I say it.

Adele is stunned, and her hands grasp mine. 'Oh my God! When?'

'Two months ago.' To my horror, my face crumples and I begin to sob, right there in the car park, then somehow we're in her car, driving out of town. Her hand goes back to mine after every gear change and all I can do is sit there with my eyes tightly shut, tears streaming from under the lids. I'm in a million shattered pieces. She kills the engine, and I realise we're outside her house.

'Come inside,' she says and I nod, fumble with my seat belt and climb out.

Inside, everything is as I remember it and I go to sit on her sofa, stumbling over the rug in front of it. She's beside me in a second, helping me off with my jacket and pulling me against her.

'You poor thing. I'm so sorry,' she murmurs over and over, rocking me gently, as if I'm a child. And it feels good, it feels like home. My bruised and battered heart bursts open.

Eventually, I can speak and I tell her the full story, everything that's happened so far. She listens carefully, her own tears sliding down and mingling with mine, on the backs of our hands. She still cares. It feels like a revelation, not to have to be the strong one, like I have to be for Mel.

Mel. I haven't seen her since the barbeque three days ago. I've been sleeping in the office on the sofa in the corner. It's uncomfortable and cold, and I hate it, but at least there's no one there to nag me constantly. I haven't seen Noah or talked to either of them. I've missed him, but I'm still so mad at Mel for her outburst. She hasn't rung me, and I don't know where we go from here. My life's gone totally to shit. We're at a standstill on finding out who Noah's father is and why Issy killed herself. Steve Jackson's told me he'll help all he can but that, without direction, we're stuck.

Adele falteringly asks about Mel and I deflect questions. I've told her everything else, but I can't tell her whether my marriage is over because I don't know myself. Part of me thinks Issy was the glue holding us together after my affair and now she's gone, what's to stay for?

When she gets up to make coffee, I go with her, wanting to be near her, and watch her move around her neat kitchen, standing with my back against the worktop. She moves with the same lithe grace that so captivated me before. I used to lie in her bed, watching her shower and dress, never tiring of the sight. Right this minute, I'm not sure what I'm doing here, but I never want to leave. After a deep breath in, I pluck up the courage to speak to her about the past.

'Adele, I'm so sorry for what I did to you. I know I hurt you, and I've no right to expect you to forgive me. I'm so sorry.'

Adele stops stirring the coffee. She probably can't see past how I let her down. I watch as she rubs her hand over her face and the tiredness is evident. She looks older, if that's possible, than she did just a few hours ago. Outside her window, it's getting dark fast, and the last rays of the sun cast a golden glow on the floor at her feet.

'Look, I don't know what you want me to say, Jon. I... I know I shouldn't have texted Mel like that but I was devastated. There I was, planning a life with you, and suddenly you didn't want to know. I thought it was a joke at first, but you cut me dead. I tried so many times to contact you, but you ignored my every attempt. It hurt, Jon, like I can't even describe. It still does. I loved you so much...'

'I'm sorry,' I whisper. In trying to do the right thing for my family, I'd destroyed the very thing I'd loved, along with my hope and happiness for the future. She picks up the cups and comes to stand beside me again, putting mine down next to me. The certainty that I still love her strikes quick and deep, and makes me catch my breath. Just as I go to pick up my cup, my hand shakes violently.

'What?' she says.

'Nothing, I'm just sorry, that's all. I wish I'd carried on with our plans and left, despite Issy telling us she was pregnant. It made no difference in the long run.'

Adele gives a tight nod. 'Thank you. It means a lot to hear you admit that.'

'So... is there anyone special in your life now?'

She sniffs. 'Not at the moment, no. There've been a couple of failed attempts at relationships but they didn't amount to much. The problem, you see, was that they weren't you.'

Her voice is small, and she looks at the floor. I don't trust myself to speak, so I just hold her. It feels like we should fall into each other's arms and kiss and end up in bed together, but we do none of those things. It's as if we both know that if we cross that line, there's no coming back. We sit together on the sofa as the sun sinks away and the shadows lengthen, until we're in darkness. Eventually, she breaks the silence.

'So what do you want to do? Next.'

I have to be honest here so I say, 'I don't know. I'm so lost.'

33

Mel

I HATE THE BASTARD! He stormed out of my sister's house days ago and hasn't been seen since. He's left me to look after Noah without a second thought. If it hadn't been for Mum jumping in to fill the breach, I wouldn't have been able to go to work. I can't believe he's left me high and dry. Or, rather, I can. It's typical of him, thinking only of himself.

My sister isn't speaking to me either, since I suggested Sammy might be Noah's father. After getting home from her barbeque and getting the pills out, a surge of rage made me flush them all away, and I got up from the bed with a new resolve, stronger and clearer. I'm not going to let myself be beaten down by this. No way! I'll stay and fight for justice for my daughter. I just needed a plan of action, a direction in which to point myself, and now I've got one. When Justin brought Noah back the morning after the barbeque, I'd shut the door in his face after letting Noah inside. He'd knocked on the door, wanting to talk, but I'd told him to go away. He'd only have told me how miserable I'm making my sister. Well, what about how miserable Issy must have been? That's what's important now.

In her session with Kim, Issy had implied that she may have been coerced. If we can find Noah's father, he is the key to finding out why she killed herself. I know it. And I also know that I think it is Sammy. I just need to prove it, so I need his DNA. When it's proved he's Noah's father, we can tell the police he raped her, and they can arrest him and find out what else he knows.

A few minutes ago, I called Pam's house, and no one answered. I'm on my way round there now. Once again, Mum's got Noah. She thinks I'm on the verge of some breakdown and so has offered to take him anytime to give me a break. I know she's worried about me; she keeps trying to find out what's going on with me, but I can't tell her what I'm going to do. Sammy's her grandson, after all, and she thinks the world of him. She doesn't believe me, anyway. She thinks I'm losing my mind. Maybe she's right, but I'll die trying to work this out, if it comes to it. The need to know why my daughter did what she did is burning me up, eating me away inside, consuming everything I am. An obsession, some would say. Well, so be it.

Outside Pam's house, I stop and look up at the windows, but all I can see are reflections from across the street in the glass. All is quiet and still. To make doubly sure, I ring the bell and wait. Nothing. After a suitable interval, I take out the key I've always had to hers and open the door. If there is anyone inside, I'll just say I'm looking for Pam. But it's empty. I step inside and stand there for a while, just listening. It's strange being in someone else's house when they're not there. Pipes creak, taps drip, wood and metal expand. It's as though the house is a living, breathing thing, an entity of its own.

Upstairs, I turn the handle to Sammy's room. I hope Pam hasn't washed his bedding, as I need some of his hair. Pulling back the duvet, I'm dismayed to see the pillow is clean and smells freshly laundered. Pam has a thing about washing bedding every few days, claiming it harbours more germs than toilet seats, which I find hard to believe. I pull the duvet back the whole way to check the bottom sheet but, again, there's nothing. When I reach across to check the gap between the bed and the wall, the mattress slews to one side under my knee. I can see the carpet through the wooden-slatted base. There's a line of hair and dust where the carpet and skirting board meet. Bingo! It seems my perfect sister has flaws in her housekeeping, after all. I reach down through the slats, but they're too narrow to get my fingers through, and I have to pull the mattress off to get my hand down the side. I grab a few stray hairs between my finger and thumb and place them into the plastic bag I've brought to put them in.

When I twist my hand to get it back through the gap, I dislodge something hard and bulky on the underside of one of the slats. Something is there, loosely taped to the wood, and it's now hanging off. I grab and pull it. It's a phone, the masking tape around it curled and dry. Why would Sammy conceal a phone under his bed? I turn it over in my hand. It looks small and old. I shove it in my bag and get up from the floor. It takes a few seconds to put his bed back together and a minute later I'm back in my car, adrenalin-fuelled and speeding away.

My next stop is the police station to see Steve Jackson. The policeman at reception, who repeatedly asks me to keep my voice down, tells me Jackson is in. I stand, waiting, hopping from foot to foot, and gripping the plastic bag with the hair in tightly.

'Mel?' He rises from his chair when I'm shown in by the officer from reception, who's obviously pleased to have me off his hands. He closes the door firmly behind him as he leaves.

'I need a DNA test on this hair. To see if it belongs to Noah's father,' I demand, thrusting the plastic bag across the desk at him. He gestures for me to take the chair opposite him, which I do.

He picks it up with a puzzled frown. 'May I ask who it belongs to?'

'Do I have to say?'

'You do, really, yes. Why? Is it a secret?'

'Okay, it belongs to my nephew, Sammy.'

'And what makes you suspect him of being Noah's dad?' He peers at the strands of hair inside the bag.

What evidence do I actually have? Just a hunch? I'll sound like some flake if I say that. Yet, don't detectives act on hunches and gut instinct all the time?

'I just know,' I mumble.

Steve sighs. I bet if it were Jon asking, he'd help like a shot.

'So, will you test it for me?' I sound like a sullen child, ungrateful and petulant. Does he know Jon's left? Suddenly all the fight goes out of me and I deflate, like a pricked balloon. My shoulders slump and I'm fighting back tears.

Steve gets out of his chair and comes to sit on the desk in front of me. 'Hey,' he says softly, placing his hand gently on my shoulder. 'What's this really about, eh?'

I end up telling him everything, other than the fact I just broke into my sister's house. I tell him about the row at the party with a small stab of satisfaction at the realisation he didn't know any of it. So he hasn't seen Jon then, and Jon never confided in him about his affair. He folds his arms and looks deep in thought, and I get the feeling he's about to impart bad news. He picks up the plastic bag, peering through it.

'This is no good for a DNA test. There are no follicles on the ends. This looks like it's been shed or cut. We usually take an oral swab for a paternity test. Could you get one of those?'

'Of course not. It was hard enough getting that. I can't take a swab of the inside of his mouth and expect him not to notice,' I snap.

'You say you've already upset your sister. Maybe you could get him to do one voluntarily, to rule himself out, if he's not the real dad,' Steve suggests.

The more I think about it, though, the more it seems a possibility. If he's not Noah's father, why shouldn't he do it voluntarily? It'll mean another showdown with Pam, but it can't make things any worse than they already are.

'Alright,' I tell Steve. 'I'll get a cheek swab. And we'll take it from there. If he raped my daughter, we'll find out, won't we?'

'Mmm,' he says. I don't think he believes me deep down. 'Is there anything else, Mel?'

I hesitate. I can't think of a way to tell him about the phone without revealing how I got it.

'No,' I say. 'There's nothing else.'

34

Jon

I'M WORKING THROUGH MY lunch hour when the door flies open and I look up to see a very irate Pam standing there. She looks like she wants to kill me, and my hackles go up straight away. I don't need this right now.

'What?' My phone rings on the desk beside me. I glance at it. It's Adele. I let it go to voicemail.

'What the hell do you think you're playing at? It's easier to find the bloody Scarlet Pimpernel.' Her scowl has pulled her brow way down over her eyes. 'Why aren't you answering your phone? We've rung you so many times.' She's still holding the door handle, her knuckles white but her face is a vivid puce.

So, after a week of ignoring phone calls from her and Justin, she's finally come round in person. She advances into the room like a belligerent bull.

'You can't just cast off your responsibilities where your family is concerned, you know. Mum's had to step in to help Mel with Noah. She can't keep doing it indefinitely. She's not well.'

I shrug.

'And where were you this morning? I came here at half seven. Mel said you were probably sleeping here. You weren't here this morning, though.'

I don't care for her tone of voice. I can make this easy for her or I can make it hard. 'Yeah? So? What's it got to do with you?'

I stare at her and her shoulders slump as some of the fight goes out of her. I flip my pen nonchalantly over the back of my hand, over my knuckles, from one end to the other, then back again. My phone beeps to tell me the caller left a message.

'May I sit down?' Her voice softens, as does her face.

I gesture loosely with the pen at the chair opposite mine and she sinks down into it.

'Everyone's going frantic. Mel's not speaking to me, I'm not speaking to her, you two aren't speaking to each other. We need to sort this out, one way or another, if not just to sort out things for Noah.' My silence forces her to continue. 'Do you know what happened at the party after you'd gone?'

I do actually. Justin texted me that night and told me. I didn't respond to the text. As a concept, I thought it was interesting. I say nothing now.

'She accused Sammy of being Noah's dad! Have you ever heard anything that stupid in your life?'

I just shrug again, and keep a deadpan expression. I don't think Sammy is responsible, but I'll keep that to myself for now. The reason I wasn't here this morning was because I was at Adele's. I've stayed there three times now, each time sleeping on the sofa. Last night, she went to bed and came back down in her dressing gown. She stretched out beside me on the sofa and just held me all night. It was uncomfortable in such a confined space, but the fact is, she was there for me. We haven't had sex. Truth is, I'm not sure I could manage it. It wouldn't seem right to be shagging anyone, not while Issy's body has been burned to a crisp, and I'm no nearer to finding any answers. Having your only child take her own life is a real passion killer. I also can't forget the photos of Issy on her phone. Adele seems to understand and accept this. I'm daring to hope she's forgiven me; she's been nothing but supportive, and I don't think I deserve her.

241

Pam's voice cuts into my thoughts. 'Are you even listening to me? Help me out here, Jon. Whatever you did or didn't do, I don't care. I'm not here to judge. I only want to work out what we do next. For all our sakes.'

That's very magnanimous of her. 'Well, I'm very grateful for your non-judgement, but what I did or didn't do is none of your business. So I don't need your forgiveness or understanding, as it happens.'

Two pink spots appear high on her cheeks. 'Look, I didn't mean it like that. We have a very real problem here. Noah doesn't understand what's going on—'

'Why does Mel think Sammy is Noah's dad?'

'I don't really know. We argued before she could explain. I told her to go, and now we're not speaking so I can't ask her.' She chews her bottom lip. 'You don't think he is, do you?'

I don't speak at first. She wriggles like a worm on a hook under my stare.

'My feeling is that he isn't.'

Her face sags in relief. 'Oh, thank God. I haven't told Sammy what she's been saying about him, so he doesn't know yet, but I'm terrified she's going to confront him. He'd be devastated. You know he thought the world of Issy, but not in that way. They were like brother and sister.'

'I'm not sure what you want me to do about it, Pam. Mel's her own woman. Plus, truth is, things have been shit between us for years. You might as well know. I'm not sure there's a way back for us.'

It sounds shocking when I say it aloud, but now it's out in the open, it seems obvious. Too much has happened, and Mel can't or won't forgive. I can't spend the rest of my life apologising, and now I've seen Adele again I don't think the affair was a mistake. If I had a life with her, perhaps things would be easier, better, and I would be happier.

'I want us all to get together and talk it through in a civilised way. Mel can ask Sammy outright. I can't believe I'm saying this, but it may be the best way. He can take a DNA test to prove it. Plus, Justin wants to see you. He misses you. If you won't see all of us, would you maybe just meet him? He says you don't answer his calls either.'

'I'll think about it,' I tell her, knowing I will meet him. I could do with the ear of my best mate. To tell the truth, I'm sick of things in my head going round and round and nothing resolving itself. I haven't really been ignoring him. I just needed space and some time to sort myself out.

There's a knock on the open door, then Adele appears.

'You left this at mine this morning...' Adele tails off, holding up the sandwich she made for me after breakfast. 'Oh, sorry, I didn't realise you had a client.'

Pam's eyes glide from her back to me. Her eyes widen, then narrow slightly. She suspects who it is.

'I'm not a client,' she snaps. 'Well, I'll have to go. I'll talk to you later, Jon.'

Then she hurries out of the office, her heels echoing crisply on the tiled floor.

Adele turns to watch her go, then hovers uncertainly in the doorway. 'Sorry. Was that bad timing? I phoned to say I was here, but you didn't answer. Perhaps I shouldn't have come.'

I stand up and walk out from behind the desk. 'Don't be daft. I'm glad you came. Come here.'

She looks relieved and smiles as I gather her into my arms, breathe in the smell of her and kiss her properly, to see how it feels. It feels good. She seems surprised but pleased and moves closer to me. We fit together perfectly. I kiss her again, for longer this time and my nerve-endings are sparking like mad. I don't want to ever let her go. Eventually, she breaks off, breathless.

'Wow,' she says. 'That was nice.'

'Shall we go for some lunch?' I ask, holding up the limp sandwich in its plastic bag. 'We can do better than this.'

'Really? That'd be great. I've got this afternoon off. I didn't feel well earlier, thought I had a migraine coming on, so I said I was going home, but it's much better now. They

243

don't need to know that, though, do they? I thought I'd surprise you and drive over here.'

I pull her into me and kiss her again, long and hard, running my fingers through her beautiful hair. She looks ruffled and sexy when I let her go.

'Wow!' she says. 'I might do this more often.'

I take her hand as we leave the office, not caring if anyone sees us. I know the jungle drums will be beating now when Pam gets started. If she and Mel aren't speaking though, she can't go running to her, so it may be a while longer until the shit hits the fan. And I just don't care anymore.

35

Mel

MAYBE THIS IS A mistake. Pam rang me and begged me to come round, so here we are, around Pam's kitchen table. But with Pam and Sammy on one side and me on the other, it's more like me on trial, facing the firing squad. Olivia's got Noah; God knows how she's coping, but she seemed keen enough and he was happy to go with her. She promised him they could do some dancing. He's also got his Game Boy as a backup. I feel so bad that he's being pushed from pillar to post lately, but it was too much of a risk that he might overhear something if I brought him, and I didn't want to ask Mum again. She's exhausted, and Elaine, the childminder, is on holiday. I don't know if Jon is coming and I haven't asked. So for now, it's them against me.

Sammy is lolling back in his chair as if he hasn't got a spine, with his legs spread wide and his feet planted firmly on the floor. His arms are folded tightly over his body and he's looking at me mutinously. So he already knows then. A pack of cigarettes is on the table next to him and he picks them up, peeling off the cellophane. 'So, Mum told me what you think. That I'm Noah's dad. That's fucking disgusting! And sick!'

He shakes his head and looks off to the side, and I'm unsettled to see his eyes glisten. Have I made a terrible mistake here? He looks so hurt. He pulls his knees in and sits up straighter. Just then, the door opens and we all turn to see

Jon coming in. He looks about as happy to be here as I am. He avoids my eye as he takes the seat next to me. I notice he hasn't shaved lately. Not surprising, if he's sleeping at the office.

'Have I missed anything good?' His sarcastic tone is not lost on me. He looks pointedly at his watch. 'I'm up to my ears in it.'

'Just the fact I've been accused of kiddie-fiddling. Nothing major, you know.' Sammy spits out the words and throws his arms in my direction.

I've never seen him like this. But then, I've never accused him of getting my daughter pregnant either. From the corner of my eye, I see Jon shake his head.

'Oh, God,' he mumbles.

'Is that what you think, too?' Pam asks him.

'No, you know it isn't. I told you. And I told Justin the same yesterday on the phone. Anyway, where is he? I thought he was going to be here.'

So Jon's talked to Justin then? Can't say I'm surprised. They've probably all been tittle-tattling about me behind my back. So much for family loyalty.

'Some meeting he couldn't get out of. He's back tomorrow,' says Pam.

'Lucky bastard,' mutters Jon, looking off to the side.

'Why do you suspect me, anyway?' Sammy asks. 'What have I done to make you think it's me?'

I swallow hard, hoping my voice doesn't shake. 'I've seen you around Noah. You act more like his dad than his uncle.'

'That's just bollocks.' He pulls a cigarette out of the pack and clamps it between his lips, then removes it, glancing at his mother. I notice his hand tremble.

It sounds lame now the words are finally out there, and I wonder again if I've got this hideously wrong. It could be grief and depression clouding things. But I have to stick with it now. 'If you want to prove it's not you, take a DNA test. That'll sort it out, one way or another.'

'Right, I will then. What do I have to do?' Sammy glares at me.

I open my bag, pull out the DNA testing kit I bought online, and place it on the table between us. 'Go on then.'

Sammy glances at his mother and opens the test, fumbling with the seal on the packaging. The test is fairly simple, by all accounts. Swab cheek, place in bag, seal and send off. Within seconds, it's done, and he's pushing away from the table.

He looks at Pam. 'I'm done with her,' he snaps, not looking at me. 'I'm off out.'

He storms out of the room, and I push my hands under the table so no one can see how unsteady they are. My mouth is dry and I swallow down the knot of tension rising in my chest. It's done now and whatever happens happens. I have to know. If it turns out not to be Sammy, we're back to square one. Now I'm thinking it can't be him, or he would never have agreed to the test. This is such a mess. My head is packed with thoughts tumbling over each other, and I can't make any sense of the confusion. Pam stands and walks over to the door, looking back at me. Then she leaves. It's a bit rich. She begged me to come here and now she's still not speaking.

'What the hell has got into you? Are you intent on upsetting everyone?' Jon asks, twisting round in his chair to look at me.

I stand up. 'How dare you! What about you upsetting me? How come I'm the one raising Issy's kid on my own? You haven't even seen him. He keeps asking for you, and I don't know what to tell him.'

'I'll see him when I sort out somewhere to live. I can't have him at the office, can I? There's no room. It's not a fit place for a kid.'

My knees buckle and I fall back into the chair. So that's it then: confirmation that he's not coming home. 'Somewhere to live?'

He flushes slightly and takes a breath in. 'Well, you don't want me to come back home, do you?'

Don't I? I don't know what I want anymore. He sounded like he'd made up his mind.

'I don't know anything anymore. But I can't cope with Noah on my own.'

'I do want to see Noah, course I do.' His voice softens. 'I want to help look after him.'

We both sit there awkwardly.

'Maybe we can call a truce,' he says.

'How?'

'If I move back in. I can't sleep in that bed in the attic, though. I'd have to sleep in Issy's room.'

'If you move into Issy's room, does this mean it's over for us?' I can't believe I'm saying this, but I have to know what he's thinking. He seems as reluctant to admit it as I do.

He sighs. 'I don't think you're ever going to forgive me, are you? You can't move past it, and I can't change that.'

Something shifts behind his eyes, and I feel the prick of tears. He's right, and he knows it.

'I keep thinking you only stayed with me for Issy and not because you wanted me. Am I right?'

He rubs a hand over his face, the stubble sounding like sandpaper. 'I don't know.'

My heart clenches tight in my chest to hear him actually say it. To me, it's confirmation of what I've always thought. So that's the decision made for me then. He doesn't love me enough. I'll have to work out how I feel about it later. First, we have to work out a solution for Noah. I realise he's still speaking.

'So I'll move my stuff into Issy's room, then. Which means getting rid of some of her things. Or maybe we can store them in the attic for now.'

'We'll get rid of some of it. Not the sentimental stuff, just the practical things, you know. Those bags we sorted before.' The lump in my throat is so hard I can't swallow or breathe properly.

'Okay. Well... I need to get back to work now. I'll move back in tomorrow, shall I?'

I nod, unable to look at him. My husband, who doesn't love me anymore. My marriage and my daughter, both gone. What's left to lose?

36

Jon

ADELE'S FACE HAD FALLEN when I'd told her I was moving back home. We'd just had supper in front of the TV, and her hand, resting lightly on my leg, had tightened its grip.

'When?'

'Tomorrow. It was jointly decided today, at Pam's. But it's only for Noah's sake because Mel can't manage. I promise you. My marriage is over for good. I'll be sleeping in the spare room. Well, Issy's room.'

She looked unconvinced. 'Jon, what's happening between us? I have to know how you feel.'

I leaned toward her, kissed her deeply, and leaped off the cliff edge. 'I want you. I love you.'

'Are you going to tell her about us?'

'I'll have to. But what do *you* want, Adele? Marriage and kids and stuff? Because I don't think I want that, at least, not the kid bit.'

'I don't want kids. You know I never did. I don't want to go back to sneaking around, though, and seeing you in secret, like before. I want us to be a couple.'

'I don't want to sneak around either. But she's so unpredictable lately, I don't want to make things worse. Let me do things in my own time. Trust me.' I kissed her again. I wanted her and, this time, thoughts of Issy didn't make me feel guilty.

'I love you so much,' I whispered. I moved closer to her, and she responded, melting into me as if we were both liquid, flowing and fitting together seamlessly. Minutes later, we were naked on the carpet, and she was pressing her beautiful body against me, and it was as if the end of the world was coming, and we had this one last time together. It felt good and right and not shameful, as though the walls of a vast dam had burst within me, releasing all the pressure that'd built up.

And now, it's time. We've just made love again and I hate to get dressed and go, but I have no choice. At the front door, I kiss her longingly, hating to leave her. With every fibre of my being, I want to stay here.

'When will you tell her?' She chews on her lower lip.

'Soon. I promise. No more secrets. I'll see you tomorrow. I'll see you every day until we're together properly.'

She looks small and lost in the doorway, silhouetted by the hallway light behind her. I heft my bag over my shoulder and trudge to my car, once again no longer master of my own destiny. Even now she's dead, Issy is still pulling the strings, working me like a puppet. As I drive away, I get an email on my phone. I leave it and drive across town, back home, back to Mel and Noah. Back to what feels like my prison.

The meeting at Pam's yesterday was a nightmare. When Mel accused Sammy outright, I was staggered. I don't know what she thought she was doing, but she's lost the plot. Sammy isn't Noah's father. I just can't see it, and my gut feeling is no.

My overriding force is still finding out what drove Issy to suicide more than in who Noah's father is. I'm not sure they're connected, even though Mel is convinced of it. I've decided to go back to Newcastle and talk to the other people she was due to share with, plus find out if she had any other friends who might know something. Uni is due to start back in a week, so I won't have long to wait.

When I walk through the door at home, Noah, in his pyjamas, almost bowls me over when he launches himself at me. He must have been waiting for me. I drop my bag on the sofa, pick him up and throw him into the air before catching him and twirling around with him. He smells exactly like home to me when I bury my nose into his hair, and I have to close my eyes to quell the emotion that surges up into my throat.

'Grandad, can we watch Pooh?'

'Only if Tigger does lots of bouncing.' My voice cracks, but he doesn't notice.

'Silly, he always bounces everywhere. Watch me, I can bounce higher than him.'

He squirms until I put him down and is off like a rocket, bouncing around the room until he trips over the rug and falls flat on his face, squealing with laughter.

'All bounced out,' he pants. His eyes are shining and he looks like all his Christmases have come at once. Is this all it takes to make him happy—his grandad coming home? If only it was enough to make Mel or myself happy. He crawls on his belly over to the DVD, and his chubby fingers struggle to open the case. This stage is crucial; you mustn't intervene. It's imperative he does it himself.

Mel comes out of the kitchen, looking nervous and subdued, and stops after a couple of steps. Keeping a safe distance.

'Cup of tea?' she asks, eyeing the bag I've put on the sofa. It's all I've got, seeing as most of my clothes are still here, in my wardrobe. In our bedroom. In *her* bedroom now, I suppose. Mel shifts from one foot to the other and gives a weak smile.

Is this how it's going to be then, two dancers circling around each other in a series of clumsy but complicated moves I can't understand? Or two combative fencers trying to keep each other wrong-footed and off-guard? I don't know how long I can stand this.

'Yeah, okay.'

She disappears back into the kitchen and I long to speak to Adele, to say, 'Hi, I'm coming back. Coming *home*.'

Noah manages to extract the DVD and puts his fingers all over it as he inserts it into the machine.

'I'll just take my bag up,' I call and I start up the stairs.

'Grandad!' Noah wails. 'It's starting. Hurry up!'

'Won't be long. Start without me.'

I bound up the stairs and stop dead outside Issy's door. Can I do this? I've barely been in since she died. The last time was when I found the lot of them in here, sorting stuff out that day. Taking a deep breath, I turn the doorknob and go in. It smells empty, as if no one's been here for a long time. The bags Mel filled are still lined up along one wall, taking up most of the space, so I heft them onto the landing to take up to the attic later. My phone pings with a text. It's from Adele. *Good luck. LY xxx* is all it says. I'm not sure whether I'd prefer her to be supportive or jealous that I've gone back. Maybe she should fight harder for me, but at least she's not giving me a hard time. I'm stuck here for now, helping to look after Noah. Much as I adore him, and I do, just like Mel, I never wanted to be a parent to a toddler in my forties. I look around the room. How long am I going to be here for? Perhaps, in time, I can move in with Adele and we can share Noah that way. But, for now, there's not much I can do. He needs stability and we have to provide that. But I want to tell Mel that Adele is back in the picture as soon as I think she'll handle it. We both know our marriage is over.

As I go to put the phone down, I remember the email that came in as I left Adele's. I open it and don't know who it's from at first, a David Noone. Then I remember he's the other lad Issy was due to share with, and there's an attachment with it.

Hi Jon, it's David. We were due to share with Issy next year. Ryan and Michael told me they'd met with you and that you were asking about Issy's kid's dad. My girlfriend remembered seeing him in a photo she had on her phone. She was taking a picture of me that day and he was in the background with Issy. It's definitely the man Issy said was the father. She hasn't deleted it, so I've sent it to you. So sorry to hear about Issy, she was a top girl. Hope this helps.

Best

David.

The hairs all over my body are standing up now, and I swallow hard. In two seconds, the mystery will be over. What am I hanging about for? There's no turning back when I see this picture. I click on the attachment and my heart is banging so hard I feel faint. The blood pulses in my ears, whooshing noisily in my head, as the picture opens and I stare in disbelief at the man standing with his arm around Issy. It's Justin.

37

Mel

A LOUD ANIMALISTIC ROAR from upstairs startles me and I drop the tea I'm carrying. Thankfully, the cup drops into the sink but still shatters, and pieces of china scatter everywhere, along with droplets of hot liquid. I dash into the hallway and my eyes meet Noah's. He's stopped messing about with the DVD player and is wide-eyed.

'What was that?' I ask.

'Grandad shouting,' he says. "He's very naughty, isn't he?'

'I don't know, Noah. You stay down here and I'll go find out. Put Pooh on.' I'm halfway up the stairs already.

'Wanna come,' he says, setting off after me.

I stop and twist around to face him. 'No. Stay here. I mean it. Either stay and watch Pooh or go to bed. And stay out of the kitchen; Grandma broke a cup.'

Noah takes his foot off the bottom step and watches as I disappear round the corner at the top. The door to Issy's room is open and Jon is standing with his back to me, staring at the phone in his hand. I close the door behind me.

'Jon? What...?'

He turns round, and his eyes are blazing in a bloodless face. My heart lurches at the sight of him. Another roar from somewhere deep and primal leaves him.

'Jon, you're scaring Noah. What is it?'

255

He thrusts the phone in his hand at me. Just as I take it, the screen goes black, and I frantically press random keys to get the light back on. Jon sinks onto the bed, running his shaking hands through his hair. He looks like he's seen a ghost. He's muttering, 'I'll kill the bastard,' over and over.

I turn my attention back to the phone. There's a picture of a girl I don't know in the foreground and Issy is in the background. Justin is with her, and it looks like it was taken outside the uni. I recognise the quadrangle we stood outside just weeks ago.

'What's this? I don't understand.'

Jon snatches the phone, presses something, hands it back to me and barks, 'Read that.'

It's an email and as I read it, a growing horror fills me. The photo now makes sense. It can't be, surely. Not Justin. He's both our family and best friend. There has to be a mistake. One look at Jon's face tells me there isn't. I sit beside him, trying to swallow back the roiling nausea in my guts. I grab Jon's hand and feel the tremors rippling through him. His head swivels round slowly to face me.

'I'm going to fucking kill him, I swear.'

'Hang on, let's pause a minute and work this out. First, do you believe it? What if it's not true and David's mistaken?'

'Mel, Issy told them he was Noah's dad. Why would she lie? Or why would they, for that matter? And just the fact he's there, in the picture. Why is he there, standing with his arm around her?' He stands up and begins pacing, up and down, up and down, muttering. I don't know if he's talking to me or himself. 'It makes sense, her disappearing off campus regularly. He's regional manager for the whole of northern England. He's away all week in various hotels. He can be wherever he wants to be, and no one is any the wiser.'

'Disappearing off campus? What do you mean?'

'Never mind that now. I'll explain later. But it's true.'

I don't know what to say. My brain feels like mush. 'It can't be true!'

'Why not? Just yesterday, you were blaming his son, remember?'

An even worse thought occurs: what if it was both of them and they passed her between them? God forbid! Maybe, like father like son. It's a sick thought. But I never would have suspected Justin in a million years. I never did. He's the brother I never had.

Jon is raging and spitting words out like a machine gun going off. 'The absolute bastard, offering to help me find out who Noah's dad is. He's been badgering to help me the whole time, and now I know why. He must have been bricking it about getting found out. The DNA test on Sammy would have been getting way too close to home.'

Another, darker, thought floods my mind. 'My God, do you think he raped her? She was a child. And he was a grown man. And look at the size of him! Has he spent years abusing her? Think of all the times he's been alone with her, all the time she was growing up. He's been like a second dad to her. He's had free access all her life.'

Jon runs a hand over his face. His eyes are flitting madly about the room, and I'm suddenly scared of what he might do. He looks wild, manic, and for the first time since Issy died, I'm terrified of what he might do. Of what I might do. Different ways I could kill Justin are flipping through my mind, and I really think I could do it.

I think back to the email. 'Jon, when did you meet those other boys, this Ryan and Michael? It's the first I've heard of it.'

Jon looks blank for a moment, then remembers. 'God, it was that day you came home and I was drunk in the afternoon. Their visit was why I started drinking that afternoon in the first place. Then we had a big row and ended up not speaking. They told me Issy used to disappear off campus, and they didn't know where. But I do now—hotel rooms with him. Think of all the time he spends away from home. Who of us ever knows where he is? He can tell us what he likes.'

'You're right! Is there anything else you haven't told me? Let's make sure we tell each other everything from now. We've got to be together on this.'

'I don't think there's anything else.'

I flush when I remember I came back from Greg's to find him drunk that afternoon. I never told him where I'd been. Looks like we're both good at keeping secrets. My mind is whirling crazily while Jon looks like he's falling apart. If I'm to be the strong one, now would be a good time to start.

'Jon, I have something I didn't tell you, something I did when we weren't speaking. The other day, I used my key to get into Pam's house while no one was in. I got a sample of Sammy's hair and took it to Steve Jackson, but he said it was no good. While I was in Sammy's room, I found a mobile phone taped to the underside of his bed frame. It seemed to confirm my suspicions about him, but I couldn't say that at Pam's, could I? I couldn't tell them I'd broken in.'

Jon is staring at me so hard it's beginning to unnerve me.

'What? What are you thinking?' I ask.

'Do you remember that name on Issy's phone? Lamech? I'd forgotten all about it. Do you think it could be the number for that phone you found? Or am I putting two and two together and making five?'

'God, you could be right. And guess what? I nicked the phone. I've got it here.'

Jon's hand clutches my arm. 'Where is it?'

'Still in my bag. I didn't know what to do with it. I couldn't tell you. We weren't speaking, and you weren't here and... how stupid have we been, concealing things from each other when we should have been pulling together? Listen, it's just a thought, but since we don't know what Lamech means, why don't we Google it?'

Jon is on the internet on his phone immediately. He looks up, dumbfounded, and slaps himself hard on the forehead.

'You'll never guess what it means. 'Father of Noah'. Mel, it's from the bloody Bible and we never saw it, not once. It's how she listed him. If we ring it and that phone rings…'

'But why would it be under Sammy's bed? If he's innocent?'

'Justin would have to hide it from Pam, wouldn't he? And Sammy's at uni most of the time. It could be the safest place he could think of. He wouldn't want it under his own bed, would he? And Pam cleans his car out, so he couldn't risk leaving it in there either.'

Jon gets the photo up on the phone again, and we huddle over it. Justin is clearly wrapping his arm around Issy's shoulders in a sort of proprietorial way, it seems. She looks trapped, despite her smile. Again, a sick feeling engulfs me. What has he done to her and why didn't we notice? Why couldn't she tell us? Hot tears spill down my cheeks and Jon grips my hand. I know he must be thinking much the same thing.

'Get the phone,' Jon says.

'It's dead. I tried it.'

'There's a drawerful of old chargers in the sideboard. Maybe one of them will fit. I'll have a look.'

I get the phone and meet Jon by the sideboard. Noah is slack-jawed and goggle-eyed watching Tigger and Pooh, and doesn't look up. He's eating a KitKat and jams his hand behind his back a moment too late. It means he's been in the kitchen. I pretend I haven't seen and hand Jon the phone. He looks around the edges until he sees the connection then rifles through the drawer and pulls out a charger.

'Bingo.'

We have to assume this phone was only for Justin and Issy to keep in contact, so any calls to it wouldn't be on his regular phone bill, like they were on hers. That would raise too many questions for him if Pam ever saw it. And presumably it won't have been charged since she died. So I plug it in and the screen stays blank for a while, then the charging icon flashes up, but it refuses to turn on yet. Jon paces up and down, wearing a hole in the carpet. After a few more minutes, the phone turns on.

'It's got some power. Ring it,' I say.

Jon pulls out one of Issy's phone bills and dials the number on it using his own phone. Issy's phone is long dead too, and we can't wait for that to charge. The phone in my hand vibrates and dances about on my palm. It's on silent. Jon and I look at the phone then at each other. Issy's picture flashes up on the screen. She looks young and vibrant and happy. My heart wrenches painfully.

'What do we do now?' I ask.

Jon takes the phone and messes with it, but it requires a password and we can't unlock it whatever we do. I can't even hazard a guess what password Justin would use. I'm glad we can't get into it right now. If it contains messages from him to her, I don't want to read them, and I know Jon would insist.

'We'll have to take it to Steve. It's evidence,' Jon says. He looks at his watch. 'We'll do it tomorrow, first thing.'

He goes into the kitchen. He seems aimless, but I'm glad he's stopped the endless pacing. I follow and see the mess from earlier when I dropped the cup. As Jon picks the bits out of the sink, his shoulders shake and he stops, hanging his head low. His tears are infectious and before long, we're clinging to each other desperately. If we needed proof our daughter was abused, it's in front of us. Just her age alone should be enough to get Justin put away, but for how long? My hands curl into fists as I grip Jon's shirt. I want to hurt Justin badly and make him pay for what he's done. I want the world to know he's a child abuser, a monster. The family man and great dad image he portrays makes me sick. Whenever I think about it, I feel a slam into my guts, like a horse has just kicked me in the stomach. In some ways, the grief is as bad as when Issy just died. Knowing Justin must have controlled, manipulated and frightened her makes the last few years of her life all the more tragic. He drove her to her death. She must have been so desperate. If I could only have her back for five minutes, to ask her about it, to tell her she wasn't alone, I'd give anything. Anything at all.

Jon pulls away from me and sits at the kitchen table while he composes himself. I clean up the rest of the broken pieces of cup.

'I'll, er, go and unpack my stuff,' he says and stands up. He looks stooped and weary, and the slope of his shoulders is pronounced as he jams his hands in his pockets.

I watch from the doorway as Noah jumps up, saying, 'Grandad, hurry up. How much longer?'

'Not long, buddy. Five minutes, I promise,' he says, his voice thick with tears. Thankfully, Noah doesn't argue and sinks back to his position in front of the TV, sitting cross-legged and cupping his chin in his hands. Chocolate is smeared all round his mouth, and his tiny body rises and falls as he lets out an enormous sigh. My heart twists as I wonder if he is the product of a rape. Another thought strikes me: no wonder Justin is so good with him, always wanting to take him places. He treats him like a son because that's exactly what he is.

I go upstairs, where Jon is unpacking the meagre amount of belongings he's taken from his bag. He's straightened out the duvet and is laying his clothes out on it. It looks totally wrong, seeing him inhabiting her room. He looks up when he sees me and I feel I should knock before I enter. I hover in the doorway.

'Should I leave my clothes in the other wardrobe or bring everything in here?' He glances at me briefly and slides his eyes back to his unpacking.

If I was in two minds about him moving out of our bedroom, he's just confirmed that he doesn't want to be in the same room as me.

'Um...' I begin, not sure how I feel or what I want.

'It's fine, I'll bring my stuff in here, then I can get dressed in the morning without disturbing you.'

I hate this. Is this how it's going to be? We agreed to do this out of convenience only, but it's like we're strangers half the time and intimate the other. The gulf now between us wasn't there a few minutes ago in the kitchen. Perhaps we'll only get through this if we focus on Noah and the aftermath of Issy.

'Grandad!' yells Noah. 'Come on.'

'I'll go down,' Jon says quickly. 'I don't want him to see I'm sleeping in here.'

He goes past me, turning sideways so we don't touch, and is gone, leaving me alone in Issy's room. The bags of Issy's stuff I packed weeks ago are piled on the landing. I should get rid of them; it's not like she's coming back. A wave of grief has me doubled over, clutching my stomach, and I only just make it back to the bathroom, kicking the door shut behind me. I lock the door and sit on the toilet, letting the tears flood out of me, taking the pain and agony of loss and revelation with it. But no matter how much floods out, more rushes in to fill the void. I can't give in to it all the time. I force myself to gain control—I need to do some serious thinking.

38

,

Jon

I'M AT THE KITCHEN table, harbouring fantasies about hurting Justin, when Mel comes down. She's been upstairs ages. Noah's film has long since finished and he's now curled up on my lap, having just finished some toast and jam. Mel sits in the chair opposite me, and we look at each other. Her face has a grey, washed-out pallor. I suspect that if I look in the mirror, my face would look similar. Her voice, when she speaks, is quiet but authoritative.

'Noah, come on, it's past your bedtime,' she says. 'You've stayed up late waiting for Grandad.'

Miraculously he decides not to argue and trudges upstairs after patting my face, like he's checking I'm really there. At the top he shouts down, 'Story?'

'Do your teeth and I'll come up in five minutes to read one. Go and pick which one you want,' I shout. The sound of running footsteps means he agrees.

All I can think about is killing Justin, grabbing him by the neck, and throttling him until the life ebbs out of him. Or blasting his head off. One bullet is all I would need. I want to be left alone, to let the anger feed me and fortify me. I want to look into getting a gun. My fists clench and unclench by my sides, and my jaw aches from grinding my teeth. My eyes flitter about the room and I'm muttering to myself. Where do you get guns from round here? Or anywhere, for that matter?

A massive great AK47 that'll blast a cavernous hole right through him.

'Jon?' Mel sounds frightened, as if she can see right into my head and knows what I'm thinking. No; planning. I *am* going to kill him.

I look at her and see fear in her eyes. Of me? Is she frightened of me? Or what I'm capable of?

'We have to talk. I need you to listen. Please,' she says. Her eyes lock onto mine. 'There's no doubt that Justin will go down for this, is there? I mean, the fact that she got pregnant at fifteen means he's a paedophile. I'm just concerned he won't go down for long enough. That he may say she was complicit in it to get a reduced sentence. Whether that would make a difference, I don't know.'

'So? I want to see him hang. I'm going to get a gun and...'

She shakes her head wildly. 'No, that's just going to mean that both of you will end up in prison. If you kill him, and I really believe at this moment in time that you're perfectly capable of it—'

'You bet I am—'

She holds her hand up in a 'shut up' gesture. 'I know you are. I think I could pull the trigger too, believe me, but just hear me out. I've thought of a way we can get him put away for much longer, maybe even for good.'

For good? Wouldn't he get put away for good for this, anyway? I study her face. Some of the colour has returned, so much so she's now flushed. 'Go on.'

She narrows her eyes. 'I want to frame him so it looks like he's a danger to *all* children, not just ours.'

'How would you do that?'

'With your help. Do you believe he's abused other children or just Issy?'

'Just Issy. But I don't know. How should I know? I haven't thought about it.'

'I can't really see him doing this to others, but I could be wrong. And what if we're right, and it was just a sick

264

relationship he had going on with her? It won't look as bad as if he had a history of child abuse, would it?'

'Well, no, but...'

'So we frame him.'

'How?'

Her eyes glitter. 'We download images on his computer. Hundreds, maybe thousands of them. So everyone knows what a sick pervert he is.'

I'm stunned into silence. My mouth opens but nothing comes out. Every objection and reason why it won't work gets slapped down in my head. It could work.

'Here's the kicker, though. It means we have to act normal, be his friends, build bridges until we're ready to move.'

'I can't do that.'

'You have to. It's for the greater good. Just keep telling yourself that.'

'It would be more satisfying to blow his dick off. Then his head.'

'I know! Believe me, I want that too. But this way, everyone will know what he is, and he'll have to live with that, and what he's done, for the rest of his life. It'll destroy him, like Issy's death destroyed us. Isn't that better in the end? What will killing him achieve? Five minutes of satisfaction, then the knowledge that he's not alive to suffer? So let's make him *really* suffer. I *want* him to suffer. Horrible things happen to people like him, in prison, don't they? That's when the real justice gets meted out. They have some sort of moral code in there—you can murder someone but kiddie-fiddling? It's not tolerated. Jon, please, I've thought about this.' Tears glint in her eyes and she turns her face away from me.

I mull it over. It could work. With a bit of planning and us doing the acting job of our life. Outside, it's pitch dark and I get up to close the blinds. We've got what we wanted; an answer to the question of Noah's paternity. Maybe the DNA test from Sammy would have linked Noah to him; I don't know enough about it, but I think I remember reading that links like theirs would show up. He must have been shitting himself when Sammy willingly did the test. He must be the reason she killed herself, had to be. It makes sense—abused victim can't carry on. I wish I were back at Adele's now, curled up in her bed, safe from the outside world. With all this to deal with, I don't know when I can see her again. I don't know what to tell her. The truth, I suppose. That my brother-in-law, my best friend, is a paedophile who's abused our daughter, probably for years. And Noah. The victim of that abuse. The poor little sod.

I take a few deep breaths. 'I'll go read Noah's story.'

He's in bed waiting for me, sucking his thumb. A smear of toothpaste is on his cheek. I wipe it away with a baby wipe from next to the bed. He reaches up and touches my face with a chubby hand.

'What's the matter, Grandad? Why are you crying for?' He rubs away tears I didn't know were there.

'Nothing, Noah.' I lean down and cuddle him. He doesn't deserve this. I'll die to protect him. How we will ever protect him from the truth, though, I don't know. 'Right then. Which book did you pick?'

There are about ten books on his bed.

'This one,' he says, thrusting a Fireman Sam book at me.

I blink away tears and open it. 'Okay. Let's begin.'

39

Mel

ALL THE FOLLOWING WEEK, Jon and I do our best to put our personal issues aside and concentrate on the plan to make sure Justin goes down for good. The bickering and sniping has stopped, but we're not really communicating outside *The Issue*, as it's now become known. We've agreed to keep it strictly between us and not tell a soul. The fewer people that know what we're up to, the better. It is hard, though. The only bright spot is when Greg texts me out of the blue.

I make less effort than last time with my clothes. Jeans and a short-sleeved top this time. At least they're clean. A bit of mascara and lipstick make me look less like something out of The Living Dead. At least, I hope so.

'Hi, Mel,' he says when I let him in.

Noah comes downstairs, decides he's shy, and hides behind my legs. I haven't seen or heard from him since I went to his flat the other week and found out he was about to go back to work. I never did ask him how his date went.

'Hi, Noah,' Greg says, squatting down to his level.

Noah pops his head out. 'Hello. I'm going to play with my cars.' Noah runs back up the stairs and bangs his door hard. I wince at the noise.

'He really needs to stop doing that,' I say.

Greg follows me into the living room and sits down in an armchair. I take one end of the sofa and pull the cushion out from behind my back, playing with the silky tassels on the corners. The repetition soothes me.

'How is the driving going? Are you finding it okay?'

He puffs out his cheeks and blows out, pulling his mouth down at the corners. His right hand pulls at his earlobe in a self-conscious gesture.

'Erm, I won't lie: it's been hard. It's been worse than I thought it would be. I... I keep reliving what happened and...' He gulps down a breath before continuing. 'I've been having panic attacks, but they've been very good about it. They're sending me for more counselling and some training before I take another load out. They've been very understanding, but I don't know how long that'll be the case. I'm scared they'll cut my pay if I don't get back out there soon.'

I don't know what to say. I still feel responsible that my daughter messed up his life like this, even though he's told me so many times not to blame myself. At a loss, I sit and chew my lip, waiting out the silence.

'So anyway, Mel, how've you been?' He fixes me with an intense look, concern creasing his forehead.

'Oh, you know.' I flap my hand about dismissively. *Don't talk about The Issue. No matter how desperately you want to. Don't mention the DNA test and Sammy, even though I'd told him my suspicions before. Maybe he's forgotten all about it.*

'No, I don't know. That's why I'm asking.'

I clamp down hard on the words, swallowing them back as they rise up in my throat.

'To be honest, I don't know how I feel. It's hard, still adjusting to life without Issy.' My voice hitches, and I squeeze my eyes tight to stop them from sliding to the photo of her on the sideboard, the one with Noah on her knee. It's the only picture we still have out. We packed the rest away as they're too painful to look at but kept this tiny one in its silver frame out. I regularly find it face down and have to keep standing it up again. Jon can't bear to look at it, saying it breaks his heart to see her. During one argument, he said that he can't replace the horrible sight in the morgue with any amount of pictures of her and I should respect that. I shouted back that we needed to remember her as she was before the accident, not after it. We've had so many rows since she died that I've lost track of the hurtful things we've said to each other.

I open my eyes with a start when the sofa cushion beside me sinks down under Greg's weight.

'Are you really alright? Or is that a stupid question?'

It is a stupid question, really. But it's not his fault or his problem.

'No, sorry. I'm not okay, but I'll have to be, won't I?'

He holds my hand then, his fingers warm in mine. His nails are short, neat and clean. I lean towards him slightly, yearning to be enveloped in his arms, and the tang of sharp, crisp aftershave fills my senses. It smells wonderful; of spice and aromatic warmth. Of danger. Of sex. I sit up and my hand slips free of his.

'I'm fine, really. These things just take time, don't they? Anyway, let's have some coffee and a chat. That's what I really want. Take my mind off things.'

'Sounds good to me.'

'You'll have to make do with instant. I haven't got a fancy coffee machine like yours.'

'I'll try and force it down.'

He follows me into the kitchen while I make the coffee, standing behind me and leaning against the worktop.

'Any developments on what you told me, about suspecting your nephew of being Noah's dad?'

My hand shakes slightly as I spoon sugar into his cup, and it spills onto the side.

'No. I was wrong. It was just me being stupid and getting things out of perspective.'

He looks surprised. 'Are you sure? You seemed so definite.'

'I'm sure, yeah. I was wrong.'

STEPHANIE ROGERS

'So it's back to square one, then?'

'Pretty much.' I turn my face away, so he can't see the lie that's written there. 'So how was your date?'

At first he looks blank, then grimaces. 'Oh, that, yeah. Not great. I won't be seeing her again. She wasn't my type, after all. To tell the truth, it was me. I was hard work, not in the mood. I'm not ready, so I'm not bothering at the moment.'

Part of me feels glad. Is that awful? 'Give yourself time. Don't force it. It'll happen when it's right.'

He nods. 'Yeah, you're right. I know.'

We spend the next hour chatting, and I feel almost normal until he glances at his watch.

'I'd better be off. I've got to do some driver training at the depot.'

I watch him walk off up the garden path and disappear from view.

Later, at work, Olivia notices I'm preoccupied and presses hard to find out what's bothering me as we set up for the under-sevens ballet class.

'I'm worried about you, Mel. You're not yourself. Please tell me what's wrong?'

'It's just family stuff,' I say, but she's not about to be fobbed off.

'It's more than that. I'm not prying or anything, but you've looked really unhappy these last few days.'

As long as I don't mention *The Issue*, it should be okay. I can tell her enough to satisfy her curiosity. I sigh.

'Well, Jon left me, then moved back in and is now sleeping in Issy's room. But he's only moved back in to help me with Noah and to tell you the truth, it's hard. Also, I've fallen out with my sister and we're not speaking.' I smile humourlessly. 'You're probably wishing you hadn't asked now, right?'

'No, course not. I just didn't realise there was so much going on. Are you okay with it all?'

'Well, my marriage is well and truly over, and I do, honestly, think it was inevitable. But between you and me, I think he's gone back to the woman he was leaving me for before Issy got pregnant.'

Her eyes widen, and she claps a hand over her mouth. 'Oh, my God! What?'

'Yeah. It's true. I've got my suspicions he's seeing her again.'

I hadn't meant to tell her about that. It just slipped out, but now I've said it, I realise it's been on my mind a lot since he moved back in. He's different somehow, and spending a lot of time on his phone, texting or emailing or something. He smiles sometimes when he reads something and he thinks I'm not watching, with a sort of goofy expression. And I've heard him murmuring in a low voice late at night in his bedroom. Am I bothered or not? I really don't know. Naturally, thoughts of what we found out about Justin have obliterated everything else, and I feel numb about most things. I'm struggling just to function, to get out of bed each morning.

'God, Mel, after everything you two have been through. I just think to split up would be really sad.' She shakes her head, still clearly shocked.

Just then, the door opens downstairs, and a babble of excited voices float up to us. Saved by the children and their parents trooping into the studio, Olivia flicks me one last concerned glance, then the professional in her takes over.

'Hi Evie, your hair is looking lovely tonight; I love the braid. And Alice, is that a new leotard? What a beautiful colour...'

After the session, which I go through on autopilot, unable to find the usual escape or release in it, Olivia says, 'You've been miles away through all that, haven't you?'

'Was it that obvious? I'm sorry. Listen, would you mind if I get off a bit early? I've got a shocking headache,' I lie. I just don't want to be alone with her if she starts asking questions again, in case I blurt out something I shouldn't.

'Of course. I'll finish packing away here,' she says. 'You get yourself off. I hope you feel better by tomorrow. And you know where I am if you need me.'

Gratefully, I head off down the stairs and rush to my car before I can change my mind. It's a short drive home, and the traffic is light. Just as I turn the corner into our street, I see a woman leaving my front gate and getting into a car parked outside, a woman I've seen many times on Facebook. I slow down and drive past the house, glancing at the door as I pass. The woman is just starting the engine and the headlights come on. Jon is standing with the door open, and he waves to her, then goes inside when she drives off. So I was right. And she's been to my house while I've been at work. I didn't think Jon would stoop that low. I've been waiting for him to tell me he's seeing her again, but he hasn't said a word. Even though I'd suspected it was going on, it's still like a punch in the gut.

I make a snap decision, and do a quick three-point turn. If he won't tell me what's going on, maybe she will. I put my foot down, and it takes only a few seconds to tuck in behind her. I don't know where she's going, but it shouldn't take long to find out. What I'll do when she gets to wherever is anyone's guess.

40

Jon

I'M SURE MEL SHOULD have been home by now. I look at my watch again. If she's gone to get pissed with Greg Evans, I'll bloody kill her. Just lately, she seems to have lost all track of time, and comes and goes as she pleases when she knows I'm looking after Noah.

Adele had to bring my briefcase round earlier after I'd left it at her place after work. Noah wouldn't go to sleep and she had to wait in the car outside until I was sure he was sock on. I couldn't risk him seeing her and blabbing to Mel that she was here. She'd got out of the car when I opened the front door, and I'd pulled her inside, glancing up the stairs into the darkness. I put my finger on her lips and pulled her close to whisper in her ear.

'Ssh. He's only just dropped off.' I inhaled the scent of her hair, sort of fruity, like apples. We stepped into the living room doorway, out of the sight line from the top of the stairs, and I took my briefcase from her.

'Thank you. Sorry you had to come all the way over here with it.'

'It's no problem. I was missing you anyway,' she said, kissing me and pressing the length of her body against me.

'I missed you, too. God, you're so gorgeous. You make me lose my mind when I'm with you,' I whispered into her mouth.

273

She wrapped her arms around my neck and kissed me deeply. 'How long before she gets home?'

'It should be about half an hour, but I never know with her. She could walk in anytime. God, I miss you so much. I want to come home with you.'

'I love you,' she whispered. Her eyes shone in the dark.

'I love you too.' And I meant it. I do love her. I held her head in my hands and pressed my forehead to hers.

She pulled back slightly, and her lips turned down at the edges. 'I'd better go then. Will I see you tomorrow?'

I pulled a face. 'Can't tomorrow. Maybe the day after, Sunday, if I can get away.'

'Okay,' she said with a sigh.

'I'm sorry. I'll tell her soon, I promise.'

Her face is downcast, and I'm scared she doesn't believe me.

'Listen, I want to be with you, and nothing will mess it up this time. There's just something I need to sort out here first.'

'I know. And I know it must be important.'

She blew me a kiss and was gone through the front door seconds later. I stood and watched as she hurried back to her car. It feels like she takes a part of me with her whenever she goes. I don't know how much longer I can stand this for. I need to tell Mel about us but I'm dreading the repercussions. She's just so unpredictable. I'm not sure what she might do.

And now she's late again, and I'm clock-watching and wondering if she's alright. Just then, my mobile rings. I snatch it up. It's Adele.

'Hello? You okay?' I ask.

'Er, no, not really.'

'What's up? I haven't got long. She's not back yet.'

'You've got longer than you think. She's just left here.'

'What? I'm not following.' I stand up and start pacing, an uneasy prickle starting up my neck and scalp.

'She accosted me as I was unlocking my front door. She must have followed me from yours. I didn't recognise her.'

'Oh shit! Really? What did she say?'

274

'Well, she wasn't too happy, as you can imagine. She kept muttering 'I knew it, I bloody knew it,' and similar things. I said, 'Excuse me, do I know you?' and she said, 'Yes, I'm the wife of the man you're screwing.'

I sink back heavily into the sofa, trying to decide what to do next. 'This might sound stupid, but how did she seem?'

'Angry. She asked me if it had been going on for the last three or four years. I told her the truth, but she was in no mood to listen. Then she had a right go at me for sending that text to her four years ago. I tried to apologise, but she wasn't in the mood to listen to that either, I don't think.'

'Shit! This is the last thing I needed.'

'Well, in a way, it might be a good thing. Now it's out in the open.' She sounds nervous but hopeful, and I can just imagine her gripping the phone anxiously, worry creasing her lovely face.

'Yes, I might agree with that, but since Issy died, I don't think she's right in the head. I'm really worried about what she might do. I haven't told you, but I found her with a load of pills the other week. Looked like she'd been stockpiling them. But, on the other hand, yes, I'm glad she knows. Listen, it'll be okay, don't worry. And on the plus side, now we don't have to sneak about any more.'

'I didn't know she was in such a fragile state mentally, but I suppose it's to be expected after what she's been through. What are you going to say to her?'

'God knows!' I rake a hand through my hair. 'But don't you worry. It's not your fault. And what I said earlier, that I love you—I mean it. I can't wait to be with you properly. It's all I can think about. This might speed things up a bit in that department.'

She sounds relieved. 'I love you too, Jon. Do you think we'll really be together, after all this time?'

'For sure. And soon. I'm not losing you again. I've lost you twice already.'

She sighs. 'I'd better let you go and work out what you're going to say. Face the music and all. I'll see you soon.'

'Okay. Bye.'

I put the phone down. Nothing I can do now but wait for Mel to come home. This is the worst possible way for her to have found out. Why now when we've got this other thing to sort out? I need her on side, working with me, not going off the deep end. Unable to sit down, I go into the kitchen twice and start to make a cup of coffee, then abandon the process. I peer endlessly out of the window, and finally she turns up. Here we go! I stand up to face her as she walks into the living room. Perhaps she won't tell me where she's been and wait to see if I mention it. Maybe she'll act like nothing's wrong. Or maybe she'll pick up a poker and take a swing at me with it. It's like waiting for fireworks to go off when you've lit the fuse and nothing happens.

'Hello,' she says, entering the living room and putting her bag and coat over the back of the chair. 'How's Noah?'

'Asleep,' I say cautiously, trying to gauge her mood.

She walks past me into the kitchen and puts the kettle on. This is weird. I'd prefer it if she'd charged in all guns blazing. At least we'd both know where we stand.

'Do you want a drink?' she calls.

'Er, no thanks.'

I go to stand in the kitchen doorway. 'You're late tonight.'

She stiffens, and I see the tension in her back. As she spoons sugar into a cup, her hand trembles and white granules spill onto the worktop. She turns slowly, her face fixed in a hard expression.

'I followed your fancy woman home. It was quite a detour.' She folds her arms across her body, hugging herself tight.

I lean into the door frame. 'I know you did. She rang me.'

'So you're not denying it then?'

'No. No point. We've split up, anyway.'

She nods. 'True. Fast worker though, eh?'

I shrug. 'Not really. Why did you follow her?'

'To see where she lived. Ask her a few things. She swears you've only just got back together.'

'Yes, it's true. I was going to tell you but... this Justin thing...'

'Oh, really? That's the reason?'

276

'Yes. I still care about you, Mel. I worry about how you're coping and stuff—'

She cuts me off. 'You still *care* about me? Meaning you don't *love* me anymore?'

'Well, yes, I do, but it's different. It's more a caring sort of love than...'

'Sexual?'

God, why is she doing this? 'Mel, you don't want me anymore, do you? You haven't let me near you in that way in so long. Whenever I touch you, you freeze! You can't bear me near you half the time...'

'No,' she sighs. 'I don't want you like that anymore. But I still care about you.'

'Like I just said. So... we're good then, you and me? About this?'

She shrugs. 'Do I have a choice?' She turns back to the kettle, then suddenly whirls round furiously, making me jump. 'Have you screwed her upstairs in Issy's bed? Tonight?' she hisses.

'What? No! Course not. Listen, she only came round to drop my briefcase off. She was here five minutes, and she's never been here before.'

'I don't want you shagging her here, especially with Noah upstairs. Is that clear?'

'I haven't and I wouldn't! Bloody hell, woman! What do you take me for?'

The next thing I know, a cup whizzes past my head and hits the door. The crazy cow! Thankfully, it wasn't full of tea.

'What the hell was that for?' I shout, still moving out of the way of the sharp pieces exploding everywhere.

'I don't believe you! You're a liar! You've been seeing her all this time, haven't you?'

'No! I just told you, God damn it! We're done, me and you; over. We just need to sort this Justin thing out, then we can go our separate ways, try and be happy again, if that's even possible.'

'You mean, you go off with the fancy woman and I spend the next twenty years giving up my life to bring up *your* grandchild? That would be just perfect for you, wouldn't it?'

'No! Jesus! We're both responsible for him. I've no intention of leaving him. I love him, Mel. He needs both of us.' I run my fingers through my hair. What does it take to get through?

She's eyeing me like a wild horse, all rolling eyes and heavy breathing. 'Look at you, with your fluffed-up, inflated ego. You're loving this, aren't you, having some floozy throwing herself at you? I bet you were at it with loads of them, all through our marriage. Cheap tarts and hookers.'

'Don't be so bloody stupid. And I suppose you've never looked at another man for years, have you?'

She has spots of high colour on both cheeks and looks flustered. I should stop, but she's really wound me up now, calling Adele horrible names, and the hurtful words pour out in a torrent.

'You're so perfect, aren't you, you and your family? But don't forget, *your* sister's husband abused our daughter. If she'd never married him, Issy would still be here. So don't make out you're some saint, from some perfect family. *Your* sister married a paedo,' I roar.

Her face is going redder and redder. '*Your* best friend, might I remind you,' she screams. 'How come you never knew your best mate was a sick pervert after all the time you've spent with him? Answer me that. Or did you know what he was all along, but you just never suspected he was doing it with her?'

'Mel, I'm warning you...' I really want to hit her and I ram my hands in my pockets to keep from strangling her. We glare at each other, breathing hard, prepared to hurt each other with words. But what good will it do?

'Look, we need to calm down, or we'll wake Noah up,' I hiss. 'There's no point in us ripping each other to bits, is there? We've got things to sort out.' I try to relax my shoulders and breathe slower. 'Did you ring Pam today, like we said, to arrange to go round? We need to get started on this.'

She deflates, looking trite. 'No, I didn't. Look, I'm sorry for yelling; I'm just so up and down at the moment. I know it's over between us, but I'm not comfortable with you bringing her here. Not yet.'

I nod and shove the broken pieces of cup into a pile with my shoe. 'She doesn't come here. It was a one-off, to do me a favour, I swear. I'm not that insensitive. But really, I'm glad you know. I've been trying to find the right time to tell you. I don't want to sneak around or lie to you.'

I can't tell how she feels about it. She's shut down on me and her face is blank, devoid of any emotion.

'Fine,' she says in a flat voice. 'Do what you want. I don't care.'

I decide to leave it. 'I thought you might not ring Pam, so I texted Justin instead. We're going round there tomorrow afternoon. I've told him it's to clear the air, so we can all be friends again and sort things out properly.'

Mel jerks her head up and looks stricken. 'I don't know if I can face going round there yet,' she says, knotting her hands together.

'Fine. You don't have to. I can go on my own if it comes to it. Look, I've got something to show you.'

She follows me into the living room and I pull a new, still-boxed tablet from my briefcase. It's the reason I needed my briefcase tonight. 'I'm going to charge it up overnight and take it tomorrow. When I get on his own computer, not tomorrow, but soon, I'm going to pose as him in some chat rooms. Make him look like one of those stalkers; grooming kids, I think they call it. I don't know how, but I will. I need your help, Mel. We've got to act normal and get back in with them, before we can get him for good. Can you do it?'

She nods. 'Yes. I'm scared of how I'll react when I see him, but yes, I can do it. All I have to do is act normal, right?'

'Absolutely. It's going to kill me as well, you know. But we have to do it. We just need to be strong for a bit longer. You haven't blabbed to anyone, have you? I know it's hard for you, especially since Pam is who you'd normally talk to.'

She shakes her head. 'No, I haven't. I can't tell Mum, can I? We can't talk to Steve Jackson, either. He's bent the rules enough for us, but he'd draw the line at this, for sure. Will Sammy be there or has he gone back to uni yet?'

'I don't know.'

'I need to apologise to him. I don't know if he'll forgive me, but I have to try.' She stops and cocks an ear towards the stairs, listening for Noah, but everything's quiet. 'I'm so worried about what's going to happen to him, poor little mite. He didn't ask for any of this, did he? And I love him so much, despite what I say. I just never expected to be a mum again at my age.' She hugs herself tight, looking small and bereft. I don't know whether to hug her, so I don't. She might wallop me.

'I suspected, you know, that you were back on with her,' she says suddenly, her eyes fixing on mine.

'How come?'

'Little things. It doesn't matter now.'

'Sorry,' I say, sheepishly.

'It's okay. I don't care anymore, Jon. I know it's over between us, have done for some time, really. Do what you want. I just want this nightmare to end.'

Her face crumples, and she brushes past me, along the hallway and up the stairs. I'd better not try and comfort her. I'd probably make things worse. Instead, I text Adele to tell her everything's okay, then power up the new tablet. I need to set it up for tomorrow, so everything I need is installed for when I get to Justin's. Then, hopefully, we can start to ensure the bastard is put away for a long time, if not for good. Now, that's justice.

41

Mel

JON RINGS THE BELL, and I'm so nervous as I wait for someone to open it, I think I might be sick. I have a vicious tremor in my right leg and my face feels frozen, like it's been cast in ice and set in a panic-stricken expression. Jon called it my Wallace and Grommit face a second ago and told me to relax. His hand is pressing firmly on my back in a gesture I'm sure he thinks is reassuring. I'd rather he wasn't touching me at all, anywhere. Not now I know his hands have been all over *her*.

'Everything will be fine. Just act normal and remember why we're doing this,' he whispers for the umpteenth time, as if I'm an idiot. I just want this to be over. How am I going to be when I see *him*? An image of me with my hands around his neck, squeezing, squeezing hard, flashes in front of my eyes. A cast iron boot scraper is on the doorstep. I could use it to bludgeon his head in. Just then, the door swings half-open, and my sister peers out. If she's pleased to see us, she doesn't look it. She's wearing a pinched, tight expression.

'Come in,' she says, stepping back and opening the door wider. Her eyes drop to the floor as I pass. My legs stall, but Jon keeps up the pressure in the small of my back, propelling me forward.

The house is quiet. I can't see *him* anywhere. At the entrance to the living room, my feet feel stuck to the floor.

The door is closed and I can't see or hear anything from within. What if he's in there?

'Go on through,' says Pam from behind, irritably.

She hasn't forgiven me, that's obvious. This is the longest we've ever gone without speaking. We've had the usual spats all sisters have, but we always said nothing could be so bad that we wouldn't ever speak again. But then, you don't expect your brother-in-law to make your underage daughter pregnant, do you? Jon reaches in front of me and shoves the door open, then grabs my hand, walks past me and pulls me in. My heart thumps harder than ever as the room reveals itself but, it's empty; spotlessly clean and tidy, but empty.

'Where's the man of the house?' asks Jon, throwing me an irritated look. It sounds normal and jovial, but I know it's only because he can't bear to utter his vile name.

'He's just nipped out for some beer. He won't be long. I'll make some coffee.' Pam leaves and goes into the kitchen. Even though she's spoken to me, I think she's glad to escape.

Jon and I exchange a look as we sit stiffly together on the sofa. We've agreed not to mention that we're splitting up. That little gem will have to keep for another day. There's over a foot of space between us, but the gulf is much wider. Yesterday's row was awful when I got in from work, having followed his bit-on-the-side home first. I have to admit, she's as pretty as her Facebook pictures, with her blonde, perfectly coiffed hair and stunning figure. There again, she's not run ragged looking after a toddler, is she, or still grieving from burying her daughter? I don't know if she's a grandma. She certainly doesn't look like one. She might not have any kids for all I know. Even though I know nothing about her, I want to know everything. Begrudgingly, I can see what Jon sees in her. Next to dowdy, frumpy me, she's gorgeous, with that woman-in-love glow about her. Jon clears his throat and taps my arm. I jump at his touch as if it's burnt me, and he lets go.

'Relax, for God's sake!' he whispers. 'This was your idea, remember?'

'I'm trying, honestly. But I'm just so jumpy. Look.' I hold out my hand flat, palm facing down, and we both watch it. It shakes violently and I jam it under my thigh, along with the other one.

'Well, we're here. Just keep on it.' His voice is low and grim, and he looks at me. 'Mel, we can do this. We have to do this. Let's catch the bastard. But I want to kill him so bad.'

He's shaking too. His leg is jiggling up and down, and there are little pearls of perspiration at his temple. This sign of his nerves makes my own last bit of courage seep away.

'Why are we doing this? Why not just call the police? He's going to go to jail, anyway. She was underage,' I whisper, even though I know the answer. Even though he's right; it was my idea in the first place.

'You know why,' he says fiercely, and I nod, a small movement that makes me feel more positive just for doing it.

'Yes, I know. I can do this,' I mutter. My nerves are spiralling out of control. After a deep, calming breath, I say, 'God, I feel sick though. I'm so scared of that moment when I set eyes on him, of what I'll do. We both know I'm not that good an actor.'

'Well, you're going to have to be,' he says, and we both jerk as the door opens.

Pam comes in with coffee I won't be able to drink. My stomach clenches at the thought. The cups clink together as she puts the tray down. She's as nervous as me but for a different reason. She wants things to be right between us, but I can never unsay what I said about Sammy. I can apologise, though.

'Er, is Sammy here?' I ask.

Pam's eyes shoot to mine. She doesn't answer but her frown is pronounced.

'I owe him an apology. I was out of order saying what I said.'

She says nothing, but her eyes search my face.

'I must have been out of my mind. I've been suffering with depression, you see, ever since Issy...'

283

Her eyebrows shoot up. 'Oh, so you don't think he's Noah's dad anymore?'

'No. I don't think I ever really did. I was just lashing out. It was stupid of me and I'm so sorry. I know he'll probably never forgive me, and I deserve that, but I need to tell him, anyway.'

'And the DNA test?'

'I never sent it off. I threw it away.'

Her eyes glisten and she blinks several times. 'You don't know how relieved I am to hear you say that. He's out, though, at the moment.'

'Did he go out because he knew we were coming?'

'I don't know.'

'Oh. When is he coming back?'

'I don't know.'

I nod. 'It'll have to wait, then.'

Just then, the front door bangs, and I jerk violently. So does Jon. We look at each other.

'Only me,' shouts a voice. *His* voice. The voice of Satan, the devil himself. Carrier bags rustle, bottles clink and my heart goes into overdrive, and then he puts his head around the door. That face, so familiar, so smug, and suddenly I want to punch him. I can practically see the horns growing out of his head. Jon's fingers tighten briefly around my own, and he stands up, blocking my view.

'Alright?' he says, striding over to greet him. How can he do that? He looks normal, sounds normal. No one would ever know the churning inside him. 'Long time, no see,' he continues as they shake hands then clap each other on the back.

My flesh crawls, and I want to rip my skin off. Jon's just touched the hands that roamed over Issy's body. I look to where Pam was sitting to find she has left the room again and is clattering about in the kitchen.

'Hi Mel, how're you doing? Good to see you.'

Satan, in his normal human voice, is addressing me and waiting for an answer.

'Great, yeah,' I croak, shrinking back into the sofa. No forked tail lurks behind him and he isn't carrying a three-pronged fork. Just a carrier bag of beer.

'Good, good. Well, I'll just take these through into the kitchen.' He holds up the carrier bag. 'Want one?' he asks Jon.

'Nah, mate, I'll pass, thanks. A bit early for me. I'll stick to coffee.' He comes to sit next to me again, picking up his cup and passing me mine. My hand shakes as I take it, and I grasp it quickly between both hands then place it back on the table as the mug burns me.

'Too early? Since when?' Satan laughs. 'It's daylight, isn't it? I thought that was all that was required.'

'Maybe in a bit,' says Jon, sipping coffee. 'Had a bit of a gippy tummy lately.'

'Up to you. I'm having one though,' the Devil says, exiting the room. In the kitchen, I can hear them talking in hushed tones. Pam's probably telling him what I just said about Sammy. He'll be relieved about the DNA test, I'm sure. Suddenly it occurs to me that if Sammy is off the hook, will he think we suspect someone else?

'How many times do you think we'll have to do this?' I whisper to Jon. 'I just want to get out of here.'

'Me too. I'll go to the bathroom now, do a search, and start downloading things. Tell them I may be some time, that I've got cramps again and I've had to rush off.'

'Alright.'

He stands up, making sure his untucked shirt is covering the tablet that's tucked into the waistband of his jeans, and leaves. I have the urge to call him back. I don't want to be in here on my own. My skin is itching as if flies are crawling over every inch of me and my fingernails rake over my shin. Just then, the front door bangs again and Sammy shouts, 'Mum?'

'In the kitchen,' Pam calls back. Something else is said that I can't quite hear, and then Sammy enters the room and closes the door behind him. I stand up slowly, resisting the urge to wring my hands and instead let them drop limply by my sides.

Sammy's still leaning up against the door with his arms folded and saying nothing. His face is set hard. At one time, he would have thrown his arms around me.

'My son not here, then?' he asks sarcastically, glancing around. His eyes look sunken in his unshaven face, like he hasn't been sleeping well.

God. This isn't going to be easy.

'Listen, Sammy. About that. I'm so sorry. I don't know what came over me. Can you forgive me?'

He shrugs. 'Probably not, no. You were one bitch that day. I never knew you had that side to you.'

'I deserve that, I guess. But it was a mistake. We all make them. I...' I can't stand to see the hurt in his eyes and I look at the floor instead. 'I haven't been myself lately, not since Issy... I was lashing out, looking for answers in the wrong place. It was a ridiculous suggestion, and I don't know why I said it. I can't apologise enough. I'm so sorry.'

His shoulders relax just the tiniest bit, and I meet his eyes again as he speaks. 'It was ridiculous; you're right. I would never, ever have...'

'I know. I do know that, Sammy. You don't have to convince me. I was stupid. Things haven't been easy.'

'I suppose I can see that.' There's a tiny thaw in the air, and he sits down heavily in an armchair well away from me. 'I was so upset when you accused me of that.' He shakes his head. 'I never dreamed you would have thought that.'

I focus on his bare knee, poking through his torn jeans. 'And I didn't. Not really. I wasn't right in the head that day. And that's why I've come to apologise.'

'So, the DNA test—have you got the results back yet?'

'I never sent it off. I threw it away.' That's not true. I did send it off, before we found out about the Devil, and it hasn't come back yet.

No one comes back into the room; they're giving me and him space to talk and sort things out. I wonder how Jon's getting on in the bathroom. He has to start the tablet, Google child porn, check out some sites and download some images.

He can leave it downloading until we're ready to go. I hope he's right about it showing the location to the police. He says they can trace it back to this home address. The problem is we want to do it several times, plus set up an online presence for him from here before anyone comes knocking on his door. It'll look like he's gone on the internet to groom another innocent kid, seeing as he's lost the one he was regularly abusing. And I'm sure, now, they were having a relationship, based on what she said to Kim Brent. But if he started by abusing her, what possessed her to carry on a relationship with him and not tell us a thing? It sounds like she was voluntarily leaving campus to stay with him. That's the one thing I can't get my head around. I wish she were here to ask. The only thing I can think of is that he screwed with her mind, as well as her body. Maybe she thought she loved him or something.

Pam pokes her head around the door. She must have heard the chatter has dried up.

'Are we okay in here?' she asks in a tight voice.

Sammy and I look at each other, then at her.

'I think so,' he says.

'I hope so,' I say. 'I've said I'm sorry, and I hope he believes me and can forgive me. Same goes for you.' *Because I'm going to have to come round here and do this more than once.*

She doesn't answer, and an awkward silence descends once more. I have a massive urge to run, but I can't. I have to stay and fight this thing. *Act normal,* as Jon's been saying.

'So, how are things with you?' I ask her.

She takes a couple of steps into the room and stops. 'Oh, you know. Same old same old. You know how mad things get when college starts back. Carl and Joey seem to have settled back into school. I think they were happy to go back. You know how the holidays can drag on.' She's babbling on, her discomfort palpable.

I turn to Sammy. 'When do you go back to uni?'

'Tomorrow.'

I nod. He's probably relieved to be going back, getting away from everything that's happened in the past few months. I freeze when Justin suddenly enters the room, clutching a can of beer.

'Where's the little feller?' he asks, sinking down into an armchair and taking a large pull from the can.

I swallow hard and clear my throat. 'He's, er, at a new friend's house. Someone who goes to the same childminder.' *You'll never get your hands on him again, if I have anything to do with it.*

All the time I'm speaking, Justin is looking at me intently, playing his usual part, his gaze not flinching. He has absolutely no idea we're onto him. I have a vision of a serpent that lives beneath his skin, and, beneath that, the rancid, rotten core of him.

'I wanted to see him. Haven't seen him in a while.' *Since you lost your mind and we all fell out,* hangs unsaid in the air.

I can see now, without a shadow of a doubt, that the way he is with Noah is because he knows he's his son. He's so confident that Issy would have kept their secret that the urge to go there and smash my fist into his face is overwhelming, but I know I can't. A gripping sensation starts up in my chest, as if someone has reached inside and is squeezing my heart uncomfortably hard. He's so smug and self-confident. Why did I never see it before? It seems so obvious now. For the first time, I spare a thought for what Pam is going to have to go through when this all comes out. She may never speak to me again, but somehow, I doubt it. She's going to need me when she learns the man she married is a monster.

As a great wave of sorrow rushes over me, I push it away. I need to keep it together.

'Well, I'm glad you two have come round. Maybe things can get back to normal now.'

Is he for real?

'Where's Jon?' he asks, as if he's only just noticed he's missing.

'Bathroom. Upstairs. Cramps.' All of a sudden, I'm speaking in one-word sentences. Coherent speech deserts me. Come on, Jon, how much longer are you going to be? Although I know it has only been a few minutes.

'Well, I'm off. Got things to do.' Sammy suddenly gets up and goes upstairs, banging the door to his room shut. Carrying on as normal, probably. So there's no lasting damage done, I hope. He's back to his old self. He always leaves abruptly. Pam often thinks he's upstairs and discovers he's gone out without telling them. What lasting damage will be done when he and his brothers find out the truth about their father? The fallout from this will be so seismic, it's hard to predict.

The three of us sit in silence, resorting to small talk, which they, no doubt, will put down to the arguments there's been lately. Eventually, Jon comes back downstairs, pale and wan-looking. He's trembling.

'My God, you do look ill,' Justin says. 'Are you alright, mate?'

Jon shakes his head. 'No, I feel like shit.'

'You look like it. What's up?' Justin asks.

'This stomach bug I had seems to have come back. I think we should go. I don't want to pass it onto you lot,' he lies. Convincingly. That's the side of him that was able to have an affair and lie to my face about where he'd been.

'Are you coming?' he asks me. 'I'll be okay if you want to stay here?' he adds, for a touch of authenticity.

'No,' I say, quickly. From the corner of my eye, I see Pam shoot me a look. She probably thinks it's down to the strained atmosphere.

'We'll come again when I'm over it,' Jon says. 'Maybe tomorrow, if I'm feeling better. Are you around?' he asks Justin. 'So we can catch up?'

'Yeah, should be. Or we can come to you.'

'No, it's fine. We'll come here. It's about time we mended some broken fences, don't you think?'

Justin nods eagerly. 'I'd like that. To get back to normal.'

289

I bet you would, you bastard, I think.

'Bring the little guy, if you like. I've missed him.'

I'm up off the sofa and through the front door in an instant. As we walk back to our house, I turn to Jon.

'What happened? Did you manage to do anything?'

His face is grim and grey, the colour not yet returned. 'Yeah. I downloaded some pictures and turned it off before I came back downstairs.' He pulls the tablet from the waistband of his jeans and his hand shakes so badly he almost drops it. 'God, Mel, the pictures. I caught a glimpse of some of them. They were truly disgusting. I actually threw up before I came back downstairs; that's how bad they were. I'll never forget them as long as I live. The look in those kids' eyes...' He tails off and stifles a sob, stuffing his clenched fist into his mouth. His eyes are haunted by what he's seen. I'm glad I didn't see them. I don't even want to imagine them. Now it's my turn to be strong.

'I'm proud of you for having the strength to do it. We have no choice, really. It's for the greater good. Who knows if he already has pictures like this on his computer, anyway?' He probably does. His sort do, don't they?

Jon wipes his eyes and sniffs. 'Possibly. On the plus side, I'll be quicker next time. I won't have to check out the sites. I've saved them, and I can just download pictures from them without having to look at them.'

'When is next time?' I ask.

'Tomorrow, hopefully. I just want to get this over with. You don't have to come. A couple of weeks and we should have enough to finish the job.'

I can't let him do it alone.

'No, it's alright. I'll come.'

42

Jon

IT'S TWO WEEKS AFTER the first downloading session at Justin's, and I hope tonight will be the last time. It's been the most sickening thing I've ever had to do, and every time I've done it, I've felt shame and disgust. I had my doubts that Mel would manage it but, apart from the first time, she's been great. She says it's got easier as time's gone on and has convinced them she wants to make amends. And, amazingly, they've fallen for it.

Tonight she's taking Pam out for a meal. Mel suggested it was a way she and her sister could spend some time together and bond. It's a Friday night so it should be busy, meaning they can stay out longer. Mel's agreed to keep Pam out for as long as possible, and she's going to try to talk her into going to see a film as well if I need more time. I'm going round to Justin's, with Noah, for a lads' night in, plus a spot of babysitting. It's been getting harder to think up feasible excuses as to why Noah can't come round, and I can't let Justin get suspicious now. I don't want to let the bastard anywhere near Noah, but hopefully it'll be the last time. If all goes to plan, he won't see his son ever again, or at least not for a very, very long time.

Knowing I'm downloading child porn has almost destroyed me even though there's a good reason. It seems

291

somehow as if I'm buying into it, condoning it, but I try not to look at the images. If we can get one paedo put away for longer, then consequently some children may suffer less. It's the only way I can explain it. Adele has been asking constantly what's wrong and I can't tell her. Mel and I swore to keep it between ourselves so as not to incriminate anyone else, but Adele's not stupid. I've told her I'll tell her as soon as I can, when all this is over. I only hope she'll understand. For now, she's trusting me and that means everything. Mel seems okay that I'm seeing Adele again, so long as she doesn't come to the house. I think it's a relief to her that I won't be pestering her for sex anymore, not that I have in a long time. She actually used that word once, after she found out about the affair years ago. She's filed for divorce, agreeing to irreconcilable differences rather than adultery. I suppose when it comes through, I'll move out. It would just be too weird, being divorced and under the same roof. Whether or not I move into Adele's hasn't been decided, but it's looking likely. Wherever I am, Noah will always have a home with me. We come as a package, and Adele is excited about meeting him. If she's willing to take him on, then that would be amazing.

In order for that to happen, though, I have to get tonight out of the way. A few hours more, then I'll never have to spend another minute with that odious, sick bastard again.

'Come on, Noah. We need to go. Are you ready?'

Noah is sitting on the bottom step, putting his shoes on. He's been at it for ages. His little pink tongue pokes out of one side of his mouth as he concentrates.

'Ready,' he announces proudly and stands up. His shoes are on the wrong feet, and the Velcro flap is hanging open.

'Well done, mate. Can you walk in them?'

'Course.' He frowns and takes a step. 'My feet are pointing the wrong way.' He takes another tentative step, then sits on the floor. 'These shoes don't fit me, Grandad.'

I sit next to him. 'Wrong feet,' I whisper into his ear, and he beams at me.

'I'm silly, aren't I?' He pulls them off and puts them on the right way. 'They go on quick now.'

I fasten the Velcro straps. 'Well done. Now can we go?'

'Yep. To Uncle Jussin's?'

'That's right. It'll be late when we get back, so take a coat. You're having a big boy night, stopping up way past your bedtime.'

'Yay,' he yells, running up four stairs to grab his coat off the bannister. He puts it on back to front and chortles with laughter before swapping it round.

'Do you want to take anything to play with?'

'Mmm, Game Boy.' He runs off upstairs and comes back clutching it. 'I can play Pokémon to level three.'

'Brilliant. I can't. Come on, then.'

He slots his tiny hand into mine, and we go out the front door. All the way round to Justin's, he keeps up his inane chatter about this and that, what he did at the childminder's, what he's seen on TV, his upcoming birthday in two weeks' time. I listen to him carefully. He's not a damaged child. He's going to be okay. Mel and I are the constants in his life, and we'll always be there for him. He knows us as his parents now, and nothing will change that. He points up at the stars, resplendent in the clear night despite the street lights.

'Look at the twinkly sky dots, Grandad,' he says in wonder.

I laugh and look down at him. God, I love this kid so much. No one will ever harm so much as a hair on his head while I'm around. It makes me sick to my stomach to think who his father is. Surely, this sort of thing doesn't run in the genes, does it? Sweet little Noah couldn't grow up to be a monster like his father?

Five minutes later, we reach Justin's house and I knock on the door before going in. He's just coming down the stairs.

'Hey, look who's here,' he says, running down the stairs to pick Noah up and swing him around. *The doting uncle.* To think I never saw through him before. All I ever saw was my best friend. It beggars belief that someone could be as good at acting a part as him. I can't wait for this to be over and swallow down the bile that always rises now in his presence.

'I can do Pokémon level three,' Noah crows. 'Want to see?'

'I most certainly do,' says Justin. *His father.* The thought sickens and angers me. I long to fetch a knife from the kitchen and plunge the blade between his ribs, twist it and rip it up. I could gut him like a fish and it would feel so good.

'I'll make some coffee while you watch the master at work,' I say to Justin, encouraging him to go into the living room with Noah.

In the kitchen, I make the coffee and put three of Mel's strong sedatives into Justin's, making sure they're dissolved properly before taking it through.

'I've brought some biscuits as well,' I say, putting a packet of digestives on the table.

'Good man,' Justin says, patting his slightly rounded stomach. 'I'm feeling a bit peckish.'

'Can I have a biscuit?' asks Noah, helping himself.

I laugh. 'Sure. Go on then.'

Justin takes two, dunks one after another and shovels them straight in. A piece of one drops off and falls with a plonk back into his coffee.

'Bugger. Why does it always do that?' he asks, tutting.

'Bugger. Bugger,' mutters Noah, nibbling on his biscuit.

Justin pokes a fingertip at the disintegrating fragments of biscuit and sighs. It's fine by me. Hopefully, with bits of digestive floating about, it'll mask the taste, if there is any, of the tablets. I sip my coffee, watching Justin keenly. Hopefully, it won't be too long before the tablets take effect. I don't know how long I'll need on Justin's computer. Carl's playing rugby tonight, and Joey is at his new girlfriend's house. Quiet, studious little Joey has a girlfriend; who would have thought? He kept that one quiet.

'So how's things with you? Anything new happened?' Justin turns to me expectantly.

I know he's fishing for information about Adele. Ever since Pam saw her in my office that day, the pair of them have been desperate to know what's been going on. Mel and I have told them precisely nothing.

'Alright, yeah,' I say, shrugging. 'What time are Joey and Carl coming home?'

'Ah, not 'til late. Joey's 'revising' with Sophie,' he says, making air quotes around 'revising'. I force a smile, 'And Carl's friend's mum is bringing them back after they've had tea at theirs after rugby.'

'I remember 'revising', myself. I did a fair bit of that,' I say.

'Me too,' he agrees. 'Always enjoyed it, as I remember.'

I watch as he picks up his coffee and drinks half the cup. *That's it, keep going. Don't leave the last half to go cold like you sometimes do.*

'Caught up at work?' he asks. It's been like this since the fall out over Sammy. On the surface, everything's the same, but it feels like a pretence. In reality, we're circling round each other, both trying to say the right thing. Justin never said much to me about Mel accusing Sammy. I think it was a bit too close for comfort, and he'd rather it just went away with minimum fuss.

'Yeah, just about. I'm still busy. You?'

'Mad, mate. Just manic at the minute. I'm running from one meeting to the next most days.'

He thumbs the remote and turns the TV news on then, thankfully, slugs back the rest of the coffee. I sip mine, but it tastes bitter, and I put it back down again. It's not all that unusual that we sit in silence, but it used to be amiable, the easy quiet of companions. This feels stilted and forced, like we're overthinking it. I must try harder.

'If the girls go to the pictures after dinner, they'll be back fairly late. I expect I'll have to carry him home fast asleep.' I nod to Noah, who's now deep into his game. All manner of electronic noises and flashing lights come from the game console. He'll be absorbed for at least the next hour.

Justin yawns. 'I'm knackered. Been up since five. Had to drive to Preston and back.'

Maybe I didn't need the sleeping tablets then. With two, he should be out for the count before long. We gaze at the news again, and I marvel once more at how he managed to fool everyone for so long: me, Mel, Pam. Especially Pam. Mel and I have talked about it and we've realised that people largely see what they want to see. Maybe because it suits us— all of us. How many people on the news, when told that their neighbour was a serial killer or child molester, say, 'I never would have thought that. He seemed so normal. Such a nice guy.' You think they *must* know, but here's the proof. Sometimes you really don't.

I'm itching to get started and get out of here in case the boys come back early, but it takes another half hour before he's fast asleep and snoring softly. His head is drooping onto his chest, and he's well away.

'Justin?' No response. I clap my hands in front of his face. Same. Two minutes later, I'm in his office, logging onto his personal laptop. I know his password. I've watched his fingers as he's done it many times before, right there in front of me. After all, I'm no threat, am I? Good old mug Jon. The best friend. Father of the kid he was raping on a regular basis. I don't even need to wear gloves. My fingerprints are all over the computer as I've touched it many times in the past when we've used it together.

Ten minutes in, and I've set up a profile as him on some chat room and I've also used the same name to post some dodgy messages on other forums I've discovered that are definitely used for this purpose. During the sessions over the past two weeks that I've been in his bathroom downloading and researching stuff, I've found it was way easier to find than I ever thought it would be. I thought it would be the dark net I would need and was bracing myself to search it but, amazingly, most of it's right there on the normal web if you dig about enough. And I've really dug. The extent of it is shocking and my skin is crawling now, but I have to be thorough. This is my last time, with a bit of luck, then I can go and scrub off the filth that contaminates my skin, my pores, my clothes, everything. I feel defiled and like a monster myself, just from doing it. Half an hour later and I've been chatting with some girl named Holly, posing as a fourteen-year-old boy called Aaron. She says she's thirteen and likes horses. I tell her I have a horse and it just goes on from there. Then I chat to more kids, girls and boys, telling each one what I think they want to hear from the information they've given away about themselves, looking for clues, a way in. I'm disturbed by how easy it all is. Do these parents have no clue as to what their kids are getting up to? Do they even care? I really, really hope some of these kids I've been talking to are really adults posing as victims, and they've been setting me up in order to catch the real paedos. I resolve never, ever to let Noah be in a position like this. From now on, I'm going to watch him like a hawk, and he'll be allowed on the internet over my dead body.

I jump when my phone rings. Mel.

'I'm in the toilets in the restaurant. Do you need more time? Shall I take her to the pictures? She's up for it.'

'Yeah, okay, just to be on the safe side.'

'How's it going?'

'Good. If these things *are* good.'

'I know what you meant. Alright, I'll be about three hours then. There are a couple of things we can see. I'll let her choose.'

'Okay.' I ring off and listen carefully. All I can hear is Noah's game and Justin snoring louder now. Satisfied, I download some of the worst images I can find and bury them deep in Justin's computer, confident he won't find them. But the police will, when they seize his computer and look for them. I delete the browsing history for the sites I've visited, so it looks like Justin is covering his tracks. They'll be recovered when it matters and added to the damning evidence when I go to Steve Jackson tomorrow, with the photo of him with Issy that David Noone sent me.

In under an hour, I'm all finished and back downstairs. I sneak back into the room. Noah looks up and smiles at me.

'Come on, we going home. Leave Uncle Justin to his sleep, eh?'

He nods and gets up obediently. I text Mel one word. *Done.* As Noah puts his coat on, I stand and look at Justin, my former best mate, brother, and confidante. The times I've told him every little thing about my life, my family, marriage woes, kid troubles. The only thing I never told him about was Adele, and he acted so put out that I'd kept it from him. But he was keeping much bigger secrets from me.

I pick Noah up and we go out into the chilly night. I hug him close to me, inhaling the scent of him: baby shampoo and biscuits. When we're entering the house five minutes later, Mel texts back. *OK. Film just started. See you later.* It all sounds so normal, like she'll come home to her loving husband. Instead, I'll be sleeping in my dead daughter's bedroom, wishing I was in another woman's bed. How's that for normal? How did my life turn to such shit?

My briefcase is just behind the front door where I dumped it earlier, and I take it upstairs to my bedroom. Issy's room. As ever, when I enter this room, grief engulfs me and I kick the briefcase hard before throwing myself down onto the bed. For me, life will never be normal again. None of this is normal. But I need to get Noah to bed, and there's no time to wallow. He's tired and doesn't object to missing his bath. When Mel gets back, he's been asleep for ages.

'Okay?' she asks as she comes through the front door, closing it quietly behind her. 'How did it go? Is Noah in bed?'

'Hi, yes he is, and it went as planned. We've got him stitched up. It's finished.'

I expected to have to go through it, chapter and verse, but she's seems satisfied and I'm glad. After what I consider to be an acceptable amount of time watching TV together, I announce that I'm tired and am going to bed. Her lips tighten, but she nods. She knows I'll spend the next hour Skyping Adele. She must have heard me most nights but hasn't said anything. Sometimes, I think she regrets me moving back in, even if it does help with Noah. I don't think she really wants me here any more than I want to be here.

Adele's in her dimly lit bedroom when I Skype her. 'I wish you were here,' she says. She's sitting cross-legged on her bed, wearing her lacy little vest-top-and-shorts pyjamas, the ones she knows I like. The ones that do things to me. I long to remove them and curl up next to her, skin to skin. Soon, I hope we can do it every night.

'You look gorgeous,' I say, quietly. 'Take them off.'

She giggles and blushes. 'No way,' she says. 'I'm not having Skype sex with you, you perv. It'll have to wait until you're here in person.' But she slips a strap seductively down her shoulder, and I follow its journey with my eyes. Just before too much is revealed, she pulls it back up and sticks her tongue out, giving me a cheeky grin.

I groan. 'Spoilsport.'

It's all normal banter, and I hope one day I'll be able to feel normal again. She tells me about her day, and I tell her as much as I can about mine, glossing over this evening. Eventually we say goodnight, and I turn the light off, snuggling down into Issy's bed. It's just a bed, I tell myself every night. There's nothing of significance in it. It's just simple things like wood, metal and cotton. But it feels like more than that. Just the very fact that I'm in it and she isn't is wrong.

When I eventually drop off to sleep, my mind is filled with visions of Issy and Justin. At first, Issy is small again, and she's helping me to plant a border in the garden, her laughter and giggles sweet to my ears. Then Justin is there, and they're taunting me, their faces looming large in front of me. Suddenly, the scene changes, and we're all in Peter Cunningham's office. Justin is holding his hand over Issy's mouth and tearing at her clothes. Issy screams, then laughs, then she's pulling up her sleeves to show me her mutilated arms, the scars that I remember so well from the mortuary when I first discovered them. She's crying, *Look, Daddy, look,* and Justin is dragging her away. I sit bolt upright in bed, wide awake and panting. Her face fills my mind and all I can think of is the thought that's haunted me since she died: that I didn't save her. I wasn't there when she needed me.

I'm sweating heavily and breathing hard, and swing my legs out of bed to get up to turn the light on. In the darkness, I fall over the briefcase I left lying around earlier and stumble into the wall, colliding with a picture so hard it falls off and lands straight on my foot. I stifle a yell as pain shoots through me; it's probably broken my bloody toe or something. I stab the light on hard in temper. The damn picture is face down on the carpet. As I go to pick it up, I notice something white sticking out from behind the back. Paper, wedged in tight. It hasn't fallen out, but someone's obviously placed it there and not fully tried to hide it. This is Issy's bedroom, so it must have been her. I tug at it, but it won't budge.

I sit on the bed and remove the back from the picture frame, taking out the folded piece of paper. It's Issy's handwriting; unsurprising, since it was her room. I unfold it, and my heart slams into my mouth as I realise what I'm reading… Issy's last words, answering all the questions we've worked so hard to uncover for the past few months. All the answers have been right under our noses all this time. If only we'd known. Hot tears are running down my face, and I'm gripping the piece of paper so tightly my fingers are pinched and white. Before the tears can drip onto it, I cast it aside and lay back on the bed, wailing. I've never felt such pain. I feel I'm being torn in two. The door opens and Mel rushes in. She kneels by the bed when she sees me.

'Jon? What's wrong? Are you in pain?'

Her eyes widen when she sees my tears. and I push the letter towards her, sitting up while she reads it. Every bit of me is shaking, and her face is bone white when she puts it down. Tears spill down her face too, and we sit together, not speaking, until dawn comes. This is evidence, the last nail in his coffin. The mystery of *why* is finally over. If only we'd seen this before she killed herself, we could have done something about it. But it's too late now. Our life is changed forever, and forever is a long time.

43

Justin

JUSTIN OPENS HIS EYES. The sun is worming its way in through a tiny gap in the bedroom curtains, bright and harsh. Pam is awake next to him.

'Morning,' she says. 'You were out like a light last night when I got back.'

He sits up and rubs his eyes, trying to remember last night. He'd fallen asleep on the sofa, with Noah playing on his Game Boy nearby and Jon watching TV. When he'd woken up later, they'd both gone. He was so tired he'd just gone to bed. He hadn't even heard Pam come in. He'd dragged himself off the sofa and up to bed, to find Pam already there, fast asleep. He'd climbed in and zonked straight out again.

'Good night?' he asked her. 'How was Mel?'

'It was lovely, yeah. We went to see a film, some romcom thing, with Jennifer Aniston. It was okay. It was just good to be with Mel, to be honest. She was almost happy.'

Justin's mouth turns up at one corner at her words and Pam laughs. 'You know what I mean.'

Justin feels refreshed, in a way he hasn't in a long time. He knows why—it's because everything's getting back to normal. He's been so worried for so long, especially when his mad sister-in-law turned on Sammy and made him do the DNA test. Now, with all that behind them, things are going to be good again. Things won't be the same without Issy, of course,

302

but there's nothing he can do about it. He misses her, though. He'll always miss her, those nights in hotel rooms all over the place, her young, juicy body given over to him willingly for so long. Her death had hit him as hard as the rest of them, and his grief had been deep and genuine. No acting required.

'What did you and Jon do last night?' Pam is asking now.

'Same as ever—chatted and had a drink.'

'What did you talk about?'

He thinks back. What had they talked about? Couldn't remember, really.

'Just the usual stuff,' he says.

'Do you think things will get a bit better from now on?'

'I hope so,' he says. 'Although there's still a long way to go. It's early days for us all yet, especially Jon and Mel. They'll never really get over it, will they?'

'No.' Pam sits up, fluffs her pillow and leans back, adjusting the covers over her legs. 'Why do you think Mel changed her mind about Sammy like that?'

'Just saw sense, obviously. Who knows what goes on in her head? She's been bouncing off the walls since Issy died.'

'Well, I'm just glad she did. It's such a relief.'

He settles back onto his pillows. It had been so good to see Noah last night. For a horrible moment, he'd thought they were keeping Noah away from him and Pam, but he was just being daft. Yesterday, all was well. Jon was his best friend again, and Mel and Pam were on good terms, spending time together like they used to. Sammy had forgiven Mel for her outburst, it seemed, and Carl and Joey had been kept out of it as much as it was possible. Teenagers were in their own world anyway, most of the time, so it hadn't been that difficult. If they'd gone around wearing blinkers, it wouldn't have made much difference.

He sits up again, throws the covers off and gets out of bed. When he pulls the curtains back, it's a glorious September day outside. He might start a fitness regime, maybe running, or swimming, or join a gym.

'Fancy a big cooked breakfast?' asks Pam. 'With black pudding?'

He turns around. She's halfway through getting dressed. The gym can wait a few more days.

'Why not?' he says. 'That would go down a treat.'

He pulls on his dressing gown and follows his wife downstairs. All is well with the world. His family is knitting back together nicely, damaged and battle-scarred, but mending, nonetheless. Everything is going to be alright. He knows. He can feel it. The storm of the past few months has blown over, leaving bright sunshine in its wake.

44

Issy

IN THE HALLS OF residence, Issy sits with a pen in her hand, trying hard to tune out the booming bass coming through the wall from Michael's room next door. Her door is locked, and she's wearing a vest, her arms exposed. The cuts on one arm are bleeding. She can't stop picking at them. Maybe they've become infected. She runs her fingers over them; they're hot and throbbing, but the soreness is good. It makes her *feel* something. It's been such a long time since she's felt anything, the numbness that's been with her for so long having become her norm.

Ryan is with Michael next door; she can hear his high-pitched laughter through the wall. He shrieks like a girl. She shakes her head and applies her mind to the task ahead once more. She already knows what she wants to write, having been planning it for a few weeks now. The thing with Peter Cunningham had been the kicker, the turning point. She'd known then that she couldn't be saved, that she wasn't worth it. The humiliation had hit a nerve, the disgust in his eyes at the meeting. She'd repulsed him. She had told Kim Brent that she thought it was normal to do what she'd done, but deep down, she'd known full well it wasn't. Normal people didn't do such things. But she wasn't normal. She was damaged, and the damage was too great to be repaired. She was like a broken china doll that had dropped on the floor and smashed into too many pieces that no longer fit together correctly. No matter which way or how hard you tried, the jagged edges still showed. She begins to write.

Dear Mum and Dad, if you find this then it's meant to be. You know I've always believed in fate. In an hour or so, if all goes to plan, I'll be dead, and this note is to set the record straight.

First of all, I'm sorry for what I'm about to do. I know it will tear you both apart and I don't expect you to understand, but I have to do it. There's no other way. For so long, I've tried to live a normal life, but he's ruined me. I can't have normal relationships with boys my age, as I'm no longer normal.

Justin is Noah's dad, but you might well know that by now. It's wrong, but I love him, and I know you won't understand. I don't expect you to. He has been doing sexual things to me for years. I can't really remember the first time. By the time I found out it was wrong, it felt normal to me. I didn't know any different. He said it was our secret, and that other people wouldn't understand. The first time he had sex with me, I was twelve, but he'd been doing things to me long before that. He said he loved me and that's how you show love. I was scared because he said I could go to prison too for letting him do it, and you two would be really hurt and upset with me and send me away.

After I got used to it, I liked it. I loved him and wanted us to be together, like a proper family with Noah, but he wouldn't. He said he couldn't leave Aunty Pam, that it would kill her and that he loved his boys, but I still wanted to. I know how bad this sounds, so what does that make me? I tried to have other relationships with boys, but I couldn't. I was a freak. You're not supposed to sleep with your own uncle, are you? Not that I could tell anybody. I'm too damaged, and always will be. Because of him, I'm in a dark place, and there's no way out of it. The walls are just too high.

I don't want to be Noah's mother, and I'll never be able to have a proper boyfriend. Justin won't let me go. Every time I try, he pulls me back and keeps me his, but our relationship is unnatural. When I've tried to see other boys, he goes mad until it's just not worth it and I give in and stop seeing them. But how can you live like this? I can't have him properly, but he won't let me go. Deep down, he must know he won't get away with what he's done to me.

So this is the only way I know to stop it. I'll do what I have to, to end it for good. I'm sorry, I know I haven't been the best daughter. Don't grieve for me too much because this is the way things have to be. When Noah is old enough, tell him I'm sorry. It's up to you whether you tell him about his father. I know that Justin does love him lots.

Goodbye. I love you both very much. You have been amazing parents. I'm so sorry.

Issy xxx

She puts the pen down and reads the letter through, satisfied at the tone and the grammar, shaking her head at why she even cares. What do a few missing commas matter? But there again, she is doing an English degree and hates sloppy writing. She folds the note in half, then half again, and tucks it into her purse, between her Student Union card and her bank card. It'll be safe there for the next few days. The thought of losing it and having to write it again is too much. Every word has left her feeling wrung out. She picks up the long-bladed knife with the black handle and scores it into her flesh. It's hard these days to find a gap between the cuts where the flesh is unmarked, but she only needs a tiny one. She watches as the tip of the blade splits the skin and a bead of blood appears, bubbling out of the cut. Then she places the rest of the blade on her skin and increases the pressure, pressing down and closing her eyes at the sharp sting of the metal.

45

Mel

THE LAST SIX MONTHS have been long and drawn out, leading to this moment now where Justin stands quietly in the dock, awaiting sentencing. I stare at him, unable to tear my eyes away. His head is bowed, and his hands are clasped in front of him, which has pretty much been his default position throughout. He hasn't spoken a single word since being arrested. Not to confirm anything, nor to deny it. He hasn't even said, 'no comment,' according to Steve. So there's been a trial, and all the way through he has sat there mute and unmoving. Even on the stand he didn't speak, just looked at the floor. The judge got quite irate at one bit, as he ignored her questions as well; she shook her head and pursed her lips in exasperation. She isn't a woman who likes being ignored. Hopefully, it may contribute to him getting a longer sentence, the police have told us. Lack of cooperation doesn't look good to the jury.

The only time he has looked across at us was when they read out the evidence concerning all the stuff found on his computer. He raised his head slowly and stared unblinkingly at me, then Jon, for a very long time. He would have known about this before the trial, but it was the first time we'd seen each other face to face. It was as if he had to see the look on our faces to believe what we'd done. I could see him working it out. An understanding seemed to pass between him and us, and I got the feeling he knew he'd been played. From the corner of my eye, I saw a tiny movement at the edge of Jon's mouth. It curled up a fraction, and he gave a barely perceptible nod. No one else would have registered it. At that second, his eyes were locked onto Justin's, and a flicker of confirmation passed over Justin's face. Against the DNA evidence which proved him to be Noah's father, all the other evidence paled into insignificance, and it seemed Jon and I needn't have bothered with the child porn thing. The fact that he'd been having sex with Issy since she was twelve meant the prosecution could push for life imprisonment. But I hope the images on his computer helped to convince the jury he was a monster who should never get out again. The letter Issy wrote was used in evidence, and, judging by the looks of disgust on most of the juror's faces, they believed it and were as repulsed and reviled by him as we were. A handwriting expert declared the writing to be Issy's and said the document was genuine. No one had any reason to doubt what it said, in view of what it had pushed her to do.

As I sit now, waiting for the jury to return and pass their verdict, I feel as if I'm about to pass out as my heart constricts painfully. My vision blurs and I sway towards Jon, who grips my hand tightly. What if they find him not guilty for some reason?

'Not long now, love. Stay strong,' Jon whispers. He keeps hold of my hand.

We were summoned back into the courtroom minutes ago and all stand as the judge enters for the last time. My sister is at my side, hanging onto the rail in front of her, her fingers gripping it like talons. She's looking at her husband but displaying no emotion. She looks terrible, like she's aged ten years. Ever since the truth was revealed, she's been in pieces.

'I didn't know, I honestly didn't know. I'm so sorry. Please, you have to believe me,' is all she's said to me since. She's desperate for me to believe her and, finally, after much soul-searching, I do. It's hard to understand how Justin could have done something like this and she wouldn't have known but, there again, he fooled all of us. Pam saw the perfect, loving husband whenever she looked at him; I saw the amiable, fun-loving brother-in-law, and Jon saw his best friend and drinking buddy. So, if she's guilty of being blind, then we all are. We all saw what he projected himself as. I dread to think what Issy saw—it sickens me. Pam has said she will never forgive herself for introducing him into all our lives and I know, without a doubt, that she will never, ever trust another man as long as she lives. Even though I've told her that most men aren't like Justin, she no longer has faith in her own judgement. Or lack of it, as she sees it.

Two weeks after Justin had been arrested, I got to ask Pam the question that had been burning within me.

'Pam, when Justin was a child, did anything happen to him? I mean—'

'I know what you mean,' she said, 'And the answer is, I don't know.'

Justin was adopted at seven, and I knew nothing of his life before then. His adoptive parents were a sweet, childless couple in their early forties. I'd met them a few times, and seen how they doted on him. Anything he wanted, he could have. Sometimes, it was like they were making up for the bad start he'd had in life, a start none of us knew much about, as he wouldn't talk about it. His parents had split before he was born, and his mother had a string of boyfriends. He was in foster care at five. Any one of them could have done something to him, the boyfriends or the foster carers. I'd heard of foster carers being abusive before, so it wouldn't be the first time.

'I don't know. He would never speak about his early childhood, you know he wouldn't. He'd just clam up and walk away,' Pam said. 'He always said his life began at seven.'

'Do you think it's likely he was a victim himself, that he learned that that behaviour was normal?'

She'd looked at me, tears coursing down her cheeks. 'I don't know. I've tortured myself over and over with that very thought. Maybe.'

I look at him now. Was he a victim, too? It's impossible to tell. Pam had told me that the fact that she'd had sons, not daughters, had haunted her every night since the arrest. If she and Justin had had daughters, would he have done the same to them? His sons have all sworn that their dad had never laid a hand on them in that way. They've been as shocked as everyone else about what's come to light. So the question remains unanswered unless Justin ever tells us, and I don't think he will. It shouldn't matter but, somehow, it does.

Next to Pam are two of her sons, dressed in suits and still unable to process the events of the last few months. Sammy and I have had long talks about everything, and he has forgiven me for suspecting him in the light of what we now know. He stands now with his head bowed, as does Joey next to him, fidgeting with his hands in his pockets. Sammy curls his fingers around Joey's wrist, and Joey becomes still. Sammy puts his arm across his younger brother's shoulders. Carl has refused to even acknowledge his father since his arrest. Joey and Sammy haven't been to see him, but at least they don't leave the room at the mention of his name, like Carl does. Out of all his sons, Carl idolised his father the most. I guess the higher up the pedestal, the further the fall. I look at the five of us now, struggling to process what's happened to us: six lives ruined, including Issy's. Seven, including Carl.

The judge indicates that we should sit, and I sink gratefully down as my legs threaten to give way. The judge, fifty-ish with blonde, rigid hair and garish pink lipstick, looks across at the jury and asks if they've reached a verdict. I swallow the nausea that swells up inside me and dig my nails into Jon's palm. He doesn't appear to notice. His leg is jiggling up and down, up and down, and his whole body is trembling. *Please, please, please,* he mutters under his breath, over and over again, his eyes roaming from Justin to the judge to the jury, over and over again. Various counts are read out in a never-ending stream, and I register certain words: sexual intercourse... girl under thirteen.... indecent photographs... children. Over the sound of the blood rushing in my head, I register the foreman of the jury's words saying guilty, guilty, guilty, from somewhere far away. I close my eyes and hear the judge say 'life' and force them open again to see what the Devil is doing, how he looks. He's standing straight in his best suit and tie, looking the pillar of respectability, but his shirt collar doesn't quite conceal the vivid purple bruising around his neck. Whether he tried to hang himself or whether other prisoners tried to do it for him remains unclear. He won't say what happened, but warders cut him down just in time. I don't know if I'm sorry or not. I don't particularly want his suffering to be over and if he died, then it would have been. On the other hand, why should he be alive when Issy's dead because of him? Maybe he won't last long in prison.

When Jon showed me the letter Issy had written, it all fell into place, and fresh grief ripped through me. I thought knowing all the answers would help, but it changed nothing. She was still dead. We took the letter to Steve Jackson, along with the email sent by David Noone showing Justin and Issy at the uni. It was the break we'd been waiting for, and he grabbed the ball and ran full pelt with it. The investigation was set in motion, and he didn't stop until Justin was charged. He's sitting behind us right now in the court, his hand pressing lightly on my shoulder before it's gone again. I can imagine the expression of grim satisfaction he'll be wearing.

Scuffling noises break into my thoughts, and I watch as the Devil is taken away in handcuffs. He doesn't cast a glance our way. It's finally over. Steve touches my shoulder again, and I turn to see his concerned face.

'Alright?' he asks, looking first at me, then Jon.

I swallow hard. 'Yes. And thank you for everything, Steve.'

He nods. 'Keep in touch.'

'I will,' I say, and Jon says the same. And it's true; I will. Steve has become a true friend to both of us.

He goes to shake my hand, then changes his mind and pulls me into a hug, doing the same with Jon. I watch him as he leaves, knowing he'll chalk it up to more than just a victory. For him, it was personal. Jon and I look at each other as the court files out. A few people from the local press leave, presumably to file their copy. That's all we are now; just another story. Tomorrow's chip paper. Soon, everyone will forget about this, but we can never forget. Somehow, we must move on.

'Come on,' says Jon. He hugs me tight. 'It's over. He's gone. Hopefully, he'll never get out again.' His eyes are wet and he blinks tears away.

I nod slowly, wondering how my sister feels. She's still sitting with her head bowed. I leave her for a minute. Sammy and Joey are holding her hands. Maybe, like me, they're wondering if they can put their lives back together after this. Pam stands at last, with her sons either side of her. Her eyes are red and puffy and she, like me, is now a bit on the thin side. In fact, I've put a bit of weight back on since learning the answers. I'm eating a bit better. I don't sleep well, but one day, maybe I will.

'Shall I come round later?' she asks. I can see she's desperate for me not to blame her, and I don't. I blame myself for not seeing, not noticing; the very things for which she blames herself.

'Yes, okay,' I say. We've mended a lot of broken fences in the last few months, but whether we'll ever go back to how we were, who can say? We're two different people now; both of us have lost our husbands, and I've also lost my daughter.

'I'm glad he got life,' she says, and anger blazes behind her eyes. 'I hate him.'

I nod. There's nothing more to say. I hate him too.

'See you later,' I say.

Sammy and Joey hug me, and then the three of them are gone. Jon and I are the last to leave. The courtroom is now an innocuous-looking, empty room, yet such horror as has been described here today is commonplace within its four walls. I wonder if a building can absorb such evil that it becomes stained with it. The court usher clears his throat and nods deferentially as he holds the door open for us. Outside the court, we stand on the steps. A fleeting figure on the other side of the road at the edge of my vision disappears.

'So, this is it,' I say to Jon. 'The end of the road.'

Jon thrusts his hands into his trouser pockets. 'It's hardly the end of the road. And I don't have to go yet, if you'd prefer...'

'No, it's for the best,' I say. 'I have to get Noah, anyway. Will you be gone when I get back?'

'If you want me to be,' he says, and an expression I can't read crosses his face.

He's moving the last of his stuff out today. He's been living with us half the week and the other half, well, who knows? I haven't asked, but I assume it's with her. Noah talks about her, so she's in his life. I don't care anymore. Our relationship was over years ago. He makes to leave, then stops and turns back.

'We'll be alright, won't we?' he asks.

I shrug. 'We'll have to be. No option, really.'

He looks down at the ground. 'I am sorry, you know. About us.'

I nod and find I don't feel near to tears. I don't feel anything much at all. Instead, I smile.

'It's okay, Jon. It really is. I want you to be happy and you're right—you wouldn't have found it with me. I know that now. We hung on too long, each making the other unhappy. It's no way to live.'

'So, you don't mind Noah living with me and Adele?'

Ah, so there; he's said it. 'No. I don't. But she'd better be good to him.'

'She adores him, Mel, she really does. She's got all the time in the world for him.'

If that's a barb, it doesn't sting. I scrutinise his face and realise it's not a dig at me.

'Good. He deserves as much love in his life as he can get. Anyway, I'm okay, so you don't have to worry about me. Pam and I are spending lots of time together, so when Noah's with you, I'm not lonely. Plus, Olivia and Greg come round a lot. To be honest, I could do with a bit more time on my own.'

He smiles. 'That's good.'

I take a deep breath. 'You don't have to be gone before I get back. We have to work together, for Noah's sake. He has two homes now, and we have to just get on with it.'

'It'll work,' he says. 'We owe it to Noah. And Issy.'

At the mention of Issy, I can't stop the tears. We hug once more.

314

'I'll see you later,' he says and hurries across the road to where I think she's waiting, just out of sight. I'm sure I caught a glimpse of her as we came down the courtroom steps. As I watch, she steps out from nowhere and slots in by his side. At one point, she looks over her shoulder at me. Maybe one day, I'll smile at her and wave. But not today. Not yet.

I have to go to Mum's to get Noah. Up to yesterday, she had been coming to court with me every day, but the stress of it was making her ill. She was trying to keep it together for me and Pam, and it was taking its toll.

I walk slowly to my car to find Greg leaning against it, waiting for me. He's come straight from work. He's now working in a warehouse, driving a forklift, having been unable to get back behind the wheel of an articulated lorry. A car is his limit, he tells me. Plus, he says he likes the warehouse work. He comes around the car to my side. His eyes meet mine, asking the question.

'Life,' I say, and he nods slowly.

'That's right, then.'

'Yep. He got what he deserved.'

He hugs me tight. All through this, he's been a rock for me, as has Olivia, and I don't know what I would have done without either of them. He's got a new girlfriend and I'm happy for him. He gives me his time, and I know that I've found a long and lasting friendship with him. We're there for each other anytime.

'Are you going to get Noah?' he asks.

'Yes. Want to come?'

'To see Kitty? You bet.' He and my mother are thick as thieves these days. He calls her his surrogate mum, and us, his new family. We feel the same about him.

And me? I have to start my new life here, now. Justice has been done, after all, and Noah needs me to be strong. He's all I have left of my daughter. I raise my face to the warming, early spring sun and close my eyes. Red dots of sunlight play over my eyelids and the air is fresh with the promise of a new season. Then I open my eyes to find Greg standing there, watching me, patiently.

'Come on,' I say. 'Let's go get my little boy so I can bring him home.

READ ON FOR AN EXCERPT OF LOOK CLOSER, THE
WEBCAM WATCHER BOOK 1

Chapter 1

*HE WATCHES AS SHE sits on the bed, a bath towel wrapped loosely
around her. She's combing her long, damp hair and, as a tangle gets caught
in the comb, she winces then gathers it up, twists it and secures it on top of
her head. Her bedroom is dimly lit and cosy, but he barely registers anything
but her. Pleasure ripples through his groin when she stands and removes the
towel, dropping it onto the floor. Her skin is flushed pink from her bath or
shower. He settles back in his chair, gets more comfortable. The ringing
phone makes him jump until he realises it's hers in her bedroom. She bends
over to pick it up from the bed, which elicits a small grunt of satisfaction
from him.*

*'Hi. Yes. Ten minutes,' he hears her say. Ten minutes to what?
Where's she going? What's she doing? He hopes she's not going out.*

'I'll ring you later,' she says and tosses the phone back onto the bed.

*Disappointed, he watches as she pulls on her underwear; little scraps of
lace now cover her best bits.*

*He moves back instinctively as she walks over to the laptop and sits
down, her face looming large in front of him. She breaks out in a smile and
starts tip-tapping on the keys. A response, probably to a Facebook message.
She's never off it. Every night, Twitter, Facebook, Instagram, Snapchat,
Pinterest. She's a social media junkie. He leans in again, taking in the
snub nose that turns slightly up at the tip, and the eyes, multiple shades of
green, framed by thick lashes. She's so close he can see a smattering of
freckles that dot the bridge of her nose and spill onto her cheeks. His fingers
trace them on the screen, like joining the dots, while she laughs at something
she reads. When she leans back and stretches her arms above her head, her
lace-encased breasts push up and forward towards the screen, and a rush of
heat pins him to the chair.*

*She gets up from the desk, pulls on a long, floral robe and ties it tightly,
then leaves the room, leaving the lights on. He breathes out slowly. He can*

wait. She'll be back before long. He reaches out and pops the tab on another can of beer, makes himself more comfortable in his oversized office chair and settles in to wait and watch some more. He's lost track of how many he's done this to, but this one is different. Better. Special. He smiles at the thought. He remembers reading a book about the climber, George Mallory, who died attempting to climb Everest. When Mallory had been asked why he wanted to climb the mountain, his reply had been 'Because it's there.' He sits up straighter as she returns to the room and begins to dress, scrutinising her. If anyone were to ask him why he did this, his reply would be 'Because I can'.

Chapter 2

I WAS IN THE kitchen at work, playing Candy Crush Saga and waiting for the kettle to boil to make yet more coffee to keep myself awake. The people I worked with were perfectly nice and everything, but it wasn't the most exciting place in the world. Was any solicitor's office party central? My new shoes were pinching me horribly, and I had just slipped one off when someone walked in. I jumped and jammed the phone behind my back before I realised it was *him. He* was Chris, an IT contractor who worked on the floor above.

'Gotcha,' he said, laughing.

I rammed my foot back in my shoe, knocking the blister that had formed. So much for looking cool. He must have been aware of the stir he'd caused since he started working at our place a few months ago: he was totally gorgeous, with a magnificent, muscular body. Not that I'd done much looking! Word was, he worked out all the time, and he certainly looked like he did—he was all angles and hard edges. I smiled at him as he squeezed past me. His aftershave was lovely, kind of musky and lemony, and he stooped as he towered above me with his six feet one to my five feet exactly. He leaned in and peeked at my phone, still hidden behind my back.

'What score you on?' he asked, reaching past me for a mug.

'Fifty thou.'

'What level?'

'Six hundred.'

'Managed a colour bomb on a stripe?'

'Not yet.'

'Ah! That's where the big points are.'

He smiled. He had a mesmerising mouth, sort of peachy, with a full bottom lip. When he smiled, one side sort of turned up first and the other side played catch up. It illuminated his whole face. It was a slow, spreading, lazy smile that did things to people, or women, at least. I was sure he knew it.

'The kettle's broken on our floor,' he said, reaching past me again for the tea bags.

Embarrassingly, my hand shook as I poured milk into my coffee, and some jumped out onto the side.

'Oops, butterfingers!' he said, mopping it up with a cloth from near the sink.

I felt like a clumsy oik and tried not to spill anything else as I lifted the cup. How had such a simple task turned into a major feat? He dropped the cloth into the sink and eyed the carrot cake on the plate behind that I'd already cut into small pieces.

'Ooh,' he said. 'That looks nice. Can I have some?'

'Help yourself.' I moved to one side so he could grab a slice.

He shoved the entire piece into his mouth and rolled his eyes. 'That's gorgeous. Who made it?'

'Erm... me. It's for Janice's birthday.' Now he would probably think I was some kind of boring, domesticated person, bringing homemade cake in.

His eyebrows arched above deep chocolate-brown eyes. 'You made that?'

'Mmm.' I nodded and he snatched another piece.

'That's better than shop-bought. You're good.'

I felt a flush of embarrassment mix with pleasure on my face.

'Thank you.'

'So, is that a thing of yours, then? Making cakes?'

Was he making fun of me? He didn't seem to be.

'Yeah. It is, really. It's my thing.'

He looked me up and down. 'You don't look like someone who makes cakes.'

I laughed. 'No.'

It had been said before. Everyone thought of Mary Berry when they pictured bakers.

'I'd better get back,' I said.

I shoved my phone in my pocket, put my coffee on a tray, along with the plate of cake, and he held the door open for me.

'Thanks.' I flashed him a smile.

'See you later, sexy cake maker,' he said as I left.

'Bye.' I looked back at him over my shoulder. He just called me sexy! His eyes were fixed on me and I had to work hard not to hobble in the stupid shoes. Then the door swung shut, and he disappeared from view.

If I concentrated hard, I could still smell his aftershave.

FROM THE AUTHOR

I am a thriller writer living in Yorkshire in the UK. After years working as a dog groomer and musician (not usually at the same time), I discovered a love of writing that now won't go away. I recently decorated my office in a lovely shabby chic pink wallpaper, as I wanted to have a beautifully inspiring place in which to sit and plot how to inflict unspeakable suffering on my poor unsuspecting characters. Only they don't know that yet…

I love connecting with readers. As a writer, it's one of the best things about the job. It makes all the time spent thinking up stories to share worthwhile. I'd like to say a massive thank you for taking the time to read this lil' ol' book of mine. I hope you enjoyed reading it as much as I did writing it. If you feel moved to write a review, I would greatly appreciate. It really does make a difference to authors.

I strive for perfection. If you find a typo, I'd love you to tell me at info@stephanierogersauthor.com I hope you'll stay with me on this journey. We're gonna have a blast!

Printed in Great Britain
by Amazon

41252169R00189